CAUGHT IN THE CROSSFIRE

BRYNN BABNICK

Chapter 1:

Firefly ran from rooftop to rooftop of his city. Like any story, it was a stormy night, cold and dark. Stars barely peeked through the gray clouds from the painted sky. New York was always a cloudy city. Regardless, our brave hero coughed off the smog as he ran, chasing after the cloaked figure in front of him, his mortal enemy; Xenomorph.

The two flipped and soared across the skyline as Firefly was right on Xenomorph's tail, his black coat flapping in the wind like a taunt. Just when the villain was within reach, he crossed over the street, jumping, tucking, and rolling onto a nearby roof. Firefly wasted no time in joining him, flying through the air as his name implied. When he landed, his red Converse slipped on the gravel, rag-dolling him onto the pavement of the roof.

Soon it was just the two of them.

Side by side, face to face.

They narrowed their eyes at each other, *This ends now.*

Xenomorph looked down, amused as Firefly stumbled up to his feet. He laughed and laughed like a record on repeat, but was cut short when the glow of a flame caught his eye.

See, these weren't your normal heroes and villains–these were *superheroes* and *supervillains*.

With a second glance, the fire danced elegantly in Firefly's hand. The hero tossed the fireball up playfully.

Xenomorph gave a dark chuckle, "You really think you can beat me with that? News flash, I'm the great and powerful Xenomorph–unafraid, unstoppable, undefeated...and most importantly, unlimited powers," The villain declared as he magicked up his own fireball.

It was identical.

Firefly stared at him in vain through his goggles, unphased by his claim. They had been rivals for years—he already knew Xeno's whole villain speech by heart.

Xenomorph then held up both his flaming fists, ready to knock the lights out of this firecracker, "Wanna dance?" He spat sarcastically.

Firefly ducked as the villain swung, his red hoodie catching a bit of singe. Xenomorph tried again, but the hero quickly raised his arms to block him. The two went at it, hand-to-hand combat as the lightning flashed in the background and the rumble of thunder entered the streets of the city.

Rain started to drizzle from the sky, scattering puddles along the roof, reflecting Firefly's amber glow. The hero flamed up and managed to finally get a hit on his greatest enemy. Knocking the crook back and readying up another fireball. In seconds he threw the blast.

Soaring like a bullet, it got closer and closer to the villain when suddenly—

"HEY LOSER!"

The boy jumped, whipping his head up from his comic book in a tiny fright. His white hair fluffed up and fell back into place with the sudden movement.

Before being rudely interrupted, he'd been lying on the living room rug in his white-collar button-up and blue jeans. As the sound of the dripping sink came back, he stared at the peeling wallpaper remembering where he was. The flickering light of the broken ceiling fan caught his attention, but soon the smell of their stolen, park trash can took it away. He was teleported out of the super world that was his awesome comic book, and back into his crappy apartment with his arguably more crappy roommate. Although in his life there wasn't much of a difference.

"What?" The boy replied coldly. His roommate's short black and white split hair waved in her face as she packed up a little bag. Her many piercings shined in the light and she was in the brightest, ugliest prep boy uniform imaginable.

"C'mon let's go, we're going to be late for work," she said. Her face was dull and numb.

The boy scoffed, "*Pff–* I'm not going," he snarked, reopening his comic. It was just getting good.

His roommate snapped her fingers, "Yo! Loser! I'm not asking again, put down your stupid book, and let's go."

"Why! C'mon Devan, it's degrading. Working at a comic shop?" He groaned, "*Gross*! It's all the same, the hero wins, defeats the 'bad guy', and gets all the credit!" The boy threw his comic book across the room, but Devan caught it, smirking when she realized what hero he'd been reading about. She thumbed through the pages as she spoke.

"Ah~ you're just jealous Firefly beat you last week," she pieced together.

A chill went through the kid, flinching at the sentence. He turned around in a hurry, eyes widening as he looked at his roommate.

"You don't have to be fussy about it," She continued, "Just because Firefly is *sooo* much cooler and faster and always wins it doesn't mean you're any less cool, 'Xeno'–"

"HEY! HEY! HEY! *BAP! BAP! BAP!*" The boy screamed, running over to cover Devan's mouth. "Are you crazy?! You can't say that out loud– Do you want the entire apartment to hear?! 'Hey everyone! I'm Xenomorph, the villain that's been terrorizing the city for years!'" He mocked before continuing, "Is that how you want to go down?!"

Devan licked his hand, annoyed.

Xeno pulled away, "AH! Eww~ gross! You are disgusting!"

"Get over it cry baby, grab your stuff. Let's go."

"I'm serious! You don't see me calling you Thunderstorm in public! You can't do that—if my secret identity got out, Dark Legacy would be furious!" Xeno pushed.

"Ok! Relax! Can we go now?" Devan whined, blue eyes begging to go.

4

"I don't want to. I mean, how *HUMILIATING* is it that we villains have to work for Heroes Comic Store?! It's– well frankly it's insulting!" Xeno huffed, turning his back and crossing his arms. No way he was going to be caught in that hideous red, blue, and yellow sweater vest…today.

Devan rolled her eyes; she was used to him going on these rants almost daily by now.

Tired of his rambling, she used her hand to jet out a striking bolt of lightning, shocking him when he wasn't looking.

"AH! OW! WHAT WAS THAT?!" Xeno yelled as the electricity ran through his veins.

"It's your butt getting kicked if you don't suck it up and go– I'm not getting in trouble for another one of your tantrums. Now, move it before you become a human lightning rod." She threatened, getting closer and closer with every step.

Xenomorph didn't fear many things, but his angry roommate was one of them. He rolled his eyes and clicked his tongue.

"Alright, fine…" He sighed, but as Devan turned around to look for her keys, the supervillain shocked her back.

"OW! YOU JERK!" She winced.

Xenomorph just smirked, sliding on his glasses, which were only really there to protect his identity. He walked past her in his beat-up tennis shoes, draping his hands at the back of his neck like a cushion. His face was smug, as if he had done something extraordinarily cool. He hadn't.

"I love being evil," he laughed.

"Shut up and grab your bag, we leave in five," Devan huffed and stormed off. Thunder rolled in the distance, although it was a clear blue day without a cloud in the sky.

Xeno's smile faded as he grabbed his matching sweater vest and rolled it on over his collared shirt. The hideous thing itched like crazy. He pinned on his annoyingly silly name tag that looked like a cutout cartoon *KABAM* bubble.

The name read-

"LOSER! WHERE DID YOU PUT MY KEYS?!" Devan screamed from the other room.

"I didn't touch your damn keys!" He screamed back.

He finished getting ready, and soon the pair left their apartment and walked down the hall, villains hidden in plain sight. It was so quiet the building may as well have been empty. It did look the part. Dead plants, old baseboards, and even a mouse trap in the corner.

The two got into the old, clanky elevator and Devan pushed the button. Their descent began and Xeno placed on his headphones to block out the annoying elevator music.

After a few moments, the cold, metal doors opened and the lobby was buzzing with excitement. *How obnoxious.* Xeno rolled his eyes and scoffed it off as he readjusted his backpack and trudged on.

The TV in the lobby blasted an interview of Firefly answering some questions. Xeno looked around through his fake lenses, wrinkling his nose in disgust as he soaked in how many people were engrossed in newspapers and videos–all praising the heroes of New York; Rosethorn, Solareclipse, Yellow Jacket, Duality… and of course Firefly.

The nearest visible headline read *THE BRAVE AND HEROIC FIREFLY SAVES BAKERY FROM FLOODING!* Xeno could think of a few more adjectives to describe him. Like wretched. Horrid. A total cheat. A sore winner.

The teen bared his teeth in disgust, "I hope he dies," he muttered.

"I hope you let it go!" Devan grumbled, pulling his arm as they walked out of the lobby and into the sunny, bright, and bustling streets of New York.

People rushed around, bagels and coffee in their hands. Birds chirped as yellow taxis whizzed by, driving so chaotically they almost ran people over. Nothing new.

Devan and Xeno walked to the train, but not before Xeno sneakily stole a cup of coffee from someone like it was nothing.

The boy sipped the drink and irked at the taste, "Yuck! Decaf!" Xeno sneered and threw the cup in the trash. He then took another cup out of an unsuspecting victim's hands and continued walking.

"You aren't even trying to hide the fact you're a supervillain," Devan scoffed under her breath as they walked past tall brick buildings and street lamps.

"So? You get crabby without your coffee," He sneered as they approached a crosswalk. Xeno looked around and when the coast was clear he placed his hand on the light. Secretly using Devan's electricity to mess with the lights. They flickered like crazy as cars honked and crashed. Sending smoke into the air and chaos through the streets.

Devan grabbed her laughing roommate's arm and pulled him across the pavement with the crowd as they walked through the glitched lights.

After a couple more blocks the pair walked up the outdoor stairs to the metro station. Devan sat at the bench on the platform as Xeno leaned on the glass railing, burning him a little. He looked over the sight that was New York at eight in the morning. They waited for what seemed like years for their train to take them to work. Devan opened up one of her murder mystery books and watched her roommate stare at the tracks.

"You need to learn to blend in," She bluntly interrupted.

"What's the point?"

"Look you have to fight him almost every day of every week– and more often than not, you're set up to fail, might as well not blow your only safety net and just deal with it," Devan went back to reading her book.

"Well then I need to talk to the boss about getting better hours, because I am not losing to that stupid bug again," Xeno groaned as the station bells went off. He stepped back from the railing as the train pulled up in a rush. The breeze blew his white hair into his face, but he seemed unphased.

The train slowed and the door opened. Devan packed up her stuff and stepped on the crowded train, Xeno joining her. She managed to find a seat and continued reading as the city began to blur by in the train window. Xeno grumbled to himself as he had to resort to holding the belt loop at the top of the car. The villain cranked his music up so it blasted in his ears. He hated standing when the seats were packed like this.

Blues and greens fuzzed by as the villain just stared at the glass, seeing his reflection.

Although he hated people, he did like the train, it was his moment to think, and what he was thinking…was that he really wanted to swipe that stupid smug smile off of Firefly's face.

***

Meanwhile, on the other side of the city, there was another boy. His hair, brown and fluffy, and his skin peachy and full of color. He was snug-as-a-bug-in-a-rug in his bed when a woman's voice called for him.

"Lovebug, it's time to get up."

The teen stirred under his sheets. "Mmm~ coming Mom," he groaned, yawning. He eventually rolled out of bed, stretching and running a hand through his hair to get it out of his face, only for it to fall right back into place. The summer sun peeked through his window as the kid walked to the closet to get ready.

He slipped his favorite red hoodie over his head. It had a little bug surrounded by fire in the middle. He stared at the graphic, still not believing his mom made it for him.

After he pulled up his blue jeans, he walked to his desk and picked up a pair of sky-blue goggles.

The boy strapped them over his eyes, looking in his mirror, smiling proudly, as he became Firefly. The bravest, most amazing hero in all of New York.

He pushed his goggles up, setting them in the nest of his hair. It wasn't time for his hero shift just yet. He grabbed his black raincoat and backpack, made his bed, and strapped on his harness and shoulder pads. Then slid downstairs on the stair railing. He landed with a thud on the hardwood floor and ran to the hallway closet.

"Lovebug, is that you?" His mom called out from the kitchen.

"*'No mom, it's a criminal breaking in'*—yes! Of course it's me!" Firefly yelled as he rummaged through the closet. "Hey– mom?! Have you seen my guitar?"

"It's by your board!" She called back.

Sure enough, he saw his skateboard leaning against the door, right next to his red electric guitar with flame detailing.

"Awesome! Thank you!"

"Hey, wait! Don't forget your pancakes!" his mom called back.

"PANCAKES?!" Firefly quickly slid back into the kitchen, taking a seat as a plate thudded on the granite counter displaying golden, fluffy pancakes. "Mm~ your pancakes are the best."

"Don't thank me, thank your father. It was his recipe," She said as her voice dropped. Memories of her husband flooded back to her thoughts.

Firefly looked down, suddenly losing his appetite. The syrup oozed slowly, like a wound being reopened. Grief dusting the top of his pancakes. Just one big reminder of how much he missed his dad. His mom noticed.

"Oh– I'm sorry lovebug, I didn't mean to–"

"It's ok, I know," the boy gave a weak but meaningful smile and started eating. His mom returned it, walking around the counter to give him a big kiss on the head. She ruffled his hair and held his face. "You go out there and be the amazing hero you were meant to be. Like you do every day."

"Thanks Mom…" Firefly spoke softly.

"You're welcome, Firefly," she smiled, "Are you sure you want to talk to your boss about changing your name? I think it's adorable."

"Yes, we've been over this," Firefly laughed, "It was a great name starting out, but I'm older now. It's time for a change, I need something more threatening. Especially if I'm going to put that Xenomorph in his place," he groaned, hearing the villain's laughter in his ears. "I've already been thinking of names, and I got a great one."

"Alright, if you say so honey. Just don't forget to be yourself out there," She said, patting his back.

"I won't," Firefly said, putting on the black coat. He buttoned it up at the counter as his mom just looked at him. "What?" He smiled.

"Nothing just…you look like your dad, he'd be so proud of you."

Firefly smiled, "Thank you."

His mom smiled in return, "You're welcome. Now, finish your breakfast and get going, you're going to miss the bus."

With that Firefly continued stuffing his face with fluffy pancakes, covered in powdered sugar and strawberries. Once he was done with the syrup puddles, he hid his goggles in his pocket, slung his guitar over his shoulder, and bolted outside, skateboard under his arms.

He flicked the board onto the cement and hopped on, riding from the quaint suburban housing districts to the bus stop. The wind whisped by the hero's face as he passed the green trees and the sun shone through the leaves; he playfully slid his hand along the white picket fences and waved at the barking dogs. Who just seemed to bark louder when he rolled by.

Firefly skirted along the sidewalk to a stop as he waited for the bus. Not even a few minutes went by when the squeaky bus rolled up. The teen hopped on the empty vehicle and sat in the back seat. Immediately stretching along the seats as he picked up his electric guitar and started plucking at the steel strings.

As he looked out the window, the boy made a mental note of the scenery. A runner ran by, a pigeon pooped on the bench, and as he approached the city he saw the local metro was running its track. The buildings started to grow and tower above him. The light shined off the millions of glass panels. Advertisements for all sorts of things littered the sidewalks. He even saw a poster for the biggest rock concert happening that weekend.

His eyes grew, wanting to go to that concert more than anything; it was his favorite band after all. However, due to his boss's policies, no heroes go out on personal trips of any kind. It's too risky; it could reveal a super's identity.

While a shame, the hero understood. Captain Peace was a great boss and rules were rules.

What was he going to do? Drop everything and go on the adventure of a lifetime? No way, his life was just falling into place. He'd have become 'best friends' with Xenomorph before that happened.

Chapter 2:

Flip.

Xenomorph thumbed through the colorful comic pages behind the counter, laying the book flat on its face while the time passed. He doodled all sorts of funny mustaches and scars, vandalizing the heroes with a trusty red pen. He couldn't help laughing to himself as Devan stocked the empty shelves.

"Are you going to help me?" She asked, sassing.

Xeno smirked and gave a huffy laugh, "Nah, you got it."

"You're a jerk," she scoffed back.

"Easy puffy clouds," Xeno teased. As he flipped the pages again, his eye caught the ticking clock. It hadn't moved from its spot on the wall but he kept glancing at it like it was about to run away.

Tick. Tock. Tick. Tock.

Waiting for his *real* shift to start.

"You're doing it again," Devan sang sarcastically, stacking up another box of comics up on the shelf.

"Doing what?"

"Watching the time, like a psychopath."

Xeno gave her a death glare, squinting his eyes with purpose through his cold, glass lenses. He held a hand up towards the ticking time machine. Lighting sparked in his palms and in a flash, the clock was blasted off the wall. Lights flickered on and off throughout the store as the villain threw his tantrum.

Devan seemed unphased as the remains of the clock fell off the wall and lit up in a small blaze of blue flames.

"Good thing I'm a psychopath," he smirked his iconic evil smile and took off his fake glasses, closing them up.

"You are such a drama queen," Devan shrugged off, returning to her box of books.

Xeno ignored her quip and looked at the burnt clock on the floor, totaled and wrecked.

He smiled to himself, giggling as the big hand finally ticked into place on its last breath.

"It's time," Xeno announced as he grabbed his bag and walked to a shelf in the back of the store.

"Ugh, fine. Good luck loser," Devan winked and continued her grueling job.

"Thank you…but I won't need it," He smirked and pulled down on their secret lever disguised as a comic book. The entire shelf jolted and popped out of the wall, sliding open slowly to reveal a large elevator with sharp blue detailing.

He laughed as he walked inside.

"I'm Xenomorph, and I'm the greatest villain ever."

"Whatever you have to tell yourself…"

With that the elevator doors closed. As Xeno sank down into the underground of New York, he changed out of his bright, colorful uniform and started armoring up in his dark gray armor.

He then whipped out his black trench coat and swung it around as he put it on; pulling up the sleeves, brushing his hair to the side, and finally pulling out his black blindfold and wrapping it around his eyes. Still being able to see through the fabric thanks to Dark Legacy's super technology. How he was able to get advanced gadgets and materials he never knew.

As the elevator slowed to a stop Xenomorph was finally clocked in and ready to take center stage.

The cold doors split open to reveal the villain making a grand entrance for all of HQ to see. The dim room was filled with computers, machines, and most importantly villains. Everyone froze as Xeno walked through the crowd, more confident than anyone in the room. Everyone cleared the way, slowly backing up. Although Xeno never knew if it was from fear or annoyance, perhaps a bit of both.

To put it simply; Xenomorph *loved* being a villain. It was a life filled with chaos, yes–but also rewards, status, adrenaline, and power.

People cowered at him. They respected him and no one was *ever* going to take that away from him.

As he danced through headquarters, as other villains were preparing for their shift; training and running around, waiting for their days and nights of havoc. The teen spun around as he admired the sharp armor and metal mask of his coworkers. They didn't look nearly as cool as him dressed in their evil, dark colors, but nonetheless, they would send a chill through anyone's spine with just one look.

Well, anyone except Xenomorph.

He quickly snapped his jaws at a couple of villains and they flinched back at the bite. He laughed to himself as he looked them up and down. Although he was younger than a lot of the villains, he was by far the scariest. The only soul to wear all black, like he was a shadow of the night. Dark Legacy saved that color just for him, as only one other villain had ever worn black.

Xeno danced to a giant board at the end of the hall, looking through his mask. Staring at the schedule and red strings zig zagging all over the papers and pictures.

Dark Legacy always planned the villain's attacks. Where and when. Xenomorph always thought the scheduling was weird. Villains should be free to cause mayhem wherever and whenever. Regardless, he didn't question his boss. Dark Legacy was a brilliant leader, and because of him, Xeno was now the most powerful, most feared villain in the world.

Xenomorph looked at the sheet, scanning for his name.

His time slot read: *12:00 pm local jewelry store.*

Nothing big, but Xeno didn't care. He couldn't wait to play the act.

Xeno smiled, walking over to his little high-tech locker on the wall. He twisted the lock side to side until it opened to reveal a bunch of newspaper clippings of his terror taped to the metal sides. Along with dozens of old paper wrist band-tags from previous experiments and training, some spray paint cans (full and empty), and most importantly a small metal disc with straps. The kid excitedly grabbed the armor piece and attached it around his chest. Finishing his iconic look.

His blood chilled with excitement, entire body already feeling more powerful.

"Oh hell yes," he mumbled to himself. He held his hands out, creating a bubble of water, bending and misshapening it until he blasted it to a control panel. The computer fizzed and buzzed until it popped, then he teleported across the room and roundhouse kicked a rather unfortunate co-worker down on the ground.

"*AHOW*! You IDIOT!" The poor, unsuspecting villain yelled, her mind control goggles cracking on impact and her hair in her face.

Xenomorph just laughed as he floated up. His eyes glowed from behind his mask, feeling his true potential as he wielded all sorts of powers: fire, water, sound, electricity, ice. He readied up lazer eyes as he did a spin in the air when all of a sudden–

"Xenomorph!" A dark, commanding voice yelled out.

Xenomorph froze, his concentration breaking as he flinched and fell out of the air, "WHAA~!"

He knew exactly what that voice meant and *who* that voice was coming from.

"Ow!" He hit the ground, coattails folding over his face. Xeno got back up clumsily, trying to find his way through his floppy coat. He barely managed to stand straight and tall as a dark figure approached.

The silhouette had no face, only a large, black gas mask that covered any possible features. The white skull was roughly painted over it, making him feel like death himself. The black draping cape trailing out behind him also added a layered feeling of impending doom. The only other villain who wore black.

Xenomorph automatically saluted, "Dark Legacy."

Dark Legacy made little notice of the kid, but he just stood like a shadow, "Xenomorph, you know the rules, no powers inside headquarters. Remember, hold your cards close to your chest. Although brilliant work on taking out Mind Manipulator."

"Yes sir, sorry sir." Xeno smiled, not really meaning the apology, "But, thank you."

"Don't you have a fight to get to? You don't want to be late."

"Yes sir, I'm on my way," Xenomorph gave some overly confident finger guns and started to walk away.

"Wait a second, before you go and make a fool out of yourself," The villain boss added at the last minute, "I've got a tip." There was a smile in his voice. Without being able to see his face it was impossible to tell if it was a sly and manipulative one, or a genuine, sincere one. Both excited Xenomorph to his core.

"Wait, really?" Xeno asked, immediately backtracking.

"I have word that Firefly is on patrol today…"

"*WHAT*?! OH FOR VILLAIN SAKES!!" The kid yelled, his hands and hair literally flaming up in fury, "YOU'VE GOT TO BE KIDDING ME!! That's worse than fireworks- and you know HOW MUCH I HATE FIREWORKS!!"

"Calm down," he fanned Xeno's smoke and fire. If Dark Legacy's eyes weren't hidden, Xenomorph would have seen them roll, "It's just a warning. Besides, I'm proud of you, no matter what happens out there today." Dark Legacy ruffled the teen's hair.

"Aww~ really?" Xeno gushed, admiring his idol. Sure he was a villain to the world, but to Xeno, he was the greatest hero alive. He pondered on how one day, he was going to be just like him.

"Yes– you have real...power," as Xeno's eyes lit up, Dark Legacy added, "Real *potential.*"

"Gee, thanks," Xeno smiled.

"You're welcome, kid."

"Uh... I'm nineteen," he tried to correct his boss.

"Just– play your cards right and whatever you do... don't fail."

"Haha...wait–what?" Xeno asked, confused.

"You heard me. *Don't screw this up.* You have had too many close calls recently," he threatened, getting closer.

Xeno just nervously nodded, "Yes Dad– I-I mean...boss, I won't fail you again!"

"...Did you just call me Dad?" Dark Legacy asked.

"N-No!" Xenomorph lied.

In a snatch, Dark Legacy grabbed him by the face and yanked them close. He was always like that, taking people by surprise; for better or worse. Like a jack in the box, ready to jump out and snap your neck.

"Listen kid...I didn't raise a bunch of soft butterflies. You're a villain, act like it. On and off the field."

20

Xenomorph choked a bit in his grasp, coughing, "Y-Yes sir, I'm sorry."

"Just because I own you, doesn't make me your new 'Dad'. You show up, you listen and you obey. *Got it?*"

"I-I understand sir..."

Dark Legacy tightened his grip, "...And if you even *try* to go off the track I created for you, I won't hesitate to *kill you*."

And there was the Jack in the Box.

Xenomorph's eyes widened in silence. He couldn't tell if he was scared or feeling pure admiration for his boss. He always made the most beautiful threats, like poetry or if a crime was a love confession. Xeno nodded and Dark Legacy dropped him. Hitting the floor with a thud. The villain finally caught his breath again, coughing from lack of air.

"Good. Now if you excuse me, I have an important meeting to get to and I am already late," Dark Legacy shifted and left as quietly and mysteriously as he came. The fear lifted the further he got.

Xeno saluted to his back and rushed off, ready to make his appearance. The other villain's laughter from his little mistake echoed off the walls. Xenomorph stretched and thought about what his boss said, he couldn't even imagine what would happen if he stepped out of line. Rumor had it one villain had leaked some information about their organization, nothing big, just a schedule or two; and now that Xeno thought about it, he hadn't seen that villain since...

Xenomorph gulped, he did not want to be next. He ran his lines out loud as he walked to the exit, trying to copy his boss's psychotic ways. After all, he wanted to be just like Dark Legacy when he grew up.

Chapter 3:

Firefly got off the bus and was immediately hit with a piece of rogue paper. Pulling it off his face, he read the 'great' news; Governor Jaceson was running for reelection...again...

'*Yay,*' the hero thought to himself sarcastically. He crinkled the paper into a ball and threw it away, walking down the road as he hummed.

Firefly never liked the guy. Jaceson was too focused on making money. Making their fights into comic books, selling the footage to the news, and squeezing any ounce of super work like a cash cow. He never even *tried* to get rid of the villains of New York, just let the heroes clean up the streets. They do all the work, and for what? The villains still seemed to escape and cause chaos every week like clockwork. Yet, the Governor still gets all the great credit as if he's a saint.

Firefly kicked a can down the sidewalk. Looking around at the world. A few shopping districts, a cafe or two, but mostly company buildings.

Firefly looked across the road to see something new, something under construction. He couldn't tell what it was, but he steered his head around to try and catch a glimpse or a sign of some sort. Whatever it was, it looked big. After a couple of seconds of searching, he finally found a sign plastered on the chain link fence. *PROPERTY OF GOVERNOR JACESON.*

The hero's face dropped, unimpressed. Probably another hero training facility or something dumb they didn't need.

Firefly couldn't wait until he was older. How things would change. He would run for governor, would get a new name, would end the villains' chaos, and would end Xenomorph. Ugh, just thinking about that guy put a bad taste in his mouth.

Firefly slipped down an empty alleyway as he continued chugging along on his train of thought.

Man, when I catch Xenomorph for good, everything will be different.

He could finally live a peaceful life and not spend hours, days, and nights running after such a brat.

The teen unbuttoned his raincoat, stuffing it in his backpack, and adjusted his goggles on his face. Marking the time as he clocked on to become Firefly once more. He then threw down his board and skated all the way to Hero's Tower.

The building was big, flashy, and sat in the middle of the city. Firefly liked to admire the view, feeling lucky enough to frequent a building that was surrounded by such beautiful greenery. It was the pride and joy of New York, well, to him. What the citizens didn't know was that it was a top-secret hero headquarters. Sure, it was big and modern, but so were most of the surrounding buildings. From afar it just looked like any old office building or apartment complex.

No one knew the heroes worked here, heck no one knew the heroes worked together. It was of the utmost importance that their alliance stayed under the radar. It's how they are able to get all their information and tackle the villain problems so successfully.

Firefly took out his pass, swiped it, and went through the glass front doors. Skateboard in hand and guitar around his back, he walked through the building. Light leaking through from all sides of the glass walls. It was refreshing in a way.

Firefly strutted past the desk and straight into the meeting room. He pushed open the door to see a long glass table covered in maps, lines, training routines, and a work-in-progress schedule. Probably setting up the next patrol cycles. Heroes crowded the room like a convention hall, chatter and laughter bouncing off the walls.

The place was filled with joy, as it should be. Heroes were strong, positive figures. No one hated each other–

"Hello, Hothead," a girl jumped in his face.

Ok– well, Firefly hated one hero…

He looked her up and down, with dirty blonde hair swooping backwards at an impossible angle. To the point where sometimes Firefly wondered if she was wearing gel. She was dressed in her iconic purple, black, and white superhero uniform. In the middle was a little volume icon– how he despised that symbol. Of course she could actually afford a shiny, new suit.

"Hello Molly…" Firefly groaned, "What do you want?"

"It's Soundwave right now, *Hothead*," she said with a sneer, "And *I* want nothing. But Captain Peace said he wanted to talk to us."

"*US?* Oh heck no– I am not going on patrol with you!" Firefly started, the smell of something burning hovered in the air.

"Glad we can finally agree on something! I don't want to be paired with a weakling," she sassed again, "not that you're weak…just…you know…pff– sorry I can't," The hero tried, but failed, laughing.

Firefly gave her a deadpan smile, "Gee. Thanks. 'You really did try.'"

"The Captain probably just wants you to take notes on what a *successful* hero looks like," She combed the hair out of her face and posed, chin high in the air.

"Hey, I am successful!"

"Really? Then why isn't your little buddy Xenomorph behind bars?"

Firefly growled, "I'm working on it." He seethed. Fist clenched at his side, as his hair started to smoke. Trying to push that flashy hero smile, however, anyone with eyes could see the fake grin. Xeno had escaped jail over a dozen times, and it was irritating to say the least.

"Yeah? For how long? Two…three years?" Soundwave smirked, getting under his skin.

The hero started to flare up, eyes glowing red, and hair becoming a bonfire. Ready to smoke this girl, literally.

"THAT'S IT! I–"

"Firefly!" A voice shouted.

Firefly immediately snuffed out the flame in fright, despite the fact his blood was still boiling.

He didn't have to turn around to see who it was as he saw his boss's reflection in the glass. He closed his eyes, knowing he screwed up.

"Need I remind you, we are supposed to be fighting the villains, not each other?" Captain Peace softly commanded, entering in his own superhero armor. Lots of blues and whites. He looked like an angel– *heck,* he was one. Everyone knew Captain Peace was the kindest, most thoughtful, toughest, and bravest hero alive. Once the villains took over, he dedicated his life to building the hero system. A special organization tasked to defeat every last villain in New York.

"Yes…sorry Captain," Firefly turned around and weakly saluted. Looking down as he felt his stomach sink to the tiled floor he was staring at.

"You've got one temper there…you have to learn to control it before someone gets hurt…" The Captain warned.

"I-It's not my fault, *Soundwave* was bothering me–and I have fire powers! I'm a literal hot head!" He rattled off, ranting in protest.

Soundwave scoffed, "I'll say you are."

"Not. *Now.*" Firefly seethed, smoking up again. Baring his teeth as the smile grew into a frustrated frown.

"Ah~, Soundwave, great, you're here. That means I can finally give you the news!" Captain Peace smiled.

27

"News? What news?" Firefly eyes darted around nervously. Confused, after all, there was no 'news'; everyone knew everything, and nothing had changed in over a decade. Any news usually meant a bad sign...like the time the toaster oven caught fire. Rough week for the tower.

"Listen, Firefly...you are a very talented, dedicated, true hero–"

"Oh–wait," Firefly interrupted. The word hero rang a bell as he remembered the question he wanted to ask, "real quick, I was wondering if I could get a promotion of my name?" Firefly sputtered excitedly, "I already have tons of new ideas and I've got one you might like–"

"Really?" Soundwave laughed, "What could be any stupider than 'Firefly'?"

"I-It's actually very cool and...personal." Firefly drifted off but stood firm in confidence. He knew how cool this new name idea was, and it was so him, so vulnerable. It was the perfect name for a hero who sacrificed everything to be here...

"As I was saying, *Firefly*, you're a great hero and have a bright future..." Captain Peace continued, ignoring his request.

Firefly gave a smirk and closed his eyes in confidence. "Thanks. I know."

"But you haven't caught Xenomorph."

Firefly's confidence shattered like glass.

"...W-What?"

"Listen, Xenomorph has gotten unpredictable recently, if you can't catch him by the end of this week, we are going to have to demote you…"

"WHAT?!" Firefly yelled, accidentally fanning the metaphorical flames of his fury into a very real fire.

"Miss Soundwave will take your place and catch Xenomorph," The boss continued.

"AH YEAH! *IN YOUR FACE NERD!*" Soundwave boomed, sending a loud echo through the room, the glass cracked at the noise as Firefly covered his ears.

"Soundwave, *please*, behave yourself," The Captain ordered.

Soundwave smiled sheepishly, "Yes sir, sorry sir."

"Sir– PLEASE! I'm so close to catching him, you can't give *my* super enemy to *HER*!! She doesn't know him like I do! His tricks, his strategies!" Firefly yelled as the heroes started to look at him causing a scene. The kid could feel their judgmental eyes glued to him, but he didn't care as he continued to shout to the glass rooftops, "He plays dirty, she won't be able to handle that–AND DEMOTING ME?! I am your best hero!" Firefly pleaded.

"You *are* my best hero, but Soundwave caught her last five enemies in the last two months and you've caught zero…" Captain Peace tried to explain.

"HER bad guys were EASY- STUPID ROBBERS AND DUMB CAT BURGLARS, she'd stand NO CHANCE against XENOMORPH! He has thousands of powers! She would be squashed in seconds!" Firefly yelled.

"HEY! WOULD NOT! I am just better, Sparky! Admit it!" Soundwave yelled back.

"ARE NOT! I would never tell a lie!" Firefly fought.

"You are so pathetic! You're just some hero wannabe like your dad, at least he could catch a threat…" Soundwave scoffed.

Firefly froze, eyes widening as his face grew in utter appalment. Those taunting words echoed in his ears as his shock turned into pure rage. He readied up to his side, growing a fireball in his right hand.

"Say that again." He threatened.

"Stupid. Foster. Mistake." She spat and Firefly instantly threw the ball. The flames hurled toward her face, as they got closer and closer. Soundwave instinctively clapped and sent a boom straight to it, bouncing it back to its creator. Firefly ducked as the ball hit a plant and lit it ablaze. The fire alarm rang out as Captain Peace just rubbed the area between his eyes. Soundwave ran her hands through the singed part of her hair. The kid stared at the damage, really taking in how far he had gone.

The orange glow of fire lit Firefly up, illuminating his reddened cheeks of embarrassment as Tidal Wave ran over and used her water abilities to put out the fire.

"Soundwave, you're excused," The Captain ordered.

"Ha! Figures, looks like someone's in trouble~" she jeered as she walked away. Right before she left the room, she paused in the doorframe. "You know, I don't know why you're a hero…all you do is destroy everything…" she spat and left.

30

Firefly watched her go, heartbroken at those words. Was it true, was he not meant to be a hero? Or worse, meant to be a villain? Surely not! He wasn't anything like Xenomorph...right?

The kid looked to his Captain, not knowing what to say or do.

"Kid, don't take it personally..." he started, "I do see greatness in you—I know you have it. You just...need to reassess," Captain Peace spoke, smiling as he walked closer to his protege. "In the end you're right, Xenomorph is a tough villain, one of the toughest we've ever had to face...I wouldn't give him to you if I didn't think you couldn't handle it."

"Then why are you reassigning me...demoting me? Are you...kicking me out?" Firefly asked, voice breaking.

"What? No! No, no, no, no! You'll just be given an easier villain for the time being. You need a break. A confidence boost"

"I don't want an easier villain, I want Xenomorph. I've been tracking this guy down for years! I'm so close to blowing the lid off this case, I can't have someone take that away from me...especially *her.*"

"I get it, trust me."

"If you get it and know I can handle it then why are you switching me out?" Firefly asked.

"Because you're too great and talented to waste on Xenomorph any longer..."

Firefly's eyes grew big at the genuine compliment.

"You can handle yourself, but I can't deal with just 'handling' anymore. I need this guy to stop. He's been taking up your schedule for years and I can't send you out while you're occupied with Xenomorph.

It *may* all just be a test run. Who knows the audience might love the new switch. Our funds are slipping as of recently and Soundwave has been going through villains like crazy. She needs a challenge and you need a rest...but my orders still stand, you have by the end of the week to find him and turn him in..." Captain Peace explained, smiling and winking.

Firefly just nodded, out of words.

Captain Peace hugged him, rubbing his back, "Don't worry kiddo, everything is going to be fine."

"Yeah... fine..." Firefly repeated emptily.

"Now, you have a patrol on North Street today, wanna know why I scheduled you there?"

"Why?" Firefly asked, cocking his head to the side, curious.

"Because I heard super intel that Xenomorph will be there, robbing the jewelry store," Captain smirked and patted him up, hoping he'd take the hint.

Firefly smiled, nodding, "On it sir–I won't let you down this time!"

"I know you won't," the Captain smiled. "Now run along and go kick some villain ass."

"I'm going to go kick some *ash!" He corrected and started readying up for his mission.

Chapter 4:

CRASH!!

The glass shattered on the floor of an elegant jewelry store. Bathing in white lighting and covered in diamonds that reflected like chandeliers. Smoke and lightning came from the cracks as Xenomorph strolled in as if he were the guest of honor.

People started to scream and run, begging for the police or a hero, but the villain just shrugged it off. Using electricity to shatter the glass casings.

"Good thing diamonds are a guy's best friend," he quipped to the store owner, who was cowering behind the counter. Xeno didn't hesitate to grab the silver and gems from right under his nose.

Meanwhile, Firefly was running on the rooftops, patrolling when he heard police sirens. He watched the police cars shine their blaring red and blue lights as they sped down the road. He started to follow the cars and as he got closer to the store he heard the alarms.

Wasting no time, he jumped to the ground. Running against the crowd, readying up.

Cop cars and news vans started to swarm the area sloppily, as Firefly parkoured over the barricades, ducked under police tape, and slid inside as the police yelled at him.

He jumped through the broken window, tucking and rolling onto the ground. Standing tall and lit up a fireball.

"Well, well, well…" a voice called out.

Firefly turned to see Xeno lying on the counter. Wearing dozens of necklaces, a couple earrings, who knows how many bracelets, and tons of rings.

"How predictable, you're here…" Xeno smirked, sitting up. Holding his head as if he were annoyed by the bug, but deep down he couldn't wait to squash him.

"Xenomorph." Firefly started, "This *ends now.*"

"Aww~ but don't I look great?" Xeno teased.

Firefly held up the flames, "Drop the diamonds Xeno, you're coming with me."

"Mm~ yeah…no," Xenomorph drifted, smirking as he used a lightning bolt to take out the ceiling as instructed. Firefly quickly looked up to see the rain of rubble, diving out of the way and rolling onto the floor.

Xeno launched at him, pinning him down to the ground. Firefly kicked him off and threw a ball of fire like a baseball. The villain quickly summoned up a giant wave of water and sent it barreling to the ball, putting it out into smoke.

Firefly yelped as he got on the counter, avoiding the puddles.

Suddenly, Xenomorph sprouted beautiful, blooming vines from the ground and swung them around like tentacles. Knocking the hero back into the glass display shelves behind him, sending a loud crash through the room. Xeno flinched mockingly, feeling his pain but not caring.

"Ouch, man that must have hurt. For a weakling."

The display case became ablaze and the glass melted into lava as Firefly jumped out, "I'M NOT WEAK!!!" Attacking Xeno, punching him straight in the face, and then roundhouse kicking him back into the wall.

THUD!

A crack trickled up the wall at the impact as Xeno looked up, spying the support beams. Firefly came running in, anger burning in his soul. Xenomorph couldn't see his eyes, but he was sure fire was in them.

Xeno teleported out of the way as Firefly tried to pin him, making the hero miss and smash into the building. He then threw a soundwave, pushing Firefly further into the wall and holding him there in mid-air.

"Listen Firecracker, don't take this personally. I've just got a job to do–" Xeno took out a messenger bag out of nowhere and started stuffing his treasure into it with his free hand, "and you're in my way," Xeno sassed.

"Well so do I..." Firefly cited from the wall as he whipped on his hood and shot the sprinkler on the roof just like Captain Peace taught him. Water sprayed everywhere as another alarm went blaring off. Xeno braced for cover as Firefly dropped down, stumbling onto the damp rug.

"BLAH–" Xeno spat as he went invisible. Firefly shot a line of fire on the ground. It was instantly put out, making smoke out of the indoor rain. The smoke lit the villain's outline and Firefly wound up a big fireball and threw it.

BAM!

Xenomorph was knocked through the counters, causing more damage and phasing back into reality. The glass scraped his skin, leaving a couple of scratches on his face. He hobbled up from the broken cases, probably broke a rib or two but he couldn't give up. Dark Legacy was counting on him, and he refused to lose to that blaster hero again.

Firefly readied up, slowly approaching, "Had enough? Or should I keep going?" He asked sarcastically, reciting his lines perfectly.

"You just don't know when to quit, do you?" Xeno asked.

"No, heroes never quit," Firefly taunted from above him, looking like a savior in the light.

Xenomorph grumbled under his breath. This choreography wasn't working anymore, these moves weren't enough. He looked up unsure of what to do, if he continued with the scene he would lose for sure. As the light blinded him, something snapped within him and he went rogue.

"Neither do I," Xeno smirked, and used a bolt of lightning to shoot up at Firefly.

The flaming hero bent backwards, the bolt missed and hit the ceiling.

"HA! Missed!" Firefly celebrated.

"Who said I was aiming for you?" Xeno smirked as he anchored his gravity to the roof, using his momentum to take out the last support beam.

The building started to rumble, Firefly readied another blast in shock as nothing prepared him for *this*, but before he knew it a giant beam fell on him. Trapping him on the ground. He pushed, trying to get up but he was stuck. Wedged in between some rubble. His stomach crushed and squeezed as he gasped for air.

Xenomorph laughed and landed elegantly, picking up the scattered diamonds and jewelry in the mess.

"Looks like I won," He smiled.

Firefly kept panting and struggling, "H-HEY! N-NO FAIR! You have a gazillion powers!!"

"Don't be mad you're inadequate," Xeno scoffed, elbowing the cash register, opening it, and ruffling through the green money.

Firefly still struggled, "ME?! Look at you! You're a nobody who gets pleasure in terrorizing the city and destroying lives! You arc sick! Evil!"

"Yeah~! Duh~! That's kind of my job, Buggy!" Xenomorph sassed.

"But why?! Why do you constantly do this?! You are wasting your life!" Firefly screamed.

"The only waste I see here is you." He shifted. Firefly's heart fell. Shuddering at the thought.

"Now if you excuse me I'm out of here," Xeno quipped as he slung the messenger bag filled with goods over his shoulder.

"N-NO!! DON'T YOU LEAVE!!!"

"Buh bye, Firecracker!" Xeno smiled evilly, waved off, and started to leave. Climbing up out of the ceiling.

"NO!! COME BACK!!! FIGHT YOU COWARD!!! YOU– FRICKING!!! LOSER!!! I HATE YOU!!! I WILL FIND YOU AND I WILL PUT YOU BEHIND BARS YOU HEAR ME!!! I'LL HAVE THE LAST LAUGH!!! JUST YOU WAIT!!!"

"Sure you will...Hahahaha!" Xeno laughed and vanished.

"FFFFFFrick–... Enjoy your freedom while it lasts Xenomorph, cause next time will be your last look at the sun..." Firefly threatened the empty air. Struggling in the debris.

Eventually, the police came crashing through the door, readying their guns. Firefly froze, trying to put his arms in the air. Or what he could, being crushed under fifty pounds of rubble.

Easy to say the news caught his embarrassing failure and soon the whole city was buzzing with rumors of the battle.

***

Later that night, after Firefly was pulled out of the rubble by some emergency crew, he clocked out and snuck home. He couldn't dare see the disappointment on his Captain's face, or hear Molly's insufferable, loud voice.

Firefly ran behind a building, ripped off his goggles, took off his iconic red hoodie, and stuffed his clothes into his bag. Wearing nothing but his jeans and white t-shirt all the way home. A cold breeze blew in his hair, but he didn't care. All he could think about was how he failed today. Not just today– but every day! Usually, he'd catch Xeno, retrieve some of the goods, and save the day. Xenomorph would always find a way to escape but at least the damage was bearable.

Lately, it's been a different story, something in this guy–pure evil, hatred, or maybe just sick of the same routine–was different. He got away more, caused more damage, and stole more valuable assets. He was getting good, too good. Good enough that Firefly could lose his spot as a top hero if he didn't act fast.

The teen sauntered up his porch, staring at the little orange light by the door, and turned the metal knob; stepping inside as he threw his bag on the ground. He heard the echoey voice of the radio from the kitchen and followed it.

"Today, in downtown Brooklyn the horrid villain Xenomorph was caught at Diamondz, wreaking havoc, stealing, and being a threat to our kind. Luckily, Firefly was found on the case today, trying to stop his mortal enemy. Those two are sure at each other's throats! However, in a shocking turn of events, Firefly was defeated! Xenomorph got away! Is Firefly all washed up? Has Xenomorph won? Will he take over the city with a super villain army? Stay tuned to find out–"

Firefly turned off the radio, not being able to take anymore. Sure, Xenomorph was stronger, but Firefly was always smarter and thanks to the scripts he always knew what was coming next. A battle would end in bruises and blood for him, but he always won in the city's eyes. Was it true? Was this the end?

"Sorry Love Bug..." A woman's voice interrupted his thoughts. She was quietly prepping dinner, watching everything.

"It's...it's fine– it's just one bad day..." Firefly tried to deflect, taking out a little red lighter and flicking it. Nothing sparked, as it was empty. While no fire would light, it did feel good to just keep flicking, as if it were some sort of fidgeter.

"You're right, one bad day out of many great ones ahead. You'll catch him next time!" She cheered.

"...If I don't?" He asked.

His mom just looked at him confused, "You will."

"But, Mom...he plays dirty!"

"Welcome to the super world honey, they're villains, they don't play fair."

"Then how am I ever going to catch him?!" Firefly complained.

"By playing fair-*er*."

"Huh?" Firefly cocked his head to the side.

"Villains don't listen to the rules, use that against them," his mom explained.

"Pff– you don't know Xeno like I do..." He drifted. "He's callous and stubborn, and he has every power known to mankind! He doesn't even know what the rules are! They don't apply to a guy like that! How is following them an advantage?"

"Honey…you're a hero."

Firefly nodded off, not getting it, "Yeah? Point is?"

"What's your job?"

"To help people."

"But just a few of them right? A person or two?"

"No of course not, everyone…" He explained.

"*Everyone?*"

Firefly froze, knowing where this was going. "Mom…Xenomorph *can't* be saved. He's a lost cause…"

"How do you know?"

"He's made his choice! Lines have been drawn! He's a villain!"

"But do you know why?" She asked, softly.

"Of course, I don't–who cares?!"

His mom brushed his hair and held his beat-up face, "Your father saw the good in everyone…he believed everyone deserves a second chance. You're not just a superhero, you're a role model. I'm sure Xenomorph wouldn't be a villain if he were feeling good about himself, nor any villain for that matter. Yes, they need to be stopped, but what if he's just like you…?"

"What? He is nothing like me…"

"How do you know that? You don't even know who this guy is. You want to make the world a better place? Then do so lovely. It doesn't have to be battles and fighting. Just talking would be nice."

"You want me to talk...to *Xenomorph*?" Firefly asked sarcastically. "The same Xenomorph who tried to kill me today, because he's a supervillain?"

"I want you to think about what I said. Great heroes help everyone, see good in everyone. Maybe Xeno just needs to be heard out, you never know."

Firefly just listened, his mom was so wise and sweet. Giving supervillains a chance?! Granted it sounds crazy, but maybe she had a point.

What would Dad do?

"And if that doesn't work, *then* you can kick his 'ash' or whatever you say," She winked ruffling his hair.

Firefly giggled, "Alright Mom, and 'ash' is better than what you say."

"You are just like your dad," She teased, flicking a towel in his face repeatedly as he laughed.

***

"WOOOO!!" Xeno shouted as the elevator doors opened, still iced out in diamonds and jewelry. The villain threw the bag on the table sloppily as diamonds spilled out and everyone was looking at the center of attention sparkling in the dimly lit room. "Did you guys see that?! It was incredible!" He flexed, pulling on his coat all proper-like.

"You were also reckless," Thunderstorm approached. Finally in her rightful uniform, adorned in dark grays and striking white and yellow bolts running like veins down her body.

"I think you mean 'awesome'!" Xeno snuffed.

She scoffed, rolling her eyes.

"Don't hate me because I'm just doing my job; Shining bright like a diamond," Xenomorph gave a single laugh and busted a move. He had done it, he had finally won a battle against that wretched bug.

"You shined bright alright," another voice entered.

The kid looked up to see Dark Legacy coming back from his meeting. Dark cloak and mask still covering his silhouette.

"...RIGHT THROUGH THE SCRIPT!!" His boss yelled, commanding attention. Chairs started to fly up as the ground rumbled. Villains coward, but Xeno didn't back down, didn't even flinch.

"Pff– scripts shripts– I was amazing and I won!! Who cares how I did it?" Xeno brushed off and asked, hands on his hips, flipping his fluffy hair.

"You disobeyed me."

Xeno's smirk faded, "W-What?"

"This was insubordinate! Disobedience! You didn't follow orders!"

"Ok! Ok! Ok! I get it– I didn't listen, but why does that matter? I got the diamonds and defeated Firefly, that's my job!" He argued.

"Xenomorph you can't just– UGH! You displayed complete negligence and on top of that you proved you're too big a risk."

"A RISK?!"

"Yes! What if someone caught you?! The scripts are in there to protect us!"

"BUT WE LOSE WITH THE SCRIPTS!! I WENT OFF THE RAILS ONCE! AND WON BECAUSE OF IT!! ISN'T THAT A SIGN??"

"…are you *talking back to me…?*"

Xeno immediately shut his mouth, shrinking from his confident, bold stance.

"N-No s-sorry sir…"

"You better be…you're a great and powerful villain but you're still a *child.* You don't know the system like I do, what those blasted heroes could do to you. Do you wanna die?!"

"N-No sir…"

"Then GET YOUR ACT TOGETHER!!!"

Xeno flinched up.

"Tomorrow, you're going to go out there and give the biggest fight of your life! You are going to follow *my* orders, *my* rules, *my* directions– AND SO HELP ME XENO, YOU STEP ONE FOOT OUT OF LINE, SKIP ONE WORD OF YOUR DIALOGUE, AND YOU'LL DISAPPEAR, *forgotten forever…*" His boss threatened, backing him up and pinning him to the wall.

Xenomorph gulped, "Y-Yes Dark Legacy."

"Good, I already have too many loose cannons to deal with, I don't need another. Especially considering you're nothing without me…" Dark Legacy sneered and grabbed his disc, ripping it off his armor.

"GAH– HEY!"

"Your shift is over. Go home."

Xeno fell to the floor as his boss walked away, ripped open his locker, stuffed his metallic armor piece back into its place, and slammed the door shut. The sound of the metal rang in the air.

Xeno stood frozen, heart beating in his ears as he watched his boss disappear into the shadows. How could someone so great be so terrifying?

Chapter 5:

The next morning was just as sunny as the day before. The birds–or sky rats–chirped their songs and the cars blared their horns. A usual, boring Tuesday. Firefly skated to Hero's Tower after his shift at the record shop, ready for the yelling he was going to get about yesterday. His wheels slowed to a stop as the stairs approached. They looked bigger than usual, felt more like a climb; like a never-ending mountain.

Firefly slowly opened the door, trying to sneak in–even though the doors were made of glass.

He got one foot inside before–

POW!

A punch hit him straight in the face.

"GAAAAAOOOWW!!!" Firefly screeched, flaming up like a torch. He turned to see Soundwave readying up, frowning her brows and baring her teeth. "WHAT THE HECK IS YOUR PROBLEM?!" He flamed up more, becoming a living bonfire.

"YOU! YOU PATHETIC LITTLE BUG!" She yelled back.

"WHAT DID I EVER DO TO YOU?!

"You became a TOP HERO and DIDN'T DO ANYTHING TO DESERVE IT! It was just HANDED to you ON A SILVER PLATTER AND FOR WHAT?! TO GET YOUR BUTT HANDED TO YOU YESTERDAY?!" She yelled, getting louder and louder as the glass began to crack and the room began to shake.

"…You know about that?"

"THE WHOLE CITY KNOWS!! AND THEY ARE FREAKING OUT! THAT IS ALL EVERYONE HAS BEEN TALKING ABOUT! THE TRUST BETWEEN HEROES AND CIVILIANS IS ON THE LINE– *BECAUSE OF YOU!!!!*" She boomed, sending him through one of the few white walls, creating a big Firefly-shaped hole.

Firefly stumbled up, brushing the dust and debris off of him. Coughing up the cotton candy foam. It didn't taste as sweet as the real thing.

"W-What are you t-talking about?" He asked, still letting the fabric particles leave his lungs.

"Your little failure yesterday? Caused the city to go *BALLISTIC!* The press is blowing up, the internet is going crazy– and now Governor Jaceson is questioning if he even wants to keep us in business!"

"WHAT?!?" Firefly screamed, shocked out of his mind.

"WE COULD LOSE FUNDING, HEROES COULD BE CUT, OR HE COULD COMPLETELY SHUT US DOWN!" Soundwave screamed, stomping the floor. The ground tumbled at her tantrum and Firefly tried to catch his balance.

"W-Where is Captain Peace?" Firefly skipped straight to the point.

"Does it matter? Not like he wants to see you…"

"H-He doesn't?" Firefly's heart fell.

Soundwave grabbed his hood and pulled him in really close, "Just letting you know…if heroes get cut, you'll be the first to go. Trust me…" She threatened, shoving him back and stomping off.

Firefly wasted no time as he ran through the building. Sprinting as his flames flew off him. He looked through the doorways until a room filled with superheroes caught his eye. The hero tried to do a double-take but just ended up slipping on the floor.

Thud!

"Ow!" He yelped.

The room of worried supers looked down in the doorway to see Firefly on the ground.

The hero blinked open his eyes to see Captain Peace in the center of the concerned chaos circle. A disappointed frown and sorry eyes painted his face.

"CAPTAIN!" Firefly scrambled up. Waving his arms around. "S-Soundwave told me about what happened– i-is it true– I-I-"

"Yes. It's true. I have a meeting with Governor Jaceson on Saturday, …it's not looking good," he sighed.

Firefly's guilt wrapped around his neck and hung him like a noose, "S-Sir I-I am so so s-sorry."

48

"It's fine," the Captain tried to leave.

"I-I can make this right! I can catch him! I'll do it today!" Firefly pleaded.

"Kid, don't push yourself. It's ok, it's the luck of the cards..." His boss sighed.

"N-No I'll make it up to you! I promise!"

"Firefly!" Captain Peace snapped, grabbing his attention, "Let. It. *Go.* I knew Xenomorph was too much for you...and if I still had my powers I would've taken care of it. I should've never let you go out," He drifted and moved him out of the way.

His captain left in a huff of rage, "What a mistake..." he mumbled, but Firefly heard.

The clouds covered the sun as the light in the room vanished into the gloom. His heart broke at the little whisper and his eyes glossed over. Firefly went to wipe his eyes only to find his goggle lens in the way.

He stood there stuck.

Not knowing what to do or who to go to. In times like these he wish he had a friend, or his Dad.

Anger bubbled up inside of him–*Xenomorph ruined everything!*

Firefly was going to get his revenge. He would make Xenomorph pay! He would make the villain hurt like he had!

In a fury of flames, Firefly stormed to the board and looked at the wall of schedules. Smoke poured out of his ears. He saw his patrol shift and instantly ran off, ready to finally put the supervillain in his place.

Xenomorph was a dead man!

***

With more determination than ever, Firefly raced to his spot: Times Square. Covered in lights, billboards, screens, and colorful posters. It was the flashiest, loudest, touristy part of New York. He was a tad early, but surely he would get Xenomorph's attention here; but to the hero's surprise-

"HELLO~ NEW YORK~! WHO IS READY TO PARTY?!" Xenomorph boomed, sending everyone to cover their ears. He was already there–standing on top of a billboard. The villain gave a maniacal laugh and held his hand up as lightning flickered in his palm.

He then blasted all of the screens around. Fritzing them up and letting them spark in a fiery destruction. Exploding like fireworks on the fourth of July.

The crowd started screaming and running. One screen teetered and tottered until it fell. Heading straight for an innocent lady. Firefly ran in and launched at her, tackling her out of the way.

"Are you ok?" He asked as he held the woman in his hands. The girl just nodded, getting back up to run with the crowd. Screams filled the air, and Xenomorph smiled. Enjoying every second of fleeting.

Firefly lit himself up as he angrily approached, standing on a raised planter to get his attention.

"XENOMORPH!!" He yelled.

The villain looked down, *'Yay, how predictable.'*

"Uuuugh, 'great' look who came *crashing* in..."

Firefly tilted his head, confused, "I didn't come crashing in?"

Xeno pulled the air in front of him and a sound of tumbling metal followed. Firefly turned around to see a car rolling right for him.

"WHA!" Firefly yelped and jumped as high as he could, backflipping over the car, just barely. He landed back on the concrete as the car hit a random building.

Xeno watched the wreck, amused, "Ah dang, missed. Guess I'll have to try again–" he started, excitedly turning his attention back to the hero, but Firefly was already flying through the air readying a punch.

Xenomorph ducked, as Firefly swung. Missing and punching the glowing screen behind them, landing him on the same billboard. He pulled his scratched-up hand out of the glass as it sparked. Now on equal playing fields.

"Xenomorph...*this ends now!*"

"You're right, cause I'm going to destroy you!" He quipped, magicing up dozens of powers; raging water, fire, crackling electricity, plants and vines, ice, flight, and many more Firefly couldn't see on the shallow surface.

The villain swung a vine and lassoed Firefly's foot, swinging him around and flicking him into another screen.

SLAM!!

Firefly destroyed the shiny screen as the image glitched.

"Gah! Ow...that's going to hurt tomorrow," He drifted, talking to himself.

"OH I'M JUST GETTING STARTED!" Xeno readied a blast of water and aimed an ongoing stream. Firefly ducked but it didn't matter-the water had touched the inner circuits. Soon the whole TV glitched and electrocuted Firefly and the flashy video behind him. Sending the volts through the hero's veins in agonizing pain.

Xenomorph did an evil laugh as he let Firefly fall onto the top of a taxi car roof–

CRASH!!

Denting the yellow roof.

Xenomorph floated down, tearing up the ground with roots and ice. Using lazer eyes to draw a big X on one of the buildings, like he was signing a work of art.

"Had enough…Zero?" He asked the broken bug.

Firefly lifted his head. Gritting his teeth as he jumped up and attacked his enemy, pinning him to the ground. Xenomorph kicked him back into the hood of the car and began running to the center of Town Square.

The news and police showed up like they always do, fashionably late. Cameras started to roll and capture everything as Xeno jumped onto the center jumbotron, running up the wall as if he could defy gravity.

Firefly climbed after him, being able to only use his hands. Really wish he could actually fly right now. Using every breath in his lungs he scaled the displays, slowly getting higher and higher until he could start tasting the clouds. Finally the hero met Xeno at the top, cutting off the villain's exit route. Standing on nothing except a few inches of ledge.

"Xenomorph– Please, I beg of you, stop this!"

"Why on earth would I do that?!" The villain started to throw hands, punching and kicking but Firefly dodged and blocked. Trying to make peace as he dangled almost twenty stories up. All eyes and cameras staring at the two as they fought.

He thought about what his mom said, about talking. Who knows maybe there was a soul in there…deep, deep, deep, deeeeep~ down.

"Xenomorph, please listen," he blocked the incoming fist, "I need to catch you."

"Well, I need to defeat you! That's our game. You just can't stand that I'm finally WINNING!" Xenomorph yelled, finally landing a hit and sending Firefly slipping off the ledge of the building.

The crowd gasped.

Luckily he was able to grab onto the edge.

"WAAH–! No! N-No that's not it, look I–…I need to look good for the cameras, can't we work out an agreement?!" Firefly begged.

"An agreement?! You've got to be kidding me," He scoffed sarcastically. Practically laughing in his head about the idea.

"Please…I could lose my job…"

"Good! I don't want you in my world anymore!" Xeno shouted, blasting a lightning bolt at the hero's gloved hands. The hero gasped, letting go as he started to fall. Luckily a little scaffolding balcony broke his fall and screamed. Xenomorph jumped after him, readying a punch as the bug rolled out of the way.

"You know what?" Firefly snapped, tired of playing fair-er, "Why do I even try with you?!" He protested, getting back up.

Xenomorph held his ground, only because he was interested in where this was going.

Firefly flamed up brighter than ever, walking towards his enemy, "I try and try and try to give you chances, to give you mercy but all you do is screw things up for me! NOW THE CITY HATES ME, CAPTAIN PEACE WON'T EVEN TALK TO ME, AND I HAVE *DOOMED MY ENTIRE ORGANIZATION!!*"

The world froze, yet every second was caught on camera.

Xenomorph took a step back as his face dropped and eyes widened. Firefly cocked his head, not understanding the sudden shock.

"Y-YOU HAVE AN ORGANIZATION TOO?!" Xenomorph yelled.

Firefly finally realized what he said, stunned at his negligence; but then he quickly realized,

"W-Wait– *'TOO'*?! YOU WORK FOR AN ORGANIZATION?!" He pointed out.

Xenomorph covered his mouth with the sharp flaps of his coat collar.

The news started to buzz and people started to gasp and whisper.

What had they done?

"I-I gotta go!" Xenomorph suddenly declared and ran.

"WAIT– Hey! Wait up!" Firefly yelled and ran after him. He didn't know if it was a distraction from his screw-up or revenge for everything, but Firefly followed Xeno. They both jumped down from the building and fled the scene.

The two supers ran for blocks, dodging people and cars, jumping benches, and sliding down stair railings, until Xenomorph slipped into a dark alleyway.

He turned around to see...no one behind him. He breathed a sigh of relief, bending over to his knees, however that didn't stop his pulse—he had outed the organization! Dark Legacy was going to be *furious*! This was it! The end! It was over! He was dead!

The villain's thoughts spiral and adrenaline only grew as Firefly came running around the corner and tackled the villain.

"DWAH!" Xeno yelled, getting thrown onto the concrete ground. "Are you serious?! Right now?!"

"Yes 'right now'! You have an organization?!" Firefly asked, he may have already been in deep waters, but maybe if he could get some information on the villains he could be proven useful again.

"I'm not telling you anything blabbermouth!" Xenomorph stood up, shoving the bug off of him.

"W-W- HEY! You can't just–" Firefly started.

"Listen, Firecracker, I don't know how they do it in 'Hero Heaven', BUT I WASN'T SUPPOSED TO SAY *ANYTHING*!!" Xenomorph sassed, pointing fingers and getting closer to Firefly's dirty and bruised face.

"Well neither was I!" Firefly snapped, flaming up all over again.

"'WELL GREAT JOB SUPERSTAR!!' NOW WE ARE BOTH DEAD!!! ALL BECAUSE YOU HAD TO PROVE YOU'RE SOMETHING SPECIAL!!!" Xenomorph poked his chest, walking closer, anger spilling over, "DO YOU REALIZE WHAT YOU HAVE DONE?! WE–"*BLAST!!!*

Xenomorph was suddenly knocked to the brick wall with a futuristic blast and rag-dolled to the floor. Firefly flinched at the spectacle. Xeno tried to get up but his vision grew black as he passed out on the cement.

Firefly shuddered as he turned around to see where the blast came from.

There in the dark alley, with two other villains backing his side, was Dark Legacy. Holding a very unstable blaster that had clearly just been used with the way the smoke danced off the end.

"D–D–Dark Legacy?!" Firefly winced. His dark appearance alone was enough to make Firefly's legs wobble like Jell-O. He had never seen the King of Villains face to face before, but Captain Peace would tell stories of when they would fight. The long battles, all the bloodshed, sacrifices, all of it. Dark Legacy was Captain Peace's 'Xenomorph'. "W-W-What are you doing here?! What's going on?!"

"I'm here...*BECAUSE ONE OF MY WORKERS BLEW OUR COVER!*"

"Wait– one of your..." the hero looked at the limp Xeno on the floor, "You're his boss?!"

"Was…thanks to you he will be terminated…"

Firefly backed up, horrified by what that meant.

"Permanently…and I can't have any witnesses…" Dark Legacy drifted, readying up another blast from the machine.

"W-Wait! NO!" Firefly tried to run, but he was too slow and was blasted into another wall. Conking his head on the bricks. He too fell to the floor and tried to stay conscious, but ultimately failed. Darkness leaking into Firefly's vision as the last blur he could see was Dark Legacy walking up on Xenomorph and him.

Chapter 6:

Firefly slowly flickered open his eyes. The room stopped spinning and focused—however, he did not recognize it. It was dark and cold, with a single lamp above. Metal tile covering the wall like some sort of prison and some old, red stains scattered the floor. He went to get up but something held him down.

Looking down, he saw he was tied to a chair. Chains wrapping around him more times than he could count.

"Oh no...oh no, no, no, no, no, no, no!" He muttered as he struggled against the metal. Jumping and twisting.

"Hey! Buggy! Would you keep it down," an all too familiar voice called out.

Firefly looked over his shoulder to see the back of his enemy tied up just like him.

"Xenomorph?" He asked.

"No duh– 'I am actually Governor Jaceson'," he sassed, rolling his eyes. Not that you could tell.

"Would you stop being sarcastic for five minutes and tell me what's going on?! What did you do to me?!"

"How would I know?! I am tied up just like you flamehead! I didn't do this!" Xeno yelled.

"WHAT?! You don't know?! It's your boss! How could you not–"

"FOR THE LAST TIME, I DON'T KNOW WHAT IS GOING ON! MAYBE IF YOU DIDN'T EXPOSE US ON *LIVE TV* NONE OF THIS WOULD BE HAPPENING!"

"OH NO, NO, NO! NONE OF THIS WOULD BE HAPPENING IF YOU WEREN'T A SELFISH, STUCK-UP, HORRIBLE PERSON!!"

"Firefly, this is no time for compliments!" Xenomorph yelled, looking around. He could feel Firefly's face drop, unimpressed. "There's gotta be a way out…"

"Oh, there is," another voice entered. Unfortunately, it was also too familiar. Dark Legacy came from the shadows, as he did best, "however, I don't think you two will like it…"

"D-Dark Legacy!" Xenomorph started, Firefly's eyes grew as he watched, "L-Listen I can explain-"

"Explain what? *HOW YOU BROKE OUR ONE RULE?!*" He scolded, grabbing Xenomorph's chair and shaking him up.

"He started it!" Xeno tried. Firefly's face jumped in offense.

"EXCUSE ME?!" Firefly struggled.

"It doesn't matter who did it first; what matters is you did it. So now I have to kill you," Dark Legacy continued.

"WHAT?!" They both shouted in unison.

"Sorry Xenomorph," Dark Legacy smiled behind his mask, "You were a good kid, but I can't forgive a mistake this big...you have put the entire safety of our people in danger. I have to let you go...but of course you know too much."

Xenomorph froze, not knowing what to possibly say. All he could do was beg.

"P–Please Boss– I am so, so sorry..." Xeno tried. Deflating in the cold, metal seat.

Firefly's heart sank, hearing those words before, from himself. Maybe they weren't so different.

His thoughts were interrupted when Dark Legacy got into his frame of vision.

"As for you...on top of your little goof up, I can't have you going back to tell the public what you have seen and heard today—so you have to be eliminated too. No hard feelings?"

Firefly stared at him, disgusted, "Your threats don't scare me..."

"It's not a threat...it's a *promise*."

Firefly tried to hide his gulp over his determined eyes. Although they shook with fear.

"Oh and your little organization? Done for."

Firefly's act broke, "W-What?!"

"EVERY HERO UNDER ONE ROOF? PLANNING TOGETHER? SECRETS BEING PASSED LIKE IT'S THE NORMAL? YOU THINK I WOULDN'T TAKE ADVANTAGE OF

THAT?! And now that you've spoiled everything, I have to *OBLITERATE* every superhero to have ever breathed..."

Firefly stood shellshock. What had he done?

"S-See? I helped! Now we are going to win against the heroes!" Xenomorph tried.

"Helped? Xenomorph you only made things worse! You've been a pain in my side since day one and now that you've completely put our lives on the line I have enough reason to finally kill you!" Dark Legacy slipped a small laugh.

"...What?" Xeno's voice cracked, "But you said I had potential..."

Firefly gave a small frown, he didn't know villains had hearts or that they could break.

Dark Legacy approached his protege and ripped the disc latched onto his armor.

"NO!" Xeno screamed, trying to grab at it; but the chains, still cold and heavy, held him in his place.

"This belongs to me...besides not like you'll need it anymore. Oh and by the way those chains...fireproof. There is no way you guys are getting out."

Firefly's eyes widened at the fact. He immediately tried to burn the chains but all they did was turn a bright, glowly orange. The metal began to heat up until it started to burn him.

"Ow...ow!" He yelped quietly, blowing on the chains. He stopped his power, and waited...but the cold links didn't change. Not even a single metal drip.

"I'll be back later to finish you, I have some messes to take care of thanks to you! Although, letting you wallow in your failure and guilt makes the torturing process more fun. I mean how does it feel boys? ...You are both worthless nobodies who have doomed your own kind."

Both boys froze, really taking in what he said. Every word, like bait. It was somehow fueling, like some sick twisted addiction— but it hurt just as much. How could they have possibly screwed up that badly?

"You two are such failures..." Dark Legacy said as he left, slamming the door behind him.

Silence took the room as the two supers just stared at the floor, taking Dark Legacy's words to heart.

"...Great! Now we are going to die and it's all your fault!" Xenomorph blamed.

"*MY* FAULT?! HOW IS THIS *MY* FAULT!?"

"YOU'RE THE ONE WHO SPILLED THE SECRET!"

"YOU DID TOO! BESIDES IT'S YOUR BOSS WHO IS GOING TO KILL US! MY BOSS WOULD NEVER EVEN THINK OF SUCH A THING!" Firefly yelled back.

"I ONLY SLIPPED UP BECAUSE OF YOU! YOU ARE SUCH A CLUTZ!"

"LISTEN! The blame game isn't important right now, there are bigger problems at hand."

"BIGGER THAN OUR LIVES?!"

"You heard him! Every hero will be killed! Our entire super society: gone! Wiped out! Hundreds of lives are at stake!"

"BLAGH! Such a hero thing, and in case you have forgotten—I'M A VILLAIN! So that's a win for me!" He sassed.

"WELL DO YOU WANNA DIE?!"

"OF COURSE I DON'T!"

"THEN WE NEED TO GET OUT OF HERE! QUICK USE YOUR POWERS!"

"...W-What?" Xenomorph did a double-take.

"USE YOUR POWERS! I can't do anything, it's fireproof!"

Xenomorph gulped, "Y-Yeah...right...my powers...um..." he drifted.

The villain concentrated, yanking up his hand just enough. His hand sparked as Firefly watched from behind. Soon a beautiful flame appeared and danced on his hand.

"Fire," Firefly deadpanned, "SERIOUSLY?! Did you not hear me?! IT'S *FIREPROOF*! DO SOMETHING ELSE YOU IDIOT!"

"I CAN'T!" Xeno snapped.

"W-What? WHAT DO YOU MEAN 'YOU CAN'T'?! You are Xenomorph! You have every power created!"

"NO! ...N-No I don't..."

Firefly's silence spoke volumes, looking the villain up and down as his jaw slowly started to fall.

"I–...I don't have every power created. That disc gives me everything..."

Firefly stood shocked, "W-What...? But right now– you did pyrokinesis!"

Xenomorph twitched his head.

"Fire," Firefly repeated.

Xenomorph sighs, "Well obviously, cause you're right here..."

"I don't follow—do you have powers or not?"

"I do, it's just not what you think..."

Firefly looked at him weirdly, squinting his eyes and mouth in a squiggle.

"Truth is...I'm a mimic..."

"A what?" Firefly asked.

"A mimic. I can copy anyone's powers...when they are close."

"..." Firefly stayed silent, not believing his ears.

"That disc is a piece of tech created for me. It has the DNA of every super ever born...allowing me to copy anyone's power at any time. It's less restricting. Without it...I am nothing."

Firefly's head sulked, they were trapped.

The seconds of silence dragged on forever until Firefly had an idea.

"W-Wait! What about someone else?"

"Someone else? You're losing it kid."

"No, think about it, we are in your headquarters, correct?"

"Yeah~? I think so, never seen this room though."

"Then it's filled with villains! Surely one of them has got to walk by, then you can mimic!" Firefly announced.

"Oh! Yes! Finally you're smart!"

"Yes– wait– Hey!"

"Relax Firecracker, just shut your mouth and let me concentrate. I've never reached for someone that far," Xeno shrugged off as he focused at the door. Closing his eyes as he tried to search for someone, anyone.

"Anything yet?" Firefly bugged.

"No, knock it off."

"...How about now?"

"Dude!" Xeno snipped, opening his eyes.

"Sorry! Sorry!"

Xenomorph tried again, and suddenly he felt the smallest wave of power. It was bright and destructive, but more precise.

Before Xeno said a word he instantly looked down at his chains and two red, blazing lazers came from his eyes. He focused as he sliced the chains down the middle, cutting them perfectly.

He stopped his glowing eyes as the villain jumped out of his chair, "Yes! Boom! Xenomorph wins again!" He started dancing, moonwalking away.

"Um? Hello?! Aren't you forgetting something?" Firefly sassed, gesturing to his chains.

"Nope!" Xenomorph smiled, hand on the door handle.

"HELP ME!" Firefly demanded. Flaming up.

"Why would I do that?!"

"Because I will scorch your face off if you don't let me go this second!" Firefly yelled, bursting into flames.

"Alright! Alright! Yeesh!"

Xeno snarled and walked over, using his lazer eyes to cut through the metal. Soon Firefly was free and he stood up, simmering down.

Xeno instantly punched Firefly in the face and tried roundhouse kicking the red blur, but Firefly jumped over Xenomorph's leg and elbowed him in the chest. Xeno stumbled back, but managed to grab and throw one of the metal chairs at the glowing bug. Firefly somersaulted under the incoming chair, snatched Xeno's arm, and threw him over his head.

"AH–!" Xenomorph yelped and fell with a splat to the metal floor.

"What the heck was that for?!" Firefly yelled, looking over the tired super.

"Do I need a reason to destroy you?"

"Get up." Firefly demanded, giving the broken body his hand.

Xenomorphed shoved it to the side and got up by himself, "Alright, fine, looks like we are done here so; Adios, Buggy! See you next week–" Xenomorph tried to walk off but Firefly grabbed his collar and yanked him back.

"Are you crazy?! You can't go out there—they will kill you!"

"…Oh right…that thing. Well I'll just hide until it blows over."

"You really think this is just going to 'blow over'?!"

"…Maybe?"

"Look Xenomorph…" Firefly breathed, not believing what was about to come out of his mouth, "I know we have our…*differences*, but we need to work together."

"WHAT?! Oh HELL NO!"

"C'mon! We have to! Otherwise…neither one of us is getting out of here alive…"

"…" Xeno thought, crossing his arms.

"Look what we were able to do when we worked together–" the hero gestured to the broken chains on the floor, "I know we aren't a team, but we have to try."

Xenomorph scoffed, "I could do this on my own, you just want to work together because I know the way out."

"…That may be a really big factor," Firefly sheepishly admitted. "But c'mon you need me!"

"Excuse me?! No, I don't, I don't need anyone!"

"What are you going to do?! Go out there and fight every guard and villain? With what power?"

"Theirs, duh!" Xeno sassed as he continued to walk away.

"So you are going to fight hundreds of villains who have been mastering specific powers for decades? You have little to no experience with any of them—ESPECIALLY without that disc."

"…Crap…" Xeno stopped in place, hating his point.

"I could be an extra set of eyes, arms, and another head! Plus…" Firefly stepped closer, "With me right next to you, you have a guaranteed power source~." Smiling wide to sweeten the deal.

Xeno looked into his perky lenses, full of stars and sunshine. Yuck. Finally he caved.

"UUGGGHHH!! Fine, you can come with me as my hostage! But we are in my territory, so you have to do everything I say! And once we are out–we part ways!"

"I mean I was hoping we could be more like team captains~...?" Firefly trailed off as he noticed Xeno's face already turning red with fury. "Yo-ok...you are in charge."

"Great!" Xeno commanded as he walked to the door. He jiggled the handle but it was locked, and the villain cussed.

"Language."

Xeno let out a whole slew of curse words before, "Say language one more time Bug Boy! I dare you!" He erupted, flaming up himself.

Firefly looked up to avoid eye contact as he slowly backed away, checking out the wall. He felt the cold metal and backed up, getting an idea. The hero readied up and shot a fireball at the wall.

The ball of fire bounced back as Firefly ducked. Xeno saw the red fireball from the corner of his eyes and dodged.

"WHA! HEY! Watch where you shoot those things!" Xeno yelled.

"Sorry! Sorry!"

Xenomorph watched as the fire hit the chain, the flames floated up, leaving a trail of smoke. His eyes wandered up to the ceiling as he smelt the burning clouds.

"The ceiling!" Xeno exclaimed.

"What?"

"The ceiling, we can climb out from the ceiling! Give me a boost!"

"Ok! Ok!" Firefly quickly spat and kneeled down. Readying his hands as Xeno took a running start and hopped on the hero. Firefly stood up, holding Xenomorph's boot as he reached the ceiling tile. Blasting the styrofoam to pieces with a fireball.

Little flecks of wood and rubble rained down from the sky as Xenomorph grabbed the scaffolding and pulled himself up.

"Good! Now pull me up!" Firefly said, holding out his hand.

Xenomorph froze, looking down at the little bug.

"…Xenomorph…?" Firefly's face fell a bit.

Suddenly the door handle jiggled.

Dark Legacy had returned. Firefly quickly shoved one of the metal chairs to the door, turning back to still see his frozen rival.

"Xenomorph please!"

Xenomorph looked at the door then back at his enemy, torn.

"Please…I don't want to die…" Firefly begged with sad eyes. Barely visible through his goggles.

Xenomorph felt something new inside of him. However it wasn't another power, it was something warm and fuzzy. Empathy.

After another few uncomfortable seconds, Xenomorph resentfully reached down and grabbed Firefly, pulling him up through the ceiling.

Firefly sighed with relief, "Thank you…"

"I'm going to regret that. Let's go!" Xenomorphic commanded as they crawled through the vents. However, he couldn't help but think of Firefly's words; *Thank you*. No one had ever thanked him before, it felt odd, light even. Regardless he pushed it off and continued to lead the way.

When Dark Legacy finally busted the door down he was shocked to find his two captives gone with burning chains on the floor and a hole in the ceiling.

"What the-?!" He screamed at nothing. He turned to Sniper who was guarding the door. "WHERE DID THEY GO?!"

"I-I don't know!" The villain defended.

"Sound the alarm!"

"Yes sir!" The villain protested and shot lazers from his eyes across the hall. Breaking a container with a big, red switch. Glass shattered everywhere as the switch was pulled.

Red lights covered the entire headquarters as an ear-shrieking siren went off. The HQ went into lockdown as villains started readying up to find the two boys who had been caught in the crossfire.

Chapter 7:

Xenomorph kicked through a vent and the grate fell to the floor. Sending a loud metal twang throughout the empty room. The villain jumped down gracefully, hitting the shiny tile, and readying up–

"DWAAAH!" A voice yelped and Firefly came crashing on top of him.

"GAOWW! Can't you do anything right?!" Xenomorph groaned as he pushed his hostage off.

"Excuse me! I've never crawled through a vent before!" Firefly snared, standing up and brushing the dust off.

"Then you need to get out more!" Xeno scoffed as he stood up. The sirens were still going off, but they were distant. They looked around to see the huge, empty room they had landed in. The only thing around was tons of decked-out sports cars of different colors and patterns.

"Bingo!" Xenomorph got an idea and ran to the coolest car among the lot. It was slick and nice, a real black sports car with a spoiler. Blue and white racing stripes running down the middle and flames flying off the sides.

He wasted no time in elbowing the front window, shattering the glass.

"What are you doing?!" Firefly yelped.

"Getting out of here!" He smiled, lifting himself into the broken window and into the car. Fumbling on to the seats, the villain climbed behind the wheel.

"Get closer, Sparky!" Xeno chirped.

Firefly, confused, took a step forward. Xenomorph harnessed the nearby fire powers and used his finger as if it were a blowtorch. Burning the plastic and revealing the exposed wiring of the car. He started ripping and welding, attaching and burning.

"*Now* what are you doing?!" Firefly asked again, watching this felt like a crime but knowing his 'partner' it probably was.

"Hot wiring the car," The villain exclaimed as the car jumped to life. Engine roaring and lights flickering on. Xeno hopped back in the seat as he cheered, "WOOO! Let's go!"

"Go?! You're going to steal it?!"

"Technically, I'm borrowing it~"

"Xenomorph, you can't steal a car!"

"Why not?!"

"Because it's wrong!" Firefly fought back.

"Look Firecracker– this is the only way out, so do you want to sit here and wait for Dark Legacy to find you or are you going to hop in? I'm leaving with or without you!"

72

Firefly stared at the car and then at the lone door that led back into the chaos and unknowns of his demise.

"Please forgive me, Captain," He prayed as he hopped clumsily through the window, falling on Xenomorph.

"Hey— get off of me! Passenger Princess!" Xeno shoved him to the passenger seat as he fumbled over. Firefly buckled his seatbelt good and tight.

Xenomorph pulled the stick, looking out his mirrors and windows.

"You ready for this?" He asked sarcastically.

"Nope, not in a million years," Firefly braced as he held the back of his seat.

"Let's go!" Xeno smiled and floored the gas. Firefly let out a scream as Xeno crashed the car straight through the garage door. Everything felt like it was in slow motion. Debris and metal pieces flew everywhere as the sun finally hit their faces. Flying through the air like a bird.

Firefly kept screaming. Begging to hit the concrete soon, while Xenomorph never felt more free in his life. Like wings he never had. With a bounce and a screech they hit the street and the car went racing down the streets of New York.

Xeno aggressively jerked the wheel right and left, drifting the car as much as he could as the speed only grew.

"X-Xenomorph! You could slow down now!" Firefly tried to scream over the noise of the wind and honking horns of other angry drivers.

"Why?! This is awesome!" Xeno steered right and the car went rocketing through traffic. The blur of buildings and plants whizzed by in seconds as the wind flapped in his hair. Adrenaline pumping as he smiled wide, drifting and clipping the curb. He started pressing buttons until the radio started blaring some girly pop song, "Oou! Niki Minaj!" He kept his eyes off the road as he steered, about to hit someone.

"XENOMORPH!" Firefly grabbed the wheel and steered away from the innocent and their dog on the crosswalk.

"What?! Not a fan? Fine," He yelled over the car speakers, changing the music to something more epic and metal—fit for a car chase.

"No! Slow down!"

The car bumped around as they started scraping taxis and running over outdoor tables.

"F-Funny thing...I can't," Xenomorph laughed nervously.

"You can't?!" Firefly held the handle at the top of the car in concern.

"What does the yellow light mean?" Xeno asked, staring at the traffic light in front of them, fastly approaching.

"It means it's going to turn red! You need to stop this car!"

"Crap! Ok we are speeding up!"

"What?!"

"I just gotta make it across before it turns red!"

"Who would risk that?!"

74

"I would if I knew how to drive!" Xeno shouted as he ran the yellow, turning left as he continued to drift through the road like a street racer.

Firefly took a breath, "Wait a minute— *You can't drive?!*"

"Do you think villains can get driver's licenses?! That would reveal our secret identities!" Xenomorph turned again.

The sound of a cop siren interrupted their arguing and Xeno looked in his rearview mirror to see four cop cars trailing him. The red and blue lights flashed as Firefly started breathing faster.

"O-Oh no! Oh no! I-I-I c-can't go to jail! I-I CAN'T GO TO JAIL!!"

"NO ONE'S GOING TO JAIL!"

"But you need to pull over!"

"Why in the world would I pull over?!"

"BECAUSE IT'S THE LAW!"

"WHY IN THE WORLD WOULD I RESPECT THE LAW!" Xenomorph yelled as he pulled the emergency brake, swerving the car to the side.

"WHAT *ARE* YOU GOING TO DO?!"

"LOSE THEM!" Xeno yelled, flooring the gas and going down another way, crashing into some police tape and weak fencing. Driving them straight through a random construction site. Xeno dodged metal pipes, support beams, concrete and more as he spun up dirt; creating a smog screen for the cops. Across the sandy lot was a giant wooden plank, sitting up against metal poles.

"RAMP! RAMP! RAMP!" Firefly helped, contorting his body as much as he could to become one with the plush seat.

"Good eye!" Xeno playfully punched his shoulder as he rammed the pedal. Hurling towards the dusty plank. Breaking the speed limit–and speedometer.

The police cars cleared the dust but halted with a screech as the car drove up the ramp launching the two supers into the air.

"WOOOOOOO!!!!" Xeno let go of the wheel putting his hands in the air as if this was some sort of game.

"AAAAAAAAAAAHHHHH!!!" While Firefly screamed, closing his eyes and praying to God.

The newfound flight sent them soaring out of the construction site and into a plaza. People watched as the car flew overhead. Getting out there phones and snapping pictures.

Soon the car landed as Xenomorph grabbed the wheel and did several donuts. Smoke covered their cool car which was dented all over. He finally stopped the car, but kept cheering.

Firefly held his mouth, "I think I'm going to be sick–" although the poor guy couldn't tell if he was going to throw up due to the car sickness or the fact he was working with Xenomorph.

"Say no more, Sparky, I got you," Xenomorph declared, readjusting the stick and speeding off to who knows where, but he only got about a block before Xeno crashed the car into a telephone pole.

Both supers froze as the engine smoked up, slowly looking at each other as they both realized–

"Run!" They shouted together and hopped out of the car and ran away. Sure enough the wires from the telephone pole wisped down and caught the car on fire, exploding it as the two supers didn't dare look back.

"I know where to go!" Xeno declared, still leading the way–

Gag! Firefly thought. Yep, it wasn't car sickness.

Chapter 8:

Firefly grabbed a red bag of hot spicy chips. Aluminum packaging rustling in his hands. He picked up another obnoxiously bright red bag of chips, thinking.

The two ended up at a convenience store. The lights were dim in blues and purples; not that he could see much with his hood on. A classic black and white checkered the floor. Music played just barely, however it was boring and lifeless. Nothing like Firefly's situation. The store was mainly empty with the exception of the worker asleep behind the counter.

The kid couldn't decide between extra heat or super spicy.

However his thoughts were interrupted when a metal can hit the floor.

The hero spun around to see Xenomorph holding a pack of toilet paper, spray paint, and a carton of eggs.

"Really?" Firefly deadpanned.

"What? We came here for supplies. That's why I brought us here in the first place."

"We came here for the essentials! Like food, water, bandages, toiletries!"

"Duh~ why do you think I got toilet paper~? Besides I'm not splurging, I got one ply," Xeno explained.

"You got vandalism stuff– put it back!" Firefly demanded, putting back his chips.

"Pff– I don't have to listen to you," He sassed, sitting up on an aisle shelf. He plopped his stuff to the side as he grabbed a colorful bag of sour gummy worms. Popping the bag open and eating them elegantly.

"Hey! You have to pay for those!"

"Who says I wasn't?" Xenomorph smirked.

"BECAUSE YOU'RE–"

"Shh! Easy Firecracker, let's not go spilling our location," Xeno teased.

Firefly turned his anger into a whisper, "Because you are a villain. Once a villain, always a villain."

Xenomorph smiled, "Hm, flattering."

"Just– put it back."

"Come on~ I'm just a teen, this is hardly 'villainy'."

"I beg to differ," Firefly seethed.

"It's just some stealing and pranking, I bet even you have done some!" Xeno teased.

"…" Firefly shifted his eyes, looking down at the nauseous tile.

"Wait– wait– wait…seriously? You've never done a prank? Please tell me you've at least broken a rule or acted out– or something!"

"What? No! That would be irresponsible!"

"…You are such a goody-two-shoes." Xenomorph scoffed. "You haven't ever let your anger just– explode? Just once?"

"What?!" Firefly flamed up, "Why would I do such a horrible thing!"

"Because then you look like that," Xeno smirked, gesturing to the fireball. "You keep holding it in, Sparky, you're going to crack."

Firefly breathed, took out his lighter, and flicked the flint, relaxing, "I'll never crack."

"What is that?" The curious villain asked.

"Nothing! Just something to calm me down…"

"You know it's not working, right?" Xenomorph asked, tilting his head.

"Yes," Firefly huffed.

"If it doesn't work, why do you still have it? It's broken."

"It's– …It's personal." Firefly brushed off.

"Weird~… You seriously haven't done anything bad?"

"No! I'm not like you! Well– ok– I may have jaywalked once—but that is it!"

"Man…if we are going to continue to work together I've got to fun you up!" Xeno declared, hopping off the shelf.

"Whoa! Whoa! Whoa! What are you talking about? We are done! Parting ways!"

"Well yes, but you saw what happened today. We are on the *city's* radar now."

"That's because~ you raced the cops and drove up a ramp!" Firefly flamed up again.

"Regardless, you are still my hostage until the heat dies down. *Then* we are done."

"You just want me for my power." Firefly deadpanned.

"Maybe, but I also can't leave you like this. You're so sad and depressing! Such a mess, yuck! So I guess we are…'sticking together' blah!" The villain whined.

"Excuse me? What are you talking about?"

"We are going to have some fun," Xenomorph waved the toilet paper around.

"What?! Absolutely not. What we need is a plan!"

"Exactly! A plan of attack, so who we TP-ing?"

"No one!"

"Really? No one? There is no one you hate?"

"…" Firefly looked away, feeling guilty for his answer.

Xenomorph smirked, seeing the cogs turn in his head, "So where we going?"

***

The night fell and stars painted the sky as they always did. Firefly shook like a wet cat at the sight of Molly's house. It was nice, two stories, elegant windows, dark gray with white trim and a black roof. Her front lawn was huge and lush. A perfect target.

Xenomorph blew a bubble with his gum (that he stole) as he stared at the opportunity. Tossing the roll in his hands.

"So what's so special about this place~? Who are we messing up?"

"Shh! We are not messing up anyone! This was a terrible idea and we should go back before someone catches us."

"Ugh! Don't be such a square Firebrat. Now come on, spill, whose the target?"

Firefly held his breath, really debating on whether to tell this guy or not. He didn't even know why he was still with him, why he was even here! He didn't even know the guy. Maybe a safety precaution? Who knows when Dark Legacy would come back, he'd need anyone on his side...anyone.

"It's...Soundwave..."

"Whoa?! The hero?! *YOU HAVE BEEF WITH A HERO*?!" Xenomorph boomed, but instantly covered his mouth.

"SHHHH!"

"Sorry, mimic stuff," He bashed.

"Ok, yes! It's Soundwave, she is ruthless and gives me a hard time, happy?" Firefly sassed in a whisper.

"Very much so," the villain grinned.

"Now let's go! I don't want to be seen with you!" Firefly started shoving and pushing Xeno away from the house.

"'Gee, love you too pookie…'" Xenomorph sneered sarcastically, as his feet scraped across the trimmed grass. Not even bothering to walk.

"The deal was once we are out we split ways! Your words! 'Xeno'."

"Don't call me Xeno, Firecracker!"

Firefly rolled his eyes.

Xeno slipped out of the hero's grip and stood in front of the house, "Listen, I want to cause chaos! You brought me to a hero's home and I'm not leaving until I destroy her property! Mwahahaha! –With toilet paper and eggs!" he declared dramatically.

Firefly cocked his head to the side, watching his stage presence.

"You're a lot less threatening in real life…"

"Please, I'm plenty threatening. Anyways, you're free to go! Cops are away, no villains in sight, I just thought you'd want revenge on your enemy before you leave," Xeno smirked, handing him a toilet paper roll.

"*YOU'RE* my enemy!"

"Awwwww~ really?!" Xenomorph smiled, practically shifting an octave and stars in his eyes. Not that Firefly could tell behind that blindfold. He stared at the mask, wondering what color they really were.

"That's the nicest thing you've ever said to me!" He played out dramatically, acting like he was going to cry. Voice cracking, "H-Hold on! I need a moment–"

"You are such a pain– I'm not doing your stupid 'TP' thing or whatever this is."

Xeno cut his act, grudging over as he stuffed the roll into the hero's hand, putting him in a throwing position to guide Firefly.

"Just throw the roll," he commanded nicely. Like he cared, although nothing could be further from the truth. He just wanted to mess up the place.

"I'm not doing it."

"Throw the roll or I'll kick you," He said sweetly, grinning ear to ear.

Firefly flinched and threw the roll. The fluffy white fabric bounced through the tree, leaving a beautiful trail as it draped over the branches and landed on the car.

Something awoke in Firefly, he felt...good!

"Whoa...that felt amazing– what was that?" He turned to his partner in crime.

"That was called *revenge*! Fun isn't it? Now try an egg, preferably at the door," Xeno gave him an egg, moved his aim and Firefly pelted the egg at the door. It cracked on impact and the yoke oozed all of the door.

Firefly couldn't help but smile a bit, this was fun! He'd also be lying if he said this wasn't karma.

"Yes! Bullseye! Here, you take the carton. I'll take the spray paint and we will tp this crap-show together!" Xeno took the spray paint, shaking it as the metal ball inside clanked. He started to run off but something caught Firefly's mind,

"Wait–...together?"

Xenomorph froze, covered in the shadows of the branchy tree, "I-I mean…at the same time," he tried, but it was weak.

The villain ran off into the dark and started tagging the car. Firefly shrugged it off and continued to splat eggs at Molly's house. It still felt great! Even after the fifth egg.

After Xenomorph finished the car's new paint job, he moved on to the garage door and the house; thinking about what he said. *Together? Ew- why would I ever say that?* It's not like they were friends—heck they don't even know each other. Just two strangers who hated each other in a predicament. Nothing more.

Regardless, once the eggs were gone and most of the paint cans were empty the two ran to each other to meet up. Xeno came up covered in splotches of neon paint, even on his face.

"So? What do you think?" He gestured to the house where he wrote *'U R DUM!'* in purple spray paint.

"It's…definitely not what I expected." Firefly thought out loud.

"Should I do more? What about 'idiot'? Or 'meanie'? *gasp* What if I wrote 'Loudmouth'?"

"Hey! That would be mean…do it," Firefly smirked and Xeno jumped for joy as he wrote in the paint.

"Should we sign this? It's a work of art."

"Oh heck no! We can't let anyone know we were here! The cops *and* Dark Legacy are after us, and as soon as Soundwave wakes up to *this* she might be too…we gotta lay low."

"Fine! Fine! We may lay low, but the tp will flow~!" Xeno swagged as he threw a roll.

"Hand me the one ply," Firefly spoke dramatically and the villain gave him his wish.

The two started running around the yard, throwing toilet paper at the house and at each other. Covering every inch in poo poo paper. Once the rolls were finished they threw the cardboard at the house. Xeno made some jokes, but Firefly didn't budge, he could never encourage this...but he did have to admit; he was having the time of his life.

After about an hour the rolls were up and the house looked like a Halloween mummy. With toilet paper everywhere, eggs splatters, and colorful paint in big scribbles. It will come out...hopefully.

"How ya feel, Sparky?" Xeno asked, nudging him a bit.

"I feel alive!"

"See! Villains are totally in the right!"

"Oh no, no, no, no! This was just a prank, this isn't anything like robbing a bank or hurting people."

"But it's a start~!"

"A start? No, the end! I am not turning into a super villain like you."

"You sure~ you'd be a great one," Xenomorph teased but the words went straight to Firefly's head. Ringing in his ears.

Was it true? Was he a bad person...a bad guy? It couldn't be, he was a hero. Not a villain! Never a villain!

"W-We should go!" The hero stuttered.

"What?! But we didn't get to dance on the lawn yet? That's the best part!" Xeno started breaking down as he cheered. Firefly had to hand it to him, the dude had some moves.

"WOOP WOOP!! WOOOHOOO!!! *I'M GOING TO LIVE AND VANDALIZE FOREVER!!*" He boomed. Shattering the house's windows and setting off dozens of car alarms.

The villain covered his mouth quickly.

"XENO!"

"Oops!"

The red and blue flashing lights returned as a police siren grew from the horizon.

"Run!" Xenomorph said.

"Not again!" Firefly followed, keeping on his trail.

The boys ran through the neighborhood streets, trying to lose the cops. Xenomorph hopped onto a car and slid down the front, Firefly followed him on the safe sidewalk and soon they reached a little park. Running across the grass in the dark as the flashing lights and noise still followed.

However, the park was ending as a chain link fence started to block the path.

"Over the fence!" Xenomorph commanded.

"What?! I can't jump over the fence!"

"You have already said that about the car and TP-ing– DO I NEED TO SHOW YOU HOW THIS ENDS?!"

"That's trespassing!"

"IT'S NOT TRESPASSING IF WE ARE LEAVING– GO!"
Xeno commanded.

Firefly booked it across the grass, gaining speed. Xeno followed as they passed by a mini construction set. It was small, working on a pipe or something in the ground. But four orange cones wrapped in yellow tape surrounded it, shining off of the moon.

Xeno couldn't resist and did a double-take, running back.

Firefly jumped on the fence and climbed up the chain. Heaving himself over as he sat on the top. However when he looked back down he didn't see Xeno behind him.

"XENOMORPH?!" He looked back to see the cops getting out of their parked cars, running across the grass straight towards them as Xeno picked up a traffic cone and ran with it over his head. Screaming like crazy.

"What are you doing?!" Firefly shouted.

"I've always wanted to steal one of these!" He yelled and smiled.

Firefly froze. Despite the cops closing in, lights still flickering, and Xenomorph screaming like a girl, a warmness bubbled inside of him. Checks puffing up and letting his guard down.

For the first time, since being stuck with Xeno…he laughed.

Xenomorph noticed and was confused but couldn't help but mirror the smile, aiming at the laughing hero.

"Catch!" He shouted and Firefly got pelted with the orange rubber cone. He caught it, but lost his balance as he fell off the fence, landing on the other side in a pile of garbage.

"Good catch!" Xeno cheered as he climbed up the fence, hoisting himself over and jumping off into the same mess. The cops slowed down, losing the boys. The flashes and voices faded as the two breathed. They both looked at each other and started laughing in breaths, sighing with relief.

Xeno stood up brushing the dirt off, holding out his hand to Firefly.

Firefly reached for it with a smile- *maybe this guy wasn't so bad after all*.

"What are you doing, give me my cone idiot," He smirked. Not really meaning it—well at least the idiot part. He did very much want his cone back.

Firefly's hope and face dropped as he tossed him the cone.

"Yes! Mr. Coney! You're ok!" Xeno smooched the cone.

"Hilarious," Firefly smirked, teasing.

"Don't play coy with me...I saw you laughing, I'm...glad you had fun," Xenomorph said, putting on the cone as a hat and smiling, really trying—for whatever reason.

Firefly stood up, shaking his head with a dumb grin on his face.

"C'mon, let's get out of here before they find us," Xenomorph commanded, raising his finger in the air only to turn around and lead the way. Firefly followed, still chuckling behind.

Chapter 9:

Ring...ring...ring...

Firefly fiddled with the payphone's wire in his fingers as the buzzing continued. The white light of the box being one of the only lights in Central Park. Xeno leaned on the phone impatiently as Firefly started to bang the phone into his head.

"This is taking forever~. We need to keep moving" The villain whined.

"I know– just hold on–," in seconds, Firefly was interrupted with a nice, soft,

"Hello?"

"Mom!" Firefly started. Xeno immediately shot up in surprise.

"Lovebug? Is that you? Where are you?! Where have you been?! It's so late! What is going on?! Are you ok?!" She started rambling.

"Mom– Mom– Mom! I can explain!"

"...Ok, go on..." The women on the other side of the phone waited. Xeno just kept looking at the box and then back at the hero, trying to understand it.

"Firstly, I am ok. Secondly, I may or may not have been kidnapped by Dark Legacy–"

"WHAT?!"

"BUT IT'S OK! We managed to escape, and right now we–"

"We? Who's we?" She asked, giving that motherly tone that meant he was in trouble. The phone started to slip from his palm, terrified.

"Um..." Firefly slowly looked over to his co-hostage who just violently shook his head and made slashing gestures with his hand. Firefly sighed, knowing he couldn't lie, "...Xenomorph?"

"What?" Firefly's mom asked, not believing her ears.

"I know it sounds crazy! But he was in just as much trouble as I was, so we have a truce going until this all blows over and everything is ok."

The other line remained silent.

Firefly's face turned red as his voice started to crack, "Look, Mom, I messed up...big time."

Xenomorph's face softened as he listened.

"The heroes are in danger because of me, I blabbed our secret; and in return...Xeno blabbed his."

"I wouldn't say I 'blabbed'," Xeno mumbled.

Firefly shot a look at him, "Shut up," before redirecting back to the phone, "Point is, Dark Legacy is now after *both* of us and...we...ugh...we–"

Xeno grabbed the phone, "We are stuck together. This is an exchange of safety and nothing more. I need his power and he needs my knowledge. So what your idiotic son is trying to say is: We are fine ma'am, and we are going to continue to lay low until we figure out a way out of this mess your son created."

Despite the jabs, Firefly couldn't help but smile a bit as he slowly grabbed the phone back.

"Yeah, what he said...are you mad?"

"No," The woman replied, almost as if she were smiling, "I mean, I am very worried, but I'm not mad. But sounds like you have a plan to fix everything and are helping someone who really needs you right now." She hinted.

Firefly looked over at Xeno, who was back on lookout-duty, thinking about what his mom said just yesterday. With that, questions started to spill over. Who really was this guy? Why did he become a villain? Why is he the way he is?

Firefly's thoughts broke as he returned to his mom, "I don't think it's safe for me to come home, but I'll keep updating you. We will fix this and save everyone. I promise."

"I know you will, please stay safe Lovebug! Be the amazing hero you were meant to be."

Firefly smiled, "I will," and hung up. The line dropped with a buzz as Firefly put the phone back on the box.

Xeno didn't really know what to say, but he felt bad for the tired hero.

The villain cleared his throat, "So… shall we keep moving?"

***

The two walked in the night, quiet and peaceful. No words were said, but they walked side by side like it meant something.

The trees were dark and fluffy. Leaves ruffled in the wind. The only strong lights were the floodlights of a basketball court. Firefly noticed a singular basketball rolling on the empty court and he took off running.

Xenomorph watched as Firefly ran onto the court, picked up the ball, dribbled it, and shot a free throw. It sank in the hoop with a swish. Thudding back on the ground as Firefly picked it back up to dribble.

Xenomorph smiled and headed over.

The villain walked onto the pavement and watched as the ball made another basket. Firefly caught it and turned around staring at the villain under the floodlights.

"You're…not so bad," Firefly finally said, checking him the ball.

Xenomorph caught it, "What?"

"…" Firefly gave a nervous laugh, not knowing what he was talking about.

"You're weird, kid," Xeno checked the ball back.

Firefly just held his breath. Finally, he grew the courage to just spit out the question that's been nagging him all day–

"Why are you a villain?" He rushed out.

Xenomorph froze, "I-I'm sorry?"

"A villain? Why are you a super villain? I mean you don't seem evil, so...why become a villain?" Firefly asked, tracing the lines of the ball.

Xenomorph scoffed, "Because I want to be one."

"...Do you?"

Xenomorph felt a tug. Goggle lenses begging to open up instead of eyes...*wonder what color they are?* Did it matter, I mean they were enemies...for life. Nothing would change that.

"Like you'd want to know, Sparky," he sassed.

"That's why I asked Xenny~."

"...Stick with Xeno." The villain deadpanned.

"Noted. But seriously...do you ever think about going good?" Firefly asked.

"Pah! No! Why would I?"

"Well...you don't really have a life to go back to..."

Xenomorph looked at the ground.

"I mean...are we just going to wake up tomorrow and...fight each other again?"

"...I...I don't know." Xeno stuttered, looking for an answer.

"So why are you a villain?" The hero tried again, this time more stern.

"Firecracker– stop it–..."

94

"No, seriously!"

"Sparky, I'm warning you!" Xeno threatened, flaming up.

"Why are you a villain?!" Firefly pushed his buttons.

"BECAUSE I DIDN'T HAVE A CHOICE!" The villain erupted, sending out a fiery burst. Turning around and crossing his arms. *This was a mistake.*

Firefly didn't flinch, as he was too shocked, "…What?" he dropped the ball, which bounced and rolled away from him. Just like his thoughts.

Xenomorph sighed angrily, turning back around, "I was *forced* to be a villain. Dark Legacy brought me in and I was never able to leave. The end!"

"W-Wait what?! No, that can't be 'the end'?"

"Well it is, why do you care?"

"…I don't know…I mean, what do your parents think?!"

Xenomorph's tight body sunk, becoming more loose as a sad frown formed. Looking at the green concrete. Not knowing what to say.

There, written on his face, was Firefly's answer.

"…Oh…I'm– I'm so sorry…"

"Whatever…it was years ago…"

"Do you wanna talk about it?"

"Pff– of course not! Why would I tell you anything?"

"Because 'if you keep holding it in you're going to crack'." Firefly quoted, bending down for the basketball and checking it at him once again.

Xenomorph caught it, staring at the hero. The breeze blew fast as Firefly tried to give a sympathetic smile. No one ever cared to listen to him before, heck, no one ever cared about him.

Why was this time any different? A weird pull grew in Xeno's stomach, but he swallowed it as his mouth opened.

Firefly patiently waited.

"I-I…um…"

"It's ok, take your time, I won't bite."

"That I know of~." Xeno threatened.

"Relax, who am I going to tell?"

"All the superheroes? Your boss? Your family?"

Firefly gave a tiny laugh, "I um…actually don't know a lot of the superheroes."

Xenomorph flinched in surprise, "What? Really? But your Firefly?"

"Yeah…but everyone thinks I'm just a teacher's pet who didn't earn their spot fairly… and super hero work keeps me pretty busy anyways…"

"You don't even have one super friend?"

"No, so I wouldn't tell the heroes and my 'family' is just my mom so…you're all good. No heroes, family, or friends…"

"…*Just* your mom?" Xeno questioned.

"Yeah," Firefly sighed and took a seat on the side bench, "I…don't have a dad either– if that somehow makes you feel better?" He baited with a smile.

Xeno's face softened, "…It somehow does."

96

Firefly smirked.

"N-No! No not like that– I mean, I'm sorry for your loss– but it makes me feel–" Xenomorph tried as he stuck the ball under his arm.

"Whoa, you feel things?" Firefly asked sarcastically.

"Yes you Ding Dong," Xeno sassed back with a smile, "But it makes me feel…not…alone."

Firefly's smirk softened, seeing a whole new side to this vill– to this super.

"N-Not that I feel alone– because that's ridiculous. Villains don't feel alone," Xeno rambled as Firefly stood up, walking to him. "that would make me pretty weak and worthless if I had feelings– or if I missed my dad because–" His voice started to crack as something interrupted him.

It was a soft and warm hug.

Firefly squeezed Xeno tight, "I miss my dad too, it's ok…you don't have to talk about it if you're not ready."

Xenomorph stood shocked. Usually he'd hate this sweet, sappy garbage. However, this time felt unusual.

"I–…I…I think we need a plan."

Firefly broke the hug, realizing Xenomorph wasn't ready yet. Which is fair, based on the little he did share, it was hard to talk about. Besides it's not like Firefly was ready to talk about his past yet either.

"Ok, what did you have in mind?" Firefly asked, switching topics.

"Well we can't be walking around as Xenomorph and Firefly. Between today and tonight we've caused way too much attention…"

"Good idea, let's just slip into our secret identities." Firefly started as he started taking off his harness and hoodie.

"What?! Hell no! I am not revealing my identity to you." Xeno yelled, stopping him and tugging the red piece of fabric back on.

"Well then what do you suggest? We can't go out looking like supers, and if you don't want to go as normal people then you are out of options."

Xenomorph thought a bit, his overly bubbly sidekick was right...they needed new disguises.

A light bulb flashed as he snapped his fingers, "I got it!"

***

The next day, Firefly pulled back a purple curtain, stepping out of a fitting room as he was bombarded with Xenomorph's laughter.

A pair of yellow party shades blocked his vision in plastic slits. His nose itched from the big rubber nose, smelling nothing but rubber. Bright, nauseous colors painted his hair in rainbow order. Not to mention the wacky yellow and rainbow-spotted bow tie that was strangling him.

Xenomorph just kept laughing his head off, falling out of his chair. Firefly sighed, not impressed. This wasn't even helpful. He was still wearing his firefly outfit, armor and all.

"PAHAHAHA! I can't take it– you–HAHAHA! You look ridiculous!" Xeno wheezed.

"I look like a clown." Firefly deadpanned.

"Well– duh, but now you have hair paint and a goofy nose– HAHAHA!!!"

"'Haha'. 'Very funny'. Where's your outfit?"

"Oh, simple, watch," Xenomorph strutted into another changing room at the back of the costume store and slipped into some classy clothes. A white button-up with a nice, blue sweater vest, suit pants, and a slick black tie that swayed side to side. Instead of his fake glasses he put on some nice, dark shades and walked out. Looking like some prep boy, probably because that was the costume he chose.

"What do you think?"

"How come you look cool!"

"Because I'm a chick magnet...and you're a clown," he joked and gave a striking pose to the employee who was tied up next to the counter. Her mouth being hidden by a random piece of costume fabric as she just shook there, nervously.

Firefly groaned, there was no way he was going to let this super cool outfit slide. Although, he knew if he wanted to get Xenomorph out the door he'd have to wear this; otherwise they'd be here all day.

"Ugh, I'll make you a deal. I'll go out in this... 'outfit', if I get to pick yours."

Xenomorph squinted his eyes behind his shades, tempted by the offer.

"Hmm...what did you have in mind?"

After a quick costume change (and leaving some money on the counter), Firefly dramatically left the costume store, blasting his music through his phone. It was dramatic and punk as the hero went through the streets in slow motion.

He looked back, waiting for his– whatever he was. On cue, Xeno walked out, still rocking his black shades, but now was wearing a full blown superhero costume. With bright colors, underwear on the outside, and a tacky cape that made him puke in his mouth. Regardless, he dramatically walked to Firefly, giving a deadpan stare. The hero held up his fist and after Xeno's eye roll they fist bump.

Taking the streets, music blasting, Firefly did some finger guns at a group of girls sitting outside, but they all just gave him weird looks. Xenomorph did the same, flexing his muscles in the suit but no one gave them the time of day.

They both gave a chuckle and continued down the street. They may have looked stupid, but the disguises worked. In a way, no one dared to make eye contact with them.

"Ok...so now what?" Firefly asked.

"Now– we need an actual plan..." Xenomorph started.

"Yeah...we are starting to get a lot of looks." Firefly looked around at the swarm of people.

"You mean you are– I look great!" Xeno flexed again.

"You are a teenager in a kids costume."

"The most classy teenager in a kids costume to ever walk the streets of New York," Xeno started before a door opened and caught his eye.

He walked over and peered into the glass windows to spy a little cafe passing out paper cups and baked goods. The interior was comfy, wooden brown and dark greys. However, nothing could hide the smell of coffee grounds and lemon loaf, "OOO! Coffee!" He exclaimed and headed inside.

Chapter 10:

A steamer filled the air and the coffee grinder went off as the people behind the counter continued to bustle, creating an oddly calming atmosphere.

Firefly followed him, "Coffee?! We are supposed to figure out what to do, not drink decaf–"

"Decaf?! Eulgh! It's like you want to wear that nose," Xenomorph gagged.

"Let's be honest– you don't need any more caffeine! We shouldn't be here." Firefly quipped back.

"Coffee helps me think," the villain explained and then turned to the counter, "One iced white mocha with extra whipped cream please. Oh and a hot caramel macchiato, and a brown sugar latte."

The cashier looked at him oddly, but wrote the order on the side of the cup, "For…?"

"Oh– silly me, it'll be Super Jerk," The 'hero' then turned to his comrade, "Do you want anything?"

"…I'm going to have to pay, aren't I?"

"Very much so."

"Ugh, fine. I'll have a…peach tea, extra honey, extra hot," He ordered and started talking out of his wallet.

"Wow man, you don't hold the heat," Xeno teased.

"Not like I can have anything else…" Firefly drifted and paid. He then packed up his wallet and walked to a table.

"Wait…what?" Xeno followed him.

"Hello…*Fire*fly?" Firefly sassed, magicing up a tiny flame in his hand but extinguished it immediately, "I would just melt anything else."

"Melt? Wait…so you never had chocolate?!"

"Nope."

"What?! …Your life is miserable!"

Firefly deadpanned, sitting down, "Gee, thanks."

"What do you eat for comfort? I'd go crazy without chocolate."

"I like marshmallows, they are great toasted."

Xenomorph laid in the chair causally, squinting his eyes, "You look like a marshmallow guy."

"Thank you?"

Soon four cups plopped onto their table.

"Order for Super Jerk," the waitress announced, setting down the cups.

"Thank you, ma'am," Firefly added.

Once the waitress was gone Xenomorph started going crazy, chugging down on his three coffees.

"You done?" Firefly asked sarcastically.

"Almost," he sassed as he took another sip. "Alright now."

Xeno took out a pen from who knows where and grabbed a napkin, "Ok, what's our plan?"

"Me?"

"Yeah, let's hear the awful ideas first," Xeno smirked, starting to write on the napkin.

Firefly scrunched up his face, he liked Xeno better under the flood lights. It's like he came alive at night.

"Well...we need to get to the hero league and warn them Dark Legacy is coming. Then they will protect us."

Xenomorph stopped writing, "Are you crazy?!"

"What?" Firefly asked, not seeing the problem.

"We can't go to them! Hello?! I'm a villain, they will lock me away forever or worse, kill me!"

"You don't know that."

"I do! Once a villain, always a villain, right?" Xeno shot him a dirty glare.

Firefly was taken aback, forgetting he ever said such a thing.

"L-Look, you can't go back to the villains...*they will* destroy you, and you can't run forever. Plus hundreds of innocent heroes are at risk because of my mistake– I have to fix it," Firefly started, being genuine, "But I *can't* do this alone, I need to get to Hero's Tower and warn them! Please...please come with me. We could make you a hero!"

"Ew! Gag! What if I don't want that?!"

"...Ok, then you don't have to be one right away or...at all, but I promise– swear on my life...you help me with this, I won't let anything bad happen to you. Consider it immunity..." Despite his goofy appearance Firefly poured out his heart and Xenomorph's face softened at the offer.

"You...aren't going to lock me up for good."

"No. Honestly, I don't think I even wanna fight you anymore. You're not a villain– just human."

Xenomorph sighed, thinking of every option. He absolutely hated that this guy was right, couldn't run, couldn't hide, couldn't go back. He was stuck with this hero.

"Fine...I will help you."

"Really?!" Firefly cheered.

"Easy Firecracker! I'm not on your side, not your hero– not even your little sidekick. I'm just here to avoid Dark Legacy's rath...consider me... a vigilante of sorts– for now!"

"Works for me! Ok we need to get to Hero's Tower fast!" Firefly spoke, already standing up.

"Whoa! Whoa! Whoa! With what proof?"

"Huh?"

"Listen, Buggy, you just exposed both of our organizations on live TV, ditched them, and now you're running back to the tower with a villain in hand raving about Dark Legacy's plan– when in reality we have no idea what he is going to do!"

"Shoot, you're right...we will be cooked in seconds."

"That is if we're not jumped first at the front door," Xeno sipped his coffee.

"Then what do you suggest we do?"

"Well~," the villain continued writing with the pen, "what we need to do is get close to Dark Legacy. Once we do, we can do some recon, find his plans, and *then* go to Hero's Tower." He dropped the pen as if it were a mic.

Firefly was mortified with his plan from across the table, "Go near him?! Sorry– I think you're missing the point! We are supposed to be staying *away* from him! He is trying to kill us in case you forgot and–...you're not even taking notes..." He yelled before realizing.

"No I am not," Xeno smiled, still drawing.

Firefly swiped the napkin.

"Hey!"

"This is a comic book doodle." Firefly announced as he felt the soft edges of the napkin.

"I like to doodle, is that so 'evil'?"

"No it's just...really good." Firefly stared in shock at the piece. It was detailed, accurate, full of action– and amazing. Who knew a villain could be so artistic. "Is this supposed to be me?" He asked, holding up the napkin, trying not to smile.

"...Maybe. It's not my fault a reference is right in front of me. Besides, your hair is such a mess, I couldn't resist not drawing it," Xeno smirked.

"Wow, this is actually impressive. When we make it out of this alive–"

"*If," Xeno corrected.

"*WHEN we make it out of this alive, you should do a comic. Something fun and exciting."

Xeno nodded, carefully taking the compliment but then–

"THE COMIC STORE!" He shouted standing up and pushing his squeaky chair back. The whole store stopped as he grabbed everyone's attention.

"Uh– now I really think you've had too much caffeine…" Firefly tried to bring him down.

"Let's go! I have an idea!" He grabbed his white mocha and started to march out.

"Wait what?! Dude! Where are you going?!" Firefly grabbed the napkin and raced out after him.

Xenomorph entered the busy streets as he started heading to the metro station. Taking off his tacky costume and tossing it on a bench, revealing his under armor.

"I still don't get it," Firefly tried.

"Thunderstorm!"

"T-Thunderstorm?! We are going to see *the* Thunderstorm?" The hero stuttered.

"Yes, she's my roommate and co-worker. She's probably dying to see me."

"Are you sure?" Firefly asked, uneased by the sudden change. He was already dealing with one villain, two would be a nightmare.

"Positive, she's not always the warmest person, but she does have my back…at least a bit…I think."

"And how does the comic store fit into this?" Firefly continued to walk, dodging a stroller.

"She works there," Xeno shrugged, taking another sip of his drink before crushing the paper cup and throwing it in the air.

Firefly caught it and put it in a trash can (like a decent person).

"Wait, that means...you work at the comic store?"

"Unfortunately," The villain shivered.

"More like ironic," Firefly chuckled, "You sell books about heroes? That's not what I'd picture your day job like, but alright. At least the drawing makes sense."

"Listen, kid, Dark Legacy gave me the job. I was forced to take it! It was this job or nothing, it's not like anyone else was going to hire a villain," he scoffed, flipping his white hair.

"Dark Legacy seems to force you to do a lot..."

"Well he's the king of villains and I'm either stuck or dead, so pick your poison! Besides I bet you work at a tacky fast food place or something."

"I actually work at the record store, not too far from here," Firefly smiled with pride.

Xenomorph turned around, "Really? Music?"

"I mean yeah! I love music, I even left my guitar there yesterday."

"You–...you play?"

"Yeah, I find it relaxing, as well as awesome. Man, I'd love to go to concerts, but Captain Peace won't let me go out for personal time."

"'Captain Peace seems to force you to do a lot...'." Xeno mocked.

"Hey, it's different. Captain Peace is protecting our identities, he cares for us."

"Eh– never trusted that guy. Always shifty."

"More shifty than Dark Legacy?" Firefly sassed back.

"Speaking of! Thunderstorm probably knows where he will be this week: his meetings, patrols, parties–"

"Parties?"

"Yes–...please tell me you know what a party is." Xeno asked, turning around and grabbing the hero by the shoulders. Acting like it was the end of the world.

"I do know! ...Just never been."

Xeno facepalmed, "Kid, I've got so much to teach you. Come on."

The villain grabbed his arm as he ran down a few more blocks, crossed under the raised tracks, and up the stairs into the metro station.

The train was already starting to leave so the supers started to book it. Xeno jumped over the cueing system and Firefly went through normal, ready to pay.

"You pay for that, I will kill you!" Xeno shouted as he ran.

"Aww~ but my moral compass."

"Screw your moral compass, train's leaving," Xeno yelled before he cussed.

Firefly put his wallet away and ran after him, "We have got to talk about your cursing problem."

With a bit more running, both supers jumped onto the train just as the doors were closing. Stumbling inside the empty car. The sun leaked through the windows as they fell on top of each other.

Xenomorph immediately pushed Firefly off of him and stood up. Taking off the rest of his hero costume and untying his iconic coat from around his waist and putting it back on. Popping the sharp collar around his neck. That felt better.

Firefly stood up, whipping the paint from his hair, taking off all his junk, and putting back on his goggles.

"Hm. Empty train today, nice!" Xeno smiled, holding the leather loop. Although, he leaned back to see people in the train car next to them.

"Finally, a quiet place...I can't tell you how weird it felt on the street. Everyone staring at you, like there's something wrong with you."

"Tfft– well...welcome to my life..." Xeno softly mumbled as the train continued to move.

Firefly wanted to say something, but couldn't think of anything, so he just took a seat as the train glided on the tracks. Watching the buildings blur by as they always did.

It felt odd, New York through a whole new perspective. Firefly's version was clean and sleek, shiny and new, in order, but this new side felt extravagant. Running from the cops, convenience stores, coffee shops, costumes, and late nights. It was like a party, but it felt so freeing. Like a city he wanted to protect instead of one he just *had* to. How could Xenomorph not like this?

Xeno stared at the window as the seconds ticked by in silence.

Firefly stared at him; in a way, maybe his mom was right. Xenomorph needed to be saved too, he was just like anyone else. Except instead of crashes and bad guys he needed to be saved from his horrible boss and a life he was trapped in.

Firefly opened his mouth to speak but was cut off by–

"Do you feel that?" Xeno demanded.

"N-No what?"

"We are not alone...Get down!" Xeno launched and tackled Firefly to the ground.

Suddenly a big vine covered with sharp thorns smashed through the window. Sending glass shattering as a woman in a green super suit and flowers breached the train. Her brown curly hair blowing in the train's breeze. Firefly recognized her as Rosethorn, his super co-worker. Along her side was a male with brown, fluffy hair in a yellow pilot jacket with jagged, black stripes and fragile wings wilting down his back; Yellow Jacket. As well as another male, golden hair and strong blue eyes, decked in reds and whites, and golds; Mighty Strength.

Heroes, and they did not look happy.

The two teens stared up at the threats.

"...Can I cuss now?" Xeno asked.

"Y-Yeah..."

"*F*CK!*"

Chapter 11:

The three heroes stood their ground, glaring at the two rogues on the floor of the train. Xeno on top of Firefly, protecting his head in a way—although he'd never admit it if you asked.

"There you are!" Rosethorn yelled, hair flapping in her face as her thorny vines only sharpened to express her anger. With bright flowers flying in the fast breeze.

"W-Wait Rosethorn? What are you doing here?" Firefly asked in a panic, standing back up and flinging Xeno to the floor.

"'What are *we* doing here?!' What are *you* doing here?! Firefly, you've been missing for over twenty-four hours after exposing our organization! On top of that, you two are wanted by the city!" The woman yelled.

"What?!" Both supers yelled together.

"'Wanted' seems a bit extreme," Xeno scoffed, also getting back on his feet.

"Really?" Rosethorn sassed pointing outside as a billboard just so happened to flash their images on screen, with the words wanted in big red letters. Stamped across the front as if it were a punishment.

"Governor Jaceson announced it this morning," Rosethorn smirked, "not to mention Captain Peace has…choice *words* with you," she continued.

"H-He does?" Firefly stuttered, heartbroken, but he quickly shook it off, "Listen, I'm going to fix everything, just give me some time!" He pleaded his case.

"Fix everything?! Oh no, no, no, he wants you *gone*."

"…W-What?" The world seemed to blur away as any sounds faded in and out.

"Firefly you are under arrest, for exposing the super society, theft, reckless driving, vandalism, trespassing, and fraternizing with the enemy."

Firefly's heart dropped, frozen in shock as the metal cuff dangled in the air like an unfinished sentence. Rosethorn framed the silver circles around Firefly's head from afar. Perspective was a beautiful thing. Bullseye.

"Whoa, I wouldn't say we are 'fraternizing', that's a little strong, more like tied together under the threat of death," Xeno added.

Rosethorn, "Shut it Xenomorph. We are taking you in too for your crimes against humanity," she readied up, sprouting two vines from the floor around her boots and pulling on the cuffs like a threat.

"B-But I haven't done anything wrong!" Firefly begged.

"Tell that to the Captain." She spat coldly and threw a vine.

Xenomorph gasped, knowing he wasn't going to move and shoved the fiery hero out of the way. Firefly fell on the seats, shocked, as Rosethorn grabbed Xeno instead and dragged him close.

"And you...you are going away for a long time..." She threatened in a whisper.

"Yeah...I don't think so," Xeno quipped and used one of Yellow Jacket's nuclear explosions and blasted the three heroes back.

The battle was on.

The three heroes hit the wall as Xeno fell back, tumbling on the floor.

Firefly ran to him and picked him up, "What are you doing?! We can't fight them!"

"We have to!" Xeno yelled, readying up a fireball.

"But they're heroes! They are loyal and friendly—the good guys! We just have to talk to them!"

"And I want to live! You heard them, we are both going to jail if we don't fight. Besides, they don't seem so 'loyal' and 'friendly' to me!"

Rosethorn groaned as she got off the wall readying another round of vines.

"DUCK!" Xenomorph said, pulling Firefly's hoodie down with him as the vine swished above them, barely missing. The leafy whip got stuck in the wall as it squirmed in place. "Look, you can stay here and do nothing if you want, but I'm fighting!"

Xeno stood up and used super strength to tear the vine apart, then casted his own sprigs at the heroes. Catching Mighty Strength out of three, holding him up in a jungle of vines.

Yellow Jacket dodged and blasted an explosion towards his face. Incoming quickly, Xeno braced for impact, shielding with his arms.

Suddenly a big burst of fire stopped the blast, exploding it before it even reached Xenomorph– only he didn't create it. He looked around to see Firefly walking up to his side, readying up.

Xeno dropped his arms, speechless.

Firefly just looked at him with determination, nodding.

Xeno grew a smirk and grabbed Rosethorn in a root, lassoing her up and swinging her around the train as Firefly ran and launched at Yellow Jacket, knocking him over and tackling him to the ground.

The hero shot around wildly as Mighty Strength bursted out of the vines, luckily Xenomorph caught him out of the corner of his eye. Throwing Rosethorn at Mighty Strength, crashing them together. He then readied a green, nuclear blast while Rosethorn got up from the ground and grabbed Xeno's arm with a vine, aiming the explosive at Firefly and Yellow Jacket.

"Firefly! Watch out!" He yelled as Rosethorn pulled his arm, setting off the blast.

Firefly looked behind him as the blast came soaring, he and Yellow Jacket quickly dove out of the way. The blast hit the train wall, exploding and exposing them to the outside. The wind picked up as Firefly soon went flying out the hole,

"BUGGY!" Xenomorph yelled,

Firefly quickly grabbed a handlebar and held on for life.

Xeno kept watching the teen struggle to stay on the side of the train. Air filling his hair and hood.

"Yellow Jacket! Take care of him!" Rosethorn commanded as she sent another branch at Xeno, shoving him to the ground.

"On it!" The hero replied, opened his robotic wings, and flew out. The bee made a loopty-loop, and smash-landed right next to Firefly.

The boy's eyes grew wide at the threatening wasp. He pulled himself up the car, rolling onto the top of the train–*WHAM!*

Yellow Jacket jumped him, pinning him to the roof. He went in for a punch to the face but Firefly rolled his head out of the way.

Yellow Jacket managed to punch a hole through the roof but tried again. Firefly rolled the other way until he kicked the other bug off.

The bumblebee flew back a little bit, but pulled out his obsidian dagger and dug at the train's metal roof. Sparks flew as he slowed to a stop.

Meanwhile, inside Xenomorph kept flipping around the cabin and dodging the vines. Mighty Strength pulled a pole off and ran at Xeno. Throwing it like a spear, it clipped the villain's collar and stuck him into the door. The hero grabbed the villain's collar, pulling him up from the floor.

Xeno's boots searched for the ground as Mighty Strength grabbed his head and smashed it into the door's glass window.

SMASH!

116

"Arugh!" Xeno winced, glass shards cutting his face. The people in the other car very much noticed the broken door with the villain sticking out and ran. Screaming as tiny streams of blood trickled down Xenomorph's head. Mighty Strength threw him back on the seats. "Gah-!"

Xeno tried to get up but was slow and sloppy. Rosethorn grabbed him again and banged him around; denting metal, breaking windows, and breaking seats. He tried to throw a fireball but his vision was so blurry it missed and landed on the floor and caught fire to some very dry leaves. The fire spread as Rosethorn threw him into a corner.

Xenomorph rag-dolled lifelessly as he tried to lean on the wall. He struggled to stand as Mighty Strength punched him in the face. Knocking him back down for good.

Firefly threw a fireball at Yellow Jacket who flew up to avoid it. Suddenly a glass shatter rang out; The young hero readied up again, frightened, until he smelled smoke.

He turned around to see the fire coming from his cabin, "Xeno! ...Please tell me that wasn't you! Please tell me that wasn't you!" He whispered to himself and ran toward the train car. He looked back at Yellow Jacket readying up a blast and got an idea. The hero backflipped back to the smoking train, preparing for his next move.

Rosethorn, meanwhile, gave a little giggle, "You put up a good fight...but not good enough. Now you will pay for what you've done. Have fun in prison...or *hell*," She sassed, sprouting her biggest and sharpest thorns.

Once Firefly was over the flaming car he waved his hands, flaring up like a big target.

"Hey! Over here you nasty bee!" He shouted.

Yellow Jacket threw a nuclear blast and Firefly jumped out of the way.

The blast hit the roof, breaking it to pieces.

Rosethorn looked up at the rubble raining down as Firefly jumped back into the cart. Standing between the villain and the supposed heroes. Without a second thought and a fist full of fire, he punched her.

She stumbled back, screaming in agony.

Firefly stood frozen– he had never done that before.

"YOU BRAT!" Rosethorn yelled. Hair still smoking and singed as burns covered her face.

"I'm sorry, I'm sorry! Just don't hurt him!" Firefly begged, blocking the downed super.

Xenomorph flickered open his eyes, barely breathing, the blurry image was hard to see but he knew exactly what was going on.

"Are you crazy?! He's been harassing the city for years! Stolen millions of dollars! Hurt people! He kidnapped you! He's a villain! Heck, he's *YOUR* villain!"

"He didn't kidnap me! Dark Legacy did!"

The room fell silent, apart from the fire crackling and the metal chugging of the tracks. Fear spreading at the mere mention of that name.

"We are trying to find out what he's up to!" Firefly continued.

"*WE?!*" Mighty Strength asked.

"Look– I know he seems scary and evil but I promise he's not as bad as you think. We are heroes, we are supposed to protect and save everyone...*that includes villains.*"

Xenomorph stayed speechless on the floor, not believing his eyes.

Rosethorn used a vine and in seconds grabbed Firefly by the neck and backed him to the wall, thorns cutting up his skin. Her vines twisted hard around his throat.

Firefly vision started to blur, choking.

"I am a *real* hero...*that's my job*. And I must stop the evil in this city...starting with *you*." She threatened as she squeezed harder. Firefly started to black out, coughing and yanking on the sharp vines. Flickering his eyes closed as he turned a scary shade of purple.

Rosethorn tried to twist it more, smiling as she secretly enjoyed this, but out of nowhere Xenomorph rammed into her. Knocking her, Mighty Strengthen (who was a collateral damage domino), and himself out of the hole.

The stems untwisted at the surprise and dropped Firefly on the floor, leaving him gasping for air.

"XENOMORPH!" He screamed from the floor as the three went falling.

Xenomorph concentrated as he shot a vine around the handle, swinging himself back up into the air. Mid-flight he used a nuclear explosion to shoot down Yellow Jacket who was still high in the sky.

Gravity kicked in as he swung back down, still holding the vine as he forced another sprout to pop out of the ground. Blooming a blue flower which caught and devoured Rosethorn and Mighty Strength.

Still in motion, the villain heaved himself back into the hole, rolling onto the ground and landing dramatically in the burning train.

Xeno quickly took Firefly's hand, pulled him up from the ground, and ran to the door. Reaching his hand through the shattered window, he opened the door. Jumping over the couplers and shoving Firefly into another car.

The villain turned around, flaming up a ball of fire and shot at the lone coupler. Disconnecting the train.

The flaming car slowed away into the distance as the victory finally set in; they were safe.

Xeno breathed, hating those jerks even more as he limped inside the car.

Firefly was already getting off the floor when he entered, "Oh thank god, you're ok!" Firefly ran and hugged him.

Xenomorph tried to hug him back, for whatever reason, but was too exhausted. His head felt light and the room started to spin.

"O-Of...c-course...I am..." he tried.

As Firefly pulled back to look at his beat-up face, Xenomorph's knees buckled and he collapsed.

"Whoa! HEY! NO! Xeno! Oh no, no, no, no!" Firefly screamed, falling to his side. "Don't die on me!"

Xenomorph breathed calmly, "Relax! I'm not dying, I just need a minute. Man...those heroes did not hold back."

120

Firefly looked at him, waiting for a bit,

"…You didn't have to do that."

"…Yeah well…neither did you."

Firefly sighed, oddly feeling guilty for this guy, "Yes I did. I made a promise. I'm not going to let anything bad happen to you…even though…I kinda already failed…"

"Eh– I've been through the worst." The villain shrugged off

"…We need to get you to a hospital." Firefly suddenly rushed out.

"Oh no–! That will not be necessary, I am fine." Xeno sat up, whipping the blood off his face with his sleeves.

"I don't care what you say! We are going!"

"I can't! Do you know what a hospital is? It's a government-funded facility. No one there will help and we will be arrested on the spot! Trust me…I've tried before." He muffled

"You…you can't go to the doctors? H-How do you heal? How do you get bandaged up? How do you guys get better?"

"Supervillain hospital…at HQ."

"But I…I can't get you there…" Firefly's voice cracked, feeling dcfcatcd.

"Exactly, so no hospital. I promise, I'm fine."

Another uncomfortable silence fell between the two.

"…Why did you do that?" The villain interrupted the quiet.

"What are you talking about?"

"I mean…besides your promise, why did you fight the heroes? Why did you protect me? They were right, aren't I a villain?" Xeno asked, barring his fangs a little.

"Because…*you* were right. Despite working together for years, they turned on me in an instant. They didn't even bother to listen or care– just straight to violence the first chance they got. They were not loyal and kind, not true heroes, not people I'd ever want to stand with! That's not who I want to be, besides if I had to choose to stick with someone–…"

"…"

"Never mind, just dumb moral stuff…I guess."

Xeno laid back down and looked up at the ceiling, secretly begging Firefly to finish his sentence. For the first time in years someone stood up for him, defended him, sacrificed for him; and he didn't know why, but he'd do the same thing. Heck he *did* do the same thing, what was happening to him?

***

The train slowly made its last stop and then headed to the train yard to recover from the accident. Aware of the fiery chaos that had just ensued. Thinking the dangerous supers were left in the fires of the burning train car. So the train continued, slowing down at the lot, filled with tons and tons of empty train cars. Firefly slowly stepped off, landing on the rounded pebbles. Xenomorph jumped down, joining him. They trotted along the gravel, admiring the maze of trains. Both still confused and wanted to know more.

Firefly peered around a red cargo train, "Ok...we have to be careful. Now we have villains, cops, and heroes after us! Heck– you heard Rosethorn, our faces are all over New York. Like some wanted criminals..." Firefly's voice started to crack as he continued ahead.

"Mm, not much of a difference," Xeno tried, looking up at the clouds.

Firefly froze, turning around, "How do you just do that?"

"What?"

"The entire city hates us! They think we are evil! And it doesn't even phase you?!" Firefly shouted, flaming up as Xeno coughed from the smoke.

"Does that bother you?" The villain asked, still not a care in the world.

"YES!"

"Why?"

"Because we aren't evil!"

Xenomorph eyes widen, "...We?"

"I-I mean– me– I'm– I'm not evil. In the media's eye– at least I wasn't..."

Xeno swallowed his warmth, returning to ice, "Look man, the city views me like that every day. 'Captain forbid, the city spreads a couple rumors'." He sassed, taking the lead.

"But– why? Why do you just sit there and take it?" Firefly asked, calming down the flames.

"What else would I do?" Xeno questioned back, picking up a pebble.

"I don't know…"

"I revolt or defend myself, I'm 'attacking the city', if I conform 'I have been tamed' and get thrown in jail, it's a lose-lose situation…not like I could get out if I could," He skipped the stone against the floor as the rocks clinked.

"Right, sorry, I've just never been painted as the villain before…"

Xeno turned around, "…Well, welcome to my life."

Firefly took a breath, really thinking, what they had done—or rather what they hadn't done. Xenomorph was framed and forced to do this, and they sat by and just added insult to injury for years before even finding a solution or attempting one.

"…What I'm asking is: How do you just accept that you're the bad guy?"

"…Because nothing will change."

"But we *could*! We could change things!"

"Firecracker. Let it go," Xeno smiled, trying to shut it down. Poor hero was already in the mess, the last thing he wanted to do was drag him deeper into the pool.

"I'm just saying people shouldn't be labeled as good or bad–just people! I mean if you're not so bad who knows what other villains are like. Maybe they just need to talk too."

Xeno looked at the bug, hope in his lenses bouncing with excitement. It was admirable.

"Firefly...the line between heroes and villains is more blurred then you could possibly imagine. And the city is scared of it. We are all just scary people, with scary powers fighting each other. It's best to just leave things alone. We get you to your Captain, show him the plans, you defeat Dark Legacy, and everything returns to normal," Xeno started walking off.

"For me, what about you?"

"...What about me?" Xeno asked as he continued balancing on the tracks.

"Well what would happen to you?"

"...Don't worry about it. Come on, the comic store is just up ahead."

"Wait what? No! I want to worry about it."

"Why? It's not like you care what happens to me." Xeno called his bluff.

"No, I–..." Firefly stopped himself, not really knowing what to say. Why was this so complicated? Xeno was right, the lines were blurring and he couldn't see where Xenomorph stopped and where the guy underneath began.

"I defended you...because I'm a hero." Firefly started again.

Xenomorph stopped and listened patiently.

"Because I made a promise, because it's my job to protect people...but you– you saved me...even when you didn't have to. I can't pretend that didn't happen," Firefly looked at the ground, kicking a pebble into a grass bed.

"Well—try."

Firefly's face dropped, unimpressed.

"Fine…let's just say you have my back, so I have yours. Case closed," Xeno strolled away.

Firefly smiled a bit, watching the silly guy groove a bit despite being thrown around the train car.

Suddenly the blur became clear;

This was not a supervillain.

Chapter 12:

Firefly quietly followed the villain through the lazy streets, dodging the few stragglers, as they approached a colorful hole-in-the-wall store. Peering through the windows, there were thousands of comics stacked on top of each other. Along with lots of action figures, posters, and lots of other super memorabilia.

Looking above was a striking red, white, blue, and yellow sign in classic comic book text surrounded by a big, star-like bubble. This was definitely a superhero comic store. The hero still couldn't wrap his head around how two villains worked here.

Xenomorph opened the door as the little jingle bell went off.

Firefly was right behind him—the store was pretty much dead besides a single girl behind the counter and a younger boy. The girl's hair was short, rough, and in black and white. She had fair skin, face covered in metal, and cold, dead eyes. She was wearing her tacky uniform that made Xenomorph itch just by looking at it, although Firefly thought it looked kinda cool.

She was resentfully helping the young kid check out, "That will be 4.99," she said coldly.

"Aww, I only have three dollars," the little boy whined.

Xeno grabbed the cash and shoved him the comic book, "Deal–now scram kid! Stores closed."

With one look at the villain the kid went screaming out and Xeno smirked a bit.

The woman's eyes and mouth dropped, "Xeno?!"

"In the flesh baby!" Xeno flexed his muscles, "Missed me?"

"Hardly! Where the hell have you *been*?!" The lady screamed.

"Here, there, being awesome– the usual," he teased.

Firefly leaned around his figure, "Um...hello?" He tried, giving a tiny wave.

The worker gasped, grabbed Xeno's sharp collar, and tugged him in, "...Are you INSANE?!"

"Yes," He smiled, seeing nothing wrong.

"YOU BROUGHT A FLAMING HERO IN HERE?! NOT JUST ANY VILE HERO, FIREFLY?!"

"Um– excuse, ma'am, but could you– like, kick his butt later? I know he seems bad, but he's really not that dangerous. We are looking for Thunderstorm, she works here?" Firefly tried to explain.

The lady slowly turned to Xenomorph, eyes twitching as if she was going to explode.

"Hehe...Devan?" Xeno smiled nervously.

"YOU TRAITOR!" She yelled and casted a blast of lightning, hitting Xenomorph and knocking him into a comic shelf. The shelf wobbled and fell as comic books flew.

Firefly flinched up, "...O-Oh– y-your Thunderstorm," the hero kept smiling trying to be polite. He held out his hand and Thunderstorm grabbed it hard. Electrocuting him–sending tiny little watts all over his body as the lightning infected his brain.

She let go, death staring him.

Firefly was still staticing up as he tried to recover, "Not a fan?"

"What. *The hell*. Are you doing here?!" She yelled, holding up a replica of a very sharp and big sword.

"I'm with Xeno! I'm with Xeno!" He rushed out, shielding himself. "Wait– where did that come from?!" He peered over his arms.

Thunderstorm, ignoring Firefly's question, looked at Xenomorph, who was still getting up.

"Gone soft loser?"

"Hardly– I'm just helpi–*using...I am just using him." Xeno lied and deflected. Although, he wasn't quick enough and Devan knew the truth.

"Why?! He's a nasty hero! Did you forget what they have done to us?! What he has done to you?!"

"Relax Dev! I remember, trust me he will get his karma...but I *don't* want to die so I kinda need him."

"Yeah!" Firefly smirked, finally feeling like he had the upper hand.

Thunderstorm rolled her eyes and scoffed, "That still doesn't explain why you brought him *here* and *EXPOSE MY IDENTITY*!"

"Oh, don't worry, I won't say anything," Firefly promised.

"You...won't?"

"Nope, lips are sealed," The hero did the gesture with his hands. Sealing his lips.

Devan leaned over the counter as Xenomorph approached, "What's wrong with him?" she whispered.

"I don't know, I think he got hit in the head on the train..." The villain whispered back.

"He knows he's a hero right? He is supposed to defeat us."

"While, yes, I may be a hero, I don't like to fight dirty," Firefly chirped in.

Devan just busted out laughing, "PAHAHAHA!! Good one! 'Don't fight dirty'! HaHAAA!!"

"What's so funny?" Firefly asked, tilting his head to the side.

"Come Buggy, you can't say you guys have never fought dirty." Xenomorph interrupted.

"W-We haven't. We play fair, it's you guys who play dirty!" Firefly defended.

A crackle of lightning sparked in Devan's eyes as storm clouds started to roll into the store. Thunder clapping as her face grew dark. Firefly immediately knew he screwed up.

"Oh?! Like today on the train?!" Xeno argued.

"That was different! ...Wait...that *was* different."

"Oh yeah? How so?!" Xeno sassed.

"No– no…I mean…their moves. We have never trained moves like that– I mean…Rosethorn almost…killed me…"

"Ahh~ so he's gone to the dark side, one of us," Devan declared.

"W-What? No!" Firefly yelled.

"You almost got killed by a hero? You're a Villain." Devan smirked, now feeling like she had the upper hand.

"It can't be that cut and dry– wait– …say that again?" Firefly asked.

"You're a villain?" She repeated, confused.

"No, no before that."

"You almost got killed by a hero?"

"We've never done that…" Firefly spoke softly, stunned.

The villains looked at each other.

Devan stared down Xeno, "Show him."

"Show me what?" Firefly asked.

"Oh no, no, no, it's embarrassing! And stupid, and I was just bored! They're a secret."

"'WELL XENO! YOU ALREADY EXPOSED YOUR JOB, YOUR ROOMMATE, AND MY IDENTITY. WHAT ELSE DID YOU WANT?!' DO YOU WANT ME TO EXPOSE YOUR NAME–?!"

Xeno jumped to cover her mouth, "NO! NO! No! No…no–"

"What are you guys talking about?" Firefly asked again.

Devan looked at Xeno again, making her eyes bigger to nudge him with her cold look.

The villain rolled his eyes, "Fine!" He hopped over the counter to a tiny shelf hanging on the wall. Taking a couple comics off and slapping them down on the counter.

"What is this?" Firefly asked, picking up a book.

"It's a comic, stupid," Xeno snared.

"I know that! I mean why are you giving it to me?"

"Read it." Xeno softly demanded, almost like it was an offer.

Firefly picked up the comic, "I've already read Super Soundwave: Episode 7. Spoiler alert; she fights Mind Manipulator and Soundwave wins…'yay'." Firefly 'cheers' as he tossed the paper book back on the counter.

"But you haven't read this version…" Xeno re-slides him the book.

Firefly confused, relooked at the cover again, Soundwave was drawn a lot scarier, well scarier than she already was. The hero was sticking it to Mind Manipulator but it was graphic, to say the least; and not the picture kind.

"Soundwave's WRATH" it read.

Firefly opened the comic and read. It was a classic, Soundwave chasing after Mind Manipulator, catching up, Mind Manipulator catches her, Soundwave escapes in a climax, and the two go to battle for the honor.

However, the ending was a lot bloodier than he remembered, especially for Mind Manipulator. In a last attempt, Soundwave shouted a sound blast to avoid being manipulated, cracking the building behind her. The building fell on Mind Manipulator with a *SPLAT!*

Firefly flinched, but kept reading.

Soundwave got rewarded with flowers and thanks and interviews while Mind Manipulated was holding on for dear life in the background.

Firefly closed the book speechless.

"She almost died that night," Devan started.

"O-Ok not good, but it was one time. And it's Soundwave!"

"That's true, she's a brat!" Xeno added, excitedly. Smiling wide as if he were actually contributing something.

"Ok! Then what about me!" Devan snapped and passed the other comic

"*Yellow Jacket's Death Trap!*"

Firefly picked it up, the same story followed through. The chaos, the chase, the capture, the fight– but this time to 'defeat' Thunderstorm he blasted her into the street and popped the tires of a moving car, sending it screeching towards her. Thunderstorm was hit with a *SLAM!* as the car ran her over.

Yeesh! A car crash...not the way to go out.

Yellow Jacket got rewarded and Thunderstorm passed out alone on the paved street. Firefly carefully closed the book.

Devan looked at his guilty face, "Yeah...that's what I thought."

"B-But that's impossible, we are trained to use these moves to try and protect everyone! We wouldn't give you more than you can handle– it's our nature, our conduct!" Firefly stuttered.

"REALLY?! Tell that to my three broken ribs!"

"But you're alive! Besides! I'm innocent! I'd never do anything like this!" Firefly flamed up offended.

Devan stared at him, ready to break him.

"Devs– you don't have to–" Xeno started, but she already dropped one more comic on the table.

Firefly looked down and his pulse ran cold at the words.

'*Firefly Revenge!*'

"W-What…?"first

Xenomorph looked away, hiding something no doubt.

Firefly quickly opened it up, not even bothering to read what it had been about. Straight to the end.

He froze when he saw the little comic book Xenomorph and himself on the top of the firework factory.

"This…this is our first fight…" Firefly thought out loud.

"…Yeah it was." Xeno agreed, sounding distant as he crossed his arms.

The comic Firefly fell through the ceiling and Xeno went after him. A bit of fighting here and there, when suddenly Firefly tied Xeno up with a rope. Hanging him on a crane inside the factory.

"Hold on– I– I don't get it. You escaped that night!"

"Did he?" Devan sassed sarcastically.

Firefly turned back to the comic and Xeno tried to shoot him with a blast of sound from the rope, but he missed.

However, it did scare Firefly into flaming up and jumping into a box. Setting a box of fireworks on fire.

"…I– I didn't do that! …did I?"

Devan pointed to the page. "Keep reading."

Firefly went back to the book as the comic Captain Peace called his name. The little Firefly shot a dirty look at Xenomorph, stuck out his tongue, and left.

Captain Peace opened the door, congratulating the hero.

The little Xenomorph shouted to wait, crying for help, not to leave him there. But as the ink-outlined Firefly looked back, Captain Peace pushed him away, the Captain smiled evilly at the villain.

As the door closed a giant, colorful, loud *KABOOM!!!* went off. Lighting a beautiful sight above New York as the color stars exploded.

Firefly and Captain Peace raced inside but the villain was gone and the building was destroyed. On fire, burning away as the rubble rained down and the rope swung with no one tangled in it.

Captain Peace said something corny like 'We will get them next time', and they both left. Determination filling their tiny, drawn eyes.

However, the last page reveals where Xenomorph really was. He didn't run away, didn't escape, he was blasted into a box. Bleeding out as a firework had impaled him and blew him up, trapped behind rubble, as good as dead.

Firefly closed the book.

Heartbroken.

He looked over at Xenomorph, his bandana having a couple of wet spots where eyes would be.

"So? Now what do you think…?" Devan asked.

"X-Xeno, I promise– I had no idea…" Firefly's voice shrank, reaching for him.

"I know, it's fine, it was a long time ago…" Xeno pulled away as he hid his cracked voice.

"That doesn't make it right! I had no idea I lit the fire, I thought it was you! And even then, we left you behind. That's– horrible…I'm horrible."

"BOOM! Yeah, you are!" Devan gloated.

"Devan!" Xeno snapped.

"What?! Isn't that what we wanted?"

"W-What is this series? I've never seen it before," Firefly cracked, wanting more answers.

"That's because it's not published. We call it Point of Villain…it reveals what *really* happened, and not any of your fluffy, superhero garbage they lie about." Devan explained.

"But w-who made it?"

Devan nodded over to Xeno. Firefly slowly looked up at the guy.

"I told you…I like to doodle…"

"Whoa…that's amazing– I mean not the idea of you guys getting hurt but the art, the action, the story. People need to see this!"

"Whoa! Easy Firecracker! You do realize if these got out to the city, it would trash you and every hero to walk this earth!" Xenomorph reasoned, not knowing why. He'd love to watch that dumpster fire burn.

"…I stand by what I said. People need to see this," Firefly stood his ground. Xenomorph was taken aback, shocked at the offer, the sacrifice. "I have to get this to the Captain!"

"Wait what?!" Xeno shouted.

Firefly started grabbing the books- "Don't you see! You are innocent!"

"What?! No! No! I'm not innocent, devilishly handsome and a great dancer yes– but innocent?"

"You were forced to be a villain!" Firefly protested.

"YOU TOLD HIM THAT TOO?! 'GEE X IS THERE ANYTHING YOU DIDN'T TELL HIM?!'" Devan yelled.

"You knew?! AND YOU DIDN'T HELP HIM?!" Firefly pointed fingers.

"WHAT WAS I SUPPOSED TO DO?! I AM IN THE SAME BOAT!" Devan yelled, thunder clapping.

"…Wait– both of you are being forced to be villains?"

"Do you think we wanted this?!" Devan raged. "Do you think we want to be hated by the world?! News flash kid– …we are *all* forced to be villains. Cause if we don't…"

"We disappear…" Xeno finished.

Firefly's heart sank lower and lower.

"WHICH THIS HERO SHOULDN'T EVEN KNOW IN THE FIRST PLACE!" Devan shouted, smacking the counter.

"Devan, please, I had no choice and now I need your help!"

"MY HELP?! Why?! To help HIM?! After what he's done to us?!"

"I get it sounds crazy, but I need you to trust me."

"TRUST YOU?! I don't trust anyone! I mean did you tell him about the secret base?! Our training?! Your dad being a hero-?!"

Xeno grabbed her, covering her loud mouth, "SHHHHHHHH!!!"

"...What did you just say..." Firefly spoke, barely. World breaking.

"NOTHING!" Xeno covered up.

"Y-Your dad...WAS A HERO?!?"

Xenomorph grew lightning in his eyes as he shot a blast at Firefly faster than light itself.

Firefly ducked, dropping the book, but Xeno purposely missed, shooting the power box. Causing all the lights in the store to burst.

Firefly stood surprised in the darkness. The little sunlight hitting Xeno's very angry face.

"...You said I didn't have to talk about it yet..." he threatened.

Firefly took a breath, lighting his hand on fire to create a light, "You're right...you can tell me when you're ready, if you want. Although regarding the firework incident I wouldn't blame you if you didn't...but, believe it or not I at least respect you...'like' may be strong, but definitely respect. And just remember, I made you a promise."

Xeno's face softened at the hero's apology.

"You guys sound so clingy." Devan chirped in, removing Xeno's hand from her mouth.

"It…it doesn't matter– we have a mission," Xenomorph shrugged off, coldly.

Firefly's fire died a bit, wallowing in shame.

Xeno turned to his co-worker, "Devan. Please. I need to know where Dark Legacy will be this weekend."

Devan narrowed her eyes, "Why?"

"We need to find out what he's planning. He will destroy every hero left on earth, and more importantly me, if we don't tell someone!" Xenomorph shifted his focus.

"Sounds awesome! Why would I help you interfere?!" Devan smirked evilly.

Firefly flamed up, having enough of her bull crap. This girl was wedging her way into Xenomorph's head, breaking the little trust they had.

Firefly picked back up her comic. Showing her the mess of blood on the pages.

"Did you enjoy this?!"

"NO! YOU JERK! Why would I ever–"

"This is what's going to happen to dozens of supers if we don't do something!" Firefly snapped, smoking up. Both villains lifted their heads in surprise. "I know you think they probably deserve it and I can see why, but no one deserves death. You can be better than them…"

Xeno looked at Devan, "Devan, please. For me?"

Devan sighed, "Fine, but…you have to do something for me…" she smirked.

Xeno smiled, "Ooo~ Villain Dare?"

Devan smiles back, "You know me too well," She stomped on the floor as a ring of lightning bursted out. Thunder rolling as her eyes glowed a shady purple, "Villain Dare!"

"Challenge Accepted!" Xeno yelled.

"Whoa– what the heck is happening?" Firefly asked as the lights flickered back on.

"Villain Dare! We never trust each other so when we really want something we will do a devious favor in order to claim our reward!" Xeno explained, evil laughing.

"…That sounds awful!" Firefly sympathized.

"Oh no! It's *tons* of fun, and we get what we want. Ok so Dev; you give us Dark Legacy's whereabouts and we…?"

"Hmm…I want one hundred bucks."

"Oh, that's not so bad," Firefly sighed, taking out his wallet.

"*From the store across the street.*" She finished dramatically, pointing across the way to a small hardware store. With little, red awnings, wooden crates of fruit in the front, and a little spinning display of postcards. It looked so homely, so innocent.

"What?!" Firefly yelled. "You want us to steal?! You're insane!"

"Do it or I'm not giving you Dark Legacy's coordinates," She threatened.

Xeno interrupted the two, shoving Firefly to the side, "We will! We will! Game on!" Xeno stretched, excited to be back in the game.

"What?! You can't be serious," Firefly argued.

"Do you want to save all hero kind?" He asked, but it was so sassy and rhetorical. What was the point of even answering.

Firefly shut his mouth, lowered his head and nodded.

Xeno and Devan shook a firm handshake. The deal was set in stone.

"Then let's go rob a store!" Xeno shouted, pointing to the ceiling.

"Hang on, first– Little Miss Thunderbolt tells us where Dark Legacy is hiding," Firefly demanded.

"Smart! There's no way we can come back here after we ransack the place, oou! Do you think the cops will come back?!" Xenomorph asked excited–too excited. Like he was getting a puppy for Christmas.

Firefly avoided eye contact—or rather mask contact, "Do not–… do not make me more nervous than I already am."

"Cmon Buggy, lighten up! This will be good for you!" Xeno tried.

"Wow~. Partners in crime I see," Devan boasted.

"He's not my partner," Firefly defender.

"Awww~," Xenomorph whined, pretending he cared.

"If you say so, firebutt," Devan fired.

Xeno wheezed, "PAAAAAH! That's a good one!"

"Dark Legacy! Now!" Firefly continued.

"Ok! Ok! Rumor at HQ is that the Governor is throwing a party this weekend to talk with the hero leader and address the– well– you guys situation."

"Sweet! We are in a 'situation' now," Xeno chirped in.

"Dark Legacy will be there in his secret identity form trying to snipe some information, but I have no idea what that looks like, so good luck!"

"Where and when is this party?" Firefly asked.

"Friday night at the governor's house, but remember it is linked to the venue. This isn't some small house party, this is going to be huge!"

"Aww, man! I don't have anything to wear," Xeno joked, although he was so dramatic. Firefly rolled his eyes, picturing him in a stunning suit, not that he'd admit that Xeno would rock it.

"Ok, I held up my end, now it's your turn…" Devan threatened with a smile, enjoying this way too much.

Xeno bounced up and down as Firefly sighed.

"Fine~!" The hero groaned, picking up a random backpack off the floor and stuffing the handmade comics in there.

"Hey, that's mine!" Xeno whined.

"Great! Even better!" Firefly sassed, grinning ear to ear like he was going to lose it. "Now come on…we– *gulp* have a s-store to rob."

"Hell yeah!" Xeno sang.

"This is going to be fun to watch," Devan smirked. Watching Firefly leave in pain.

The hero didn't notice her look, all he could think was, *What in BLAZES did I get myself into?*

Chapter 13:

In a blink of an eye, Firefly was suddenly in the store across the street. Sweating profusely as he tried to keep his head down and his hood on. Staring at the ground trying to figure out how to get out of this mess. The aisles felt like they were closing in as he could hear his heart beat like a drum.

Thump. Thump.

Thump. Thump.

Thump. Thump.

He *couldn't* believe he was doing this. He was a part of a robbery—heck an accomplice! Nothing had happened yet, but it would! Then what?! He was already seen as a threat to the public; how was this going to help?

As Firefly drifted into his thoughts, Xeno wasted no time. He was a bit loud as he started grabbing spray paint, soda bottles, and mints. Scooping them off the shelf and into the backpack with the biggest grin on his face.

"Really?!" Firefly whispered-yelled.

"What? We can take whatever we want! Enjoy it!" Xeno explained, eyes drifting to the shelf. "Ooh! Sour gummy worms!"

"Again with the gummy worms?!"

"Hey! They are my favorite." Xeno waved around the bag as he defended.

"Because they're as sour as you?" Firefly asked rhetorically.

"Yep, pretty much," Xeno answered, unphased. He gracefully opened the bag, sticking his hand inside for another piece of sugary bait. "C'mon, don't you want something?"

"Want something?" Firefly puzzled.

"Yeah, for yourself."

"Absolutely not! Besides I don't need your sour worms," Firefly insisted, trying to walk off.

"Well what about marshmallows! You know, because they're your favorite," Xeno tried, with a big smile.

Firefly froze, turning around in pure shock.

"You...you remembered?"

"Of course I did..."

Firefly felt the corners of his mouth rise a bit, giving a warm, genuine–

"It was so oddly specific, yet so weirdly insignificant it was almost impossible to forget it." Xeno smirked.

Firefly's nice smile dropped into a deadpan. Not amused by this guy's antics. Things were supposed to be going well since the metro. Why was Xeno acting weird? Weirder than usual?

It's like the night before never happened, erased. Firefly decided not to get into it. *At the end of the day, this guy was still a villain...right? Yes? No~? Ugh!*

"Oou! Oou! Oou! Check it out!" He grabbed a pair of cool sunglasses and tried them on. Giving some fun faces, "Pretty sick, right? Here you try some!" Xeno pushed a pair of sunglasses on his goggles.

Firefly looked in the mirror and hated to admit how awesome they looked. He gave in a bit and the two did some supermodel poses in the reflection, until Firefly realized how wrong this was (robbing the store, not being supermodels),

"Wait– no." He took off the glasses and turned to his crime scene.

"Why don't we just leave?!" Firefly whispered to Xeno who was wiping sour powder from his lips. "We got the information we needed, we don't have to do this!"

"Um~, yes we do! Otherwise we would be breaking our deal~ and lying~. That's not very 'heroic'," Xeno teased, tossing a gummy worm at the hero's face.

"I I can't even with you," Firefly groaned. Why was this guy always twisting his words?!

Xenomorph looked over the shelves, watching as the worker left the register unattended to head to the back. He pushed 'his' glasses up. The villain's mouth curled up, *ecstatic* to be back.

"Alright, let's go," Xeno patted Firefly and ran down the aisle.

"No! No! Xeno!" Firefly called after in a whisper, chasing him.

Xeno slid over the counter and got to the register, grabbing a screwdriver and jabbing it into the little slot. Hitting some buttons, and voila! It opened with a clink.

"Xenomorph! Seriously! Stop!" Firefly argued on the other side of the counter. "I thought you hated being viewed as a villain?"

"I do." He replied, tossing the tool away.

"Then what are you doing?!"

"Hey, I hate being *viewed* as a villain, I never said I didn't like being one," Xeno smirked as he grabbed stacks and stacks of cash, stuffing it in his backpack.

"...You're unbelievable."

"Thank you, you're so nice!" Xeno smiled, tossing him a stack of cash, "That's Devan's cut."

"What?! Then what's the rest of it?!"

"Our cut! You think we are going to rob a store and not get at least 80% of the profit. I'll split it...70/10."

"First off—if we were doing this...it would be 40/40 even. Secondly, we are not doing this! This is wrong!" Firefly flamed up.

"Ugh~! You're such a buzzkill..." Xenomorph groaned when suddenly–

"HEY!" A voice called out.

Both supers whipped their heads around to see the employee. Eyes grew as Xenomorph quickly tossed Firefly the bag.

"Run!" He jumped over the counter and ran.

"I'm getting tired of running!" Firefly yelled as he followed, quickly yelling back, "So sorry!" To the worker.

The employee pulled an alarm and a siren went off. Xenomorph elbowed over a shelf to block any brave employee's path. Firefly quickly slid under the falling display, nearly being squished.

The two teens sprinted to the door, but once they pushed the glass open, cop cars started surrounding them.

The red and blue flashing came back like a bad dream as Firefly closed up, shaking. Frozen in fear.

Xenomorph smiled at the chaos, ready to draw his rifle like a cowboy at dawn, but when he looked to his partner the smile vanished. The fear was getting to the hero, and for better or for worse he needed to get his Firecracker out of here.

"Over here!" Xeno grabbed Firefly's hand and ran. Pulling him over to a parked ice cream cart and swinging him around. Shoving the hero into the open cooler compartment.

The police started to shoot as Xeno jumped on the cart and pushed. Trying to dodge bullets, until one nicked him in the shoulder,

"Ahrg–!" He winced as the cart went racing down the street.

"Hand me Devan's cut." He spat.

Firefly groaned and sprang up from the icy box, handing him the money with his face covered in strawberry and chocolate smudges.

"Devs! Catch!" Xeno threw the wadded stack at Devan (who was watching the masterpiece from across the street) and she caught it.

Xenomorph managed to snag a gun out of an officer's hand and stood up, shooting back at the uniformed enemies.

"What are you doing?!" Firefly asked.

"Getting away!" Xeno exclaimed as he slammed his boot on one of the tires. The rubber wheel snapped and flew off as the cart hit the pavement and swerved, sparking against the road.

"Hold on!" The villain yelled, holding the colorful umbrella. They made a sloppy left turn as the cop cars came chasing around the corner.

The cart scratched paint off of an unsuspecting taxis and cars. Flying down the street as the silly, little ice cream music played.

Soon the villain spotted a big, obnoxious billboard with their smiling governor. With a roll of the eyes, he tucked the gun in his back pocket.

"Ready?!" He continued as he eyed up a billboard. Firefly followed his eyes and readied up.

"JUMP!"

They both jump for the metal sign.

The world felt slow for only a moment as they both grabbed the bottom of the board.

Firefly pulled himself quickly as Xeno struggled. Groaning as his fingers start to slip, until-

"AH!" Xenomorph fell.

It was only a few seconds as Firefly dove and grabbed his hand, yanking him back up.

"Woo! Nothing beats this, Buggy!" Xenomorph cheered.

Firefly, on instinct, cussed and screamed, "I hate you!" as he dragged his partner onto the scaffolding.

"Oh my god your first curse word! I'M SO PROUD OF YOU!"

Firefly covered his mouth, ashamed. Getting a glimpse of the street as cops tailed each other. "The police are gaining on us!"

"Hand me your cut!" The villain demanded as he ran across the billboard.

Firefly followed and reached into the bag and handed him a couple stacks.

Xeno paused, looking at it, "This isn't what we talked about," He deadpanned.

"Just shut up and take it!"

Xeno smiled more, with one hand he unwrapped the rubber band around the stacks, and jumped across the road while letting go. Spreading the money through the streets, flying in the winds like a plague of locusts.

"WOOOOOHOOOO! That should keep them busy!" Xeno laughed, tucking and rolling to stick the landing.

"Just run! I don't want to get caught!" Firefly begged as he did an aerial to catch up.

"You need to chill out–…wait," Xeno dug around in his pockets as he ran.

"Now what are you doing?!" Firefly asked, already knowing he wasn't going to like the answer.

"Got it!"

"A way out?!"

"No! Better!" Xeno held up a chocolate fudge stick.

"What is that?"

"It's ice cream." Xenomorph explained.

"I know what it is! How is that going to help us!"

"It's going to help you."

"HOW IN THE WORLD–MMM!" Firefly started to flame up before Xenomorph shoved the fudge stick into his mouth.

"MM! …mm? Mmmm~!" He licked it a few times as they ran, fire extinguishing as he felt the steam fly away; being replaced with a refreshing chill. He actually liked the popsicle.

"Better?"

Firefly smiled and nodded, nomming on the fudge stick. He liked chocolate, who knew?

Xeno and Firefly kept jumping and climbing on roofs, sliding down sharp angles and tight-rope-walking on fancy accents and dirty gutters. Xenomorph reached back into his coat and pulled out a popsicle of his own, licking the rocket pop.

The two ran into a rooftop greenhouse. Firefly tripped over a bucket of water and bumped into Xenomorph. Knocking them both in a planter box. The two paused in the dirt breathing, looking up at the sky.

As Firefly's heart slowed, Xeno started to laugh. The hero looked over shocked. However, the laughter was too contagious and he soon followed.

Suddenly a blur flew over them, and their laughter stopped. Firefly gulped down the remains of the ice fudge.

"Oh relax– it's probably just a bird," Xeno sassed as a flying planter box hurtled towards them.

"AAAAAHHHHHHHHHHHH!!"

"AAAAAHHHHHHHHHHHH!!"

Both boys screamed bloody murder as they scattered. The boxes smashed together and exploded into splinters.

In a jump scare, Mind Manipulator jumped in front of Xenomorph, grabbed him by the throat, and pinned him down.

"Crazy lady! Get off of me!" Xeno screamed.

Firefly hid behind a nearby wall only to see Sniper and Magnet on top of some neighboring building roofs.

Sniper blasted him with lazer vision, causing him to keep running.

Magnet quickly jumped down and used his power to pull the metal roofing and piping to him. Flinging it around to try and crush the pinned-down Firefly. Xeno kicked his catcher off and ran, joining his teammate.

Firefly looked back, took a deep breath, and screeched his shoes to a stop. Turning around as he flamed up.

"Uh?! What are you doing?!" Xeno yelled, stopping as well. Police raving beneath them in the cracks of the alleys.

"I'm going to fight the supervillains—that's my job!" Firefly yelled as he ran towards the danger.

"...He's going to die." Xeno whispered to himself, but eventually followed the teen back into battle.

Firefly launched and kicked Mind Manipulator again, sending her into another garden box. He smiled and laughed, feeling confident.

Magnet flung the water bucket at Xeno and it unfortunately stuck to his head. While Xenomorph struggled, Firefly kept backflipping and dodging lazers until he met with a soaring AC unit.

Firefly managed to duck, "Ha! Miss!"

"Did I?" The magnetic villain taunted.

Firefly looked back to see Xeno finally remove the bucket, but got slammed by the metal box off the roof. As Xenomorph screamed, he managed to grab a closeline, but it snapped and swung him crashing into a window.

"Dude, watch out!" Firefly screamed, jumping down the fire escape to meet up.

"I COULDN'T SEE! There was a bucket on my head, Firecracker!" Xeno yelled as he brushed the glass off of him.

"Oh. Fair." Firefly said, but as he was trying to help his friend out of the building–

WHAM

He was greeted by a hard, metal punch from Magnet. The red and grey villain punched him over and over as Xeno scurried away from the window. Finally, Magnet grabbed Firefly and dragged him to the top of the roof. Rag-dolling him to a solid floor.

Firefly coughed and tried to block from the ground but Magnet had the upper hand.

In seconds the gauntlet grabbed the hero's throat as metal objects from inside the house started to fly up and stick to the plaster; including a lot of sharp knives Xeno had to dodge. Unfortunately, one cut his cheek as it zoomed up to stab the drywall. He winced, but quickly used the magnetic power to pull the bullet from his shoulder.

"Careful up there! You're going to dent my crib! Honestly! It's hard enough to afford a place in this economy without annoying neighbors!" Xeno started before the ceiling started caving in, revealing the concrete, wood, and metal poles of the building. He stared at the architecture before he got an idea. "Poles...magnetic poles– *Gasp* wait– I'M A MIMIC! Hey Buggy get ready!" He yelled.

Firefly kept holding the metal hand away from his face, "What?!"

Xeno looked to the ceiling to see the dents.

Feeling around for the magnetic power he readied up his hand. Magnet slammed his fist into the concrete again, missing Firefly's face, while Xeno punched up into the same spot.

"WHA-" Magnet yelped as he immediately went flying up into the sky and hit a power line, shocking him as he fell back down onto the road. Crashing onto a police car's hood. The cellphone tower fell into the streets with a loud and flashy crash.

Some of the cop cars crashed or braked hard, screeching their tires. Other police cars swerved around the sparking log and continued their chase.

Firefly lifted his head in surprise, he leaned over and stuck his head through one of the broken side windows, "How did you do that?!"

"Magnets that have the same poles repel each other when pushed together!" Xeno said as he went to the balcony.

Firefly stood surprised yet again, "How do you know that?"

"How do you not?" Xenomorph sassed as he jumped back on top of the building.

Firefly paused as he noticed the villain's cheek and shoulder, "Oou~ ouch, are you ok?"

153

"I'm fine–" Xeno quickly cut off before Mind Manipulator jumped into the battle. With a ready pose her goggles started to swirl.

Xeno quickly shot his arm out and covered Firefly's eyes, shutting his own, "Don't look!"

"'Don't look'?! HOW ARE WE SUPPOSED TO FIGHT?!"

"I CAN FIGHT! ...Just not well."

Mind Manipulated seized her chance and kicked Firefly off to another roof.

"GAAHH!" He screamed and went flying back.

"BUGGY!" Xeno yelled as he looked back, which gave Mind Manipulator the perfect chance to punch the traitor right in the face.

Xeno cussed under his breath as he closed his eyes and readied his fist, but with no sight Mind Manipulator beat the crap out of him.

Firefly managed to climb back up as he watched his teammate get absolutely destroyed, taking hits like a champ.

Mind Manipulator went for a swing in the face when–

"Duck!" Firefly called out and Xeno did.

Mind Manipulator missed her shot, turned around, and her frown grew at the bug. She pinned Xeno to the wall of another building, twisting his arms behind his back. Firefly ran to save him when she turned on her goggles once more and looked into his eyes. The flaming hero was too late in looking away.

"Whoa~." He slurred as he felt his body being taken away. He stared into the beautiful green swirls until her voice interrupted.

"Let's see you help now– Firefly~" She taunted and gave a squeaky laugh. Suddenly, with her hand she commanded the hero to launch at his friend.

"AH!" He yelped and punched Xeno in the face against his will.

Xeno got knocked out of his crumpled position and crashed into a vent, "Ow! Hey!"

"It's not me– It's her!"

"What?! I told you not to look!" Xeno wailed with his shut eyes. Standing up as Firefly punched him in the gut. "Gaow!"

Firefly's leg went for a swing, "Jump!"

Xeno did and avoided the kick.

Mind Manipulator then commanded the hero's hand to punch.

"Block!" Firefly yelled and Xeno blocked.

"What are you doing?!" Xeno tried, still blinded.

"Being your eyes, she's on your left, three o'clock!" Firefly said as he kept trying to fight his body, yet he still attacked his villain.

"GAOW!" Xeno yelped again as Firefly's fist smashed into his face. Lazers raving around as the two danced.

"I SAID ON YOUR LEFT!" Firefly yelled.

Xeno cartwheeled out of the way, slid on the floor, and knocked the mind controlling villain back with his whipped-cream-and-dirt covered boot.

Firefly stood still without instructions as he yelled, "Upper cut!"

Xeno did so and knocked her goggles right off, shattering them into scraps.

Firefly breathed and relaxed as he felt he finally had control of his body.

Xeno opened his eyes and kicked her off the roof, she tumbled against the bricks on her way down and landed in a trash bin. *SMASH*

She plucked a banana peel off her ratty hair, she growled in anger.

"WOOOO! That's for leaving the coffee filters in the machine every day!" Xeno cheered, waving his fist in the air and stomping on the goggles. He then looked to the roofs for that last pesky villain.

In an instant, he saw Sniper and shot a lazer back at him—bullseye.

Firefly ran back to Xeno and panted, resting on his knees.

"Awesome job, Buggy!" The villain cheered as he patted his back.

"I think I'm going to throw up," Firefly muffled.

"This is living!" Xeno cheered, picking the hero up by his hood to keep running. However as they made it to the edge of the roof, a police helicopter floated up in their way, blocking the two. Both boys froze as the police and S.W.A.T. finally made their way to the roof. Busting down doors, surrounding the two, and aiming their weapons.

Firefly slowly raised his hands as his pulse skipped a beat.

"Ugh– typical, wait till after we do the dirty work to arrest us," Xeno sassed as he also threw his hands up. Both gave a frown as they were caught red-handed.

Chapter 14:

The police soon cuffed the supers with some weird glowing blue cuffs that seemed to nullify their powers and took them downtown. Shoving them through the front doors.

Paper ruffling and stapling noises filled the air as people hurried around. The whole building seemed to be in quite the panic.

The police captain squeezed Firefly's wrist tight as he pushed the boys to the front desk.

"I found them, call Governor Jaceson and the heroes. Once the paperwork is filled we can lock them up for good," The captain commanded.

The officer behind the counter nodded as he put two paper packets on the counter.

"Sign these please."

"Yes! Of course officers, right away–" Firefly started as he rushed to grab a pen.

Xeno grabbed his wrist, "Hold on! What exactly is this…?"

"It's an arrest warranty, inventory listing, and the super packet."

"The super packet?" Firefly asked. He had never heard of such a thing.

"Oh hell no– not signing that crap," Xeno huffed, pushing the packet away.

"What? Why? What's the super packet?"

"It's a *stupid* amount of papers and apologies that we have to go through when a villain is arrested. Special cuffs and cages for power diffusing as well as jumps priority to the government!"

"That doesn't sound so bad, sounds ethically moral if anything…" Firefly mumbled, rolling his eyes.

"It also gives them consent to treat us like *GARBAGE*! Experimenting on us and our powers like we are some rats! Using shock collars, drugs, and even suffocation; straight up torture methods to make us obey or get any information for the heroes. Last time I was here, I barely could walk out, with all their so-called 'interrogation'!"

"What?! That sounds ridiculous, why would you ever have to sign that?!"

"Because it's the rules you created! Plus, Dark Legacy makes us. He says it makes us look less threatening and that way the heroes aren't all up in his business! Easier for him to break us out apparently. Point is—Dark Legacy is not here—so no! I'm not signing your stupid contracts!" He tried to cross his arms with his cuffed wrist, and both cops looked angry.

"L-Listen we are in a very tight situation right now, can you please just lay low and sign the thing. I promise whatever they have planned we will go through it together," Firefly tried to land on everyone's good side.

Xeno sighed, "Fine!" As he grabbed the sharpie and started singing away. When he was finished he held up the papers and instead of his signature and precisely marked box he wrote some cuss words in big, bold, black letters. He smirked, feeling proud.

Firefly just sighed and face palmed softly, feeling embraced and defeated.

Next thing they knew the snaps of mug shots were taken (Firefly looking more nervous than ever while Xenomorph just rocked the camera) and the metal bars slammed closed. Locking them up behind the cold gate. Firefly grabbed the bars as the realization finally hit him. He was in jail. He was in trouble. He was a villain.

"Screw you! Some real 'protectors of the city' you are!" Xenomorph jeered at the policemen as he took out another fudge bar. "Want one?"

"Are you kidding me? No! ...Oh who am I fooling, of course I do," Firefly replied, yanking the ice cream from his hand. After a couple seconds of angry silence—and chocolate—Firefly continued, "You are *unbelievable*."

"*Excuse me?*" Xeno asked, rhetorically as he heard him clearly the first time.

"You couldn't just listen to me for once!"

"I did us a favor! I think it's pronounced 'thank you'."

"WHAT IS WITH YOU?!"

"With me?! You're the one who doesn't know how to stay safe, Firebutt! Running into villain battles, signing weird contracts, not to mention you don't know how to have fun."

"You— YOU— YOU ARE SO IMMATURE AND SELFISH! IT'S LIKE YOU DON'T EVEN CARE HUNDREDS OF PEOPLE ARE GOING TO DIE!" Firefly screamed, although he didn't set a blaze like usual.

"WHO SAYS! I wouldn't be here otherwise!" Xeno yelled, also wanting to flame up and smoke him.

"WELL THEN ACT LIKE IT! CAUSE FROM WHERE I'M STANDING, YOU COULDN'T CARE LESS ABOUT THE HEROES."

"YOU'RE RIGHT I DON'T, YET I'M STILL HELPING YOUR INCOMPETENT ASS! BESIDES, YOU COULDN'T CARE LESS ABOUT ME SO WE ARE EVEN!"

"I NEVER SAID THAT—!"

"'WELL YOU ACT LIKE IT'!" Xenomorph mocked, sticking his tongue out and making a horrible impression.

"UGH! YOU ARE *INFURIATING*! I KNOW YOU WERE FORCED TO BE A VILLAIN, BUT WHY ARE YOU ACTING LIKE THIS NOW?! I THOUGHT WE WERE GOOD! I THOUGHT WE HAD EACH OTHER'S BACK!" Firefly raged

Xeno's head sprung up, offended, "I DO HAVE YOUR BACK!"

"YOU DIDN'T HAVE MY BACK AT THE DESK, OR THE SHOP, OR EVEN AT THE COMIC STORE!" Firefly listed, counting on his fingers.

"CAN YOU SHUT UP!?"

"NO! TELL ME WHY YOU'RE ACTING THIS WAY!"

"WHAT WAY?!" Xeno screamed.

"LIKE A VILLAIN!"

"*BECAUSE THAT'S WHAT I AM*! A VILLAIN! WHY DO YOU CARE?! YOU'RE A HERO! YOU ARE JUST GOING TO GO BACK TO YOUR PERFECT LIFE AND JUST FORGET I EXIST!"

"WHO SAID THAT?!" Firefly yelled back, now confused.

"I DID! I'M SAYING IT! YOU WOULDN'T CARE IF I DISAPPEARED!" Xeno shouted in his face.

Firefly's anger vanished, taken aback by that statement.

"What...? Yes I would, why would you think that?"

"BECAUSE YOU'RE A HERO AND I'M A VILLAIN! THAT'S HOW THIS WORLD WORKS FIRECRACKER!" The villain raised his hands to gesture at the sky.

"But you don't have to be a villain!" Firefly protested.

Xeno sighed, "...Yes– I do."

"No you don't."

"Yes I do!"

"What if you were a hero? Like your dad!"

"**GO TO HELL**!" Xeno yelled as loud as possible, trying to flame up but with the cuffs he couldn't. Firefly flinched at the villain, near inches away from his face, sending a cold death stare behind his mask. While fire never lit, he did reek of smoke, like he was ready to blow if he could.

A few seconds of silence went by and Xenomorph turned away, resting on the bars.

"...Sorry." Firefly started, fidgeting with his hands, "...I just...I *get* that Dark Legacy used you for his games...forced you to be that horrid villain running through the streets. But...you were right back there: he's not here, and I have your back– so I don't understand why you wouldn't try to be a hero or at least a better per–"

"It's the only thing I'm good at," Xeno interrupted as Firefly froze,

"What?"

"Being a villain...it's the one thing I'm good at," Xeno spoke softly, not turning around. "I can be free to do whatever I want...not be worried about what people think. I can have fun and get rewarded in treasure and loot and just *live*. And I'm *good* at it...besides it's not like the city will see anything different...so what's the point. Just because I don't like the way people treat me doesn't mean I don't like who I am."

Firefly paused.

Xeno's voice cracked, "I'm sorry I'm such a 'horrid villain'. I know you...and my dad...are '*so~*' disappointed in me...but I don't care." He lied.

Firefly's eyes widen, finally seeing that side of Xeno again; the same one under the floodlights. Despite looking at his back. He chose his next words carefully, as to not spook the baby bird.

"...I'm not disappointed in you."

162

"Then why do you want to change me?" Xeno asked, still not understanding.

"Because…I…I *see* good in you…"

Xenomorph slowly turned around not believing his ears.

"I don't know how– or why, but I see it. And…after all of this…I can't imagine going back to fight you. I don't want to fight you."

"Aren't you a superhero, isn't that kinda like your whole thing? To fight villains." Xeno sniffled.

"My thing is to save people, and that includes you. Besides you aren't a villain, not to me, not anymore."

Xeno tried to cover up his surprise, but failed miserably. Feeling his heart tug at his frie- um…partner in crime.

"I just thought, maybe…I could give you something…to make up for all that lost time. Provide you with a better life, a second chance. Xenomorph I do care. I know you don't believe me, but I do. I wouldn't be here otherwise," Firefly ended, reciting the villain's words against him.

Xenomorph stood quiet, not even knowing how to top that.

Firefly sighs, "I don't know what I'm doing," he leaned on the wall and slid down, falling to the tiled floor "I am not such a great hero. I wish I was…but I'm not."

Xenomorph looked at him on the ground, not aware of what to say or do. His world was turning backwards and his brain was scrambled. After a while, he finally found the words,

"That's stupid, you have defeated my ass more times than I can count," Xeno comforted, sitting in front of him, "You're *the* Firefly."

"Truth be told, I actually don't like being 'Firefly', I wanted to change my name." Firefly sighed.

"Whoa, really?" Xenomorph asked, surprised.

"Yeah, Firefly was Captain Peace's pick, mine's more personal, more inspiring– more me."

"Let's hear it."

"Oh no– you wouldn't care."

"What if I do? You can't decide that for me and we've got nowhere to be, so spill," Xeno chirped excitedly.

"Well...I was thinking: *Phoenix*."

"Ooo~ nice!" Xeno smiled.

"Sounds better, right?"

"Totally, and more threatening! I'd *actually* be afraid of Phoenix," Xeno laughed.

"See you get it!" Firefly laughed along.

Xeno stopped his giggles as a thought popped into his head, "Why didn't Captain Peace like it?"

"I haven't been able to tell him, he's been so busy...plus I'm making such a mess for him to clean up." Firefly defended.

"Why do you have to answer to him? Like I know you guys are all on a team, but why can't you just pick your own name?"

Firefly sighs, finally ready to talk, "Because like you...I'm also *forced* to be here. Forced to be a hero."

Xenomorph's mouth dropped, "WAIT– WHAT?! B-BUT YOU LOVE BEING A HERO!"

"It's true, I love being a hero but that doesn't mean I wasn't forced. Whether I wanted it or not, I was pushed into the hero program, I'm just glad I liked it. I wanted to be one more than anything, I was willing to do whatever it took." Firefly explained, he didn't wanna admit it at first, but he actually related to Xenomorph. Feeling trapped in a world you love.

"Why did you want to be a hero?" Xeno bugged, a million questions flooding his head.

"My dad, following in his footsteps."

Xenomorph deflated.

"Oh– I'm sorry. I didn't mean–" Firefly rushed.

"It's ok, I'm fine. Just…can't relate. My dad was always there for the city…and I'm always trying to destroy it…" He drifted.

"I mean it's not all perfect, New York does have overpriced pizza…if that isn't a cause to destroy the city, I don't know what is," Firefly chuckled.

The laughing died out and a few seconds later, Xeno got the courage to do the unthinkable,

"I'm sorry…"

Firefly looked up, utterly shellshock, "W-What did you just say?"

"I'm sorry…for being a pain." He repeated, a bit louder.

"I'm sorry too…" Firefly started, "For trying to change you, honestly I wish I was more like you."

"Really?"

"Yeah, you're so confident and brave and just do whatever you want! It's amazing...I can't even leave the house for a personal trip..." The hero explained.

"Why not?"

"Heroes rules."

"Oh, right."

"Yeah," Firefly sighed, curling up.

"...I wish I was a bit more like you," Xeno started, Firefly looked up.

"What?"

"Yeah, you see the good in everything, you are open to learning and are loyal...man Devan would never."

"Devan is awful," Firefly laughed.

"Right?" Xeno laughed with him.

Firefly giggled as he thought of something, "Maybe...we are more alike than we are different."

Xeno smiled, "Maybe we are, Buggy."

"...What if...we helped each other." Firefly thought out loud.

"What do you mean, I'm already helping you?"

"No– I mean, I wanna be more like you, yes?"

"Yeah, I guess?"

"And you want to be more like me."

"Ok, well don't say it out loud, I still have a reputation to protect." Xeno looked around to make sure no one was listening.

166

Firefly rolled his eyes playfully, "I mean, what if we stuck by each other a little longer and learned from each other? You could help me be more confident and adventurous and I could help you be better and gentle."

"Really? You...*want* to do that?"

"Like I said, my job is to save people...and you're not so bad to be around," Firefly smiled.

Xeno smiled back, sticking out his hand, "Ok, I am in."

Firefly shook his hand and they both stood up.

"Permission to cause chaos?" Xeno asked confidently.

"Wait– what?" Firefly's record scratched inside his head.

"Well we've gotta get out, right? We are sitting ducks here. The government, Dark Legacy, the heroes; one of them is going to find us here eventually. We gotta go save the crappy city!" Xenomorph smirked.

"Well, Yeah! But we can't just walk out."

"Oh~ but what if we can?" Xenomorph walked backwards, heading towards the bars.

"What are you doing?" Firefly asked.

"Do you trust me?"

"What? Xeno–"

"*Do you trust me?*" The villain repeated.

Firefly nodded, sighing as he couldn't believe what he was going to say, "Yes, I do."

Xeno smiled and fluffed his hair, taking out a random lock pick behind his ear.

Firefly's eyes widened as he meticulously maneuvered the silver blade into the cuff's, unlocking them, "Stay here. I'll be back," he took off his coat and threw it on the floor.

Looking at the prison bars, he harnessed the fire with him. Lighting up like a candle.

The bars turned orange as they bent and melted and Xenomorph squeezed through, escaping.

He reached back and grabbed his coat and put it back on with style, "When I give you the signal; run," He explained as he started to burn Firefly's cuffs through the other side. They too soon melted away and became a gloob on the floor.

"Wait– what signal? What about you?" Firefly tried but Xeno left before he could get answers. Firefly groaned, smiling a bit, "Man, I hate him."

Xeno confidently snuck over to the evidence locker, grabbing their backpack. Zipping it open to reveal his plan.

He then slinked over to the employee closet and spied a bunch of navy blue uniforms on hangers. He grabbed one random one off the coat rack and ran back to the cell, slipping the uniform through the bars,

"Put this on," Xeno commanded and ran away.

Firefly, confused, did what he said and buttoned up the police uniform, attached the radio, and clipped on the name tag– sorry Officer Jay. Firefly then tied his hoodie around his waist and ran his hands in his pockets– feeling something. He pulled the object out to reveal his little red lighter. The hero smiled, putting the pieces together and started flicking the empty light.

168

Firefly watched the main office from the little view he had. It was quiet, too quiet. The officers shuffled around like chess pieces on a board as they filled out paperwork.

Suddenly a spray paint can rolled into the room. Everyone stood in silence until–

SPLAM!

The can exploded, sending a big colorful cloud of pink paint. Soon another boom went off exploding a neon green cloud. Then an orange one, then a purple, then a cyan one.

As the officers screamed and ran Xenomorph arose from the painted smoke, covered in colors himself.

"WHO'S READY TO PARTY?!" He yelled as he set a spray can on fire and threw it at the radio, exploding the box and turning it on. Blasting a really sick punk band that Firefly just so happened to want to see in concert.

The villain laughed and danced as the police officers went running. Throwing more exploding paint cans around, making a masterpiece on the walls.

Firefly guessed that the parade of colors was the signal and slipped through the bars, making a run for the door like the rest of his fellow men in uniform.

Xenomorph took one of the bottles of soda, opened it and put three mints in it, sending the liquid bubbling like a geyser. Making even more of a mess. He set off about five more soda bottles before he was out of ammo.

He laughed and looked around as he spied Firefly booking it, but not out yet.

"Crap." He whispered to himself.

He looked around and spied the fire extinguisher. The villain grabbed the extinguisher and pulled the pin like a grenade. Grabbing a rubber band off a desk and tying it to two parts of the handle together. The white foam started to spray him, but he quickly grabbed the container and swung it around. Spraying the fuzzy soap everywhere.

Firefly ran, but got hit with a face full of extinguisher foam—ironic. Luckily he ignored it and headed to the door.

Pushing it open, escaping, ducking into a nearby alleyway, and catching his breath.

Last thing Xeno did was throw a fireball at the fire alarm. Setting off bell alarms and the sprinklers.

His work was done and so he too ran and left. Bolting it outside as he looked around for his Firefly.

However his search was interrupted when a spray paint cap hit him in the head.

"Ow!" He turned around at the source and saw the hero hiding behind a garbage bin.

Xeno ran over, sliding over the top lid and falling on top of the hero.

"Ouch!" Firefly yelped.

"Sorry!" Xeno apologized as they both got off each other and took a breath. Panting as if they were dying dogs. Laughing a bit.

Firefly couldn't help but feel the deja vu of yesterday. Man how so much has happened, how so much has changed.

Chapter 15:

Xenomorph shook the spray can, making the rattling sound as he sprayed the wall. Throwing his whole body into it as he was in the middle of a statement.

Firefly sat across the way, back in his hero gear, reading the comics he had taken and watching the villain do his work. The sun went down and the stars were out. Back in their usual place. The two were just waiting for the heat to die down...again.

Firefly looked up at the wall as Xenomorph stood on the box and kept at it.

"...You are really good at art."

Xenomorph turned around, "What?"

"Your art, it's impressive. Do you ever think about doing something with it?"

"Oh– no, no. Art is just a hobby." He shrugged off, nervous for some reason.

Firefly showed him the comic, "You call this a hobby? Man, it's incredible!"

Xenomorph froze, pride welling in his chest as he smiled, "...Thank you."

He went back to it, spraying a couple more lines as he stopped, thinking, "H-How about you?"

"Hm?" Firefly stopped reading.

"Do you...art?"

Firefly chuckled, "Nah, I just play music, I guess that's kinda art."

"Nice man, you mentioned you had a guitar. What genre do you play?" Xeno went back to his mural.

"...*Xenomorph*," Firefly smiled, "Are you...trying to get to know me?"

Xenomorph dropped the can. It clanked on the floor.

"No! No! No! That would be ridiculous," Xeno leaned on the wall, trying to act cool but failing miserably.

Firefly smirked, "Lots of indie pop, rock, metal, punk, you heard of Boys of Mayhem?"

"Yeah, vaguely," Xeno replied as he took a seat on one of the wooden boxes.

"Man, I love them! I could play their music all day long," Firefly pretended to rock out as Xeno smiled, watching the silly teen.

"They sound cool, how did you find them?" Xeno asked.

Firefly stopped, slowly putting down the air guitar, "Oh um, actually my dad was a big fan."

"O-Oh, I'm sorry…"

"It's ok…"

Xenomorph bit his tongue, but it didn't help, "Do you miss him…your dad?"

Firefly smiled, "Of course I do, I miss him every day. You?"

"I…" The villain paused, picking at the wooden crate he was sitting on, "…yeah I do."

"Did you want to talk now?" Firefly offered.

Xeno shook his head.

"Do you want me to talk?" Firefly asked.

"You would do that?"

"Of course man, if it helps, I don't mind."

"…What was he like?"

"Oh, he was crazy!" Firefly laughed and Xeno joined him in a giggle. "He was the mighty Flamethrower!"

"Oh, sick! No way!" Xeno sprung up, recognizing the name.

"Indeed way! He was the bravest hero in the city. He was reckless and risky but he did it for good."

Xeno listened, eyes slowly widened as he realized…maybe– just maybe, he didn't need to change as much as he thought to be seen as good.

"He never failed a mission and was celebrated all night long! He had hundreds of comics, and was just overall a sweet, caring guy…man, how I miss him."

Xenomorph stood quiet.

"Man, I miss all the Super Seven."

"Super Seven?" He puzzled.

"You don't know about the Super Seven?"

Xenomorph shrugged.

"The best super resistance in all of History? Seriously?" Firefly re-asked.

"No...?"

"Well, long ago there was a group of seven heroes... Flamethrower, Stratosphere, Waterspark, Wind-f-fly? A bird...one? Shoot I always forget the last ones."

Xenomorph waited for him to remember.

"Starlight, Ace Spades was definitely one." Firefly continued, trying his best.

"Whoa, 'Ace Spades' must have been pretty great if you remember him in that goldfish brain of yours."

Firefly shot him a dirty glare and continued, "Well my Father was close with Ace Spades, they were like best friends. Well Flamethrower, Ace, and someone else...but I can't put my finger on it."

"What happened to them?"

"New York was at its peak; heroes were thriving, a new Governor was elected, pizza bagels were half off, it was great! Until they all just mysteriously disappeared, never to be seen again. One day shortly after, Dark Legacy arrived and the city suffered for months. Thankfully a younger hero stepped into the field: Captain Peace! With the new rise of the Captain, they fought and Dark Legacy was banished to the sewers of New York...where he now lies."

"Oh wow, I had no idea…" Xeno pondered, taking every little detail of the story.

"They say it cost him his power."

"His power?"

"Well Captain Peace is powerless, he just runs the heroes." Firefly explained.

"What power did he have?"

"No one knows, some think it's matter manipulation, or speed, I personally think it's some sort of light ability. I mean how else are you going to destroy *Dark* Legacy?"

"Fair," Xeno shrugged.

"…Captain Peace was the only hero to survive…"

Both stood in silence until they both had the same thought. This city was a twisted place, and it wasn't getting any better.

Firefly silently seethed, flaming up.

Xenomorph flinched a bit as the fire glowed in the alley. The hero looked over to the villain who seemed scared by the fire. Firefly paused and took a deep breath, trying to calm down but to his surprise, he was met with another fiery glow.

"You're…mad too?"

Xeno lit ablaze as he smirked, "I'm pissed."

Firefly stood confused.

"Wanna do something about it?" He asked, ready to wreak havoc.

Firefly smirked back, determined, "Heck yeah."

***

The next morning the two supers strolled through town as inconspicuous as they could. Taking off all accessible armor and dead giveaways, walking around in nothing but pants and undergear.

Firefly led the way and carried the backpack as they traveled in the sunny hustle and bustle of classic New York. The taxis, the food, the coffee...the rats.

Xenomorph slowly slunk over to a guy not paying attention, holding a hot, steaming cup of coffee.

Firefly didn't even need to look behind him, "Don't you even think about it."

Xenomorph shrunk back and groaned, and suddenly a pigeon flew right into his face. Flapping aggressively as the villain screamed.

Firefly turned around and just laughed.

Soon the pigeon flew off and Xenomorph ruffled his hair, trying to poof it back into place.

"Not funny."

"It was kinda funny," Firefly joked, "c'mon lighten up Xeno, 'have some fun'." He teased and walked around the corner.

Xeno rolled his eyes and turned the corner, looking up as he saw a giant sign with music notes and records. Neon lights blaring like the fifties or whenever records were invented. Inside records were stacked strategically like an art piece. The villain squinted at the odd place, it felt like a big jukebox or an antique store. Which it probably was, *does anyone even use records anymore?*

177

Firefly held the straps of the bag as he breathed and walked in. Slowly opening the door.

Xeno followed and looked around. The place was covered in music posters and fliers. Stars and old records filling any leftover space on the wall. A nice dim, golden hour glow shined overhead from some fairy lights. It felt old, rustic, but safe.

Firefly walked to the back of the store to a sound booth designed like a phone booth, pulled out his red electric guitar, and his bag filled with spare clothes and other hero supplies. He rocked out on the metal strings as Xeno watched. Surprised at how fast and well he was playing it.

"Got it, ok, what's the plan?" Firefly asked, repacking all their supplies into one bag. Medical gear, the comics, spare clothes, leftover snacks, the napkin, emergency money, and anything else Xeno had pick-pocketed beforehand.

"Plan?"

"Yeah, the plan for getting into the party tomorrow?" He continued casually, ruffling through the backpacks.

"I-I thought you had one, why are we here if you don't have one?" Xeno wailed.

"Oh! Well, I just thought after the 'little– um– ROBBERY' we couldn't go back to the comic store and we need a place to stay." Firefly explained, sarcastically.

"Ah right– I guess so."

"Our houses won't be safe if the heroes and villains are after us, but no one knows I have this job so we will be safe in here. Like a little base– ha, get it base?" The hero pointed to the electric base on the wall.

"Ha. Ha. Very amusing... I am not even going to ask why I had to sleep on a cardboard box last night instead of coming here," Xenomorph raised a brow, sassing.

All Firefly could give was a nervous laugh, embarrassed he didn't think of the idea sooner. It would've been comfier.

"*But as I was saying*, the plans for tomorrow?" Xeno asked.

"Aren't you the mischievous one? Shouldn't you make a plan?" Firefly returned.

"Aren't you the one who is supposed to be defeating villains? This is your territory, Firecracker."

"Hey, I am just learning to be fun, you are the expert in chaos so cause chaos," Firefly smirked, putting him in checkmate.

"Ugh...I hate when you're right. I am better than you in every way." Xeno gave in with a smirk, pacing around to think. Firefly hopped onto the counter and started strumming as the villain walked around the room. Sinking into the plush, blue carpet.

"Well if we can get disguises, we can sneak in as some rich assholes or something." Xeno thought out loud.

"We can get the disguises from the party store, if they have a superhero suit they have got to have normal suits," Firefly chirped in.

"Yes! Oh my god, your brain works!"

Firefly cocked his head confused, "Yes? It does?"

"I knew taking you in was a good idea."

"You didn't– you know what, never mind. Point is we can get disguises, but how do we sneak in?"

"Duh– you're talking to a stealth professional," Xeno flexed, posing up for the hero as his pride bubbled over.

"Really?" Firefly asked, deadpan and sarcastic.

"Yeah!"

"Because you stole a sports car and caught the attention of the cops, we toilet papered a house and caught the attention of the cops, you robbed a store and stole an ice cream cart and caught the attention of the cops, then you blew up their station using spray cans which–"

"CAUGHT THE ATTENTION OF THE COPS– OK! I get it...so I'm a bit flashy! It's the villain in me! Haven't you heard of presentation!" Xeno sassed.

"This mission needs to be flawless!" Firefly argued.

"...But I'm taking you. So mission failed." Xeno jabbed at him.

"Har. Har. I'm serious, you need a stealth test run..." Firefly suggested.

Xeno rolled his eyes but once they landed they slowly caught the poster behind Firefly. It was a rock and roll advertisement for that band Firefly was talking about last night. An all-out party, loud concert happening tonight. Just a few blocks away.

"...A warm-up..." Xeno smirked, getting the picture. Cogs turning in his head.

"Yes! Exactly!"

"Ok! I am in! Let's sneak into the Boys of Mayhem concert!" He announced, pointing at the poster.

180

"Yes let's– wait– WHAT?!" Firefly turned around, looking at the poster. "Dude are you crazy?! Trespassing at a concert?! The biggest concert in town?! Big mistake! That place will be crawling with security!"

"So, it'll be a great warm up!" Xeno smiled, liking the idea more.

"I was thinking you could just try and get to the back room of the shop," Firefly tried.

"Come on, where's Funfly?"

"Never say that again."

"Only if you come with me to the concert. I mean, it's your favorite band, right? Wouldn't you want to go?!"

"Well– yes– but I'm...I'm not allowed to go on 'personal' trips, remember? Captain's orders. I'd never be able to see them in concert."

"One, that's stupid. Two, you're not even working for your captain right now. Three, it's not a personal trip if it's practice for a mission!"

"I guess so..." Firefly thought about it, trying to bend his conscience.

"Did I mention four?"

"What's four?"

"That it's stupid."

Firefly chuckled a bit, looking at the villain through his lenses then back at the poster.

"Well…I did always want to go…and I do know all their songs by heart," Firefly strummed a song on his guitar and Xeno could only guess it was one of theirs.

"See~ c'mon…please…partner in crime."

"You're not my–MMMM!" Firefly steamed up, hopping off the desk to be on the opposite side of the counter, "Fffffffine~! We will sneak in and out only for a *test*, we will listen to one song and leave as *training*."

"And get a pretzel."

"What? No, in and out–no pretzels."

"What?! But I want a pretzel, also one of those glowy, light-up sticks those people swing around." Xeno begged.

"Xeno. Focus. Mission."

"Firefly. Focus. *Pretzel*."

The supers got up into each other's face, inches away from each other.

Firefly's mouth twisted into a frown.

"Can I have my pretzels?" Xeno asked again.

"NO!"

Xeno stared at him, blindfold scrunching like a death stare.

"…Only if you behave," Firefly gave in softly.

"Yes! Deal!" Xeno stuck out his hand, from the other side of the desk, like a transaction being rung up.

Firefly took it, deja vu. Shaking the hand up and down staring into his blindfold. He couldn't help but mirror the smile on the villain's face.

182

Suddenly a bell rang out through the store and the next thing Xeno knew, Firefly grabbed his shirt and pulled him over the counter, hiding him.

"GWAH-!" The villain spat as he hit the floor but Firefly shoved his hand up his mouth.

"Quinn! What are you doing here?" Firefly stuttered.

Xeno immediately shut up.

A girl lifted her head, her auburn hair falling into place as her high ponytail bounced. Rocking a cool band hoodie, jeans scribbled with stars, and beat up sneakers. She took her headphones off and placed them around her neck, confused by the question.

"...I work here?"

"Right~," Firefly replied. Forgetting his co-worker, well, worked.

"What's with those goofy things on your face?" She asked, throwing her bag down and ruffling up her sleeves.

Firefly covered his goggles, "These?! Oh nothing! Just some...um Halloween prep. You like them...?" He smiled nervously.

"Yeah, they are cool!" She smiled and shrugged. Grabbing a pack of records and walking over to a shelf. Stacking them, "Are you going to the concert tonight?"

"Oh! Oh...the concert...um~ yes~?" Firefly tried.

"Nice, going with anyone?" She calmly continued, stacking more of the fragile music.

"Um– yes? No! I mean we aren't really going as a pair, it's more like a mutual thing? I mean no– but I– well– um…pretzel?"

Xeno silently pumped his fist. Celebrating his salty victory. He could taste the soft dough from here.

Quinn turned around, looking at him weirdly. Those blue eyes could shoot a guy on sight if she wanted. Although they weren't cold like Devan's, they were so big and innocent, like a baby deer.

"You know what I mean?" Firefly tried, placing his hand on his burning red face to seem natural.

"Yeah~ totally~ pretzel," She replied, snickering a little.

"Are…you going with anyone?" Firefly asked.

"Just some friends, nothing really serious or married," She said, grabbing a plastic crate and carrying it along. Hauling a bunch of books, guitar picks, and records inside.

"Yeah me too," Firefly started kicking Xeno.

The villain mouthed 'ow' as he looked up.

"My um…*partner* isn't going to be a *problem*. I mean if he's *wise* he'll *leave before she sees you*." Firefly kicked more as he tried to act casual, gritting his teeth, sending the message.

Xeno clicked the code and started nodding. Crawling on the shag carpet to get out.

"What?" Quinn asked.

"I just mean, I'm totally free! You know, I'll be going with someone, but that someone is not important!" He rushed out.

"Oh, ok! So, I'll see you there?" She asked.

"Yes! Definitely! I'll be there!" Firefly nodded as Xeno silently mocked him from the floor.

As she turned the corner the villain started climbing a shelf by the counter. Knocking stuff over, but luckily Firefly rushed over and caught it. Saving all sorts of priceless merchandise. Xenomorph eventually got on top of the self and hoisted himself into the rafters of the store.

Firefly just watched with worried eyes, as he knew this wasn't going to end well. The villain snuck across the wooden beams and retro fairy lights as Quinn continued,

"So this 'partner', is it a new friend?"

Xeno froze in the ceiling.

"F-Friend?" Firefly shook.

"Yeah, I mean it's no secret dude, you don't have many friends. If you found one, I'm happy for you," Quinn responded, still stocking stuff in its rightful place.

"I-I mean..." Firefly looked up at the ceiling where Xeno was staring at him, waiting for an answer. "Well, 'friend' is a bit strong..."

Xeno deflated a bit. Although he didn't know why.

"–but, I hope someday we could be," Firefly finished, smiling. Xeno smiled back and turned away to continue scaling the ceiling.

"Oh yeah?" Quinn chirped.

"Yeah...I mean he's a bit rough around the edges but, I think he's really...nice." Firefly ended as his co-worker made her way back to the front.

Xeno got far, but soon the beams ended into nothing but a jungle of fairy lights.

I'm about to do something stupid..., He thought confidently as he held onto a light cord.

"Why don't you come help me in the back now that you're here, if you want," Quinn offered.

"Oh! Totally!" Firefly hopped the counter and started leading Quinn away from the room in a rush, but just as they were approaching the back door–

"GAAAAAHHHH!!!" Xeno fell. Tangling himself in lights he bungeed right in front of them, barely missing the ground, hanging like a chandelier. He slowly spun in the flickering lights as the two workers just froze.

"…'Aaaaahhh!' It's Xenomorph!" Firefly tried but it was so forced and dull.

"Really, dude? Even I'm not buying that," Xeno spat.

"Xeno!" Firefly snapped between his teeth.

"Is this your new friend?" Quinn asked.

"What?! Oh…noooo~!" Firefly tried.

"Best buds," Xeno chirped.

"I am going to strangle–"

"Cool." Quinn smiled.

"Wait– what?" Firefly froze.

"That's cool, nice to see you made a friend. He's the one you're taking to the concert, right?" Quinn asked.

"Bwa… you… you do know who this is right?" Firefly asked.

"Yeah," Quinn shrugged.

"And...you don't see a problem with it?"

"Or want to scream?" Xeno asked, butting in.

"Nope. I trust you man. Any friend of yours is a friend of mine. If you say he's cool, then he's cool. Nice to meet you," She smiles, sticking out her hand to shake.

Xeno grabbed it and shook it, still tangled in the lights.

Firefly just stared, jaw dropped at how odd everything was. The realization of just how far he'd gone finally hit him. He befriended a super villain.

"I like her!" Xeno declared from the ceiling.

Chapter 16:

The rest of the day was spent waiting for nightfall in the store. Firefly strummed his guitar in the back, sitting on the steps that led to the second floor of the place. It was an old, worn out staircase, but he didn't care. It was his favorite place to practice, mainly for the acoustics.

After what felt like hours of strumming and humming, Xenomorph clumped down the stairs, bandaging himself from yesterday's fiasco. He stopped as he saw the hero just sitting there. Tapping the railing covered in twinkly lights to think.

Firefly ignored the feeling of being watched and continued. After a while, Xeno quietly sat down next to him. Firefly screeched the steel strings to a halt and looked over confused.

"Shouldn't you be robbing the store by now?" He sassed.

"You'd think, but nah, I'm good, it's all junk," Xeno teased back, "...Shouldn't you be kissing Quinn?"

"What?!" Firefly gripped the neck of the guitar tight and turned bright pink.

"Aw c'mon! I saw the way you looked at her and s-s-stuttered to her," Xenomorph joked.

"Shut up~! You sound just like my mom." Firefly shoved him away.

Xeno laughed, but it slowed as he wanted to ask something, "What is your mom like?"

"What?"

"Your mom, what is she like? I mean I have heard about your dad, but what about your mom?"

Firefly's silence spoke volumes, not believing the person in front of him. He still couldn't see his eyes behind that pesky fabric, but he could picture them begging to know more.

"I mean, she's great. She is nice and supportive. Super caring and giving. Open minded, a great role model. I mean she's just any other amazing mom." Firefly said, going back to play with the strings and tuner. "I still update her every once and a while."

He strummed a little tune, thinking that was the end of it.

"I...I never met my mom." Xeno broke the air and Firefly froze. "And when my dad died I was taken in by the foster care system, that's where Dark Legacy found me and the rest is history..." He played with the ground, trying not to make a big deal out of it. Not sure why he was telling him in the first place.

"...Whoa," Firefly whispered under his breath, the villain was alive once more. "No one tried to take you in first? When my dad died I went into the foster system for a few months too. It was a hard time for my mom, couldn't take care of a child on her own at that moment...but she scooped me back up as soon as possible."

"...You went into the system too?" Xeno sat up.

"Yeah...I was...how weird is that?" Firefly gave a soft laugh at the irony of it all. He knew they were starting to seem similar, but now it was just uncanny.

"...Well...no mom ever came for me. Just Dark Legacy and a lot of weird testing." Xeno looked at his wrist, expecting to see another band or tag with silly numbers he didn't understand. But for once, nothing was there.

"...I'm so sorry."

"Why, not your fault," Xeno snuffed out the apology.

"Well– no but...I don't know. I guess I just thought villains had...better lives? I mean you steal diamonds and have gadgets and hijack cars, how are you not on top of the world right now?" Firefly asked.

"I wish I knew, and I wish we had better lives. It's not as black and white as you think." Xeno explained.

"I see that now, I'm sorry for what I did."

"What?"

"Sorry for the fighting, the name calling, everything. I was a horrible hero...I didn't even *know you*. I just started attacking you because I was told to! ...Man, I'm an idiot..."

Xenomorph felt that warmth in his heart again, empathy. Could it be? Empathetic for a hero of all things? He was supposed to be the cruelest, darkest, coldest person alive, but he had been around the fire too long. And now this fire was melting his frozen heart.

"You are not the bad guy..." Xeno suddenly said out of nowhere.

Firefly stopped, flabbergasted by the masked vigilante.

"You didn't know, we were just forced and told to do stuff—like me. If anyone's the bad guy it's me."

"Maybe...it doesn't have to be either of us..." Firefly thought out loud.

Xeno stood in silence considering it. He was no hero, he'd never be one. Mind already made up, but maybe he didn't have to be the villain everyone thought he was; and based on Firefly's dad he could still be chaotic, reckless, and fun. He wouldn't have to change all that much.

"Honestly, I don't know about you, but I'm not going to let anyone tell me who I can or can't be!" Xeno declared, standing up.

"What are you going to do?"

"*WE* are going to expose Dark Legacy for everything! To the whole world! Once he's gone and every villain is free, they can make the choice of what they want! Then we will take down the hero force–"

"WHAT?!"

"We will take down the strict, blind hero force and they can choose! These organizations are dumb! We can be more than what they tell us!" Xenomorph pointed at Firefly, "I'm already helping you with Dark Legacy and exposing him...all you gotta do is promise to make life better for the villains and heroes after this." Xeno declared.

"…I thought you wanted to run? To have nothing to do with this? 'Just avoiding Dark Legacy'."

"Well…guess you changed my mind…" Xeno smirked.

"So…you want to be a hero?!" Firefly sparked, excited. The warm orange glow encased the stairwell as his eyes grew big within the lenses.

"Whoa! Hold on now– that's a big claim– and honestly, I don't know what I want. I guess I just want things to be fair and better for other villains, …and I'm so sick of running. Like literally I might throw up." Xeno held his mouth as if he were about to gag.

Firefly smiled, *I knew there was good in him.*

"So deal? I help you, you help me?"

"Deal," Firefly shook his hand. Xeno jumped up and down, stretching and twisting as he started down the stairs again.

"But for the record…" Firefly continued

The villain looked back at him.

"I think you'd make a great hero."

Xeno smiled at the thought, call him crazy, but after this week maybe being a hero wouldn't have been that bad.

"Thank you."

***

Soon the sky melted away into oranges and pinks. Xeno geared back up with his coat and armor as Firefly was going to wait until they left. Keeping what little cover he had left.

Firefly packed some water into their black backpack and wrapped his electric guitar around his torso. Tossing the bag to Xeno as the villain caught it and swung it around.

"You boys heading out already?" Quinn asked, bag in hand and coat on, jangling her keys.

"Yeah, we...want to get there early," Firefly lied—well technically it was true. This whole week was filled with 'technicalities'.

"What about you? You look ready to go?" Xeno sassed and Firefly kicked him. "AHH! Right in the knee! You jerk!" He jumped around, holding his injured leg.

Firefly smiled, ignoring him.

"Well, I'm clocking out, but I was going to go have dinner with some friends before the show, see you there?" She asked.

"Yes! See you there!" Firefly started and pushed Xeno out the door.

"Aren't you forgetting something?" Quinn asked.

Both boys froze.

"Your kiss goodbye?" Xeno asked.

Firefly playfully swatted him away like a bug.

"No, your sweater," Quinn said, taking out Firefly's red sweater from behind the counter with his iconic logo of a lightning bug on fire.

...crap

They both thought.

"I-I-I can explain! That's not mine!" Firefly spat.

"It-it's mine!" Xeno grabbed it, "I totally killed Firefly today, it was crazy and bloody– you should've been there. You would've loved it," the villain tried.

Quinn just smiled at the two, Firefly rolling his eyes.

"Right~ so it just so happens Firefly and Xenomorph are both wanted criminals right now who have been spotted together," Quinn smiled more.

"Yes~?" Firefly tried.

"Oh please dude, you don't think I know your Firefly?" Quinn dropped her act.

"WHAT!?" Both boys yelled.

"Yeah? You think it's a coincidence how you're always running late when Firefly has a fight. Or that time the shelf just 'magically' caught fire?" Quinn laughed.

Firefly blushed, embarrassed about that time, "It– It wasn't me, it was the matchbox...it fell?"

"You seriously still trying to deny this?"

"No, no I'm not," Firefly gave in, taking the hoodie from Xeno and slipping it on. Then he reattached his harness and armor pieces. "Since when?"

"First day man, you can't hide much from me."

"...And you aren't going to tell anyone?" He asked, shaking.

"No, of course not."

"You don't find this weird? Or odd?"

"No, not really. Supers have to have outside lives. Trust me man, you're secret safe with me. You too Xenomorph," She winked.

"Seriously?!" Xeno asked, confused out of his mind, "I am a delusional maniac who is a super villain and a threat to the city– and he's a human blow torch who fights the supervillains–! And you're just cool with it?!"

"XENO!" Firefly slapped his hand over his mouth. "I'm sorry Quinn, he's still learning his off button."

"It's cool man, see you at the concert," She waved and left. The bell jingled off and soon Firefly felt his hand growing hotter and hotter until–

"YAOUCH!" He pulled his hand away as Xeno smirked. "Did you just burn me?! With your mouth–?! How?!"

Xenomorph breathed and fire came rolling out like a dragon, "Mimic stuff!"

"I– you– ...wait– I can do that?"

"Beats me, all I know is I can! Let's go Buggy!" Xeno grabbed him from his harness and tugged him outside.

Golden hour hit the city like a virus, a beautiful, breathtaking virus. Crowds of people with branded hats, glow wear, and posters heading in only one direction. It was going to be the biggest bash of the year.

Firefly and Xenomorph left the store and tried to blend in, hiding behind what they could and ducking low. They hadn't even walked a block yet before something caught Xeno's eye, smiling as he rushed over to a brick wall. Firefly noticed his absence and looked over, but his pulse ran cold at what he saw.

Dozens and dozens of wanted posters for him and his accomplice.

"Sweet! Look, your first wanted poster!" He tugged Firefly's mug shot down. Staring at it with pride.

"Oh no, no, no, no, no," Firefly started ripping them all down. Xeno just admired his image. The duality was crazy, Firefly still scared as heck and Xeno not afraid at all. Posing like he wanted to be there. Peace sign, tongue sticking out, and everything.

"You ok man? It's just paper," Xeno tried.

"No! No, I am not alright! how are you alright?!" Firefly flamed up.

"Because I'm a supervillain~? This happens like...all the time?" Xeno sassed.

"But I'm not a criminal! Heck you're not even a criminal!" Firefly protested.

"Hey! I am a very respectable criminal, thank you very much!"

"But this completely tarnishes your image! We will never get around town like this!" Firefly started casting a fiery beam destroying all the posters.

Well except one; a copy of Xeno's floated down as the villain took it. One of Firefly and one of Xeno; a matching set. He folded them up and tucked them away into the backpack. Thinking of what to do.

Firefly continued, huffing tiredly, "Not to mention...now everyone hates us."

Xeno rolled his eyes, "Captain forbid someone doesn't like you," he sassed.

Firefly turned around, "What?"

"Kid, you wanna be more like me? More confident? Rule one: don't care what anyone else says!"

"Well you can't just ignore everyone!" Firefly put the villain in checkmate.

"Ok...fair, but you also can't listen to everyone...you can't please everyone, it's impossible. So just please yourself and the people who matter to you will see you for your true worth. Just because you don't see eye to eye doesn't mean you have to change," Xeno said.

Firefly stared at him, taking in the advice like he needed it to survive.

"Wow that's...actually really insightful..." Firefly drifted, shocked.

"See? I can be just as fluffy as you!" Xeno smirked.

Firefly leaned on the wall and slid down, feeling defeated.

Xeno's cocky smile softened away as he approached the hero, "Hey man, don't care what anyone else says. I mean, there's only two people who know what's really happening..."

"Who?"

"You and me."

"..."

"And I don't think differently of you because of some crappy government photography portfolio. Do you?"

"...No," Firefly mumbled.

"Then the only two people who have a reasonable opinion are both in favor of you. So why are you worried?" Xeno smiled, offering his hand.

Firefly smiled and took it. Xeno pulled him up and the hero couldn't help but rush him with a hug.

"Thank you."

"...Anytime Firecracker," Xeno patted his back a bit, still not familiar with a hug. The villain pulled back, "Now, let's go crash a concert!"

"Yeah!" Firefly cheered.

"But... 'oh how are we going to get there'?'" Xeno teased dramatically.

"What do you mean? We are walking," Firefly corrected.

"But that's no fun..." He joked as he did some cool dance moves and backed up by a cool motorcycle. Chained to a bike rack.

"...No...no! Bad Xeno, we are not stealing another car."

"But it's not a car! It's a bike!" Xeno beamed and winked, not that you could see under the mask.

"Xeno...that's wrong."

"*Exactly*..." Xenomorph lit his hand on fire and dangled it close to the chain. The metal started to drip like liquid as Xeno made some dramatically shocked faces.

"Dude. No. Stop it– stop it– don't you make me get the spray bottle!" Firefly told off.

"You're a spray bottle and a real wet blanket," Xenomorph barked back.

198

Firefly took a deep breath, "You said...you wanted to be better."

"Yeah! Better! Not less fun!" Xeno hopped on the bike.

"Xeno!"

"Listen, Buggy, I am racing this thing to the concert whether you like it or not. Do you want a ride?"

Firefly hesitated for a bit, but he knew how this would go, so he sighed and hopped on.

"Then we return it!" Firefly insisted.

"Yeah! Yeah! We will return it, probably in multiple pieces but that's ok," Xeno teased.

"What?!"

"'Oh wow, would you look at that!' My hand is turning on the handle–" the bike vroomed alive, "And I'm pushing the gas–"

SCREECH!

Firefly screamed and Xeno laughed as they raced the bike through the New York streets. Revving the engine loudly and creating smoke clouds. Almost hitting a couple taxis, but it's ok because they were just taxis. Like the car version of pigeons—which they also almost hit.

They zoomed pasted green and red lights and when they went over a bump, Firefly hugged Xeno tight. Clinging onto him and shutting his eyes tight. It felt safe, who knew a 'supervillain' could be this comforting?

Xeno was surprised by the sudden jolt, seeing Firefly's hands wrapped around his armor. It felt...amazing. To finally have someone trust him like that. With the wind in his white hair, Xeno knew at this moment…he *did* want to be friends with Firefly.

Chapter 17:

Xeno got to the theater and popped a wheelie as Firefly yelped. He finally stopped, clunking forward a bit. Both boys' ears rang from the speed, although Xeno liked it.

"Ok, where do I park her?"

"…did you just ask me where to park?" Firefly asked.

"Yes! Pay attention!" Xeno shouted.

"You want to follow the rules of the road?" Firefly lifted an eyebrow, smirking.

"…I will chain you to the fence." Xeno threatened.

Firefly shrunk and pointcd, "Over there."

"Thank you!" Xeno smiled and rode the bike to the parking lot, sneaking to the back behind an unused ticket booth for cover.

The two supers jumped off the bike and snuck to the chain link fence. Xeno quickly climbed over it like nothing and Firefly hesitantly followed. From there they hopped barricades, hid behind bushes, and avoided security guards till they made it to a safe spot.

They started to stroll into the quad. Fans started to spill in, spotting in little groups. Everyone had the same black and red shirts and hats like they were multiplying.

"See? That wasn't so bad. Easy even," Xeno bragged.

"We are only halfway, we still have to get into the place without tickets…which means even more security."

"Yeah, yeah," The villain shrugged off.

Firefly suddenly took notice that all the people started to stare and whisper. He took a deep breath, remembering to shrug it off. However, the more he looked he noticed they weren't talking about him.

"X-Xeno…"

"Yeah? What's up?" Xeno asked as he started to break dance on the bricks. Heading to the doors as this was looking like the easiest warm up ever.

"I-I think you should change."

"What?! I thought you were cool with–" Xeno started.

"No-no your clothes." Firefly corrected.

"…Oh, wait why?"

"Because this is supposed to be a stealth mission and people are staring," Firefly argued.

"So?"

"Don't you understand? If they catch you now, we won't get into the concert."

"Pff–is that all? News flash, they have to catch me first," Xeno scoffed.

"Xeno if they catch you we could be separated."

Xeno stopped, "Separated? You're...you're worried we'd be separated?"

"Yes! You are my only lead and the only person I have on my team right now. Please, I beg, wear a disguise, just until after the concert." Firefly held his hands together, praying.

Xeno sat there, contemplating.

"C'mon, you said it yourself. You are the master of stealth," Firefly tried with a smile.

"...Ok, fine– only for you though!" Xeno commanded as he strutted away to find something. Firefly followed close behind as more people started to show.

The two went around the side of the building and Xeno popped open a vent. Being familiar with vents by now, Firefly snuck in and Xeno followed, closing it back up. The teens fumbled around in the metal tunnels, pushing and shoving until they finally saw light. Firefly kicked the vent open and they were transported into the ginormous stadium lobby.

With ceilings so high it felt impossible and marble covering the floor. Food and drink stands every few feet and so much merchandise it was practically a mall. Neither supers had seen anything like it. It was like heaven.

"Whoa~..." they both mumbled together.

Xeno spied a merch booth. Girls and guys fanned around it, exchanging ruffled money for some sick band clothes. They actually looked nice, something Xeno would actually consider wearing...

"Wait," Xeno thought out loud as he ran to the booth.

"Xe-mmm Hey! Wait! We really should've thought out code names," Firefly called and chased after the villain.

Xeno slid on the ground next to an unattended box and dug out some t-shirts and put on a band hat. Covering his white hair. As he took off his coat and put on the shirt, something near the booth caught his eye.

Xenomorph got up and pushed and shoved to the front of the line. Excitedly hopping up and down. The cashier froze at the sight. Xeno didn't care; his eyes wandered through the booth and spotted a sick letterman jacket.

It was breathtaking. Sky blue with a hood and white sleeves. There was a white X on the front where a pocket would be and on the back were these angelic white wings. The graphic dripped like it was graffiti and Xeno couldn't take his eyes off it.

It screamed his name, like it was *made* for him.

"I'll take that one!" Xeno declared, pointing to the jacket on the mannequin.

"Oh, sorry bud. Those are still in beta." The guy behind the table explained.

"Beta?"

"Yeah, it's still in the process of being designed and hasn't been released yet, so therefore it is not for sale."

"Then why do you have it up?" He questioned.

"It's more of an update or a sneak peek at the new line," The worker kindly offered. "The band's idea."

Firefly finally caught up to Xeno, panting like a dying dog while wearing his own band shirt over his hoodie, barely hiding anything.

"Ok~ well can I just have the beta?" Xeno tried. This was making no sense to him, but so did the exchanging of money.

"No, sorry."

Xeno narrowed his eyes and leaned over to his partner, whispering, "This guy is being a jerk. Can you please tell him that?"

"What?! No I can't say that, that's rude."

"Well I can– HEY BUDDY–!" Xeno started, but Firefly dove in front, covering his chaotic villain.

"Sorry sir! He's just really excited, ignore us, we will be leaving now…" Firefly tried, walking Xeno out of line as the whispers grew and people started taking out their phones to either call nine one one or record.

Firefly felt the hundreds of eyes staring at him; it was suffocating.

"Dude! What the hell?! I thought you wanted me to change outfits or whatever?" Xeno protested.

"I do, and I appreciate the attempt, but you can't go around fighting vendors."

"What?! What's the point of living anymore!" He groaned.

"'Touching.'" Firefly said, sarcastically.

"C'mon man, that jacket wasn't half bad."

"Agree! It was super cool, but you heard the guy, not for sale." Firefly stood his ground.

Ding

Xeno's lightbulb went off in his head, "Got it! Not for sale, why don't you go get me my pretzel and I'll scope out the area?"

Firefly sighed in relief, "Thank you."

And just like that Xeno headed off into the crowd. Firefly tried to remain calm as he remembered what happened at the police station. He *trusted* Xeno, he may not have believed himself but he was going to keep saying it until he did. Besides no trouble yet, they must have blended in with all the red and black.

Firefly walked over to a little food bar. The sun was still spilling in from the glass windows as the line went by. Finally it was his turn and he did in fact order one big soft pretzel with cheese. The vendor gave him his treat, covered in the crystal salt and he turned around.

However a girl's face was waiting for him (and was pissed) like a jump scare!

"GAH!" Firefly yelped, almost dropping the pretzel. He looked closer at the girl. Swoopy dirty-blonde bangs and dead hazel eyes, "M-Molly?!"

Molly dragged him out of line as Firefly held onto the pretzel for dear life. She herself was in jeans and a band t-shirt under her long sleeves. Nothing like her super suit. She dragged them around a corner for some privacy.

"What *the hell* are *you* doing here?!" She threatened under her breath. Getting in his face.

"I-I…"

"Oh–you are *so dead*. Do you know how much trouble you are in?!" She continued, smiling as she enjoyed it all.

"But I thought…"

"First you expose the system, then you are working with the *villains!* Then you vandalize my house–"

Firefly eyes widen as she pieced the puzzle together,

"–Yeah, don't think I didn't know it was you! And now you are fighting our heroes and are a wanted criminal running around with Xenomorph, trying to break into a concert!" She yelled, getting louder by the second. Any louder and she would start sonic booming.

"Shhh! Please! Molly it's not like that–wait–why are *you* here?" Firefly redirected.

"Don't change the subject!"

"Heroes aren't allowed to go on personal trips…" He drifted, trying to figure it out.

"It's not a personal trip, it's a sound assignment!" She lied.

"There's no such thing! All our assignments and exercises are inside the tower!"

"Fine…*You're* not allowed to go on personal trips."

"Wait what?! Why me?!"

"BECAUSE YOU DO STUFF LIKE *THIS*?!" She yelled, throwing her hands and causing a scene.

"Molly please! Be quiet! I can explain!" Firefly yelled in a whisper, trying to take back control of the volume.

"No! Why should I be quiet?! Worried you'll get caught, YOU VILLAIN!"

"NO! No, we aren't villains, this is just a big misunderstanding!" Firefly tried.

"I'm sorry–*WE?!*"

"Listen, we've had everything wrong! Xenomorph isn't the bad guy here!" Firefly defended.

"REALLY?!" Molly shouted and pointed to Xeno. The villain snuck up behind some girls and took their light-up wands from their hands. They yelled and tried to take it back, but he just played a sword fight with the other girls for a bit before running away. "THAT'S NOT A VILLAIN?!"

"He's learning! Give him some credit! He wants to help!" Firefly held back, getting angry on Xeno's behalf.

"Unbelievable, you actually think he's a good person."

"HE IS!"

"HE IS NOT! YOU'RE EITHER WITH US FIREFREAK; A HERO OR WITH HIM...a villain."

Firefly thought about it long and hard. He thought about everything, the battling, the talks, *all* of Xeno's advice...

"Then...I'm a villain now."

Molly stood speechless.

"*I am not one*, but if you're forcing me to choose...then I'd rather be seen as a villain for doing the right thing than keep playing your stupid game of hero. Not one hero has supported me this week, came looking for me, stood up for me, helped me...but he's done all that and more! He's done more for me this week than you've ever done in our lifetime of working together. So yes! If I had to choose– I'd pick him! One hundred percent, because he actually has my back!"

Molly just continued to stand there.

"You don't know what is going on! What we've been through! What we've learned! What I saw! ...No one will understand except the Captain, because you are all such blind and ignorant heroes and I don't want to be a part of a team like that..." Firefly finished with a death glare. Sending the message.

"...Captain is *furious* with you..."

"I know, but I don't care, he needs to know what's going on. So are you going to help us?" He asked, already knowing her answer.

"You are insane."

"Then please get out of my way...I have a *real* mission to accomplish."

Firefly shoved her out of the way and began to walk back into the setting sun of the lobby.

"...You are going to get yourself killed one of these days." She threatened.

"Then...so be it. I'd rather live a life worth living, than be just alive and cold like you..." Firefly added without looking back and marched on. Anger bubbling up inside him but he tried to hold it down. Molly, with a sour frown, took out her phone and dialed for back up.

Meanwhile, Xeno had escaped the crazed fan girls and snuck over to the merch booth once again. Crouching down the side as he poked his head up. Looking at the jacket. He tried to pull a power from somewhere but no one was close enough.

"Alright, an old fashion robbery," He whispered to himself as he put back on his villain coat. Xenomorph waited until the worker was turned around and busy.

In an instant he hoisted himself over and tried to grab the jacket, but it was on the mannequin tight. A single pull sent the entire bodice crashing down, sending a loud *CLANK* through the air as everyone turned to look.

"Hey!" The worker called out.

"Oops," Xeno mumbled and grabbed the jacket, launching himself back over the booth's fabric fencing and ran. He slipped on the marbled floor and bolted as he heard.

"SECURITY!" Being yelled, bouncing the echo off the walls.

"Shoot! Shoot! Shoot! Buggy is going to kill me," He mumbled to himself as he dodged people—who were already scattering out of his way.

Firefly still walked, looking at the floor until,

"FIRECRACKER!!!" Xeno yelled.

Firefly lifted his head to see Xeno being chased by security.

"What did you do?!" The hero immediately spat out.

Xeno grabbed his wrist and ran, "I got the jacket!"

"What?! But it was not for sale!"

"Exactly! It was for 'steal'!"

"No! That's not what that means!" Firefly couldn't help but laugh a bit and ran as Xeno dragged him on an escalator.

Two ran to the second floor, security still on their tails.

Firefly saw the pretzel in his own hand and frisbeed it. Hitting a cop straight in the head.

"What was that?" Xeno asked, curious as he kept booking it.

"Your pretzel," Firefly smirked.

"MY WHAT?!"

"Xeno! Ditch your coat, put on the jacket!"

"Now?!"

"YES NOW!"

Xeno took off his big, draping coat and stuffed it in the bag as they sprinted. Putting on the new jacket. The wings being a bigger taunt to the security still behind them.

"Ready?" Firefly asked.

"R-Ready for what?"

Firefly grabbed his hand and jumped over the railing and off the second floor.

Xenomorph screamed and flew in the air, as Firefly focused up. Landing perfectly on the modern art light fixture that hung above the lobby. However, there wasn't much to grab of the cubed lights, darn minimalist.

Firefly looked at the ground to see thousands of people watching them, especially Molly. Who gave a death glare in the audience. Firefly watched them all as it finally clicked. They saw him as a villain, whether he said so or not.

Firefly turned around to see Xeno struggling to hold on to another piece of the light, rope breaking and security still right behind them. Trying to catch them in the suspended air.

The epiphany finally hit him, time seemed to slow in the golden air as he realized he didn't care what anyone else thought, the only thing he really cared about was what his teammate thought, his partner.

Firefly instantly shot a fireball at the snack vendors and sent popcorn exploding everywhere like a hail storm. The crowd went crazy! Either running away from the hot kernels or trying to snag some free tasty popcorn. The perfect distraction.

In all the chaos Xeno slipped and fell off the chandelier, "AAAHHH–!"

"XENOMORPH!" Firefly screamed and parkoured over to him, sliding on a shape plane and grabbing his hand just in time. The wire strained more as Xenomorph panickly breathed.

"Hey! Hey! Hey! Calm down…it's going to be alright." Firefly soothed.

Xeno nodded and suddenly.

snap!

Both supers froze as the wire dropped and then fell to the ground.

"AAAAAAHHHHH!"

"AAAAAAHHHHH!"

They screamed together and if the light could scream it would've too.

The two supers, along with the art piece, crashed into another booth with a smash. Bending fabrics, snapping wood and sharp poles, scattering band goods everywhere, and shining distorted light and glass.

The security finally surrounded the booth and the cops had just arrived outside.

It was game over.

However when the police stepped inside the damaged booth, they found no signs of either the hero or villain. Bunch of mangled and destroyed parts. But not one superhuman.

Chapter 18:

Both boys laughed and ran down a dark hallway. Firefly's heart was beating in his chest, as he couldn't believe he just did that. Xenomorph led the way, not really knowing where he was going, but anywhere to avoid security. Xeno stopped at a door that said *'EMPLOYEES ONLY'* and tore down the plastic sign, tossing it to the ground as he jiggled the lock doorknob.

"That was insane!" Firefly breathed, a slight smile on his face. But to Xeno, it was huge.

"Did you enjoy causing chaos?" He asked rhetorically, smirking a bit. He brushed behind his ear to take out his lock pick once more and played with the door,

"Haha...maybe– maybe I did," Firefly laughed.

Suddenly a big bang went off, and another and another. Tapping in some sort of rhythm. Soon a guitar started to shred revealing a melody. People screamed and cheered as the lights dimmed even more until it was almost pitch black.

The show was starting.

"See! We made it! Super stealth!" Xeno sassed, opening the door and walking down the hallway. Neon lights flashing and shining.

"'Oh yeah, so stealth'," Firefly scoffed off with a smile. He was secretly very excited to see his favorite band in concert. Already humming the tune of the starting song.

All of the sudden a bright light shined behind them.

"FREEZE!" Someone yelled.

Both boys froze. Sticking their hands up and slowly turning around to see security.

"You two are under arrest!" The guard yelled.

"Ah crap," Xeno mumbled, "Permission to cause chaos?"

"Permission granted," Firefly nodded.

Xeno threw a blast of fire on the ground, creating a wall between them. He grabbed Firefly's hand and ran.

They somehow got to the backstage of the show as the band kept going. Stage crew running around, costumes on racks, cords along the floor, as equipment got pushed around for the next song.

The band sang and the verses echoed through the building. Xeno dodged managers, electrical boxes, and stage props with Firefly right on his tail.

Firefly accidentally smashed into a vanity mirror, but brushed off the glass and kept running.

Security finally managed to pass the wall of fire and continued to chase after them.

The band kept singing, not even knowing what was going on behind the stage.

"Hey, I think I know this song," Xeno yelled over the base as he ran, picking up the little bits and pieces of words he had.

"…Wait– HOLY CRAP THIS SONG IS MY FAVORITE!" Firefly yelled, smiling wide.

Xeno looked behind him and the cops were catching up. He then looked forward to see the wing of the stage, and through the black curtain's slit saw Boys of Mayhem playing.

There was their chance to escape.

As the verses grew and the bridge started up, Xeno jumped on the steps, running to the crack in the fabric when Firefly grabbed his hand and yanked him back down.

"Whoa! What are you doing?!"

"We gotta go!" Xeno declared.

"On stage?!"

"Listen, I don't want to be separated! So you could either get caught by the cops or live out your dream of performing your favorite song with your favorite band!"

Firefly stood speechless, not knowing what to do.

"I'm going up there, are you with me?" Xeno asked, holding out his hand, but Firefly just stood there like a statue.

That was his answer.

With a bit of a deflated heart and a sad look he took off. As if on cue, Xeno slid on stage and grabbed the mic from the singer.

216

Xenomorph sang the chorus with all of his heart and lungs, as he had made it just in time. The villain breakdanced all over the stage, creating his own little choreography. Firefly's mouth dropped as the music didn't stop. The band just looked at each other, but intrigued they continued. Whoever this guy was, was good. Xeno looked like a professional dancer and a part of the show.

Xenomorph continued the second part of the chorus, still loud and strong as the crowd cheered. Lights shined in his face as the vibrations made him feel alive. By far one of the best feelings in the world, far better than any super villain junk.

Firefly, still shocked, heard a bang behind him and turned around as the cops were approaching.

Firefly threw a fireball at a rope and a sandbag fell. Knocking a security officer unconscious.

Xeno continued, getting nervous as he started to lose the words. He heard the song once or twice, but it was nowhere near his favorite.

Firefly backed up as he kept throwing balls of fire in defense. Until he felt nothing but plush curtains. Turning around to see his partner on stage.

With no other choice, Firefly grabbed a mic. Looking at it, hesitating as he looked to the stage, back to the struggling cops, back to his partner in crime. Grabbing the microphone tight he knew what he must do.

In another brilliant cue, Firefly ran into the light, standing next to Xeno as he bolted the chorus. Xeno turned to the hero, absolutely shocked that he came around. So shocked he couldn't even sing, but luckily someone else had that covered. Firefly followed Xeno's steps as both boys danced in unison. Firefly nodded to him as he metaphorically passed the mic.

Xenomorph smiled and picked back up the rest of the chorus. Yelling into the mic, still dancing in perfect rhythm with his partner. Both supers danced their hearts out and sang like no tomorrow. Partying the night away as friends would...as friends did.

Xeno screamed the bridge as everyone jumped and cheered. Taking out their phones to film the spectacle; although Molly was just shocked and no hero ever answered her calls.

Firefly slid to his right and accidentally knocked the guitarist off stage with a yelp and a thud. He flinched at the scare as the guitar crashed to the floor, he quickly picked it up admiring the sleek thing. The song started to die out without the guitar player, and so with all eyes on him, Firefly grabbed the guitar and swung it around. Plucking his steel strings and started playing to the beat. The song picked back up like usual and went on. Everyone still having a great time.

However, Firefly caught a glimpse of the cops waiting in the wings. He kept playing and carefully danced his way to Xeno to send a message.

Xenomorph eventually noticed too, and both boys looked at each other, knowing they were stuck on stage. Millions of eyes glued to them. Xeno looked around and spotted a fire cannon about to go off.

"Firecracker, the canon, to your right!" Xeno yelled.

"What?"

"*Fire* it!" Xeno gestures as he readied up a little flame in his hands.

Firefly saw the cannon and got the message. He did the same and readied up.

They chanted as Firefly started shredding on the guitar—having fun as he jumped up and down. Xeno sung the repeating bridge and on that last high note, didn't back down. Sliding on his knees, pointing to the ceiling as he held the note perfectly. The villain taking center stage.

Firefly shot his ball of fire at the cannon and Xeno shot his own. Both sides of the stage exploded in a blast of fire as the beat dropped. Scaring the officers away from the curtains.

The two supers sang the chorus together for the last time as the crowd roared with excitement. Xeno still dancing with the mic and Firefly still rocking it like crazy on the guitar. Dancing their little routine like they had practiced it a thousand times. Back to back they sang the last lines of the song and rocked out to the last notes. The song slowed, and the drums and the bass faded. A roar of applause filled the stadium.

"THANK YOU NEW YORK!!!" Xeno cheered, throwing his hands up as the song dropped out of the air.

Firefly grabbed his jacket and yanked him backstage as the crowd kept cheering.

Both supers tripped off stage and fell on each other, but they just laughed their heads off as the band started playing the next song.

"Holy crap! That was amazing!" Firefly bursted.

"Tell me about it! Ugh! That was awesome! Is that how you

feel when you save the world?!"

"That was even better!" Firefly flamed up in excitement.

Both *heroes* laughed.

"We should go before the popo comes back!" Xeno started, helping up Firefly. Lending out his hand, for real this time.

"Yea," Firefly scoffed.

"See! Easy! Get in, one song, get out– Boom! Who is your stealthiest friend?! I am!" Xeno danced.

"...You're my friend?" Firefly asked, smiling wide. He could have never imagined Xenomorph being his first friend out of everyone, but for some reason, he didn't mind at all.

Xeno froze, "I–...I mean..."

Firefly walked toward the stuttering villain and hugged him tight.

"What are you doing?" Xenomorph asked, remaining still.

"It's a hug, silly."

"I know– but why are you doing it?"

"Because we are friends," Firefly smiled and squeezed.

The corners of Xeno's mouth started to rise as a smile painted his face.

Firefly pulled back to see Xeno's happy face, shining from the spotlights,

"Shall we go?" He asked.

"Indeed we shall, *WOOOOOHOOOOO*!" Xeno boomed and instantly covered his mouth. A speaker fell from the scaffolding up top.

220

Firefly tackled Xeno out of the way as the speaker came down with a crash. Flying into a million pieces.

Xeno still covered his mouth, shaking.

"What– what's wrong?" Firefly asked.

"I-I boomed, S-Soundwave! She's here! Somewhere!" Xeno stuttered. Firefly had never seen him so nervous before.

"Hey, it's ok, don't worry about her."

"You...you knew?" Xeno backed up.

"Yes...yes, I did– but listen–"

"Did you sell us out?!" He started panicking. Already tasting the betrayal,

"I told her to get lost," Firefly explained calmly.

"You–...you did? Why?"

"Because she made me choose, it was a stupid choice and I didn't like what she was saying so I didn't care," Firefly smiled.

"W-What was the choice?"

"It was between being a 'real hero' or you."

"...What did you choose?" Xeno's voice cracked, too afraid to even hear the response.

Firefly smiled, "Dude. You really think I'd get up on stage in front of the entire city and sing like that if I chose the hero's life?"

"So you didn't choose Soundwave?"

"No dude, I chose you," Firefly ended, being so soft and light it was like talking to an angel.

Xeno sniffled.

"Are you crying?" Firefly asked.

"NO! No! No, that would be ridiculous," Xeno sniffled more, whipping his cheeks.

"You are such a soft goober," Firefly sighed, wrapping his arm around Xeno and together they walked out of the wings. As one, as friends.

Chapter 19:

The laughing teens strolled out to the empty lobby. The broken light fixture was still on the floor in shattered pieces. Without the light, the night was a beautiful, blue starry sky. Making the lobby look like another dimension.

However they didn't get far before–

"Hey! Vigilantes! Freeze!" A security guard shined a light on the two. Police started showing up from the shadows.

Both supers looked at each other, smirking, already knowing what was going to happen.

"I'll race you to Fifth Avenue," Xeno challenged, stretching.

"Bet, see you there slowpoke!" Firefly agreed and bolted.

Xeno followed him as the cops yelled and shouted. Firefly dodged a guard's tackle as Xeno slid off his back, making their way to the exit.

The two pushed the glass doors and sprinted under the moonlight. Running into the streets and dodging cars. Taxis honked at their stupidity, but they didn't care.

The police tried to catch them, but when they finally got to Fifth Avenue they quickly ducked in an alleyway and they were gone.

They continued walking and got far, maybe too far. The cars stopped driving along the roads and the skyscrapers shrunk. Soon neon store signs and broken lamp posts became the sight. The green bushes and porch lights lit the yard as the two ran alongside a chain link fence.

The boys slowed as a silver shopping cart came into view, just resting alongside the sidewalk. It looked empty and sad.

"Whoa~ sick!" Xeno shouted and hopped inside the basket.

"What are you doing?"

"Riding in style~!" Xeno finger gunned and rocked the cart side to side.

"What?" Firefly smiled, confused.

"You've never ridden a shopping cart before?"

"Nope, can't say that I have," Firefly chuckled, he should've been frustrated or annoyed, but he was too happy from his adrenaline high to care.

"Ok well tighten those goggles and push."

Firefly tightened his mask, tugged the cart off the fence, and started pushing, "Ugh! You're heavy," he groaned.

"I won't be for long," Xeno sassed.

"Wait– what?" Firefly kept pushing.

"Speed up!"

224

Firefly started to run.

Xeno's new jacket flapped in the wind and spied his target ahead, "Hold on!" He yelled and grabbed Firefly's arms, pulling him onto the back of the cart. Firefly hopped on and soon the cart started to roll.

Firefly looked over Xeno's head to see them plummeting down hill. Xeno raised his hands up. Screaming just for the heck of it, and for the first time so did Firefly.

They both wooed and cheered as they rolled down the pavement. The cart sped faster and faster until they were invincible. Flying down the streets, living their lives.

Firefly opened his eyes to see metal debris lying like a ramp.

"Ramp! Ramp! RAMP!" Firefly screamed.

Xeno laughed, feeling the deja vu, "Good eye!" He recited back and aimed for the ramp.

"Xeno, not again!" Firefly yelled as they went barreling up the ramp.

They both screamed and flew in the air. Disobeying gravity as well as everyone else. Firefly's feet left the cart but Xeno reached back for his arm, holding on tight and not letting go.

The cart began to fall like a star as reality had finally stolen them back. They both looked to their crashing sight to see water; lots and lots of-

SPLASH!

Both boys started sinking until they felt the tiled floor at the bottom. Xeno quickly grabbed Firefly's hand and sprung up. Launching from the water like a buoy. Gasping for air as they flailed around in the tides.

Finally, they were able to tread water and look around. But they both froze at the sight.

A backyard filled with people all dressed up in suits and dresses. Catering, fairy lights, tables, decorations, music– well there *was* music. All the guests stared at the two as Xeno looked over to a sign on an easel.

Congratulations Newlyweds

Xeno looked back at the group, "Um…congrats?" he tried with a smile.

Firefly's little rush ended, as reality hit him like a ton of bricks. The hero sunk into the water, embarrassed. Peaking over the ripples, showing only his goggles.

***

A couple minutes and two towels later, the boys were out of the swanky pool and dried off, sort of. The party continued as Firefly ruffled his hair with the towel. He pulled off his hoodie and hung it to dry along with the backpack, Xeno's villain coat, and Xeno's new jacket. Luckily a lot survived, and he was happy he went with a waterproof bag.

The hosts were extremely nice, for some strange reason. Letting the boys stay a while and dry off. Firefly, while shocked, took the offer.

After all it was shelter, food, water, and the concert was on in the background on a giant screen.

Firefly walked over to the drink table where Xenomorph was already pouring himself a glass of champagne.

"Dude, can you even drink that?" He asked, already assuming the answer.

"Yeah, idiot, I know how to digest a liquid," Xeno sneered jokingly and continued to pour the bubbly syrup.

"No– I mean, are you of age to drink."

"Who needs to know?"

"...Are you under 21?" Firefly asked again, not impressed.

"Ha! That would expose my secret identity, Firecracker, nice try," He put the bottle down and sipped the golden liquid. The glass danced in the light as Firefly took those words a bit too literally.

"...Well, what if we did?"

"Did what?" Xeno asked as he took another swig.

"Tell each other...who we are."

Xeno spit out the drink, "WHAT?! ARE YOU CRAZY?!"

"All I'm saying is...we are cool now, right?"

The villain tightened his grip around the glass, not saying a word.

"I mean we are friends, we are going to stop Dark Legacy, and we are going to make the hero system better—so what's stopping us from telling each other? I mean the heroes all know each other..."

"...So do villains..." Xeno added, although he didn't know why he wanted to contribute.

"So, what's the problem?" Firefly smiled.

"...I...I don't know– just not ready for such a big step in this relationship...?"

"Oh calm down, you act like *we* are the newlyweds," Firefly joked and Xenomorph chuckled.

"But seriously, I...am not ready. People know me as 'Xenomorph, the great, scary villain!' and that's it."

"But you are more than just Xenomorph, and you know it, and...I know it. Someone once taught me to not care what anyone else says, the people who really matter to you will see who you really are," Firefly cited back.

Xeno stood quiet.

Firefly waited a bit, "What are you so afraid of?"

"...N-Nothing. Nothing! I am Xenomorph! I fear *nothing*!" Xeno downed another glass of alcohol, "WOOO!" and ran off.

Firefly rolled his eyes as the villain bolted to the dance floor. He heard a laugh behind him and turned around to see a guest leaning on the door frame.

"Ah~ distant one?" The stranger asked.

"Excuse me?" Firefly asked.

"Your friend doesn't seem to like being vulnerable," The gentleman sipped his red solo cup.

"Oh– yeah– we...are working on it," Firefly tried.

"I'm Jay," the guy stuck out his hand and Firefly shook it.

"I'm– uh–" The hero froze not knowing what to say, he was wanted after all.

"I already know who you are, Firefly, it's an honor." Jay smiles. He had very tan skin, green eyes, and swift brown hair. He looked so nice in that suit he could've been a spy for all Firefly knew.

"Nice to meet you Jay, so…you're not afraid of my friend and me?"

"Are you kidding? You guys are all over the news!" Jay laughed, Firefly paused. He already knew this, but it was all slander and threats; what could possibly be funny about that.

"…That's good?"

"Well it wasn't really at first, but your concert tonight? Totally mind shattering! You both rocked the stage and are blowing up!" Jay explained.

"W-Wait really?! People saw that…and liked it?"

"Liked it? Saw it?! It has over a million views, we were just watching it in the living room. You both were amazing!"

"Wow, thank you! Nice to know not everyone is trying to kill us." Firefly chuckled

"Ha, don't worry, I'm clocked out."

"Ha…uh what?" Firefly tried, but it was no use.

"Oh, sorry, I am a cop," Jay whipped out his shiny badge as Firefly froze. Mind running on how this was the end, they were cornered, caught! "But don't worry," Firefly shook his racing head in surprise, "You're secret safe with me. Like I said, I am off the clock and I really don't understand why the entire police academy is after you. Xenomorph I could see, but you've been protecting the city for years! I knew something was amiss, and I am on your side," Jay smiled.

"Oh thank you, Officer!" Firefly groaned in relief.

"So what are you doing here?"

"We just got lost. Shopping carts in the air– you know how it is." Firefly tried to explain.

"Alas, I do not, but it sounds like a heck of a time."

"It actually was! I just wish...well..."

"You wish 'Mr. Dark and Scary' would be more honest." Jay smirked, winking.

"...Is that obvious?"

"Yeah, a bit, but it's ok."

Firefly sighed, rubbing his head, "I don't know why I care so much. Call it the hero in me. I just know he's hurting...he'll feel so much better if he just– talked to someone, and I've told him everything about my life. I just thought he trusted me."

"I wouldn't call it the hero in you, but I'd call it the *friend* in you."

Firefly whipped up his head in shock.

"I mean, I'll never know what is going on between you guys. I mean your enemies one minute, then friends the next, I don't need to know your business...but do you ever think he's not telling you *because* he trusts you?"

"What are you saying?" Firefly questioned.

"I mean, if I had to think about it; he is a villain. Probably doesn't have a lot of people to go to. Then this hero comes along, and *viola~* the first reliable person that won't stab him in the back. Maybe he's just trying to protect that. I see a lot of criminals come in every day, they are always cautious of their loot and families, even if it costs them their lives."

"Whoa. Thanks Jay…I've actually never thought about it like that," Firefly watched as his friend danced on the dance floor taking another cup. Firefly giggled to himself, no matter what crime he had done no one could deny what a good dancer he was.

"Just give him time," Jay continued.

Firefly scoffed playfully, "I know, he'll open when he's ready…it's just getting hard to keep pushing this off–"

"No, I mean wait like an hour, he'll be so drunk he'll tell you anything."

Jay laughed as Firefly chuckled a bit, trying to decide if drunk Xeno was a good thing or bad thing.

"Welp, I better get back to the party. Here is my number, if you ever need some help out there on the field." Jay handed Firefly a little card with a ten digit number. The metallic paint shined in the light as Firefly observed it.

"Thank you Jay," Firefly said.

"You're welcome," and with that Jay walked away, waving to some other people.

Firefly grabbed a table and watched the party for a bit, admiring the scenery and fairy lights. Thinking about what Jay had said, really trying to see the world through Xeno's eyes.

Eventually Xeno came over holding many glasses and cups. He plopped them all down and fell into the chair sloppily.

Firefly looked at him, stunned.

"Dude~ you would not BELIEVE HOW MUCH I've drink!"
He slurred.

Firefly tried to hold his composure, but he bursted out laughing,
"Are you drunk?!"

"I'm a poet." Xeno declared.

"Are you drunk?" Firefly asked again.

"Perhaps-aybe...?" Xeno tried.

"Ugh, Jay was so right," He groaned with a smile. "What am I
going to do with you?"

"Uh~ duh~ we are going to stop Lark Degacy."

"You mean Dark Legacy," Firefly helped.

Xeno took another drink and chugged it, "WOOO! Party time!"
He tried to get up, but Firefly grabbed his arm and sat him right back
down.

"Oh no, you are sitting this one out, and drinking some water,"
He parented.

"What?! But I've just swam in water!"

"That doesn't count."

"Brooo~ lighten up!"

Firefly smirked as he lit himself ablaze.

"That's not what I meant–...woah~ dude the light is dancing on
you..." Xeno whispered.

"You are insane," Firefly smiled.

"Not as insane as you, Bestie."

"...Wait– what?" Firefly uttered softly, thinking he still had
water in his ears.

"Yeah! You crazy! You fight your whole team for me, standed up~ for me. I–...appreciate the level of insanity coming out of your mouth."

Firefly gave him a deadpan smirk, "Ironic. Considering the level of insanity coming from your mouth."

Xeno got on the table, "You are my Buggy! You hear that everyone, he is my best friend! So nobody~ hurt him or I'll screw you up and then you go boom!" Xeno readied a fireball and the people around backed up, frightened, rightfully so.

"Whoa! Ok, ok! Calm down dude, you are way too drunk to be scaring people right now," Firefly helped him off the table.

"I drunk I scared them, and I am not think," Xeno slurred.

"...Sure, buddy," Firefly dragged another chair over and sat him down. The hero took a seat next to the villain but Xeno leaned onto his shoulder. Eyes flickering close.

Firefly noticed, "...Did you mean what you said? About us being best friends?"

Xeno yawned, "Of course I did silly," he laid his hand on Firefly's knee, "Nothing is happening to you on my watch...you aren't going anywhere," and drifted off for a quick nap.

Firefly just smiled, rubbing the sleepy villain's head, guess he really did just need a little time.

"Can I have more alcohol," Xeno asked in his drowsy state.

"No."

***

Despite Firefly's answer, after Xeno's power nap he did sneak off and had a couple more drinks and dances.

Eventually the party was over, wrapping up when Firefly found Xenomorph again. The guest slowly left and with nowhere to go, the supers grabbed their stuff and headed off.

They walked down the pavement—well Firefly walked, Xeno clumsily wobbled. Tripping up along the way, but Firefly kept catching him. That repeated and catching soon turned to just holding him up as they walked.

Firefly didn't know the outer cities too well; he just wandered aimlessly. Too bad his only map was drunk. They soon wound up at Battery Park. Which was huge, and they seemed to walk forever, but they eventually stopped by the playground to rest.

Firefly was tired of walking for two and just decided to stay there for the night.

"Cool, playground!" Xenomorph yelled and ran over, immediately dangling on the monkey bars.

Firefly should've been concerned, but he just chuckled as the villain played. The hero stuck his hands in his pockets and watched his friend. Xeno flipped himself upside down and stuck out his tongue. His dark cape draped down, covering a bit of his face.

Firefly laughed and watched him climb all over the play structure and slide down every slide.

"Woo! C'mon your turn," Xeno said as he hit the bottom, kicking up sand and dust with his boots.

"What? Oh no, I'm good."

"Dude, it's a slide." Xeno offered again.

"Well one of us has to be responsible, and since I'm the one who's sober, I should stay watch."

"I'm totally soomber!"

"Mhm, yeah, sure." Firefly toyed with him.

"Please, one slide?" Xeno begged.

Firefly rolled his eyes and went up the stairs. Walking through the miniature fort of colorful plastic and metal, and went down the twisting, yellow tube slide.

"Woohoo!" He cheered as he got to the bottom. "There, happy?"

"Who cares if I'm happy, are you happy?"

Firefly smiled, "…Yeah, I am."

"Then success!" Xenomorph shouted as he went running back, climbing on another set of bars. Firefly followed him as Xeno dangled. "Hey…did you mean what you said?"

"Huh?"

"About identities and junk…" Xeno monkeyed across. The bars were child's play, nothing compared to his training.

"Of course man," Firefly sat down on the metal steps.

"…Why do you care so much?" Xeno asked.

"What are you talking about?"

"You…seem to care a lot about well…me…" Xeno tried.

"I mean, you care for me right?" Firefly asked, even though he already knew the answer.

"...No comment," Xeno shrugged off.

Firefly chuckled as Xeno climbed to the top of the monkey bars, scaling up the plastic castle tops of the playground. The hero looked at him genuinely, not sure of which of the many questions to ask first. He grabbed onto the railing and swayed a bit,

"Now that we are alone, can you please tell me what you're afraid of?"

"I told you, I'm not afraid of anything."

Firefly just raised a brow at him, not believing his answer for one second.

"I am the fearless, most powerful villain alive and I–!"

BOOM!

"AAAAAAAAAAHHHH!" Xeno screamed and fell off the playground as a colorful blast exploded in the sky. He hit the sand as Firefly flinched for him. "Ouch!"

"Whoa! Are you ok?" Firefly ran to him but another colorful blast went off right behind the hero and Xeno scooted back. Breathing heavily and shaking, trying to feel the grains of sand beneath his gloved palms. "...Xeno?"

"I'm fine– I'm fine..." He lied.

BOOM!

Another rocket went off painting Firefly's face in a scary red shadow.

"AAAHH!" Xeno screamed and punched him in the gut.

"OOF! Ow...ow...ok, that hurt," Firefly whimpered, grabbing his stomach.

Xeno covers his mouth, "Oh my God—I'm so sorry; instinct!"

"It's fine, what are you..." Firefly began to ask as he looked up at the sky. Dozens of fireworks went off and lit up the night. He thought it was beautiful, but he could tell Xenomorph didn't feel the same way. "Oooo~...come with me."

"What?"

Firefly dragged him through the sand and up a grass hill, "Yep, let's go!"

"Where are we going?"

"We are conquering your fear," Firefly stated as he stopped at the top of the hill, just under a tree.

Xeno looked at him confused, but shut up and watched. Firefly sat down under the tree and patted the soft spot next to him. Xenomorph slowly joined him in the cool grass, looking up at the stars as a giant burst went off.

The villain flinched back but Firefly caught him. The fireworks went off one after another and Xeno flinched less and less. Finally seeing the beauty of these things. Like a work of art glazing the night sky in light, it was beyond majestic. Nothing says New York like a fireworks show.

Xeno relaxed and found himself lying on Firefly, like a brother would. Eyes fixated on the bursting colors as the Statue of Liberty stood proud on the horizon. A view that could never be matched.

"See? Not so bad," Firefly added.

"Yeah, ...not so bad," Xeno got comfortable, which ironically made Firefly physically uncomfortable; poking him in the ribs and all.

"…Could you maybe take your elbow off my stomach?"

"Not a chance," Xeno smiled.

They watched the show for a bit and Xeno moved and stretched out in the grass, watching it all on his back. The only noise going off were the booms of the fireworks, until–

"Fireworks aren't what I'm afraid of," Xeno announced out of nowhere.

Firefly joined him in lying in the grass, "What? But I thought–"

"I mean, they are, but it's not the *big* thing."

"…What's the big thing?" Firefly asked, looking at him from the ground.

Xeno didn't take his eyes off the sky when he answered, "…Being alone."

Firefly's eyes widened.

"Pretty stupid right? A villain afraid of being alone?"

"You're not a villain, and you're not alone," Firefly said.

"But I could be…"

"…Does this have to do with the 'Xenomorph' thing?" Firefly asked.

"…Possibly?" Xeno tried, but immediately sighed as he wasn't even believing himself, "You get one shot to make a good first impression, and I blew it. The whole world knows me as 'Xenomorph, the hated villain'. With a city as close minded as this one…you don't get to fix what you've done…but then– this, uh, person came into my life…"

"Oh really?" Firefly asked rhetorically, playing along.

238

"Yeah– oh man, he's such a weirdo."

"Hey!" Firefly smirked and Xeno giggled.

"What! I'm not talking about you," the villain lied. "But...this um...person—that you don't know—...I don't know, he just means a lot to me and it's my first time having a friend, and...villains don't get second chances."

"Ok...but you did, so what's there to be afraid of?"

"Making a mistake."

Firefly listened to the silence of that answer.

"Call it the villain in me, but I'm very overprotective of what I think is mine. If I want something I take it! And I took something that I really, *really* want...I just don't know if I'm going to be able to *keep it*."

"I wouldn't call that the villain in you..." Firefly started, remembering Jay's words.

Xeno looked at him confused.

"I'd call it the friend in you."

"...I...I don't have such a side." Xeno denied.

Firefly laughed, "Are you kidding? You do! Would a villain defend others like crazy? Would a villain help other villains live better lives? Would a villain help someone achieve his dreams of going to a concert? Would a villain tell an entire bachelor party that we are best friends and that you aren't going to let anything hurt me?"

"W-What?! I never said that! ...Did I?"

Firefly nodded.

Xeno covered his face, "Ugh~ last time I get drunk with you."

Firefly giggled, "I didn't mind, it was nice to know what you were truly thinking for once."

Xeno looked at the sky, tapping his thumbs as he bit his tongue. However his teeth weren't strong enough,

"My dad...he...he was a great superhero," Xeno started as Firefly jolted up, basically having a heart attack. "He...had the power to shapeshift into anything. The Mighty Mocking Bird. He was incredible, and my biggest inspiration. I wanted to be just like him, but then one day he went out for a mission...and he didn't come back."

Firefly held his mouth as tears watered up in his lenses, knowing the feeling too well. Although something felt familiar about the story he didn't dare interrupt.

"I found out on the news what *really* happened. I tried to live in peace as long as I could, but eventually Governor Jaceson and his crappy staff found me...put me in the system. They did all sorts of weird testing and DNA analysis. I don't know what really happened, it's fuzzy...but I somehow was found out by Dark Legacy, he took me in. Gave me a place, a roommate, a job, and all I had to do was perform his little scripts and dance from his puppet strings."

Something clicked for Firefly– a light bulb he never wanted to go off. He stood up being too shocked.

"Wait...so your entire villain life...is a script?" Firefly asked.

"Yeah...pretty pathetic...right?"

"...Do you have schedules?"

"...Yeah?" Xeno sat up.

"Practiced routines?"

"Yeah?"

240

"Lines you have to say?"

"Yes–? What is going on?" Xenomorph questioned.

"I-I have schedules, routines, and lines."

"So?"

"Don't you get it?"

"No…?"

"Someone is *faking out fights*."

"What?"

"Xenomorph— *we have been scripted the whole time.*"

Chapter 20:

"Wait– what?! I don't follow."

"Think about it! How are you and I always at the same place! I just go where my schedule is and you're magically there!" Firefly clarified.

"Because that's where my schedule says to goooo~..." Xeno dragged out until it clicked.

"We are being set up! Someone is playing with us like– like– ACTION FIGURES!"

Xeno stood up, "Whoa…"

"Don't you see?! You were forced to be a villain—and I was forced to be a hero—and then we were *forced* to fight each other! We go without rules for a week and we haven't even fought once! We are nothing but a puppet show!" Firefly threw his hands up in the air.

"WHAT?! But who would do that?! And why?!"

"I…I don't know, but I have a feeling Dark Legacy is behind it." Firefly seethed.

Xenomorph's world started to spin as his vision blurred. His whole life; a lie. He was supposed to be the most feared villain in the world, but if everything was an act: who was he? His thoughts spiraled as a ringing went off, slowly creeping up to him. When suddenly—

"Hey," Firefly grabbed his shoulders, snapping him out of it, "We are going to stop him!" Firefly threw out his fist, hoping his teammate was still on board. Xenomorph paused, looking down at the fist. Thinking it over, he bumped the hero's fist determinedly.

The villain started to march away, ready to put an end to his maniac boss before Firefly pulled him in and hugged him.

"…I'm so sorry about your dad…" Firefly muffled.

Xenomorph's anger disappeared like smoke.

"Thank you for talking about it…" Firefly ended.

Xeno hugged him back, "Thank you for listening."

"Any time…'Bestie'," Firefly snarked.

Xeno pulled away, waving his finger, "It was once and I was drunk."

"Whatever you say," Firefly joked.

The villain rolled his eyes playfully, "Are we kicking Dark Legacy's ass or what?"

"*Ash and heck yes, step one: disguise! We need to get back to the costume store!" Firefly announced.

"Great, let's go!" Xeno announced and went running down the grassy hill. The two passed the playground before– "Oh! Wait!"

The villain ran up the steps and slid down the twisty slide again. When he arrived at the bottom he sighed in relief.

"Ok, now I'm ready…let's go!" He declared and with that the super team was off to get to the bottom of their twisted city.

***

Soon the sunrise dripped into the sky, as a new day began. They walked back to the busy streets. The buildings grew and the cars began to swarm up in the morning traffic.

The day seemed to pass by like nothing as the supers hid their faces in their hoodies and collars, Xeno tugging along the backpack. Avoiding eye contact with anyone.

Eventually, they got to Times Square—ironic. Firefly, with his covered face, quickly bought some breakfast pastries for the two as Xeno waited off to the side. As the bag of sweets was secured, one of the jumbotrons went off with the breaking news intro.

The reporter appeared on screen with Governor Jaceson. They talked frivolously in the background.

Screw that guy. Firefly thought as he walked, Xeno stuffing his face with a croissant. That guy did nothing except stick a big, red target on their backs and for what? Money? A reputation?

His messy, dirty blonde hair and untrustworthy, shifting blue eyes painted his sculpted face.

"Good morning New York! Today we are here with Governor Jaceson with news on the vigilante story!" The report broadcasted as the city streets started to slow to pay attention.

"Vigilante story?" Firefly also slowed down.

Soon Firefly's and Xeno's wanted pictures flashed on screen.

244

Firefly's mouth dropped. His worried face captured perfectly in black and white while Xeno just looked like he was enjoying the chaos as always.

"Yes, so as you may have heard we have two supers who went *rogue* this past week," The Governor started.

Firefly grabbed Xeno's collar, pulling him back.

"Ah— what?" Xenomorph asked.

"Shh! Watch…" Firefly muffled.

"Now Governor, when you say 'rogue' what do you mean? Because Xenomorph has always been terrorizing the city. For years he's been rogue!"

Xeno groaned.

"Well yes, but he's always been predictable. Banks and heists, maybe an attack here or there but we've always had intel on where he was and what he was up to. We've always sent the heroes to stop him…and we've always stopped him— well until recently…" the Governor drifted. Firefly eyes looked the screen up and down, disgusted.

"Don't even get me started on our beloved hero Firefly, word has it he has gone to the dark side! A villain, a hero gone bad! What do you have to say about that," the reporter questioned.

"I have no words– it's utterly heartbreaking to see one of our favorite heroes betray us…" Jaceson finished as a clip of the train fight popped up on screen; not a good look for the two.

"He didn't betray you, you overly political cow!" Xeno sassed.

"Xeno, shh!" Firefly hushed.

"But that was taken out of context!" Xeno kept yelling, pointing to the screen to illustrate his point.

"I know, but quiet, people are here," He gestured over to the crowd and Xeno zipped his lips.

"Now the whole city is in quite a predicament. As they are unable to tell whether these rogue vigilantes are well– actually vigilantes!" The announcer explained.

"What do you mean? They have been caught attacking our own kind! Robbing stores, jailbreaking!" The governor ranted as a security camera of Xenomorph's little jail break party went live. The villain just smirked at his work.

"Well yes, but they crashed the Boys of Mayhem concert last night and the fans actually loved it!" The reporter showed the clip of the two boys dancing on stage. The streets seemed to dance along, enjoying the show—well everyone except for the Governor, who was just shocked at this information.

"That– that doesn't mean anything! These two are still dangerous! Monsters! Criminals!"

Firefly looked down feeling guilty.

Xeno noticed and nudged him, "'Oh my goodness, Governor Jaceson, stop I'm flattered'," He joked, being overly dramatic. Firefly laughed at his feminine flair.

"To my citizens, I promise this issue will be taken care of, I have a plan to capture and detain these vigilantes for good. Stay calm and go about your day, the heroes will take care of this," The governor spoke and the two supers froze a bit. The hunt was back on.

"Hey Governor, any info on those 'organizations'?" The reporter asked as Firefly and Xenomorph's mess-up played on screen. Reshouting the lines word for word.

Xeno rested his hand on Firefly's shoulder, trying to console him.

"You know what…?" Firefly started, "I'm *glad* that happened," He smiled as Xeno.

"Really? You're not upset or embarrassed?"

"Embarrassed about going on all these crazy adventures with my new friend, and finally taking down Dark Legacy once and for all? Not a chance," Firefly boasted.

Governor Jaceson looked pale, "No– no comment on the 'organizations'. Every villain and hero acts on their own—I mean sure we call them individually when needed to complete a mission but organizations?! Plotting?! That's insane."

"…That's not suspicious at all 'Governor'," Xeno sassed.

"Relax dude, no one knows any better. He does fund the hero organization, he's probably just trying to keep a cover. I mean, we *just* figured out it's all fake and we were the stars!"

"But…we clear as day exposed everyone, that's why everyone's after us right?" Xeno questioned.

Firefly thought as the big screen grabbed his attention,

"My only concern is: keeping my people safe and catching these juvenile delinquents!" The Governor sneered.

"Wow, he's got so many nicknames for us, it's cute," Xeno scoffed.

"I'm sending out all heroes today to do a city sweep and perimeter search. We will catch them before the big Gala tonight. Then I will disclose any other questions about this... 'situation'." Jaceson continued.

"Sweet! Still a 'situation'!" Xeno quietly celebrated and started doing some small, little moves in place.

"This weekend will be the *end* of this madness and we will shut down any signs of Firefly and Xenomorph," Governor Jaceson finished determinedly.

"Well, there you have it folks, some words from our beloved Governor. Will the vigilantes be caught? Is there another side of the story we aren't seeing? Will the 'super' stars break out on their own world tour? Stay tuned to find out– and remember we will be filming live at the Gala tonight!" The reporter finished and the newscast ended.

Firefly looked off the screen and immediately spied Yellow Jacket walking in the square, patrolling. Adrenaline shot up his body like a bullet to the brain.

"Oh crap– Governor wasn't kidding, we need to go! Now!" Firefly yanked Xeno and the two went running down the block.

"What's going on?" Xeno ran with him, already out of breath.

"You heard Governor Jaceson, he sent all heroes out! We need to find somewhere to hide!" The hero explained as he bolted, but he screeched his shoes to a stop when he saw Tidal Wave and Timetraveler were patrolling in front of them.

The two heroes hadn't noticed the 'vigilantes' yet, but Firefly wasn't going to take that chance (especially since one of them had water powers and would extinguish them in seconds).

Firefly grabbed Xenomorph's gloved hand and rushed into the nearest building he could find. Neon colored lights blurred his vision as the metal blue door swung open, slamming it behind them. Breathing as they slid a bit against the steel.

However, the neon only got brighter when they finally looked at where they landed. The carpet was soft and plushy, 80's music and colors filled the air, and people glided like magic on wooden floors. Arcade machines were being won, tickets poured out, and there was a snack bar with slushies and hot nachos.

"What is this place? Did we go back in time– did Timetraveler catch us!?" Xeno panicked.

Firefly looked to his right and spied a counter filled with roller skates. He got an idea and tucked and rolled over to the counter. Ducking behind it as he grabbed two pairs of skates from down below.

"Are you stealing?!" Xeno whisper-shouted.

"No! Just…borrowing?" Firefly tried to convince himself.

Xeno put his hand over his mouth, pretending to cry, "I taught you so well," his voice cracked.

Firefly rolled his eyes and pushed the skates. Passing a pair to Xeno.

"Here, put these on," Firefly commanded as he started lacing up his own pair.

"…Wait– what?" Xeno asked.

"The heroes are everywhere, we go back outside now we are done for. We need a place to lay low and hide, and we gotta fit in,"

Firefly explained and got up, getting the feel of his skates. It was just like his skateboard after all.

"O-Oh…you want me to put those on?" Xeno asked, stuttering.

"Yeah, c'mon let's go– and take off your cloak of darkness or whatever!" Firefly skated off into the rink. Taking off his hoodie and tying it around his waist so no one would recognize him from the floor. Xeno gulped, but ultimately took off his gear, put on his bag and skates, and wobbled to the floor. Looking 'super cool'.

Firefly had already completed his first lap, dodging people, when he noticed Xeno holding the wall tightly. The hero skated to him.

"What are you doing? They could come in at any second—we need to blend in! Hide in plain sight, you gotta skate!"

"I can't skate Firecracker!" Xeno yelled as he stumbled.

"…Seriously…you can't skate?" Firefly asked, springing up.

"Yeah! What's it to you?!" Xenomorph snapped as he wobbled on his wheels.

"Nothing! I just thought…I don't know, I just assumed you could," Firefly explained.

"Well I can't, and now if those heroes come in here I'm going to make a bigger scene when I fa–AAAALLLL!" He started before eventually tripping up and falling to the floor.

Firefly gasped a bit.

Xeno tried to get up, keyword; tried, "See!" He teetered on the skates, rolling like crazy, "I can't do it."

"Sure you can, watch, I'll teach you," Firefly grabbed his wrists and held them. Slowly snaking his legs to go backwards.

"You skate?"

"Yeah, skateboard. It's pretty similar. Just think about it like dancing…" Firefly started as he turned and slid next to Xeno. "Instead of stepping forwards, you're going to step diagonally, or sideways."

Firefly did so and skated a bit.

Xeno watched him as the disco ball-spotted lights spun around, he soon followed the steps and began rolling forward.

"Nice! Now, when you skate you want to bend a bit forward, make sure you're balanced. If you stand too far back you will fall on your ash."

Xeno froze, smirking, "Did you mean–?"

"Shush! No! Language! I'm trying to speak Xenomorph, give me a break. Now all you gotta do is move your hands with your body and you're good!"

"Ok…how do you turn?"

"Easy! You're just going to lean to one side, just a bit. The pressure will be enough to steer, you can also use your outside leg to help guide you," Firefly coached as they rounded their first corner.

Xeno wobbled a bit, but was able to make the turn.

"Yes! Way to go man! Awesome job!" Firefly celebrated and cheered.

"R-Really?"

"Yeah really, now follow me we are going to do it again!" Firefly lent out his hand and Xeno took it, Firefly stayed backwards as Xeno made the second turn (with help from his hero).

After a while of practicing, Firefly let go and Xeno was able to soar on his own. The two went round and round, laughing as they raced. They eventually took a break, had a slushie, played some arcade games, and blended right back into the skating crowd. They were having so much fun they failed to notice that not one hero came in.

Firefly tried some tricks, showing off as Xeno tried to copy, but he just ended up flailing his arms and losing control of his skates.

"WWAAAAHHH!" He screamed

"I got ya! I got ya!" Firefly tried catching him, but–

CRASH!

Xeno slammed into Firefly and both boys crashed into each other, falling onto the floor. Xeno on top of Firefly like a dog pile. The boys just sat there for a second before laughing their heads off on the hardwood floor.

"Dude! Skating is awesome!" Xeno cheered.

"Right?!"

They laughed until Xeno felt the swashiness of water in his stomach. It wasn't nauseating, it was more like the calming salty waves on a beach. He also felt the ticking of the clock and felt nostalgic for some reason. Xenomorph pondered in his weird moment until it hit him like a ton of bricks.

He gasped.

"Hey, you ok?" Firefly asked, stopping his laughter. The hero tried to sit up but he was tackled back down to the ground. "Wha-!"

"Shh! Get down!" Xeno commanded.

"More down than I already am?" Firefly asked rhetorically.

"Tidal Wave and Timetraveler are close!" Xeno

whispered-yelled.

"What?!"

"I feel them! They could be here any minute! We need to hide!"

Firefly looked around and spied a photo booth near the bathrooms, "This way!" He commanded as they raced on wheels to the box.

Firefly drew back the curtain as Xenomorph crashed inside, ramming into the back wall.

"OW!" He yelped.

Suddenly the front door opened and Tidal Wave and Timetraveler came walking through. Firefly immediately hopped in the booth and closed the curtains.

Pressing his finger to his lips as he shushed the villain. Who was trying to de-tangle his body. Firefly guarded Xeno and readied up a small ball of fire just in case.

However, no one ever came. With a peak from the curtains Tidal Wave and Time Traveler left and the boys were safe. Firefly sighed in relief and extinguished his flame.

"Are they gone?" Xeno asked.

"Yeah…good thing too. I have a feeling since we are 'off the script' they are too…"

"That's why they were so much stronger on the train! And on the roof!" Xeno added.

"Exactly, we wouldn't stand a chance," Firefly looked back out the curtain as Xeno sunk a bit.

"…I'm sorry."

Firefly whipped his head back, "…What?"

"If I had a real power or my disc we would've stood a better chance, I'm completely useless now…"

"What? No, are you kidding? We wouldn't have gotten this far without you! You had all the escape plans, knew where to go, all the ideas, the disguises. And let's be honest, the heroes would annihilate me! You saw me on the train."

"True," Xeno played along, trying to be sassy.

"Dude, you are my friend, powers or not. And you are the farthest thing from useless," Firefly chuckled, not believing he'd ever have to convince a 'villain' that.

"You mean that?"

"Of course I do."

"Thanks man," Xeno ruffled Firefly's hair like a noogie.

Firefly giggled as he tried to fix his messy hair, flipping it back to place, "You're welcome."

Xeno stretched, ready with new determination, "Alright! Let's get back out there, but first…" he ruffled around in Firefly's pockets.

"W-What are you doing?"

The villain pulled out his nice wallet, "Sweet! I was so worried Devan stole it."

"Wait– what?"

Xeno plucked a dollar from the wallet and slid it into the dispenser.

"What are you doing?"

"I'm taking a photo," He explained calmly as he set up the

machine.

"Why?"

"Duh~ because I want one. Plus it's your money."

"Gee, thanks," the hero deadpanned.

"Anytime, now smile!" He side-hugged his friend and smiled.

Firefly rolled his eyes playfully, smiled with him and the flash went off.

"Now silly faces!" Xeno got in the face of the camera and stuck out his tongue, holding peace signs as Firefly laughed in the background. The flash went off again.

"Ok! Ok! Cool crime-fighting one!" Firefly spat and the two boys were back to back. Firefly crossed his arms as Xeno held up his fist, filling them with fire. The white light blinded them a third time.

"Ok, now wh-AHHH!" Firefly tried to ask before Xeno jumped on him, doing a horrible piggy back ride. Firefly busted out laughing as he tried to regain his balance, but the forth flash went off and they both went tumbling out of the machine with a yelp.

Once they hit the plush floor they continued to chuckle as the machine spewed two slips of photos.

Xenomorph immediately picked them up, admiring how great he looked, "Sweet! These look sick!" He passed on to Firefly.

"You want me to have one?"

"Yeah, if you want. There's two for a reason," Xeno addressed.

Firefly took it, looking at his friend in the little boxes of the photograph. Worth the dollar.

"Why are you so weird?" Xeno asked.

"What?"

"You're looking at them weird, ...you know what a photo is right?"

"Hey! I do!" Firefly jokingly punched Xeno.

Xeno snarked, "Then what's the problem, Buggy?"

"There is no problem," the hero smiled.

"What are you on about...?"

Firefly chuckled, "I mean, I'm just...happy? Surprisingly? It's nice to actually have a friend and get to know the real you."

"...The real me?" Xeno puzzled, twisting his head a bit as he held up his confused smile.

"Yeah."

"Did you conk your head when we fell?" Xeno panicked and immediately started checking his head.

"No! No! I just mean, you aren't the 'horrible' villain I thought you were, you're pretty alright and I'm happy I stopped being an idiot and realized it."

Xenomorph's face softened, was it surprise? Horror? Or just plain out genuineness.

"You are such a sappy tree," The villain finally said, although that's not what he wanted to say.

"Pff– alright 'Bestie'..." Firefly teased.

"I was drunk! That doesn't count!" Xeno pointed fingers.

"Sure~ deep down I know you have a heart, I will find it eventually Mr. Villain. Can't hide it from me!"

"I– no...?"

256

"Dude, I promise…I'm not going anywhere," Firefly smiled as he started taking off his skates.

Xenomorph opened his mouth to say something but he closed it, not knowing what he could possibly say. He genuinely cared for this kid but he didn't know why. Deep down, he did have a heart; a heart telling him he was going to screw everything up. This wasn't his life, his world, he was a villain…right?

Chapter 21:

"Your turn," Xeno said as he picked up a slice of hot pizza.

"Never have I ever–" Firefly started before a flying pepperoni hit him smack in the face, making him jump a bit.

Xeno giggled as he readied another one.

"Dude, you're supposed to throw it after I say the sentence. And that's only if you've done it!"

"I know," Xeno threw another one. Firefly was not impressed. "This is just more fun," Xeno readied his next shot.

The hero rolled his eyes and continued, "Never have I ever...been to Coney Island!"

"What?!" Xeno dropped the pepperoni, "No fair, I wanted to throw one!"

"Too bad! Neither of us has been, so you don't get to pelt me with pepperoni," Firefly did a small victory dance at the table.

"Ok, ok, never have I ever..." Xeno thought as Firefly grabbed a pepperoni, "Gotten an F in Chemistry."

"Hey! That's lying!"

"No, it's not!"

"You just said something I have never done so I don't get to throw," Firefly grumbled.

"No it's true, I aced Chemistry!"

"...Really? You?" Firefly asked sarcastically.

"Yeah! Villain Chemistry. Someone is willingly going to teach me how to blow stuff up and you think I'm not going to pay attention?" Xenomorph asked rhetorically. "How do you think I made the paint bombs?"

"Ok, fair," Firefly thought, "What about math?"

"...I don't wanna talk about it."

Firefly laughed, "Ok, never have I ever...had a pancake without syrup," Flinching up as he knew the sliced lunch meat was coming.

Xeno froze, "...What's a pancake?"

Firefly's heart skyrocketed, "WHAT?! You– you don't know what a pancake is?!"

"No...not really? ...Is it like a death ray?" Xeno asked, really hoping it was a death ray.

"What?! No," Firefly chuckled, "Pancakes are the most delicious thing in the world!"

"Better than pretzels?!"

"Better! It's a soft, sweet, thin cake that you can top with whip cream, syrup, powdered sugar, bananas and strawberries! And you can eat it for breakfast! Ugh! They're so good, how have you never had one? My mom makes them all the ti– ...oh..."

Xeno looked at his friend spin his majestic tale of 'the

pancake'.

"Sorry..." Firefly apologized.

"It's...it's fine..."

"...What's it like?" Firefly asked, filling the awkward air.

"Hm?"

"Being a villain, I mean I know you claim to 'love it' but I don't really think that's true..."

"Why do you care?" Xeno sassed.

Firefly gave him a deadpan stare, "Seriously?"

"Right! Right, we are um...friends now."

"Exactly, and you can't escape it," The hero smiled, "C'mon, I genuinely wanna know."

"Curiosity killed the cat you know..." Xeno warned.

"Then consider me a dead cat," Firefly smiled, taking a swig of his soda.

"Well...what do you wanna know?"

"*Everything.*"

Xeno huffed a breath of air, really thinking of what to say. Firefly waited patiently and Xeno looked around in the pizza place they wandered into. It felt like they were in Italy. The smell of pizza, the murals on the walls, the bright colors. Scenic. Enough to make Xeno forget where he really was for a second.

"Well, there's pros and cons..."

"Cons?"

"...I hate being looked at like I'm some sort of monster. Or the fact that I can't go out to certain places, get a normal job, or not be stuck in the same crappy apartment. Plus all the training and testing. Everything is forcefully handed to me. Choices are made for me, and I don't get to live like a normal teenager. I take orders from the only adult figure in my life…who also may be a psychopath."

Firefly gave a tiny giggle at the jab, but he was still listening. Hung on every word. As if it were an epic battle. Because deep down the hero knew it was; a battle between good and evil. All within one person.

"I guess that's it, …wait, Devan. Huge con."

Firefly gave another laugh, "Alright, …pros? If there are any."

Xeno gave another pause, "…Freedom."

"What? …But– I thought–" Firefly started, taking his teeth off his plastic straw.

"It's a different kind of freedom, Buggy," Xeno chuckled, "When I put on the mask I can be and do anything. Sure, I am a villain, but I just let go. My intrusive thoughts take over and it allows me to do the impossible! And I don't care what people think! I don't know, man, the rush and adrenaline of barely escaping every time, cops on your tail, loot in your hand, fear in everyone except you–…*it feels like your invincibile.* And…no one can take it away."

Firefly's face softened, wishing he had something even close to that.

"I'm not bound by any laws or rules, the only limit is me…and it feels amazing. My emotion pours into my work and it's like…like I'm creating a masterpiece. Each day, drawing a new sketch, drawing this character. Day by day I create a force to be reckoned with. I create a movement, an idea, and *that's* what I love. I know it sounds cheesy…"

"Very, chill dude, the pizza is getting jealous," Firefly snarked and Xeno threw another pepperoni at his face. Deep down however, Firefly loved every word of his confession.

"…What do you like about being a hero?" Xeno asked.

Firefly froze, not expecting those words. Heck he never even thought about them himself.

"Huh…I um…I don't know…I've been so focused on becoming one…I guess I never really thought of anything else," He answered honestly.

"Cons…?"

"Pff, well that's easy. I never get to go anywhere. I have all these strict rules I have to follow too, practices, rehearsal lines…as a hero in the organization we have to be *perfect*. Any flaw is a weakness and any weakness is defeat."

"That…doesn't sound like fluffy-hero positivity?"

"It's not supposed to be."

"What happened to 'Anyone can be a hero' and 'Do the right thing' or 'help others and be kind'?"

"Well those are *my* mottos, that's what I…secretly carry with me, but most heroes in the organization don't think like that. I mean we are all forced to keep an image up. We break that…we are useless."

"Flaws don't make you useless? They make you human– well superhuman…" Xeno claimed.

"It's not that simple, Captain knows what he's doing. We have one fumble and the city panics, like earlier this week…"

"Oh~ so that's why you wanted me to cave back at Times Square."

"Yeah, sorry. I just couldn't disappoint anyone. Heh, how ironic is that, now I'm disappointing everyone," the hero smiled off, trying to find the humor in his misery.

"...You're not disappointing me..." Xeno tried.

Firefly looked at him, feeling like he was missing something. Like the last piece to a puzzle.

"Pros?" Xenomorph continued, brushing off his kindness before Firefly could acknowledge it.

Firefly shot back to life, "Pros, right," he cleared his throat, "Well, I *love* helping people. Protecting them. Even when they don't know it. Like a guarding angel, you know. You just feel there's something bigger than yourself. You are hope, you are light, you are good, you could be anything... I like being under the mask too," he grinned, trying to help the villain a bit.

Xeno listened to him, wondering if he'd ever felt hope before. He searched his brain for a sign, a moment, but he realized the only times he'd ever felt that same light of hope was when he was with his partner in crime. Strange.

"Plus it helps me feel closer to my dad. Knowing I'm following in his footsteps...he'd be proud. I hope..."

"...I bet," Xeno corrected.

Firefly played with the top of his straw as the two just smiled at each other, pure genuine leaking from the mask.

"Man, must feel nice to feel that," Xeno tried.

"…Well who says you can't?"

"Firecracker, I'm not hero material. Even *if* I wanted it, it would never happen. Besides all the strict rules and schedules, perfect grades and image—it's not me."

"Who says it has to be?"

"Duh~ you, just now, when you were talking about the hero's life?"

"Yes, but that was before."

"Before?"

"Before we change everything!" Firefly smiled.

"Whoa– wait– you remembered?"

"Yeah! Once we prove to Captain Peace Dark Legacy's plans and that you're not evil, the world will change, remember? No more organizations! And then whoever is puppeting us can't pull the strings. No more schedules and lines, no more faked moves. We could be heroes– *real* ones! Everyone will have a place, even you."

Xeno's eyes widen behind his mask, trying to imagine if such a place existed.

"I mean…if you wanted. I just thought once this is over, well…I didn't think you'd still want to run after everything…I thought…maybe we could be…like…a duo," Firefly shyly offered, playing with his straw, swirling around his water.

"Seriously?"

"Yeah! I mean…I don't want you to leave…"

Xeno bit his tongue, carefully choosing his next words, "I…will *think* about it…"

264

Firefly launched out of the red booth, "YES! YOU ARE GOING TO BE A HERO! WITH ME!"

"I said I'd *think* about it! And that's only if this all works out and you stay one. I am not becoming a blah- 'hero' by myself."

"Ok, ok, ok, deal!" Firefly jumped.

"And sit back down, you're making a scene, Firecracker!" Xeno whispered his demands. Firefly sat down as the villain picked up a slice of pizza from Firefly's side.

"I~ wouldn't eat that if I were you, 'you'll make a scene'." The hero teased.

"Tfft– really? Eating a piece of pizza, you're 'hilarious'," Xeno raved sarcastically and took a bite. However, the bite was brutal.

Xeno instantly flinched at the spice, it felt like he tasted the sun. He swung his arms around for his cup, but it was clumsy. He managed to finally grab it and chugged it down. But the soda did nothing except make it worse.

The villain started banging the table in pain as his red cheeks puffed up in pain. Firefly laughed and slid him a glass of milk that was on the table. Untouched.

Xeno slurped it down, finishing the whole glass in one whole take. He sighed in relief as the burning extinguished. Xenomorph opened his mouth to speak but all that came out was smoke.

Firefly watched him, enjoying his entertainment, "I warned you…"

Xeno tried again, tears welling up as he fanned his tongue, "What…the hell…was that?" His voice cracked and squeaked as if there was no voice left.

"Ghost peppers and hot chili flakes, I like my pizza hot," Firefly smirked.

"You like everything hot," Xeno croaked, "even your women."

"Wait– what?"

"H-How did you know...about the milk?" Xeno coughed, changing subjects.

"I know milk is the only thing to soothe the pain, so I ordered some."

"But– you– you didn't even flinch when you ate this piece of melting lava," Xeno explained, panting.

"It wasn't for me silly, it was for you!"

"But– but– h-how did you know?"

"You've been stealing stuff since the day we met, I think I know you by now," He smirked, taking another bite of his pizza.

Xeno looked down, tapping his finger on the table. He mumbled something.

"I'm sorry...what?" Firefly asked rhetorically.

"Thanks for the milk...or whatever," Xeno shrugged off.

Firefly smiled, "You're welcome."

The fire continued to dance in the villain's tongue, until he had a burning question; Xeno shook off the heat, "Do you...like having fire abilities?"

"Oh...um– woah...that's um...a question," Firefly stopped to think.

"Is it that bad? You don't have to answer," Xeno gave him the option to back out.

"No it's ok, it's- it's just not…simple. I *do* love having powers, especially my dad's. Fire is so amazing, and warm and it's light! It's everything a hero should look up to, but others see it as destructive and harmful…"

"Really? Fire is fun! I love arson!"

Firefly wheezed, "NO! I didn't mean it like that– just– you were right about controlling my temper. When I get mad…" Firefly thought of Molly, and instantly became a living torch, "I flame up and become this *monster*. If I'm not careful…I could be real dangerous."

Xeno's eyes widened, never thinking he'd ever connect with a hero in such a way. This bug kept surprising him, and maybe that wasn't a bad thing.

"You thought I was dangerous once," the villain started.

"Tff, that's different."

"How?"

"You choose– ok– not choose, bad wording; but you were dangerous because of your actions, you do things on purpose…mine…well mine is purely based on emotions. I can't control it anymore than you can control the weather," Firefly chuckled.

Xenomorph looked down, curiosity still running through his veins, "What would happen if you went full Firecracker?"

"What?"

"Like if you just let go, intrusive thoughts took over, you just for once gave into your emotions? What would happen to you?"

Firefly laid back on the booth, staring at the ceiling and at one bright fluorescent light.

"I don't know, I could only guess."

"What's your guess?" Xeno kept prying, not because he was being snoopy, but maybe (just maybe) because he genuinely cared. If something were to happen to this kid on his watch, he'd never forgive himself, especially after *everything*.

"My mom calls it...blowing a fuse."

"Oh, like a mental health thing? You just get really mad and go crazy? Nice pun."

"No– no, we'll yes, but it's more than that. I...hypothetically would blow up..."

Xeno spit out his drink, coughing, "PFFFF–! AUGH–kak–BLOW UP?!"

Firefly slapped his hand over the villain's mouth, "Quiet! Yes, I'd blow up. I mean I'd still be intact, just pure fire, flames, and anger. Like a bonfire...with a desire to kill."

The villain removed the gloved hand from his mouth, "You're not capable of that," he was confused, but also dead serious. His Buggy wasn't capable of hurting anyone.

"I could be, who knows, I could literally destroy the city for all I know, I might not even be human anymore...just fire. Rage would run through me and then: game over."

"But this is a hypothetical, you don't even know if this could happen!"

"I have a pretty good feeling," Firefly fiddled with the silverware on the table. Making it spin around.

"How in the *world* would you know?!"

"…Because I almost did," Firefly barely spoke.

Xeno froze, "…What?"

"…The…the day my dad died…"

Xeno's pulse ran cold.

"When I found out he wasn't coming home– I–…I was a wreck," Firefly started. Tears welling up but putting on his strong smile, like a true hero. "I got so angry and bitter I…I burnt down our old house… My mom was there… she said I had literal fire in my eyes and I wouldn't listen…granted I didn't even hear anything except for the flames and my own heartbeat. I screamed and cried and I…hurt a lot of people…close neighbors…my mom…I would've taken the whole city out with me if my mom wasn't fast and used a fire extinguisher on me…" Firefly giggled, trying to be lighthearted on the darkest day of his life.

Xeno covered his mouth in shock, gasping, "Dude–back at the police station– the fire extinguisher! I'm so, so sorry! I didn't know!"

"Hey, it's ok! Trust me…the foam is actually quite comforting. …It's *me* that I'm afraid of…"

Xenomorph just sat there, not knowing what to say to that.

"That's why I have to be in check at all times, I can't let anything get out of hand otherwise…the city could be lit a blaze…all because of me," he drifted, sinking into the booth. His tough smile faded into a weak frown.

Finally, Xenomorph knew what to say, "You haven't flamed up in a while…not since Devan," he smiled.

Firefly smiled back, "...I haven't been angry or felt hurt in a while."

Xeno smiled, wanting to say something but he snapped out of it, "Anyways, the plan?"

"Right!" Firefly grabbed a napkin and Xeno's doodle pen and wrote out the blueprints of the Governor's venue, "So once we get our disguises we will sneak into the party. Play the scene a bit, fit in–"

"Drink," Xeno added.

"No...no drinking."

"Awww~ but it's the Governors biggest party of the year. They will be serving all types of fancy, expensive, alcohol," Xeno whined.

"No. We have a mission, stay focused. Anyways once the Governor gives his big speech about the 'vigilante problem' we'll sneak off. Try to find some clues."

"How are you so sure we will find something?" Xeno asked.

"Devan said Dark Legacy will be there in his secret identity form, this speech is a great distraction for any hero...or *villain*. Dark Legacy will strike and that's when we will catch him."

"How are you so sure? What if we don't?" Xeno asked again, poking holes in his plan.

"Then we go to plan B."

"What's plan B?"

"*Expose the system.*"

"Wait– what?!" Xeno shouted, choking on whatever drink he had left.

"The foster care system, you were tested on, correct?"

"Yeah?"

"And Dark Legacy adopted you."

"...I guess– I don't know if I'd say adopted–"

"Point is– that trade, it's a government deal—whether they knew you were super or not! There has to be some sort of paperwork in that house detailing your foster agreement!"

"Would my records even be in that house?" Xenomorph asked.

"The government wouldn't have dozens of super files just lying around some office. This secret was kept good, too good. It has to be somewhere protected and hidden. The governor's house is the most protected place in New York. If we can get our hands on that, we can prove to the world that Dark Legacy forced your hand!"

"Wait, really? You'd think my records would work?"

"Yes, trust me. One way or another, this party will give us exactly what we need to take this puppeteer and Dark Legacy down, and then we can go to Captain Peace!"

"Ok, I'm in!" Xeno smirked, but his confident grin turned weak and unsure.

"You ok?"

"Y Yeah totally, just...a lot riding on tonight," He played with his sleeves, not really sure why. He was never this scared of anything.

"Are you nervous?" Firefly asked, surprised that Xenomorph could ever be nervous.

"What?! No! I never get nervous!" He whined.

Firefly just waited, not believing it.

"...Maybe."

"Well...what's your 'fire extinguisher'?"

"Huh?"

"You know to calm down, what gets you relaxed?"

Xeno perked up as he had the perfect place in mind.

Chapter 22:

CRASH!

Xenomorph swung his bat as glass shattered everywhere. Obliterating the beautiful vase that once stood in place.

Firefly guarded himself, even though his goggles did the job for him. The angry rage music filled the air as Xeno danced around in the shards of glass that he'd call his masterpiece.

Firefly looked up, seeing the nauseating spray paint on the wall. Xeno rested the bat on his shoulders, laying his wrist on the wooden weapon.

"So, what do you think?" Xeno smirked, feeling much better now that beauty itself was in millions of pieces on the ground, just like New York had always been.

"A rage room? Seriously?" Firefly asked.

"Yeah! Oh come on, you have your foam, I have my bat!" Xeno commanded as he took another swing shattering an old TV screen. "Woo! Feels good."

The villain then tossed the bat and Firefly caught it, stumbling it in his hand.

"Try it," Xenomorph chirped.

"What?"

"Try it!"

"Oh, no."

"What? Come on!"

"No, I really shouldn't," Firefly convinced himself.

"Why not?!"

"I am a hero, I don't break things!"

"That's ridiculous,"

The two fought over each other like a bickering couple, barely waiting to take turns. Squabbling.

"Dude!" Xeno finally shouted, calling his attention, "You are *supposed* to break things here, everything is either getting destroyed or getting tossed out anyways, the only difference is letting out your rage. Come on, I wanna see fire ...literally."

Firefly's body dragged, scraping the bat on the ground as he thought.

"Just try it, you might feel better," Xeno teased, smiling.

Firefly sighed as he picked up the back and walked over another glass vase, perfectly positioned. It sat there, shining in the light. Glaring off rainbows in every direction. It was perfect.

Firefly wound up the bat and swung as hard as he could. Sending the vase shattering and flying to the wall where the glass shards exploded like fireworks in the night sky. Firefly froze from fear– not realizing he had that much power in himself.

Xeno also froze, but had the biggest, jaw-dropping smile on his face, "That…was …AMAZING!"

"R-Really?"

"Yes! Do it again! Do it again!" Xeno begged.

Firefly smiled a bit and looked around for something else, with another swing he hit a table.

"Woo! Go! Destroy him, Buggy!" Xeno yelled as Firefly beat the table senselessly. Whacking it until the wood cracked into splinters and the table split in half.

Firefly then threw a fireball at the remains of the tacky furniture. Lighting it like a blazing bonfire.

"HOLY– THAT WAS INCREDIBLE!" Xeno cheered, throwing his arms in the air.

"Woo! That felt good!" Firefly added fuel to his fire. Panting in short breaths.

"See?! Wanna break something else?" Xeno did a little move.

"…I wanna break New York." Firefly glared, spreading an evil grin across his face.

"Oh yeah?

"I'm ready to turn these streets upside down! To take down Dark Legacy and whoever is behind the setups! I'm ready to expose everything!" Firefly announced, never feeling more alive. "Let's set the Phoenix free!"

There was a fire in the hero's eyes. Xeno smiled, it wasn't a nasty, dangerous fire of destruction. It was a fire of pure passion and hope, one he'd only wish to have.

"Crashing New York? I love it, sounds like you need some help...*Phoenix*," Xeno sarcastically drew out, fluffing his white hair back. Letting it poof right back into place.

"Heck yeah, but first..." Firefly spied a bookshelf filled with breakables and wielded the bat over, beating everything within the shelves.

"YEAH!" Xeno added, kicking the boxes and books left on the ground as Firefly went off. The two went crazy, tearing up the room, breaking everything in sight, shattering any last piece of perfection on display. As the supers created havoc, Firefly took his last swing and shattered a fragile mirror.

After everything was destroyed Xeno lay on the ground, panting; looking up at the cciling. Firefly huffed and breathed heavily as he tossed the bat away. Slowly joining his friend on the ground.

Both caught their breaths, trying to think of any words to say.

"Tomorrow, everything will change," Firefly promised, still staring at the crappy ceiling.

"Yeah, it sure will Firecracker," Xeno grinned.

"Should we get going?" Firefly asked, still panting like a dying dog.

"In a few, I need a rest," Xeno drifted.

"Me too. Man, being destructive is tiring."

"I know right? Try doing it on a daily basis!" Xeno scoffed.

"Hey, like I said, it's no picnic being a hero either," Firefly mocked.

276

"Really? You guys get pancakes and fame and praise! Sounds pretty lucky to me," Xenomorph breathed.

"It's nice in front of the cameras…but behind, I feel just as trapped as the villains I send to jail…" The hero drifted, not knowing where that came from.

Xeno looked over, silently holding off for his partner in crime to continue.

"People want perfection, people need perfection, I am not perfection…" Firefly drifted, staring at the shattered glass on the floor, still sparkling, still beautiful. Just not together.

"No one is perfect…have you seen me?" Xeno asked, making a funny face.

Firefly laughed.

"No, seriously! What is my deal man?!" Xeno continued poking fun at himself.

Soon the villain's laughter slowed, "But, no one is perfect, not even heroes."

"Never thought I'd be hearing *that* from a supervillain of all things." Firefly softly admitted.

"It's a coping mechanism, made it up so I can do whatever the heck I want and chalk it up to human nature," Xeno explained, cold and calculated. Like it was just a general fact of the universe.

Firefly chuckled, "Still, heroes don't see it like that. You need to be flawless because you need to seem more than human. Only then, you can achieve hope."

"You don't seriously think you need to be Mr. Perfect to

277

'achieve hope' or whatever, right?" Xeno sneered, quoting in the air.

"No, I don't. But anyone else with a mask and a cape will say otherwise," Firefly sighed.

"You never did fit in with them, did you?" Xeno asked, already knowing the answer.

"...Nope. You?"

Xeno stared at the ceiling, thinking. Sure, no villains ever got along but some were definitely closer than others. Alliances were made. Favors were done. Teams and partners created. And Xeno was a part of none of it.

"Nah...I don't like to fit in," He bragged, trying to spin it.

Firefly hummed, "Neither do I, maybe...we could not fit in together."

Xeno's eyes grew, but he pulled back his heartstrings, "Ulgh, barf– you're such a fluffy hero."

Firefly patiently waited, knowing his friend all too well.

"...But, sounds...nice I guess," Xeno finished.

Firefly smiled, "...Wanna spray paint the walls?"

"Yes!" Xeno hopped up, feeling more excited than ever.

The rest of their rage room session was spent painting away. Firefly didn't know what to paint so he just scribbled up and down. However, when he looked over he saw Xeno actually painting something. Measuring with his hand, flipping between paints as a real shape started to form.

Firefly stopped his can, sat down, and saw Xeno spraypaint a bright red and orange bird, wings spread wide as he wrote 'Welcome to *the revolution'* in black.

Firefly felt more connected to the name now than ever, ready to rise from his week of ashes into a phoenix.

***

Xenomorph took a right turn on the sidewalk as Firefly followed. The villain scooped up some old newspapers and opened them, pretending to read to hide his face. He handed a stack to Firefly but the guy couldn't keep his head down. The city lights sparkled like another world as neon blared everywhere. With all this running around Firefly felt like he was truly getting to know his city. Instead of just maps and routes he started to know places, shops, landmarks, and so much more that made the place feel alive.

Soon, Firefly and his villainous partner snuck back over to the costume store like it was nothing. The two made eye contact with the same employee and she immediately put her hands up.

"You're going to keep quiet and do your job before you get tied up again, understood?" Xenomorph threatened with his hands making up a gun and the employee shook her head. The boys soon hid in the back corner once again as they got ready for tonight. Only this time, Firefly would be choosing his disguise. He found a rather fancy suit and a black silk tie. Buttoning up the white collar shirt and ruffling on the blazer.

"HYYYAA!" Xeno yelled as he bolted out of the dressing room curtain. He too had a fancy suit on, only in dark blue, and a motorcycle

279

helmet. You know, something totally natural and practical.

Firefly sighed as he carefully swapped his goggles for some nice shades, ones Xeno was also supposed to wear.

"What are you doing?" He asked, tired of asking that question.

"What? Don't I look cool?" He asked, posing.

Firefly hated how he wasn't technically wrong, "Dude, you are going to get us caught."

"Come on Buggy, it hides my *obvious* hair, besides everyone loves a cute biker," Xeno blew a kiss and did a little dance.

"What if someone flips up your visor?" Firefly started.

"Duh– then don't flip it up, Firecracker. I could say the same thing about you and your glasses," Xeno smirked, not that you could see it behind the helmet.

Firefly wanted to be mad, but Xeno did a silly little dance and he couldn't resist chuckling,

"Ok! Ok! You win, just be careful," Firefly warned as he started packing up.

"Weird they would have such fancy suits here?" Xeno tried to carry the conversation as he looked down at a palette of paint.

"Probably some spy costume or FBI, don't think about it too much."

Xeno quietly dug his fingers into some face paint, "Say, Buggy?"

"Yeah?"

"You don't look exactly ready for war…"

"Ready for war?" Firefly turned and was immediately greeted

by Xeno's fingers striking two lines of black paint on his cheeks. Firefly gasped at the cold paint, freezing in place at the scare.

"Now you are! Let's mess up some politicians! Woooo!" Xeno cheered as he grabbed the backpack, stuffed his suit and mask inside, and took off.

Firefly couldn't help but giggle as he followed behind, not even bothering to wipe away the war paint.

Chapter 23:

Without a ride, the two walked across town to get to the venue. The sky grew dark and Firefly was focused, as he always was. Planning moves, making escape strategies, trying not to panic.

Xeno was just being silly, hopping on the white street lines as if he were a bunny rabbit, swinging around lamp posts as they started to flicker on, and splashing in puddles. He always seemed to enjoy life, savoring every minute. Whether he was doing it on purpose or not: Firefly had no idea, but he wished he could enjoy life like that. Here they were, walking to a death trap and Xeno still danced every step of the way.

Xeno kicked his feet around until he noticed Firefly's cold demeanor.

"Hey, relax, don't think of it as a mission, think of it as a party!" Xeno said as he slowed down, walking next to his partner in crime.

"W-What?"

"You're nervous," Xenomorph stated.

"How…did you–?"

"I know nervous when I see it, Buggy, and you get nervous a *lot*!"

"Ok, fair, but how are you *not* nervous? You were tense a couple hours ago? I mean we are purposely walking towards Dark Legacy and Governor Jaceson—who also wants us dead! How can you remain calm?"

"Rage room."

"Right…" Firefly ended, sounding defeated.

Xeno could tell that wasn't the answer Firefly was looking for so he took a deep breath and tried again, "I'm not worried…because I have you."

Firefly's eyes widened as he looked at the helmet. The helmet looked back. Glazing the villain in mystery.

Eventually, Xeno looked ahead and kept walking.

Firefly stopped under the next lamppost as Xeno could feel his presence lingering behind. He stopped as well, turning around.

"You ok, Firecracker?" He asked rhetorically, acting like he didn't care.

"How do you just– do that…?" Firefly paused as the wind blew.

"Talking? It is a pretty simple concept–"

"No, no! How do you just say…stuff!"

"'Say…stuff'?" Xeno repeated, not getting it.

"Just– ugh– you always know what to say, and how to live. Despite everything. How do you still have hope and still have fun?"

"Whoa easy Buggy, fun is a villain's game."

"Not really…it's just, a life thing…you know?" Firefly tried.

"I'm going to be honest– ...no, I have absolutely no idea what you're saying. Are you tripping?"

Firefly chuckled, "Maybe, just...it takes me weeks to come up with some sort of fluffy, inspirational, hero junk to tell the media...and you just say it like that." The hero snapped his fingers to demonstrate the point.

"You try too hard man, I just say what's on my mind. No harm in that," Xeno smiled through his disguise.

"Exactly! How do I not try so hard?"

"First step is to stop asking stupid questions like that," Xenomorph sneered.

Firefly deadpanned, "'Haha. Very funny,' but still how do you not worry about death or getting caught?"

"I don't know. Don't really have time to think about it, too busy living," Xeno answered, bouncing on the tips of his boots a bit. With that he continued forward, still dancing on the sidewalk as he slid.

Firefly couldn't tell if the conversation was over or never happened in the first place, but in an odd way, he liked not knowing. Maybe that's what Xeno was talking about, he didn't know the villain under the mask, he didn't know this whole week would spin out of control, he didn't know about the staged fights...but he still was having fun, the most fun in a long time.

The hero breathed, guess it was true. Why worry? Xeno couldn't control the world, not to mention his life; but he kept going strong, dancing to whatever pop girl was running around in his head this time.

The corner of his mouth began to rise as he followed the dancing queen down the concrete, trying to follow in his steps. However he wasn't a very good dancer—or one at all. A quick learner yes, but without a guide he looked like a fish out of water. Since that first night, he always was.

"Do you want food?" Xeno asked out of nowhere.

"Food? Like, right now?"

"Yeah," Xeno asked, nudging Firefly a little.

"Aren't we going to a party?"

"Nah~ I mean—well, yes, but it's a fancy party. There will be like bite size foods and cocktail weenies...haha," Xeno laughed at himself.

Firefly chuckled, "Oh, ok. Well sure, food sounds great, what are you thinking?"

***

Next thing Firefly knew Xeno ran down the street and had stopped at a brightly lit, neon fast food drive-thru. Firefly looked at the restaurant in all of its...um 'glory'. Xeno soon walked on the paved road and completely missed the door.

"Um...dude? Where are you going?" Firefly asked, following behind.

"Drive-thru, it's faster," Xeno explained as he walked through the drive-thru in his fancy blue suit and biker helmet.

The neon red, yellow, and blue glow shined on him as he got to the menu board, staring at all the options. Firefly was so confused, but his stomach wasn't. It growled and he didn't want to not eat, and Xeno was ordering anyway.

Firefly hurried to Xenomorph's side to look at the flashbang that was the white menu screen.

"Hmm, I'm thinking a number two, no pickles, with fries, a root beer, and a toy."

"Seriously? You want a toy?"

Xeno slowly turned his helmet, "...*More than anything*..." he announced dramatically.

Soon the speaker buzzed as a gentleman came on.

"Hey guys, welcome to Super Burgers where our service is as fast and strong as a real superhero! My name is Michael. What can I get started for you today?" He cheered through the metal box.

Xeno deadpanned at it all, it was so– blah. Regardless he still readied his order, and his demand for a toy.

"I'll have a number two, no pickles, and a–" Xeno started.

"I'm sorry, sir, you guys need a vehicle to enter the drive-thru," Michael said, sounding less cheery.

Xeno looked behind them, "But there's no one here."

"Sorry guys, rules are rules, if you'd like to order you can come inside."

"Wha– my bike is literally right over there!" Xeno pointed out of view.

"What? No, it's not–" Firefly added.

Xenomorph covered his mouth, "Shush."

"Guys, please come inside," Michael begged, he wasn't being paid enough to deal with this.

"Ok! No problem, sorry Michael," Firefly started to shove Xeno, but he stayed still as a rock and stopped Firefly with his hand.

"Oh no...we aren't going anywhere until I get my burger...and *my toy*."

"Sir, aren't you too old for a toy?" Michael tried.

"Say that again mister!!" Xeno readied up a ball of fire, ready to aim it at the voice box. Firefly quickly grabbed his hand and yanked it down.

"Aye man! Cool it," Firefly tried.

The villain breathed, "Ok, sorry, clearly you can see us. We probably look ridiculous."

"Yeah sorry guys, everything is on tape," Michael drifted.

"And where exactly would that be?" Xeno asked.

"On the corner of the building?"

Xeno looked to see the little camera, "Oh yeah~ I see it," he chuckled, "Silly thing~ haha, man I bet you can see everything, like THIS!" Xeno threw his free hand up ready to send an unfriendly gesture before Firefly blocked him, pulling his hand back down.

"Hey! Easy, man! Michael, I am so sorry!" Firefly struggled against Xeno who was raving about ketchup and hamburgers and stupid service.

"This happens twice a week, you're fine," Michael sighed.

"Look, my buddy is just not comfortable with people, as you can tell. Can we please just walk through? Just this once, we will tip you obviously," Firefly tried.

Michael sighed, "Alright and for you, the nice one,"

"Oh um one number four, extra crispy, a side of hot fries and–,"

"A Chocolate milkshake!" Xeno yelled.

"What?!"

"Alright, that'll be $13.99 at the window," he spat like nothing.

"Yes! See Buggy, flawless planning," Xeno calmed down as he approached the menu, pressing on it like a threat, "A don't you dare forget about my toy 'Michael' if that is even your real name?"

"Sir, the window…I beg of you," Michael whined defeatedly.

Firefly quickly strolled on the road that led to the window as Xeno followed, giving the 'I'm watching you' signal to the camera.

Firefly quickly got to the window and they were soon handed a bag and two drinks, by a kid with black hair and tired eyes.

"Thank you so much, I promise we will never bother you again," He rushed as he quickly stuck a wad of cash into the jar.

"You remember my toy right? And no pickles?" Xeno grilled the worker.

"Yes sir. Everything is just how you want it, now please leave," Michael begged starting to close the little, glass door, "A bachelor's in Political Science better be worth it," he mumbled as the window shut.

Firefly and Xenomorph walked down the drive-thru road and out onto the curb. They both sat down as the night slowly grew darker. Watching the sky, taking out their perfectly constructed burgers, and unwrapping them. Xeno took a swig of his soda as Firefly pondered.

"Why did you get me a chocolate milkshake?" He asked,

picking it up.

"Because you need chocolate, plus it seemed to calm you down back at the ice cart. We went to the rage room for me, only seems fair," Xeno shared a small smile as he lifted his visor halfway so he could eat.

"You remembered?"

Xeno took a big, juicy bite of his burger, "Of course I did," he said, mouth full. No pickles, Michael nailed it.

Firefly took a sip of his shake and it did feel amazing. So cool and refreshing, yet so sweet and silky, how he missed chocolate.

Xeno ate some fries as he looked up, stars finally starting to peak out, "What's your favorite moth?"

"Excuse me?" Firefly choked on his milkshake.

"Your favorite moth? Which one is it?" Xenomorph repeated.

"I don't believe I have one?" Firefly smiled, confused.

"Mine's those really fluffy, white ones with the big eyes," Xeno answered as he took another bite.

Firefly laughed, "That is not how you ask a question, bro!"

"What?! Ok, you do better!" Xeno challenged.

"What's your favorite color?" Firefly asked.

"That's such a basic question! But blue, next question."

"Well, mine is red, thanks for asking," Firefly sassed.

"What's the worst seat on an airplane?" Xeno asked.

"Beats me, haven't been on one. Super hero stuff…"

"Same," Xeno laughed as Firefly joined him.

Firefly munched on his fries, "Ok, Ok, what's the most annoying thing to do in public?"

Xeno bursted out laughing, "Probably what we just did," he fell onto his friend as they both cracked up. The villain breathed as he started again, "Do you believe in astrology?"

Firefly paused, really thinking, "In a way...yeah, but not like most people."

"What does that mean?" Xeno asked, sipping his root beer.

"I don't really believe in zodiacs or stuff like that, though it is interesting. But I believe something is in those stars, maybe stories from old heroes, legends we haven't found yet, or just someone helping us through life. Who knows, maybe they are just a physical depiction of our dreams and wishes, spread across the sky..."

"...I'm an Aries," Xeno said, after a while.

"Pff– that makes *so* much sense," Firefly smirked.

Xeno looked back up, "But your answer is pretty cool too I guess."

"...What do you want to be remembered for?" Firefly asked, ready to finally meet the real person under the helmet.

Xeno froze on his straw, "Wow...that's a bit...deep ain't it?"

"Sorry, too much?"

"No...just...I don't know, haven't really had to think about it. I don't really get a say in my life," Xenomorph answered depressingly as he took another bite of his burger. "What about you?"

"Hmm, I guess I just want to spread good and virtue. I know I can be a better hero once this whole ordeal is behind us, you know? I just want to leave a legacy people can look up to. Say 'I want to be like him', I want to help others. Make an impact...and other 'fluffy' stuff like that," Firefly poked fun at himself, knowing Xeno would already do it.

"Sounds nice," the villain nodded.

Firefly stood stunned, "No jab? No joke? Nothing?"

"Hey, I'm one to talk. I've got nothing on that, I wish I had even a fraction of an idea."

"Well aren't you going to be a hero when this is over?"

"Hey, that's still a maybe."

"A maybe is not a no," Firefly smiled.

"Regardless, I don't know what type of hero I want to be...not that I want to be one," he 'saved'.

"Oh yeah, totally," Firefly sassed, giving him a hard time.

"We'll just, everyone has their thing: honesty, kindness, hope," Xeno gestured to Firefly, "and those just...aren't me. I'm chaotic and fun and reckless– not a very good role model, maybe I wouldn't make a good hero either," he drifted in thought as he chewed on the top of his straw.

"Hey, don't say that, you would be an awesome hero! Sorry about my question, you don't *have* to be remembered as something if you don't want to, that's ok."

"...The strange thing is I do. I just can't for the life of me figure out what," Xeno thought, what would his *thing* be? What would he be known for?

"...I bet the middle seat on a plane sucks," Firefly tried to lighten the mood.

"Oh yeah?" Xeno asked.

"If it's anything like the bus; yes. I bet my life on it," Firefly snickered.

Xeno joined him as they both continued to eat and ask the most random questions on the most random night.

Chapter 24:

Soon the questions ended and the burgers were finished. The boys grabbed their bags, got up, and continued on to Governor Jaceson's party; Xeno dancing all the way there.

Firefly watched him behind his shades until they both turned the corner and their mouths dropped.

The venue was everything you could have dreamed of. A giant glass cube, cut with beautiful detail and covered in what looked to be diamonds. Layers of floors inside with flooding yellow lights, making the whole party look like a Hollywood event. A red carpet led to the front doors, red rope blocking off the paparazzi. Greenery and plants dotted their way around gracefully. It was grand enough to be a museum or a billionaire's mansion.

Both supers froze as they looked at their sparkly, shiny, glamorous demise.

"Ok...this is it," Firefly tried being confident.

"Totally, we got this," Xeno started as they walked across the street.

They hid behind some topiary looking as celebrities and politicians walked on the carpet. Luckily there was a backdrop for the cameras that covered the two as they hopped over the rope. Sneakily coming out from behind the backdrop and stepping onto the velvet red carpet like it was planned.

Firefly grabbed him back, "Just lay low, please...don't cause attention."

"I won't," Xeno whined.

"And the helmet stays *on*. At all times."

"Yes 'mom', don't worry, I'll lay low...low, low, low, low, low," Xeno joked as he indeed got low and hit the floor.

Firefly watched him, trying to hide his chuckle.

Xeno jumped up and they both walked down the red trail. Blinded by bright lights and camera flashes. It was sort of familiar to Firefly—given all the interviews—but that didn't mean he hated it any less. He shielded his eyes as he walked.

Xenomorph did the same, covering his helmet. The paparazzi called out to them, sticking mics in their faces and rushing questions, but the two ignored everyone and hurried up the steps.

They got into the glass container that was the party and breathed. Xeno panted forward as Firefly looked around, googling at the place. It was just as priceless as the outside.

Crystalized chandeliers hung from every ceiling space, and an installed-bar top with the most expensive bottles of alcohol. A music system set up in the back with some sort of DJ behind the spinning records. Ice sculptures instead of lampposts and waiters in white ready to serve on the dance floor. And this was only floor one!

"Yes! A bar! Thank goodness– I need a drink!" Xeno exclaimed, already heading in that direction.

Firefly blocked him, "Oh heck no. I need you sober for this mission. We are too vulnerable. Dark Legacy could be anyone…"

"Dang…I hope he's the bar lady."

"Alcohol is bad for you anyways!" Firefly snared.

"But that's my thing! Bad and fun, c'mon you should know me better by now," Xeno smirked under the helmet.

"You can have one drink– *after* we find some proof! We can't screw this up!"

"Ok, ok, deal," Xeno shook his partner's hand and walked with Firefly. He looked around to admire the fancy room, tweaking his head to the side in curiosity, "Huh, someone's compensating for something."

Firefly flinched in the confusion that was that sentence, "What does that even mean?"

"It's just really nice…" Xeno drifted.

"Ok, I hate to break it to you, but everything is nicer than your dump of an HQ," Firefly explained.

"But he's just a governor right?"

"I guess?"

"This is like, really overboard. Does the governor even make this kind of money? With all this flair, I'd think he was robbing banks with us or something," Xeno explained as he slowly spun in place, looking up at the ceiling to watch the crystal sparkle in the light.

"Huh…now that you say it, it's a bit flashy. Could be putting this money back into the city, but that's besides the point. We aren't here to look at decorations and architecture—or discuss his horrible political decisions, we are here to catch Dark Legacy. Now, what does he look like?"

"..."

Firefly looked over at Xeno who stood too still for a confident answer, "You don't know?!"

"Of course I don't! Dark Legacy never takes off his mask!"

"What?! How are we supposed to find him?! Xeno!" Firefly yelled, the smell of smoke soon returned.

"Oh like you know Captain Peace's real identity?!"

"That's different!"

"How is that different?!"

"Just—!" Firefly started to glow as little flames started to spark.

Xeno quickly noticed, and without hesitation; turned to a server, grabbed a cocktail, and threw it at Firefly. Dousing him in the fruity drink; making him dripping wet and smelling like cherries.

Firefly stood still in utter annoyance, but he knew Xeno was just trying to help. If they got exposed here it was game over. Powers were off limits.

The hero collected himself as he whipped his face with his sleeve smudging his war paint.

"Sorry..." Xeno tried.

"It's fine...I was burning up, wasn't I?"

"You looked like a fire truck on fire."

"How is that even possi—you know what, never mind. New

plan, I'll search around to find any dirt on the Governor, the files, your foster care history, anything; you stay on the floor and search for Dark Legacy, you can feel others' powers, right?"

"Yeah?"

"Good, you'll be our compass, please tell me you've spoken to Dark Legacy before."

"Yes, idiot," Xeno snarred.

"Ok then try to listen to his voice too, any mannerisms, anything is *vital* to finding him," Firefly explained.

"Wait– we are splitting up?!"

"Yes, pay attention."

"Uh– like hell we are! What if something goes wrong?!"

"Then just get out and I'll meet you back at Super Burgers," Firefly answered like it was nothing.

"What if you *don't* make it out?!" Xeno asked again with a little more panic in his tone.

Firefly was at first offended, *Wow, haha, I get it. I must not be able to get out because I'm an 'incompetent superhero' and I'm 'nothing without The Great Xenomorph'* he sassed to himself.

However, as he gathered up the words to say it, he realized it wasn't a jab or an insult, it was concern. Real genuine concern.

"Are–...are you afraid of us splitting up?"

"YES!" Xeno wailed, not believing he was admitting it, "When we split up, bad things happen! What if you're caught again? What if you get arrested? What if we are separated and we never see each other again?!"

Firefly froze.

"…B-Because then the mission can't continue," Xeno tried.

Firefly just smiled, then rushed to hug his friend, squeezing him tight, "I'll be fine, Xeno, I promise."

Xeno hugged him back, squeezing him tighter than ever before. How so much had changed, a week ago he couldn't even imagine high-fiving Firefly, now he didn't ever want to let go.

Firefly soon left the hug and just knocked on his helmet, "Stay safe ok? Meet back at the bar in an hour."

"Bar! Yes!" Xeno yelled as he ran off excited to start his happy hour. Firefly giggled, secretly bribing him on purpose.

With the rules set, it was time to start the game and so Firefly started walking around, hoping to find something.

***

Xeno ran to the dance floor which was filled with people, slowing down as he ruffled up his sleeves. Carefully scanning his surroundings. His white hair dangled in front of his eyes as he people-watched.

Xeno took each guest in,

- *Girl in red dress, black hair, brown eyes.*
- *Blonde in green dress, tight bun, blue eyes.*
- *Tall, brunette guy in black suit, blue eyes.*
- *Redhead in purple dress, big bow on the back, freckles, black eyes.*

298

- *Short, blonde guy in an obnoxious red suit, light eyes.*

- *Blue dress, brown hair, brown eyes, diamond earrings.*

Remembering the details, he slipped by the women in blue and with a sly of hand took her earrings,

- *Blue dress, brown hair, brown eyes, no earrings*

He jotted down from memory and continued, sticking the shiny, sharp, and blue jewelry in his pockets.

Xeno was quiet, stayed out of conversations and stayed off to the side. He listened out for voices and felt around for powers, but he was getting nothing; yet everything? It felt like a bunch of different powers on top of each other. Screaming in agony. Blah– it was nauseating.

He eventually grabbed another cocktail off the serving trays being passed around and swirled it, still watching. Ignoring the odd sense of chaos in the room.

People gave him weird stares, whispering, gossiping, but he didn't care. Only two people knew why they were really there, and those were the only two people whose opinions mattered.

The chatter overlapped as Xeno went to sip his drink, but he stopped himself remembering Firefly's wish. The music blared sick club music as he sighed, trying to stay focused, but all the rainbow stage lights were so very tempting.

Xeno started slowly grooving to the beat, but soon a groove turned into a full on jam session with the glass drink still in his hands. Dancing as if no one was watching, but as he was rocking out he heard something—

"Yes, I am sure everything will be fine," a voice said, but Xeno froze halfway through his sick move as he'd recognized that commanding dark voice anywhere.

Xeno saluted as fast as he could out of instinct, his heart beating in his ears. The villain looked around but saw no one facing him that was matching the voice. Slowly putting his arm down, he walked through the party again. Thoughts spiraling as he tried to find the owner of that cruel voice.

"I was dealt a bad hand with these wild cards, but I have an ace up my sleeve…"

The party started to spin, playing mind games as he grew lost within the sea of people. Circling around crowds, laughter ringing throughout the walls. The villain didn't fully understand how trapped he was until that very moment. The chains never felt tighter.

Xeno kept looking for someone, anyone! Still no red flags raised as the voice continued to talk. Mumbling about superheroes and political nonsense. He followed the voice until it left the dance floor. Someone rounded a corner. *That had to be him.* Xeno bolted around, sliding on his shoes when—

BAM!

Xeno slammed into someone different, spilling a drink on the unsuspecting victim.

"OW! Ugh– oh shoot– I am so sorry, are you ok!" Xenomorph rushed, looking the person right in the eyes but his pulse ran cold. It wasn't Dark Legacy…It was Governor Jaceson.

The governor's sour look turned into a smile as he started

wiping the stain away with a fancy, cloth napkin,

"Ah– no sweat, Sir. Happens to the best of us," The governor looked up, trying to look him in the eyes, but the biker visor was very dark.

"Say…that's an interesting piece of equipment you got on there? Any reason?"

Xeno held the helmet on tight, he wasn't wearing his bandana; if the helmet came off now it was game over.

"Nope! No reason! I just look dashing as hell! And I'm hot—really, really hot! The girls– man I can't get them off me! So it's best to just hide! I hate the attention, Mr. Governor sir!" Xeno rambled, uncomfortably.

The Governor laughed, "Haha! I get it, the lights, the cameras, the crowds, it's not everyone's thing…but…I'm sorry, you sound familiar~? Do I know you?"

Xeno gritted his teeth in fear, of course the Governor had heard him. Who hadn't heard his evil monologues?

"Oh no! Nope! I'm a complete stranger!" Xeno answered quickly, although a part of him was thinking the same thing.

"…In my house party?"

"Well– you know me– but you just don't *know* know me, you know what I mean?" Xeno tried.

"…A name, kid."

"Ah– right– I am…" he looked over his shoulder trying to find something, "…uh…" he spied the elegant bathroom door, "John…Adams?"

"…Like the second president?"

"PFF– no– that's so funny, I am messing with you!" Xeno forced his laugh and lied, looking for something else to pull from, struggling until his eyes landed on an indoor fireplace, "My name is…um…Phoenix~?"

"Whoa, how extraordinary! I can see why you went with 'John'," Governor Jaceson laughed.

'Phoenix' forced a laugh, playing along, "Well that's not my real real name– my real real name is uh– Michael…but I go by Phoenix."

"Ah I see, so pray tell Phoenix, what are you doing here?" Jaceson asked.

"Well, I am a man of the people, good sir, and I plan to hear about your diabolical plan of capturing the vigilantes," Xeno tried, trying to grab some dirt while he could.

"Diabolical?" The politician laughed, "You flatter me kid, but no we are just going to have the subjects turned in."

"Huh, that doesn't sound so bad."

The governor gave him a confused look.

"I-If I were them– but I'm not– just Phoenix," Xeno nervously laughed, mumbling to himself, "Why is it so hard to be cool right now…"

"Well I mean they won't just be taken in, obviously they will be punished and have their powers revoked."

Xeno stood still, "P-Powers revoked…? I-Is that even possible? I mean powers come from the blood, right? You can't just drain a

302

superhuman…r-right?"

"Hey, that's correct! How did you know that?" Governor Jaceson smiled and asked, impressed by the mysterious person in front of him.

"O-Oh, I heard a um, rumor…"

"Well rest assured, no one will be hurt, I have actually assembled an amazing science team and we've been working on this for months. We were originally going to use it to destroy the villains, but the vigilantes are a much bigger problem."

"The vigilantes are a bigger threat than the villains?" Xeno asked sarcastically, making sure he had that right. Sure he was flattered, but something about that didn't make sense.

"In a way, yes, Xenomorph has gone completely off the rails, nothing new for our city, but still worrying. However Firefly is the one I'm concerned about…"

"…Oh?" Xeno asked, afraid to hear the answer.

"Yeah, villains running around, cause havoc; it's life here. Classic New York, sadly. But Firefly turning evil like this—the city is in chaos. We can't trust him anymore. People are afraid and questioning all of our heroes. He puts every hero's reputation in jeopardy…he has broken all the trust the city has built and for what?

Firefly has to go."

Xeno gasped and took a step back, bumping into a nice potted plant.

"You alright, Phoenix?"

"I'm fine! I'm fine! Completely fine! Completely just

standard!" Xeno jumped.

"I hope I didn't scare you with the whole Firefly is a villain now thing. I mean, I would be pretty worried too if that flamethrowing manic was at large."

Xeno bit his tongue hard, he wanted to explode at this guy. Defend his friend as Firefly was anything but a villain, but he'd cause a scene and suspicion, then it was really game over. *Lay low*— Xeno swallowed his pride and nodded along.

"But again, I, your great Governor, have a plan and no one will be hurt. Both villains will be taken care of," The politician finished, patted his shoulder, and walked away.

As soon as he left, Xeno gave him an unfriendly gesture and retched under his helmet. Hating that guy even more than when he walked in here. Jaceson didn't deserve his power or the city. Xeno rushed away, he had to tell Firefly about the plan—or at least half of it. The Governor did keep his cards close to his chest after.

Xeno ran down the carpet looking for any signs of his Buggy. Firefly might have been furious he let Dark Legacy go, but this new target on their backs was too important. Besides they still had hours until the party was over, everything would be fine.

Chapter 25:

Firefly walked up the marble steps, entering a more house-like area; although with glass in the ceiling and art pieces everywhere, it could pass as a museum. He walked through the exhibit, passing all sorts of paintings along the wall.

Firefly did a double-take when he saw one of the Mona Lisa. He looked down as he read the plaque about the history of the painting. At the very bottom *Decoy* was edged out in gold letters.

Firefly was instantly taken back to the time the Mona Lisa was imported from Paris to New York City for a display showcase; however, it was stolen by the villains. Never to be seen again. That day was a hard loss for the heroes.

Firefly breathed as he continued down the halls, looking at more famous paintings and art pieces, he eventually came across display cases.

Tons of them, some of them being replicas of priceless artifacts and pieces of history. Others being just jewelry and bling. Firefly walked past a small display filled with diamonds, no bigger than a quarter.

The hero bent down, examining the little jewels. They were cut in many different shapes and styles; glistening in the light as Firefly rubbed his head. *Where have I seen these before?*

He stopped pondering when he found no answer and continued. Soon, he walked up to a huge, glittering red crystal. Incase in glass and under a spotlight. The flecks of gold shined like the stars of the sky.

Firefly admired the thing, wondering what it must have cost; it was almost as big as him!

"Hey!"

Firefly jumped as he turned around.

A woman approached in a green mermaid dress, her chestnut hair in a messy bun with little flowers pinned in at all different sides. She had a nasty burn mark on her face, which Firefly immediately felt empathy for.

"…Step away from the goldstone," She threatened coldly.

"Oh, sorry ma'am! I was just looking– trust me I had no intentions on taking it," Firefly backed away from the case.

The woman's mouth curled up into a smile, "Pff, I'm teasing," she padded him up.

Firefly breathes in relief, "Oh thank goodness."

"Goldstone, huh?" She asked, making conversation. "Rumor has it this heap of rock has meaning behind it."

"Oh yeah? What is the meaning?" Firefly asked intrigued.

"Empowerment, ambition, drive. It's legended to assist in aiding goals at any level. No matter how challenging, kind or cruel."

Firefly went back to staring at the thing. Out of all the rich, pricy gems in the world, why this one?

"You still trying to take it?" The lady asked rhetorically.

"Oh no! No! I'm just looking! I swear on my life," Firefly stuttered.

"I know, you are way too casual to be a thief, and there's no way *you're* carrying that out."

"Oh, are you a cop?" Firefly asked, already nervous.

"Something like that, although one could argue a cop doesn't do anything in New York. I am a *real* hero...*that's my job.* " She muttered.

However as she said that line Firefly froze, remembering those words. Like a script he could never forget. He looked over to recognize one of his own ex-coworkers. She had no mask and her smile was brighter, but it was Rosethorn in the flesh. The burn mark stained like a taunt as he realized–

I did that...

Firefly whipped his head around as he saw two gentlemen behind them, a brown haired fellow in a black suit with a yellow tie and a buff blond with a red suit Yellow Jacket and Mighty Strength.

Oh no...

The heroes are here! Governor Jaceson probably invited them as security, or maybe they're here for Dark Legacy! This is bad– Firefly thought to himself, he was a wanted criminal now, and Xenomorph...was still a villain to them.

"You ok?" Rosethorn asked

"WHAT?! YES! Yes! I'm fine! Totally fine! Will you please excuse me for a second? I have to um…go check on my friend– he's in the bathroom– he has a peeing problem!"

Rosethorn gave him a confused stare.

"You know what– you didn't need to know that, I'll just go!" Firefly started to backtrack.

"Whoa– already? I didn't…scare you, did I?" She asked, but it was more cold and dark than genuine concern. Suspicion lining her eyes.

"Not at all Madam, it was nice talking to you. I just have to run, you know how it is– Governor, drinks, um– Go New York! Woo!" Firefly rambled as he backed into a random guest.

"Ah– sorry," Firefly apologized and turned around to get out of there as soon as he could, he had to tell Xeno about the heroes. He could maybe get out of the drama, but Xeno? With no proof? He was just a sitting duck! He needed to get out of here!

Firefly finally turned the corner and sprinted off, taking off like a silver bullet.

Rosethorn watched him leave, confused, the two gentlemen looked at her ready to follow orders.

"…Keep an eye on him."

She commanded as Yellow Jacket nodded and left.

Firefly ran down the hallway as he tried to lose the superheroes, pushing past crowds and turning corners. The hero looked back, and instantly regretted it as the guy in the black suit and yellow tie was following close behind.

Firefly took a hard right and hid behind a plant, stiffening up to not be seen. Yellow Jacket walked a bit, looking around the hall, but he didn't see the suspect despite him being right there. The bumblebee turned around and walked off like nothing happened.

Firefly breathed and ducked into the closest room he could find, slamming the door shut behind him and sliding to the white tiled floor in relief. The rest of the bleaching white bathroom blinded him. What was he doing? The sneaking around? The lying? He felt so dirty, ironic considering he was in the bathroom.

Firefly sat up and walked to the sink, taking off his shades and turning on the tap. His reflection swayed in the mirror, but it was blurred and quickly ruined after he splashed the water up his eyes. He cupped the liquid and doused his face a couple more times. Rubbing his skin.

Firefly refreshed his train of thought and got a hold of himself. He needed to regroup, and not just in his mind. He sighed as he placed back on the shades and slipped out the door. Carefully watching everyone to make sure there were no more super surprises.

Firefly kept his head low, but that didn't stop him from finding more heroes through the crowd, Tidal Wave, Time Traveler, Solar Eclipse, and more. They were *all* here.

Eventually after many long halls and stairs later he got to some sort of balcony, *Man this place really was big.* He looked over the steel railing and glass planes to see the dance floor; No biker helmet in sight.

"Shoot, Xeno…" Firefly mumbled to himself as he kept a lookout. Tapping the silver railing as he tried to find Waldo— or Xeno.

"You alright?" Said a firm voice.

Firefly flinched and turned around to see Governor Jaceson right there with two drinks.

"G-Governor, sir, what are you doing here?" Firefly asked...like an idiot.

"It's my party? At my venue?" The governor tried with a smile.

"Right," Firefly smiled back, secretly face palming inside his head.

"You ok? You look stressed," The governor approached him.

"Oh yeah, I'm fine, I just lost someone," Firefly waved off.

"Oh? Well, firstly, let's get you a drink. Helps those worries disappear," The governor offered, shoving the glass into his hands.

"Oh– oh– no thank you, I don't drink."

"What? Really? That's new," He laughed, "But seriously I insist..."

"I um..." Firefly tried, but before he could do anything the Governor raised his cup for him and shoved it in his mouth. Firefly took a big sip and shuddered at the awful taste. "Blaugh– ugh– mm...that's– um... distinct."

"It's the finest whiskey around! Now maybe I can help with your little lost friend?"

"Uh~ sure~..." Firefly tried. Not that he wanted to trust the very soul who was after him, but regardless he brushed it aside. As he did need to find Xeno as fast as possible before the heroes did, "He's my height, very cocky, dances a lot, oh and has a biker helmet; have you seen him?"

Firefly went for another sip, although it tasted just as bad as the first time.

"Oh, Phoenix?"

Firefly spit out his drink, "PFF– WHAT?!"

"Phoenix, the kid with the helmet?"

"…Uh– y-yeah…I guess that is him?"

"Yeah, I was just down there talking to him," He pointed to the bottom floor, "dude seemed in a hurry or nervous. Guess you have that in common, it's a shame you two don't lighten up. I mean it's a party after all," he laughed.

Firefly pulse started to chill as worry immediately filled his stomach. *Why was Xeno nervous? Was he in danger? Was he captured?*

"Y-Yeah! Party! Woo!" Firefly tried taking another sip and started to leave, "B-But I'm going to go find him, thank you Governor Jaceson and, um, good luck with your speech!" Firefly finished and ran off.

The governor watched him go, scowl slowly creeping up as he didn't trust the strange kid. He did sound a bit too familiar after all. Something was up.

***

Firefly got to the main floor and looked around at everything, wandering the busy floor. He took another sip of his drink as the flavor started to simmer.

He kept bumping into people, apologizing as he scoured the

lands of the rich and glamorous. Spinning around with his thoughts. Although he still could not find his friend in the helmet.

Defeated, he stumbled over to the bar, where he was served another drink and took it. Letting the cold liquid run down his throat. Trying to drown his anxiety in alcohol. The taste finally started to fade as he kept going.

Firefly had just about finished his second drink when he heard giggling. He turned to his side to see two ladies staring at him. Uncomfortably.

They were gorgeous to any sane person. Long flowing dresses, wavy hair, stunning eyes, jewelry running up their limbs like veins in a beaded fashion statement.

Firefly squinted at them, for all he could see were blurs of fabrics and makeup. They weren't unattractive, but his brain started to blank as he kept drinking.

After what felt like an eternity, one of the ladies walked over. She wore a red dress and had long, black hair. Brown eyes, some loud red lipstick, and tiny white pearls hanging around her neck.

"Hey, handsome," she strung out.

Firefly looked behind him to see the handsome guy, but no one was there.

The lady just laughed, "Yes, I'm talking to you."

"M-Me?" Firefly stuttered.

"Yes~ silly!" The lady answered and got close, really close.

Firefly flinched back.

"Are you here all by yourself?" She asked.

"N-No I came with my friend," Firefly answered, confused.

"Ooo~ double bonus, is he hot too?"

"Hot? Um…I…don't know?" Firefly tried, her words strung together like gibberish. Was hot a code? Did she know he was Firefly? Or was he just missing something?

"Aww, well I'll keep you company while you wait," she offered.

"N-No no…I'm good."

The lady laughed and put her hand on his shoulder, "Ugh~ you are just too cute, so…do you have a girlfriend~?"

Firefly's heart dropped, and not in a good way, "U-Uh…n-no…"

The lady started holding his face, getting really comfy and clingy.

"Aww~ that's too bad, you're quite the catch."

Firefly gulped, "R-Really? Because I'm not 'catch' material," He kept trying.

The lady laughed again, "You're so funny, I bet you're tons of fun, I'm tons of fun too."

Firefly blushed, "M-Meaning?" He scooted back.

"Dancing! Partying! Drinking! Other things," She looked Firefly up and down, although her eyes stayed down for a bit too long.

"Oh no, no, no, no– I don't dance– or drink," Firefly defended.

"You finished that glass awful quickly, Mr. 'I don't drink'," She sassed back.

Firefly looked at the empty glass– *since when was it empty?*

"Come on, you and me; let's go!"

"S-Sorry, but no, I have to find my friend," Firefly declined.

"Trust me, he will be ok. Let's go have some fun," The lady grabbed his hand, holding it tight as if they were a thing—they were not.

Firefly never wanted to punch a civilian more in his life.

Firefly yanked his hand back, "N-No! I'm good ma'am."

"Oo~ playing hard to get, alright~…well I know what'll make you change your mind~," She sang and grabbed his face, brushing the hair out of his face and puckering up her lips as she grew closer–

Firefly could barely process what was happening until a gloved hand intercepted the kiss.

The lady flinched back, disgusted by the taste of leather. Firefly jumped back afraid of the close call.

"Excuse me!" A voice entered. Firefly sighed in relief as he would recognize *that* voice from anywhere.

He turned to his side to see his friend, still masked up and in his dashing suit, but it was him. *Thank Captain.*

"What are you doing?" Xeno asked in a squeaky voice.

"Excuse you! We were in the middle of something," the lady whined.

"Yeah, something gross!"

"Would you just mind your own business?"

"You mean the business of why are you making moves on *my* man?!" Xeno sassed.

Firefly froze, "your *w h a t…?*"

"Woah– woah– woah– wait– he said he was single."

"No~ he said he didn't have a girlfriend, so move it homewrecker. He's been off the market for three years, and I'm not putting him up for sale, he doesn't even like you anyway– so shoo!" Xeno shooed.

The lady scoffed and walked away, her friend closely followed. As soon as they were out of sight Xeno dropped his feminine pose and pitched-up voice.

"Phew– that was close…" The villain sighed, stretching.

"…What the heck was that?!" Firefly yelled, face turning pink.

"Me saving your butt, you're welcome."

"But– how– you– huh?!"

"Relax, I was faking! That's how you get girls to leave you alone," Xenomorph explained.

"…Oh, thank you." Firefly started, tapping his glass, "…Are you–?"

"No," Xeno interrupted, swiftly and coldly.

"Oh. …Really?"

"*Pff*– yes you jerk."

Firefly chuckled, "Sorry, you were really convincing!"

"Or maybe you're just into it~?"

"No~ho!" Firefly laughed off.

"Ah that's right, you have Quinn," Xeno puckered up and kissed the air.

Firefly sighed, "Sure, if that's what you wanna call it."

After a second of silence, Firefly realized–

"WAIT– WHERE HAVE YOU BEEN?! I've been looking everywhere for you!"

Xeno jumped, remembering the urgent situation, "ME?! *I've* been looking everywhere for you! We've got a problem!"

"You're darn right we do–"

And at the same time the boys blurted out;

"THE HEROES ARE HERE!"

"THE GOVERNOR WANTS YOU ARRESTED!"

"YOU NEED TO GO!"

"YOU NEED TO GO!"

"Wait–WHAT?!"

"Wait–WHAT?!"

"Ok, ok, one at a time!" Firefly interrupted, "You first."

"Ok! Ok! So I was looking for Dark Legacy, and I found him."

"YOU WHAT?! Where is he? *Who* is he?"

"I don't know! I was following his voice until I ran into Governor Jaceson, I played it cool—you know, because I'm awesome," the villain smirked, flipping his hair under his helmet.

"Yeah, I heard '*Phoenix*'." Firefly spat.

Xeno's smile instantly sank.

"Did you really have to use my name?!"

"I'm sorry! It was a reflex! I had to say something!"

"Fine– continue," Firefly rolled his eyes.

"Point is, he said he wants 'Firefly' behind bars, you've 'broken the city's trust', you need to go right now before they catch you!" Xeno blabbed.

Firefly's face dropped, as his worst fear had come true. Everyone's eyes seem to glue to him at the moment. All the guests were staring and whispering, although it was all in his head. He started to hyperventilate as another drink was passed to him from behind the counter.

"Hey, you ok?" Xeno asked.

"Y-Yeah I'm fine," He chugged the glass cup.

Xeno grabbed it from him and pulled it down, "Whoa– Woah– Whoa– are you… DRINKING?! WITHOUT ME?! What the hell man?!"

"The governor gave me one! I'm sorry, I was afraid to say no!" Firefly begged, "Speaking of; you need to leave!"

"What?! Why do *I* have to leave?"

"The heroes are here! Rosethorn, Yellow Jacket, Tidal Wave, Time Traveler, Mighty Strength, they're all here, looking for us—looking for you!"

Xeno's heart sank and panic struck him like a frozen icicle.

"If they catch you it's game over!" Firefly finished.

"…But if they catch you, it's also game over," Xeno added.

"I know, but we can't just leave– we are so close! I'll stay, you go."

"Oh frick no! I'm not leaving you by yourself here with these fluffy heroes! You'll be taken away for good, I'm not letting that happen."

Although Firefly was beyond touched, he did have a slight question, "Did you just say 'frick'?" he smiled like a taunt.

Xeno's face froze, "...N-No..."

"Aww! You're learning!"

"Shut up!" Xeno yelled, throwing the cup back on the table; dangerously close to his friend.

Firefly laughed as he shielded himself from the glass.

"But what's the plan now? I've lost Dark Legacy and you've got no proof...and the Governor and heroes know we are here! This is bad!"

Firefly looked around for something, anything. He looked behind the bartender and spied the shelves of bright bottles, different shapes and sizes,

"I have an idea and a way we can get out, but we still need more time."

Xeno looked around at the people staring at him, remembering what Devan said a couple days ago, "Ok, well we gotta start blending in."

"Blend in?"

"We are causing a scene, and we need more time."

"Ok, but what do we do?"

Xeno looked at the dance floor and immediately got an idea, "Wanna dance?"

Firefly stood still, Dejavu hitting him, "What–?" He rushed, readying for Xeno's incoming first, but it never came.

"Dance. You and me: right now."

"Oh no– I can't dance," Firefly defended.

"You–...You can't dance?! That's bull crap! What about at the concert?" Xeno asked, waving his arms around.

"I was just following you! I can't dance by myself!" The hero wailed.

Xeno looked around as people started to whisper, "Well it's time to learn," he grabbed his friend's wrist and tugged him off the barstool.

"WHAA! Xeno, I can't dance!" Firefly pleaded as they headed towards the glowing dance floor.

"If I can skate—you can dance," Xeno stated as the DJ scratched the record and another song started to play.

Firefly stood as stiff as a board.

"You have to dance, everyone's lives are on the line," The villain started dramatically as he began to groove.

"How long have you been waiting to say that?" Firefly deadpanned.

"Since we got here; now just follow the beat."

Xeno did a simple side step to the beat and Firefly followed, trying to ignore everyone's staring eyes.

"Not bad man, now feel the rhythm," Xenomorph coached as he started to wave his arms around, rolling them to the beat as he busted a move.

Firefly tried, while he wasn't as good as his partner in crime, he started getting into it.

Soon the eyes started to disappear and the boys became in sync. Dancing to the song, Firefly even started to smile a bit.

Xeno did a backflip and the crowd cheered as his feet moved

into a moonwalk, sliding around everyone and finished with an aerial.

Firefly slid over to him, "Dude, we are supposed to be blending in, take it down a notch."

The villain groaned, "Fine~," He suddenly took Firefly's hand and twirled him off into the crowd.

Firefly stumbled into someone, "Sorry– Sorry– Sorry– *Gasp*," He started before he realized it was Rosethorn.

"No worries, your friend is really good," She smiled, but it was more suspicious than anything.

Firefly gave a nervous laugh, "Yeah…you have no idea…"

Xenomorph kept dancing, even starting to break it down as the crowd cheered.

Firefly managed to skid back into the circle as the chorus came back.

"Ready?" Xeno smirked from under his helmet.

"Ready as I'll ever be…" Firefly slurred.

The beat dropped and the two danced together, doing their own thing, but rocking it. Xeno played the air guitar on his knees as Firefly just waved his hands in the air.

Firefly slowly smiled as he realized how much fun this was.

"Yeah! Go, Buggy, go!" Xeno cheered from the floor as Firefly started to get into it, almost passing as Xeno himself.

The boys let the music take over, dancing together and blending in. Everyone joining in on the fun.

Soon the song ended as the friends posed, the crowd cheered and Xeno dapped up his dance partner.

"Not bad!"

"That– that was awesome!"

"Look at that, you *can* dance," Xeno reassured. Firefly just smiled back at him.

Suddenly an older gentleman appeared on the speakers, "Ladies and Gentlemen, Governor Jaceson will be giving his live speech in a few moments, everyone please make your way to the stage."

With a screech the call on the speakers dropped.

Xeno twisted his head, "Huh, what are the odds of that?"

"This is perfect! While the Governor is giving his speech I'm going to sneak into his house."

"You mean *we* are."

"What?"

"There are heroes now and your reputation is on the line– I don't think we should split up again," Xeno commanded.

"Fine…clingy," Firefly joked, giving him a smirk.

"I'm not clingy! Just worried– for myself of course! I'm the powerless one, remember!" Xeno covered, although he was failing miserably.

"Right," Firefly smirked as he spied another tray with drinks heading their way. "Ok, then let's get a move on! The speech will only be about a couple minutes long."

"Yeesh– that's not a lot of time to ransack this place."

Firefly gulped and took a drink off the tray, tracing the top of the cup, "W-Well maybe I'm wrong. That's a big assumption, they may ask questions."

"Maybe, but we can't take that chance, we need to go right now!" Xeno explained and ran off, heading to the back of the venue.

Firefly, in a nervous state, downed the cup, tossed it away on a table and ran. Following Xeno as his vision started to blur.

Chapter 26:

The boys ran around sharp corners and down dim halls. Xeno ran up some stairs as Firefly tripped over them.

The villain turned around, "Are you ok?"

"Yeah! Yeah! I'm fine, phew– just got those butterflies, haha…" Firefly gave a nervous laugh.

"Are you nervous?" Xenomorph asked.

"Pff–imsnot nervous!" He tried and continued up the steps, stumbling a bit.

Xeno watched him carefully as they made it to the back side of the venue.

True to the rumors, it looked more like a house, with living rooms and fancy kitchens, paintings that weren't on display, and bookshelves filled with books and artifacts. Xeno walked around looking at everything.

The kitchen had a nice, sleek white marble countertop and the lights were minimalistic. There were steps and dips in the floor that didn't need to be there but were there anyways. Creating the illusion of even more floors.

The books on the shelves were all about heroes, powers, laws, and some were about blood and anatomy. A shiver went down Xeno's spine,

"Yeesh! I don't want to know about your hobbies Governor…" he mumbled to himself as he regrouped with Firefly who was holding on to a bar stool for dear life. "Ok, Buggy, what now?"

"Huh?" Firefly asked.

"The documents? Or whatever we are looking for? How do we find them? You're the legal one here."

"The legal one?" Firefly squinted his eyes.

"Like you follow all the rules! You should know what a document looks like!"

"Ok, ok, Give me a sec," he tried to stand, but ended up stumbling.

Xeno caught him, and as Firefly lay in his arms he finally figured it out, "…are you– DRUNK?!"

Firefly gave a small laugh, "Tff– no~! Just, a bit excited," Firefly tried to stand again, and he did so, but it was clanky and awkward.

Xeno's face dropped, "You totally are!"

"I am not! I am Firefly! Protector of the city! Hero to all! I do not get wasted!" Firefly started to walk away down the hall.

"I can't tell if I'm proud or upset," Xeno admitted. "Why couldn't we get drunk together?!" He complained, until a thought popped into his head. He rubbed his hands manically, "Ooh~ I am going to have fun with this…"

Xeno followed his friend to the Governor's bedroom, an echo of a cheering crowd came roaring down the hall as the speech had started, and with that so did the clock.

The bedroom was huge, a big fancy bed in the middle with red velvet covers and fluffy pillows. Not to mention tons of treasures and displays; it looked like a castle, or a resort hotel room in Europe—anything but a New York home.

Regardless, Firefly stumbled over to the drawers and started ripping them out and leafing through paper looking for anything connecting his friend to the twisted lies.

While Firefly searched, Xeno whistled his way across the floorboards, slowly making his way to the closet. He opened the door to find loads and loads of clothes. From exotic prints to silk robes to the richest white suits. There were also golden watches and a number of hats above. Last but not least, trunks of accessories and shoes.

"HOLY–!" Xeno blurted a cuss as he ran inside.

"Language!" Firefly yelled as he continued.

Xeno removed his helmet, strapped back on his blindfold mask and tried something on.

A few suits and blazers flew through the air as they were thrown out. Firefly paid no attention and kept looking. The words were blurring and smudging together, but he didn't see anything worthy. Just Governor Jacesons contracts, deals with the heroes, random bills and laws that didn't seem to have made it through.

Firefly couldn't tell if it was the alcohol playing tricks on him but the laws seemed odd. Propositions for experiments. Inner workings of child custody. Rules about supers and how they interact with police or hospitals. He was taken back to when his friend told him villains don't get access to hospitals. If this were truly a law in front of him, and not a drink illusion, at least his partner in crime would finally get better health care.

Soon, Xenomorph came out in a loud tiger print blazer, a pink fluffy boa, and a black fedora.

He tossed the feathered scarf around his neck, "Howdy partner!"

Firefly looked over, "What– are you doing?!"

"I'm having fun!" Xeno said while galloping in place, "Come on! Don't I look great!" He flexed, tipping his hat and fluffing his hair. "I wonder what else is in here."

"Xeno! I told you not to remove your helmet, besides, we've gottafin your documents– we've got no time for a flashion show!" Firefly slurred together.

Xeno smiled, "You feeling tipsy bud?"

"Stop it! I'm not drumpk!"

"Uh huh, sure~…" He picked up a top hat and walked over to Firefly, placing it gently on his head.

"What are you doing now?!" Firefly asked.

Xeno dragged him to the mirror, "Come on man! Knowing your sad, miserable life you'll never be drunk again, and I'll never be able to witness this!"

"Xenomorph, we don't have time for this!"

"C'mon please...just one."

Firefly wanted to roll his eyes but his skull buzzed and adrenaline pumped in his veins. Reluctantly, he walked over to the closest and grabbed something. Not a minute went by before Firefly slid out in a pink suit, hot pink tie and a top hat. Still rocking his shades.

"Bam! What do you think?"

"I think...you look epic. Tuxedo showdown!" Xeno declared and soon the boys were trying on everything possible. Completely forgetting their mission.

Xeno buttoned up a collar shirt with some nice jeans, and a golden chain around his neck.

Vs.

Firefly who wore an expensive blue blazer that draped down more like a cape or coattails. With a red interior and golden accents. Rocking the same blue vest and suit pants. And a golden bow tie.

"Alright~ Mr. Fancy~," Xeno sneered.

Firefly posed, flurrying his hair, "What do you think?"

"You look sick! Round two?"

"You're on!"

Xeno draped on the red silk robe with pajama pants and the governor's bunny slippers. Pretending to smoke a pipe and showing off the three expensive watches he was wearing.

Vs.

Firefly came out in a minx coat with a black velvety tux underneath. With a red tie and beret from Paris, France.

"Bunny slippers? Really?" Firefly asked.

"Shh– don't dis the bunnies," Xeno commanded softly as he moonwalked in his fuzzy shoes.

"Round three!" Firefly declared.

"Last round!" Xeno commanded and back to the closet they went.

Xeno pulled out the final stops- coming out in a bright blue Hawaiian shirt, swim trunks. Wearing pool floats, an inflatable flamingo, and to tie it all together; a snorkel.

Vs.

Firefly who came out in a black and white lined dress shirt with a black vest that was open, you could even see a couple scars from hero work. Black jeans, a stopwatch, and a black cowboy hat. To top it off big clunky boots with spurs, and a red bandana around his neck.

Xeno looked at him, "Since when do you have abs?!"

"Since when do you look ridiculous?!" Firefly snapped back with a smile, really feeling the euphoric buzz now.

Firefly just started laughing, "What are you wearing?!"

"My swim trunks! You like?"

"No!" Firefly laughed some more as he fell on the bed.

Suddenly, the background talking stopped and hands clapped, and after? Dead air.

The speech had ended–

Both boys froze and looked around the room. It was a disaster and clothes were everywhere. Worst of all they had found nothing but cool threads.

"oh no, no, no, no, no!" Firefly went off as he started searching again.

"Hey! Hey! Relax!" Xeno tried, taking off the snorkel.

"Relax?! The speech is up, and we haven't found any of your files!"

"Oh– right– paper."

"What are we going to do!? The government is going to catch us! We are doomed!"

"Hey, hey, hey! I am Xenomorph, greatest villain alive, I never get caught!" Firefly looked at him with dead eyes as that was not true at all, "And I'm not starting that train today! Forget the room! I'll go stall the Governor—you find those documents and get out of here."

"Are you crazy?! You can't go out there by yourself!"

"You wanna go, your drunkness?!"

"I am not–" Firefly started to flame up as Xeno stuffed the cowboy hat in his face.

"Trust me. If you're going to trust me at all, do it now." He calmly demanded.

Firefly tipped the hat up and nodded.

Xeno quickly got back in his own fancy party clothes, draped back on his villain coat on top of his suit, grabbed his helmet, and raced off. Firefly got back into his own clothes as well and started ripping books off of shelves and emptying drawers to find any signs of proof.

***

Xenomorph ran down the hall, about to put his helmet on when he turned the corner and stopped dead in his tracks–

Blood turning to ice as he stared down the corridor at the shadowy figure he had seen a hundred times.

Dark Legacy, gas mask and all.

Xeno's heart pounded in his ears and he gripped onto the helmet tight.

"Xenomorph~ there you are, I heard you might have been here..." the true villain taunted. He slowly walked up to a knight in shining armor. Looking at himself in the reflection. "I've been looking *everywhere* for you..."

"D-Dark L-L-Legacy– b-but h-how did you–?"

"You really think I don't know what you're up to...?" He spat coldly and took the sword from the armor. Its iron blade clashed against the steel, removing the weapon with a slicing noise.

The sound made Xeno's heart drop even more.

"Xenomorph, you've really disappointed me." Dark Legacy continued as he walked forward. Xeno walked backward, carefully stepping on the floor runner. "Do you know how much trouble you've cost me this week? You've ruined *everything!* Because of you, I have to completely start over. Don't I?" He showed off the sword, as it reflected the light.

"W-What...? N-No please–"

"Where is he?"

Xeno's mouth clamped up, refusing to say anything more.

"Come on Xenomorph...WHERE IS HE!?" Dark Legacy yelled, sticking the blade to his neck.

Xeno flinched a bit but stayed strong, giving him a death glare from behind the mask.

"How much did you tell him?"

"…"

"…," Dark Legacy scoffed, figuring it out; it was too late. Secrets were spilled, now blood had to be. "You told him everything, didn't you, you pathetic idiot!"

Xeno stiffened.

"…I'll make you a deal."

"A deal?!" Xeno asked, aggressively.

"You tell me where he is, sell him out, and you come work for me again. No punishment, you walk free from *all* of this and get to continue running around playing your villain character. Everything goes back to the way it was…" Dark Legacy baited as he flashed Xeno's disc like a prize.

Xenomorph's eyes widen at the disc, but he thought it over knowing his boss too well,

"…Except?"

"Well, except that nasty bug won't be in the way any more."

Xeno's face fell at the thought.

"But isn't that great?! Besides, do you really think anyone will listen to you anyways?! You're a villain! He's just going to leave you after he gets what he wants. So c'mon 'Xenomorph' hand him over…before I make you."

Xenomorph's world stilled at the offer, a choice had to be made. It was too good to pass up. Sure there were some cons to being a villain, but he did love it! The freedom, the presentation, the excuse to lash out and express in full rage and chaos! Adrenaline pumping as he always got away. He was invisible under the mask, but never felt more seen.

"You are a chain reaction…you cause chaos and people run and heroes fight. That is your story. You are the show. You are stuck on an endless cycle of lies and you like it! Admit it!"

Xeno flinched at the truth.

"I'm giving you a chance to take everything back, to earn forgiveness. Just hand over Firefly…"

Xenomorph thought about it, long and hard. Looking at the rug as he struggled on what to do. What could he do?

"Once a villain, always a villain." Dark Legacy sneered.

With those words Xenomorph had, finally, made his choice.

Chapter 27:

"No."

"I'm sorry?" Dark Legacy asked, not believing his answer.

"I said NO!" Xeno said, louder.

"I don't think you know what you're doing..."

"No! For the first time I do! You're right! I am a villain and I'll always be one to the city, to myself– to you! But he doesn't see me like that! He's had my back more times than you've ever had! He'd never *forced* me to do anything! He's been honest– and loyal– and kind– and genuine! Something I never got from you!" Xeno ranted.

"You're being ridiculous! Irrational! You don't befriend heroes! HEROES SAVE EVERYONE BUT YOU! They'd choose the world over you every time!! HAND HIM OVER RIGHT NOW SO I CAN SQUASH HIM LIKE THE BUG HE IS!"

Xeno's glare hardened into pure rage, standing tall and staring death in the face, "...*You stay away from him*..."

"*Is that a threat...?*"

"**Don't. You DARE. Hurt him.** *Or I'll kill you and rip you limb* *from limb...and that's not a threat– it's a **promise**.*" Xeno commanded, sending a wave of anger down Dark Legacy's back. Throwing his own words right back at his face.

Firefly gave up his world for Xeno, it was time to do the same.

Dark Legacy just chuckled, "You think you're so clever...fine. You made your choice," Dark Legacy raised the blade, "you *will* regret this. You'll lose everything you've ever loved and you'll die a weak, miserable death."

"I'd rather die standing, than survive picking up scraps for you...I know what you've been doing...and you're SICK! You've controlled me my whole life...you won't do it any longer. You hold **no** power over me."

"...I could kill you right now and have your blood spill across the floor like a flowing river...but I won't; cause I can't wait to see the look on your face when you finally realize."

Xeno stood his ground, puffing his chest up, still staring daggers at his boss– his ex-boss.

"You...are nothing but a pawn in this world. You have no idea who's running the show. You and Firefly are *nothing* compared to what I have planned. You've given me no choice...the board must be reset."

"W-What...?" Xeno's act broke.

Dark Legacy laughed, "You guys practically begged me to write your stories! So now, your story will be told *my way* whether you like it or not," Dark Legacy bent down, patronizing the super, "Your father would be so disappointed in you and no one...will trust a word you ever say."

Xeno started shaking at the statement. It cut deep, but after a shake breathe,

"*He* will," he declared, thinking of his best friend and yanking the sword out of Dark Legacy's hand using his telekinesis.

Dark Legacy flinched, but readied up.

The battle was on;

Dark Legacy gave a laugh, "You really wanna fight me?"

Xenomorph stood silent, keeping the blade ever so straight as the chandelier made the iron sparkle.

Dark Legacy laughed again, "Fine...*you're on Hero.*"

Xeno's eyes widened at the title.

With that Dark Legacy launched at the teen, who ducked and rolled on the floor under him.

Xenomorph got some rug burn from the fancy, velvety carpet as he scuttled back up, threw his helmet away and swung the blade around.

Dark Legacy didn't hesitate as he used his telekinesis to drop the chandelier that was dangling over Xeno.

Noticing the chimes, Xeno used telekinesis on himself to anchor him to the nearest wall; whooshing the little villain out of the way. The chandelier shattered into a million diamonds on the floor.

Dark Legacy shielded himself, but he lowered his arms to see a flying Xenomorph. Punching him straight in the face.

"ARG!" The masked screamed as Xeno kept punching him.

Suddenly, Dark Legacy caught his fist and Xeno let out a small gasp.

Dark Legacy threw the kid over his head and to the wall,

smashing against a potted plant. Sending dirt flying and the new hero on the floor.

Meanwhile, Firefly kept digging around in the draws, pulling them out and shaking them upside down until a bunch of files fell out. Splattering to the floor. The hero's eyes widened at the sight of every single super hero's and villain's profile laid across the floor like an unfinished puzzle.

His eyes grew at the sight, not having the words to even process what this meant. The world seemed to stop as he saw his own name, along with his coworkers, and villains he'd fight everyday. Truly the only time they were in the same room together. His eyes wandered until he landed on *Xenomorph* written in bulky marker on a folder.

Firefly wished he could take them all, but the room was trashed and was already going to alert suspicion, might as well not make a big scene. Xenomorph's case would be enough. Plus the comics and everything Xeno told him; that had to be enough proof for Captain Peace, for everyone.

He grabbed the folder, tore through the sheets of paper and signatures quickly, until he spotted Xeno's fosters record paper clipped together. Firefly ruffled through all of them to make sure everything was there and it was! The entire exchange, records, family past, and even other papers labeled 'Test'; all there in fine print. No one could deny it. Xenomorph was innocent.

The hero got up fast, too fast. He wobbled a bit, but was able to catch himself. He quickly threw off his glasses, slipped on his iconic, red hoodie over his suit, put on his blue goggle, and made a run for it.

Xeno flickered open his eyes to see a tipsy Firefly running down the hallway in the opposite direction, passing the fight. His line was far from straight and he almost tripped, but as Xenomorph looked closer he could see a stack of paper in his hands.

The documents! He found them! Xeno looked up at Dark Legacy, thinking. He needed to get back to Firefly, that *real* hero had the plan for the way out after all. *Time to take this show on the road*– no scripts, no planned moves, all pure chaos. Just how Xeno liked it.

Dark Legacy noticed his distant stare and started to turn around to see what he was looking at. However in seconds Xeno readied up a blast of fire and shot it at his ex-boss.

"AURG! OW! SON OF A– ...he's close...isn't he." Dark Legacy demanded.

Xeno leaned against the wall as he said nothing, ignoring the liquid running down his skin.

"Your mimic abilities are a dead give away. Guess I'll have to finish you off quickly. I have another hero to defeat."

Xeno got up as Dark Legacy grabbed the blade out of the kid's hands with his powers, swinging it around. Xeno black flipped and ducked out of the way, slowly backing up as he tried to make his way to the dance floor. He had moves and he was going to show them off.

Firefly ran through the crowd, squeezing past people as he made a run for the bar. Literally running into it.

"Ow!" He yelped as he fell to the glowing floor.

Xeno continued to lead Dark Legacy down the hallway, closer to the party, as he dodged one threat after the other. Surviving sword attack, flying paintings, and tossed plants. Soon Xeno heard music as he dropped to the ground, kicked Dark Legacy, and made a run for it. Dark Legacy stumbled, but recovered and bolted after him.

Firefly crawled up to the bar and was tempted by another glass, but shoved it over as his stomach grumbled in agony.

"Ulgh~ I'm never drinking ever again..." he groaned.

"FIRECRACKER!"

Firefly whipped his head around as Xenomorph had entered the party. Jumping on the stair railing, sliding down it as people started to scream and backed up, clearing the way. The villain landed with a roll, sprang up, and sprinted to his friend.

"Get behind the counter! *Now!*" Xeno pointed as he ran.

"W-What?! Why?! What's going on?"

"Dark Legacy is here and you're too drunk to fight! Behind the counter!"

"WHAT?!" Firefly shouted in fear.

"*NOW!*" Xeno yelled and Firefly clumsily rolled over the bar and fell on the floor, slamming his back to the bar to hide.

"XENOMORPH!" A voice interrupted as Dark Legacy appeared at the top of the stairs. Soon true fear struck within the building. As the people ran faster and screamed louder.

Xenomorph readied a blast of fire as Dark Legacy commanded one of the sharp glass sculptures down, launching like a rocket from the second floor; straight at his little protege.

Xeno back flipped out of the way as the glass shattered against the wall.

338

"Oops– sorry, collateral damage!" Xeno flinched and yelled at nothing.

Dark legacy jumped down. Shaking the floor.

Xeno backed up and breathed, ready for the biggest fight of his life when he felt nauseous yet a surge of power. Not just fire and telekinesis, but everything! Suddenly, he saw a few of the party guests reading up, they didn't fear him. Until it clicked, water, plants, strength, flight. *That's right! They are all here, that's why I was feeling strange before,* Xeno thought, *Firebutt said all the heroes are right here.*

Xenomorph was back, baby.

The little villain instantly pitched a blast of water, slashing Dark Legacy back into a wall. Xeno floated up and used vines to grab his ex-boss by the leg and toss him over to the DJ, crashing the music and freezing the record.

Dark Legacy used telekinesis to launch a chair at the flying villain. Xeno shielded but took the hit, crashing on top of the bar.

Xenomorph sprang up and immediately started round house kicking all the glasses and bottles left as Dark Legacy dodged the crashing glass.

Dark Legacy grabbed a vase and ran, ready to swing like a baseball bat. Xeno cartwheeled over him as the vase crashed into the marble bar. Xeno instantly dropped to the floor and kicked his legs out from under him. Then he used more vines to swing himself up in the chandelier.

However, Dark Legacy pulled it down from the roof before Xeno could make it. The vigilante fell a bit before taking flight once more.

Dark Legacy jumped up onto the bar and Firefly muffled his gasps.

Xeno pulled the villain up into the air with his own power, smashing into the glass railing of the second floor, where the fight continued.

"Ow…" Dark Legacy started, reaching under his mask to whip the blood off his lip, "You're not going down easy, are ya kid?"

Xeno readied up, saying nothing as a ball of fire raged in his hands.

Suddenly a growing vine grabbed Xenomorph and smashed him into the wall of the second floor. The villain spat out debris and dust when he looked to see Rosethorn in a dress and mask, concealing her burn mark, commanding the vines.

"Xenomorph! You are under arrest for your crimes against humanity. Stay down!" She demanded.

Yellow Jacket flew up in a fancy suit and tie and Mighty Strength soon entered in his formal wear.

Xeno lit the vines ablaze and snuck out of them. He then wielded whatever he had left, throwing a blast of fire at Yellow Jacket, a blast of water at Rosethorn—which she dodged—and a blast of time at Mighty Strength slowing him down.

However, he forgot one person–

"GAH!" Xeno yelped as Dark Legacy used his powers to shove him off the edge from afar.

Xeno held onto the edge of the second floor balcony. He freed up one of his hands and sent a nuclear explosion blasting the entire upper floor. The backlash shot him back but he broke his fall with a wave of water.

As soon as he got to the ground, a soaked mess, more heroes in dresses and blazers appeared. Launching at him one at a time.

Xenomorph instantly took them all in hand to hand combat, ducking and dodging. Throwing heroes over one another until the fight started getting flashy again.

The villain stomped on the ground sending a layer of ice on the floor. Everyone struggled, but luckily, Xeno learned how to skate. He glided around taking out the heroes one by one. Teleporting around with kicks and anchoring his gravity to walls and ceilings which allowed him to sneak a punch to many supers. He even phased through a table as one hero went for a punch, destroying the wood and scratching up their fist. Firefly tried to help by throwing some sneaky fireballs, but they were sloppy and too crooked to do anything in the teen's tipsy state.

While Xeno was fighting and rocking out to his so-far victory, a wave of heroes rushed him. In instinct he grew super size. Making a hole in the roof. A flash caught Xenomorph's eyes and he shielded himself and waved away the nosy helicopter responsible for the spotlight.

Firefly watched everything, but soon couldn't stay hidden anymore. He stood up, about to jump in with a nasty fireball when someone tackled him back onto the ground.

"Arg– hey!" He yelled as he saw Soundwave above him already readying a punch. Firefly gave a small gasp and blocked.

"I told you! You are going to get yourself killed!" She went for another punch.

"Get off me!" Firefly yelled as he reached for a bottle behind him, smashing it over her head.

"AHOW!" She yelped.

Firefly punched her and kicked her off. However she recovered and yelled a sonic scream.

Xeno looked down at the ear piercing shriek and saw the problem. In an instant, Xeno's big boot came crashing into the bar and knocked Soundwave into a glass shelf. She fumbled to the ground and tried to get up, but gave in to the pain. Staying down.

Xenomorph shrunk to normal size, "What are you doing?!"

"You need help!" Firefly insisted, jumping over the counter and started taking out heroes.

"Dark Legacy will *kill* you! Get down– and stay down!" The vigilante demanded.

"No way! I am helping!" Firefly demanded.

Xeno couldn't help but grow a smirk and nod, understanding the stubborn bug was not going to back down.

While they were distracted, Tidal Wave shot a blast of water and Firefly dodged as Xeno used super speed to run and slide out of the way; crashing through a window. Luckily, due to someone in the mess of heroes having elasticity, he stretched his arm and grabbed onto the curtain.

Pulling himself back up to the window's frame; he instantly took a duck as a hero launched out the window and quickly climbed back in after that.

Rosethorn soon jumped down, sprouting a green mess as she swung her vines like octopus tentacles. Firefly threw more fireballs but tripped over the vines, falling down but still firing his wonky shots. Xenomorph yelped and jumped over as many as he could like a jump rope.

Eventually, Rosethorn got lucky and one of her vines caught his ankle. As Xeno got dragged along the dance floor he shot a forcefield knocking her back, but Yellow Jacket pinned him to the ground, choking him as the heroes started to circle in.

Xeno huffed, getting exhausted as he looked over to see Firefly struggling against the heroes.

Getting socked in the face, kicked in the chest, and thrown around the room until he landed back at the bar. Blood scratching up his face; coughing and throwing up, as he hit his limit.

"Alright, you're done, sit out!" Xeno commanded.

"But I–" Firefly started before Xeno shot a blast of sound at him and he knocked the drunk super back over the counter for cover.

Suddenly Dark Legacy appeared over the second floor, light shining on him as if he were God. All the heroes froze at the sight of the horror of the villain. Dark Legacy in the flesh.

"Where…is he…?" The mask demanded once again, staring cold black eyes.

Xeno choked on his breath, "I'm not telling you…"

Dark Legacy just laughed, "You know he's just going to turn you in right?"

"He'd never... W-We know what you're *coughs* up to *coughs* You–" Xeno started but Dark Legacy grabbed every hero in telekinesis and sent them flying in different directions like a blast. Hitting their heads on walls, smashing through windows, smacking them on stairs. Knocking them all out in seconds.

Xenomorph breath shivered, slowly scooting back. He knew his boss was powerful, but he underestimated how powerful.

"Do you? Well I'm intrigued, go on..."

"Y-You won't get away with this..." Xeno panted, now being free from Yellow Jacket's grasp.

Dark Legacy has a sinister chuckle, "Oh but I will...just like how I got away *with killing your father.*"

Xeno froze right there, Firefly gasped from behind the counter. Covering his mouth in shock. He pulled out the file and looked at it, hesitating.

"W-What...?" Xeno asked.

"You think it's a coincidence your dad just dies and you, one of the most powerful villains in the world, end up in my care?! No! If we are going to spill secrets, then let's do it. *I killed your father, so I could have control over you.*"

***

Xenomorph stood speechless, not even grasping on what to say, the world seemed to fade away and slow, as the party blurred and everything fell apart. Flames everywhere, vines tangled, a party destroyed to the ground.

Firefly flipped to the back of Xeno's files and at the top *'Villain'* was stamped in a box. This was always his destiny. He soared to the bottom under Dark Legacy's signature, to find Governor Jaceson's signature. Firefly's heart dropped.

The Governor himself signed off on this. They were working together; everything started to click. That's why Xeno was passed over so easily, why he was tested on, why every villain had been forced to work for Dark Legacy, why the vigilante rumor is going around! The government *MADE* villains.

Firefly poked his head up to see Xeno still frozen in fear, Dark Legacy swung him around, bashing him into the hard wall. Leaving him hanging with his powers. The real villain waved his hand and soon an iron blade went flying back into his palm.

"Just thought you'd know, before I send you to him…" Dark Legacy threatened as he got closer.

Firefly decided it was time to put his plan in action, despite what his partner thought. He grabbed a bottle of alcohol, lit it ablaze, and threw it. The glass bottle flew through the air and exploded and shattered on impact.

Dark Legacy dropped Xeno, who gasped for air. He looked over as Firefly stood up on the counter preparing another Molotov Cocktail.

"HEY! Leave him alone! It's me you're after." Firefly yelled.

"How noble…" Dark Legacy started, but in seconds he used his powers and grabbed the air. Sending Firefly flying into the back of the bar. Knocking him into the expensive drinks and crashing to the floor as dozens of bottles went down with him.

"Firefly!" Xeno yelped.

"Aww~ they grow up so fast, you guys really are like your parents. How sick," Dark legacy groaned.

"W-What?! Y-You knew his dad too?" Xeno stuttered.

"Oh, Xenomorph…do you really think I just killed your dad?!"

Firefly slowly arose among the glass shards as he tried to get up, hearing everything and not being able to stand it.

"*I* killed *all* the 'heroes'. "

Xenomorph's mouth dropped as a raging fury grew in him like no other. The smell of smoke started to burn as Dark Legacy kept taunting,

"And I intend to continue the story…starting with your little bug."

"*TOUCH HIM AND YOU'RE DEAD!*" Xeno yelled, sonic booming. However, the boss didn't flinch.

"Pff, like your parents?" Dark Legacy sneered.

"How could you do that to him…? To EVERYONE?!" Xeno started to flame up.

"Because I wanted *CONTROL*! Something I lost when you two decided to run behind my back…I was trying to spare you…"

"W-What is he talking about?" Firefly asked, crawling up on the counter.

"Don't worry about it–" Xeno blurted.

"What's the matter?! If we are just SHARING might as well! I offered your little friend a chance to work for me again."

346

"X-Xeno?" Firefly stuttered, not believing it.

"AND I TOLD HIM *NO!*" Xeno sonic boomed him back and shot him with a blistering fireball which Dark Legacy redirected to the stage. Exploding the DJ booth and lighting a huge fire.

"You are BLIND?! People believe in the heroes, not us! YOU AND I BOTH KNOW YOU ARE A VILLAIN– ALWAYS WAS– ALWAYS WILL BE! YOU CAN'T DENY YOUR FATE– YOUR DESTINY– YOUR *LEGACY*!"

"YOU PSYCHOPATH! YOU KILLED OUR PARENTS! YOU ARE SENDING VILLAINS TO HERO SPOTS ON PURPOSE! YOU PLAN FOR US TO LOSE! YOU FORCE US TO BE EVIL! HOW IS THIS CONTROL?!"

"You really think I'm the *only* one pulling the strings?! You'll see…a person must see all of the pawns to win the game. You are both too dangerous to keep around, you know too much. So say goodbye to your pawn–," Dark Legacy quipped and grabbed a piece of the roof and slammed it down into the bar.

"NO–!" Xeno yelped as Firefly got down, covering his head.

The piece of roof crashed into pieces, spilling alcohol everywhere.

"NOOO!" Xeno got up to run to his friend, but Dark Legacy caught him in the air and threw him against the floor. Tumbling like a ragdoll.

As the liquid ran down Firefly's back his getaway plan would finally go into action. He grabbed his friend's files tight, made a tiny flame in his hand, and braced for impact.

Xeno tried to get up, weakly throwing punches as Dark Legacy blocked effortlessly. The fire of destruction sent a chilling orange glow on his mask. The skull painted in white never felt so unsettling. Death coming to collect his debt.

Xeno tried to throw another punch but Dark Legacy punched him in the face and the stomach, kicking him back onto the ground. Until–

BOOM!

The bar exploded into flames, knocking everyone back; including Dark Legacy.

A noise rang in Xeno's ear as he got up, pushing off the debris. Looking over at the bar that was drowning in fire.

"No…" Xenomorph thought as he jumped up and raced over, but he collapsed onto the ground, tumbling. "NO! NO! NO! Firecracker!" He yelled, looking over the bar, pushing aside flaming boards and swishing away melted glass. "Buggy! …FIREFLY!"

Firefly sprang up and coughed like crazy, lying on the table. Xeno grabbed him and pulled him over and out of the flaming bar, both falling onto the floor.

"WHAT WERE YOU THINKING?!" Xeno yelled on his knees.

"T-That…was the plan," Firefly smiles, coughing. "That was our distraction to leave…granted I planned to be outside of the exploding beverage stand…" he smiled like nothing.

The flames grew as Dark Legacy slowly rose, brushing off more debris and pelting it away in anger.

"Ok time to go!" Xeno declared, as he grabbed Firefly, wrapped him around his shoulder and they ran off with the rest of the crowd.

Chapter 28:

As the boys ran out with the crowd, the fire department soon arrived to take care of the flaming venue. Guests were being helped out by the firefighters as the hoses unraveled. A beat up Tidal Wave helped the heroes, and together took care of the fire as Firefly and Xeno ducked under the attention to escape.

They stumbled for blocks and dipped into an empty alleyway. Adrenaline was still kicking as they decided to climb up the fire escape; just to make sure they wouldn't be caught again. Helping each other up, they finally collapsed on the roof.

Both breathing and looking at the stars. After a few minutes of just catching their breaths, Firefly sat up and walked over to the other side of the roof. Sitting on the edge as he watched the flames and smoke in the distance. Wondering if he truly was the villain they feared.

Xeno noticed and soon joined him, staring at the flames.

They remained silent for a while, not knowing what to say. Legs dangling over the edge as they both thought the same thing. The mission was a success, but at what cost?

"…Do you think I'm dangerous?" Firefly finally asked, ash and blood covering his face.

Xeno looked over, seeing the least dangerous thing on earth, "No, why would you ask that?"

Firefly sighed, "The building went up in flames."

"That *I* helped make," Xeno corrected.

"With *my* powers."

"You didn't do anything!" Xeno defended.

"Exactly! I didn't help you! You fought everyone by yourself while I blew up the venue and threw up!" Firefly yelled as he curled into his hoodie. Covering his dirty face.

Xeno frowned, feeling bad for his friend, "Hey…"

Firefly looked up.

"I thought you blowing up the bar was awesome."

Firefly smiled a bit, "Really?"

"Yeah! I mean I would've never thought about that!"

Firefly laughed as he looked down, files still somehow tucked under his arm. The hero slid them out and handed them to Xenomorph.

Xeno looked down at the manila folder, he wanted to ask what it was, but he already knew. He slowly took it, but didn't open it. Just tapping the edges.

"Go on, open it," Firefly encouraged.

"I…don't feel like opening it," Xenomorph muffled.

Firefly looked at the folder, then back at the disaster piece that was the party, "Is…this because of what he said?"

"…I– …never mind."

"It's ok, you don't have to talk about it if you don't want to."

"…I trusted him."

Firefly looked at him, already expecting the next part.

"I…I wanted to be him, sure I was forced to have this life but…he made it…"

"…seem ok?"

Xeno held his face in his hands, sniffling.

Firefly couldn't believe what he was seeing. Through cop chases and battles, through epiphanies and hard talks. Xenomorph had finally broke. He rubbed his friend's back as Xeno's face appeared again. Or as much as it could with that mask over his eyes.

"I am so sorry…" he mumbled.

Firefly just stared, quietly wondering what he had been apologizing for.

"I swear…I had no idea about your dad either…or anyone else's," Xeno hiccuped.

"Hey, it's ok, I believe you," Firefly gave him a little hug and Xeno hugged him back. "If you don't wanna open it, I get it."

Xeno broke the hug gently, "…No, we…have a mission to finish, that– *monster* will get what's coming to him…I wanna tear his world down to pieces…" he said coldly, reading the front of the folder.

Firefly patiently waited as the file was flipped open.

Xeno's face fell at the sight. All of his records (or lack of records), his weird test results about his DNA, and his identity and life were all there, stapled inside. There were tons of pictures paperclipped to pages, a lot of them were him as a little kid and a lot of them contained his dad. He hadn't seen his dad in a long time and had almost forgot what he looked like

Xenomorph smiled, sniffling all over again as he saw a picture of him and his dad playing in the yard. He kept flipping to see the more legal side of things. There was all the adoption junk Xeno couldn't care less about now, but there was a page detailing his powers and how he would become a–

'Villain' was still stamped in a box in bold red letters. His fate was sealed before he even walked out that foster care door.

He kept looking until he saw all the signatures at the bottom, Dark Legacy and Governor Jaceson.

"…The…Governor ok'd this?" Xeno asked, shattered.

"I have something to tell you…and I don't think you are going to like it." Firefly started.

Xeno looked at him, giving him a bit of a playful scoff, "How could tonight get any worse?"

"I…think…Governor Jaceson *is* Dark Legacy."

Xeno's eyes widened, "…What?"

"It– just– makes sense, no one in their right mind would 'ok' this awful system! Governor Jaceson seemed pretty ticked with us on the news, Dark Legacy only shows up after his speech is over, and that would explain why he gave me a drink—he *wanted* me wasted so I couldn't fight!"

Xeno slowly came to realize, "…the corner…"

"The what?"

"I *felt* Dark Legacy! Just like you said I would! I couldn't see him, but I followed him, I went around the corner to find him and I ran into the Governor! Literally!"

"…Woah…"

"I– I can't believe it…Governor Jaceson is Dark Legacy?!" Xeno asked.

"More like Dark Legacy is the Governor," Firefly tried to joke, but it was weak and pathetic.

"That's somehow way scarier," Xeno mumbled.

"I just– ugh– I still don't understand if he's the Governor and the villain why does he hype up all the superheroes?! Why does he pay us for equipment and training and the tower?!" Firefly ranted, trying to solve it.

"Sounds like a two faced jerk to me," Xeno picked at the folder, now shut with his super villain name on the front. "So…now what?"

"Well, it's too late at night to go to the tower now, guess we will have to wait until tomorrow to tell Captain Peace everything."

"Do you think your Captain will believe us…believe me?"

"He has too, he'll believe me…and I believe you."

"…And then what?"

"And then everything will be over, and you'll be free to do whatever you want. Villain, Hero, or just normal."

Xeno couldn't believe his ears, the freedom of choice was so close. He'd never imagined in a million years he'd ever get a choice like that.

Suddenly it hit him.

He could now choose whatever he wanted, he could break any

rule 'Dark Legacy' gave him. That night, he finally said no to his boss, and it was time he said yes to someone else. Thinking it over, he quickly made his choice.

Xeno whipped the dirt and tears off his face and turned to his partner in crime,

"...Do you want to reveal our identities?"

Firefly stood shocked, "...What?"

"If you still want to."

"B-But I thought–" Firefly started.

Xeno cut him off, "I know what I said! Just...I am ready now and Dark Legacy doesn't control me anymore."

Firefly waited.

"...I don't know what's going to happen tomorrow, but if this is...the end...I want to know. I'd be kicking myself for the next ten years if I didn't ask."

Firefly just smiled, "...Yes."

Xeno smiled back, "Seriously?"

"Yeah man, we are friends now, and I want to know too," Firefly turned to his partner in crime and Xeno did the same. "On three..."

Xeno grabbed his Bandana as Firefly grabbed his goggles.

Adrenaline and anticipation building. Both hearts thumping louder and louder as they were somehow nervous, yet never more excited. Blood running cold as Firefly started,

"...One."

Xeno's hands started to shake as he gripped the bandana harder.

"Two…" Firefly said with a shaky breath,

Silence rang out the night until–

"Three!"

Xeno pulled down his mask and Firefly pulled his goggles off his eyes, setting them on his fluffy hair.

They both flickered open their eyes and froze in shock. Finally putting a face to a name. Somehow looking exactly like how the other one expected them to look, yet completely different.

A decision was made, and it was an impossible undo.

Xenomorph smiled a bit as he got his first *real* look at Firefly. Still with fluffy brown hair and bruised skin, but he had the most distinct brown eyes anyone could have. Freckles dotted his face, freckles he never noticed and his smile seemed more human than ever. For the first time seeing an actual person behind everything. His heart beat nonstop at the realization that he had a real friend.

Firefly looked at him with the same smile, tilting his head to the side as he looked at the 'villain' that was Xenomorph. Same jaw, same nose, same white hair, but his eyes– his eyes were sky blue. Who knew? His pale face made his blue eyes sparkle even more. The hero just kept observing, happy he finally got to know the guy behind the mask.

After a while of staring, Firefly stuck out his hand.

Xeno looked at it, confused.

"Parker."

Firefly– or rather Parker said, smiling.

Xenomorph's eyes widened as he took the hand slowly. Shaking it up and down,

"Xander."

"...Xander with a Z or an X?" Parker asked.

"An X? Why?"

Parker's brown eyes widened. It was odd for Xenomorph—or Xander, to actually see his eyes grow. But it was a nice kind of odd.

"Ooohh~! See, *'Xenomorph'* makes much more sense now," Parker teased.

Xander laughed, "Yeah, Dark Legacy wanted to keep the X theming."

Parker smiled and took his hand away, "Well...it's a pleasure to finally meet you, Xander."

Xander gave a small grin back, "...you too, Parker."

After that weirdly incredible interaction, they both stared back out into the city. A chill filled the air as the lights dazzled and both boys never felt more free.

On top of the world.

Away from everyone.

Finally revealing the secret that's been eating them alive since day one.

Revealing it to their best friend no less.

"So...what do you wanna do now?" Xander asked.

Parker looked over, "Excuse me?"

Xander laid down, looking up at the stars, "I mean we have a whole night left. Where do you wanna go?"

Parker rolled his eyes with a smirk, "Where do *you* wanna go?"

Xander smiled, finally seeing that eye roll was so worth it.

"Hmm…I want a pretzel."

Parker laughed, "Of course you do. Ok, let's go," Parker started to get up when Xander sat up–

"Wait–!"

Parker froze, staying seated.

"…Thank you…or whatever." Xander mumbled, genuinely smiling.

Parker smiled back, "Of course dude, you're my partner in crime."

"And as your partner in crime…I'm obligated to do this–!" Xander announced as he pushed Parker off the roof.

"AAAAAAAHHHHHH!" Parker screamed for a second before his falling was instantly stopped by the iron gritting of another fire escape.

Xander laughed a bit.

"XENOMORPH!" Parker yelled, "YOU SCARED ME!"

"Oh relax, I knew it was there, and it's Xander to you wise guy," the villain smirked and Parker couldn't stay mad at him for long. His anger vanished as he climbed back up.

They soon packed up their files and bag, and left the roof. Walking away as completely new people than when they arrived. Leaving behind one thing: their pasts.

***

The two boys, now with their identities revealed, could finally slip out of their super clothes and into their regular clothes. Parker wore his gray hoodie and his jean jacket over it. Sliding on his headphones, to further the disguise more; although no music was playing out of them.

Xander wore a collared button up in white and a preppy sweater vest over it. Pulling out his glasses and putting them on his face.

They put the file into the bag, along with all their super armor and clothes and began to walk.

No destination, no expectation, just walking. It was late and the streets were mainly empty; but it was peaceful.

The street lamps lit their way, puddles on the ground and a few rouge pigeons still flapping around.

The teens took their time as they just strolled, breathing in the cold night air.

Somehow they arrived at the subway, still as empty as above but the tunnel lights illuminated the green tile. Parker paid for some tickets, and Xander let him, although he wished Parker hadn't.

Someone's beautiful acoustic guitar filled the air, strumming a familiar soft lullaby through the station. Parker listened, humming the words as he never heard anything so beautiful.

Soon the subway arrived and slowly opened the doors. They got into the car and the subway was empty, but regardless they took their seats.

Xander watched the bricks blur by as he started to fall asleep. They hadn't really rested in days. Soon the transit went above ground and the city view was breathtaking at night. Xander's eyes started to close and he laid back into the seat.

Parker watched out the window until something fell on him gently. He looked down to see his friend asleep, resting on his shoulder. Xander started to cuddle up next to Parker, curling up into a ball on the seat.

Xander started to shiver as his real clothes were comfortable, but not really much against the element of the cold night. Parker carefully reached into their back and pulled out the blue jacket his friend stole from the concert.

Smiling Parker placed it on top of him like a blanket.

Xander felt its presence and grabbed it, wrapping in it for warmth.

The shivers stopped as Parker looked out the window, also getting sleepy. He pulled out his lighter and started flicking it as usual. He didn't expect much as usual, but to his surprise the lighter sparked,

And it lit.

Parker stopped and watched the beautiful flame for a while. It danced in an orange glow, so small yet so powerful. Like someone was telling him something.

Smiling, he blew it out and quickly pulled out his phone; he texted his mom real quick, put on some acoustic guitar in his headphones, and laid his head back.

Both boys fell asleep on the subway as it went throughout the whole city, stopping at every stop but no one got on.

It was the most peace the supers had ever felt in a while.

Chapter 29:

It had only been a few hours when the train stopped again, softly jolting the boys awake. Parker flickered open his eyes to see it was still dark outside. A lot more lights seemed to disappear as it was past midnight.

Parker grabbed his lighter and the bag and gently shook Xander.

The boy flinched up tight, refusing to get up. Waving away the hand.

"Mmm~! Five more minutes…" he groaned in his sleep.

Parker just shook him again.

"Devan– knock it off…" he mumbled.

"It's not Devan," Parker laughed.

Xander slowly opened his eyes to see Firefly there, a Firefly with no mask and no armor. Just a completely normal kid. Xander's eyes softly grew, forgetting for a second.

"You ok?"

"Y-Yeah, sorry…just not used to seeing…that," Xander

gestured to his face as he got up, slipping on his blue hoodie correctly.

"Oh 'har har' because it's so ugly," Parker sassed, playfully.

"It's…actually quite nice to see a real face," Xander smiled.

Parker smiled, he thought he knew his friend by now, but maybe he still didn't; and he was ok with that.

"Come on, this is our stop." Parker continued.

"We had a stop?"

"You wanted a pretzel."

"Yes! But what pretzel vendor would be open this late at night?"

"Who said it was a vendor?" Parker smirked as he hopped off the subway, Xander followed him clumsily, as they got off the train. Fumbling on the sidewalks of New York.

The sky still its shade of night blue, stars barely sparkling. The few trees blew in the wind and in Xander's hair. The villain stayed still and watched the world for a while, just taking everything in.

Parker, however, was already on the move, and Xander quickly caught up. They ran across empty roads and into giant courtyards. Eventually making their way to a vacant parking lot.

"So…where are we?" Xander asked, looking at the parking spaces.

"Yankee Stadium," Parker declared as he walked towards a giant baseball arena.

"Whoa," Xander ogled at the huge thing. He couldn't see inside, just the curved walls and open roofing. Regardless, it was magnificent.

Parker walked to a chain link fence gate, shaking it a bit.

Xander frowned, "Dang, sorry dude."

Parker smirked.

"What?"

"You really think I haven't learned anything from this week? Especially with the time I've spent with you?" Parker asked rhetorically as he tossed his bag over the gate, not even looking as the bag fell on the other side.

"You're...trespassing?!" Xander gasped.

"*Visiting," Parker corrected as he started climbing the fence, heaving himself over to the other side. Landing perfectly.

"I have never been more proud of you," Xander whispered dramatically.

"Just get over here, before I eat all the pretzels myself," Parker sneered as he picked up the bag.

"I'm coming! I'm coming! I'm coming!" Xander shouted as he climbed over the gate, falling less gracefully.

Soon both boys were inside the walls. The stadium was eerie, empty, calm. They walked around looking at all sorts of jerseys, bats, merchandise, hall of fame records, and mural art (before Xander whipped out his spray paint and drew a mustache on it).

Finally, they got to the food court and Xander slid over the counter and went rummaging around the drawers. Finally, after many splatters of mustard later, he found his big, soft pretzel.

Parker took it from his hands and with a little flame toasted it just right. Warming the pastry into a twisted perfection.

With Xander's snack, both teens sat down in some chairs and

watched the empty field.

Xander took a bite of the salty bread, "…Why are you doing this?"

"Hm?" Parker asked, turning his attention to him.

"You don't…'break in' to places, that's *my* thing," Xander explained.

"Oh…eh, who cares." Parker muffled half heartedly.

"…Did I break you? Holy crap I broke Firefly!" Xander joked.

Parker laughed, "No, just, thinking."

"Thinking? You do that?"

"'Haha' yes."

"Ok," Xander ripped another bite of his pretzel, "About what?"

"Being a hero…" Parker admitted.

Xander froze.

"If…the government *is* evil, been funding us to be defeated, glossing us up just for the people– what's the point in doing any of this. It's all fake…I'm fake. So why does it even matter what I do…" He drifted into thought.

Xander hesitated for a bit, thinking. He then tore a piece of his pretzel off and handed it to his friend.

Parker looked at it, and eventually took it. They both took a bite of the bread, in silence as they went back to watching the field.

"Is this fake to you?" Xander finally asked.

"Is what fake?"

"This? You and me, friends, this week?"

"Are you kidding, this is probably the only real thing in my whole life– how pathetic is that…"

Xander smiled, "I don't think it's pathetic."

"Really?"

"Yeah."

Parker paused, "Why would you ask me if this is fake?"

"Well, you said what's the point if it's all fake, but *this* isn't fake…so is there a point now?"

Parker just looked at him thinking; thinking about his mom. How he missed her, but most importantly what she said,

"…Am I important to you?" Parker asked.

"I don't know– am I important to you?" Xander recited back, taking another bite.

"I just thought, maybe I actually saved someone; and it was real this time…"

Xander waited a bit, still chewing.

"Maybe if I could actually help you, this whole thing would have been worth it, I would've been worth it," Parker thought out loud.

"You're too hard on yourself," Xander answered.

Parker looked away.

"…But if it makes you feel better, I'm having a blast," Xander smiled as he captured Parker's attention again, looking into those brown eyes, "I hate to admit but you did 'save' me, blaugh. And you are important to me. None of this is fake to me, so, I guess that's my point."

"…Seriously?"

"You are so sappy," Xander gagged, "Dude you're ok, you did good, you did your hero job! Stop being so harsh on yourself, you're enough. And you don't need to prove it to some prissy captain or organization."

Parker's smile grew. While anyone else could hear Xander's sass, only he could hear the genuine behind it.

"If you're asking me if you should still be a hero after this, the answer is yes! One hundred percent! You are so much more than a 'hero', you try to see the good in everyone and you are caring and selfless, so stop throwing a pity party."

Parker could have said a million things, however, there was only one thing he needed to say,

"...You're important to me too," Parker grinned.

Xander froze mid bite.

"And thank you for that. It's not easy losing your world."

"Tell me about it," Xander agreed.

"Ever since the heroes left, I've trained to become the best. I had big shoes to fill, a dream to live up to, expectations to meet– but...I wanted to be there. I wanted to help someone, to save someone. I wanted to be somebody to someone..."

Parker leaned his head back on the seat, looking straight up, "I don't even know who I am anymore... what am I without this?"

"Yourself?" Xander asked.

"Myself wouldn't save lives."

"...Someone sitting next to you might disagree," Xander joked.

Parker looked at him.

"I'm just saying, someone has given me friendship, freedom, protection, and compassion; and it sure as hell wasn't 'The shiny and popular Firefly'."

The hero played with his drawstrings, wanting to ask more, but deep down he already knew the answer to that.

"Now would you stop having a crisis because you *are* a hero! Sure it may not be in the way you thought, but you are one. I am here with my best friend. What is more real or to the point than that?"

"Thank you, Xander."

"Anytime, Parker."

"Who knew you had such a soft side," He teased.

"Hey! No! You tell anyone– I will kill you!" Xander sat up, waving his finger around.

Parker laughs, "Nah you won't, you need me."

"So?" Xander replied sheepishly, "You need me, clingy."

"Aww~ like soulmates! Bound to find each other!"

"Dude– we are friends, not getting married!"

"Who says friends can't be soulmates?" Parker asked as Xander lost his train of thought, being stunned by the question.

Parker tried grabbing a tiny piece of the pretzel when Xander swooped it away.

"Hey! My pretzel! Hiss!" Xander hissed and scolded.

"Hey share! I'm the one who got it for you anyways!" Parker kept reaching and soon the boys were playfully fighting and wrestling for the last few pieces of the twisted bread.

Parker grabbed a piece with an, "Ah-HA!" and ate it.

Xander chuckled, "Ok, ok fine– you fluffy hero."

Parker smiled, finally feeling like he earned that title.

"You could be one too~," Parker started.

Xander rolled his eyes as they landed on the bases.

"Make you deal...let's play. You hit a home run, I'll be a hero."

"SERIOUSLY?!" Parker grew excited.

"Yes– but if I strike you out, then I'm out."

"Deal!" Parker said, hanging out his hand.

Xander took it.

***

A few moments later the boys were out on the wet, grassy field. Xander took off his fake lenses. He stood at the mound firm as he slid on a mitten that was lying in the dugout.

Parker came out swinging a bat like a staff, approaching home. He tossed Xander a baseball and the pitcher caught it.

"Ok...three tries, you hit a home run I become a hero," He reminded.

Parker wielded up, "Heck yes~!" He cheered.

Xander readied up, standing straight, focusing.

"But I have some questions."

Parker deflated a little, "Questions?"

"Yeah."

"Ok, shoot."

"If I become a hero, I'll be safe right? This isn't like a trap where I go to jail forever?"

"What?" Parker drifted as he dropped the bat, "No, of course not. You'll be safe, I promise."

Xander threw the ball.

Parker hurried back into position and swung–

Missed.

"Strike one," Xander announced.

"W-What, I wasn't ready!"

"That's why you get three tries," Xander readied up again and Parker did the same, "If I become a hero is someone going to be telling me what to do? I don't wanna be controlled again."

Parked eyes wandered, "Fair, but no. Once we tell Captain Peace, everything is going to change. We won't have scripts and schedules and planned fights, no strings. No one can tell you what to do, you get to call the shots. Promise."

Xander threw the ball and Parker swung–

Missed.

"Strike two," Xander spat coldly as he readied up the ball again, thinking.

Parker held his bat high, staring down his friend. Focusing on nothing but that ball. He had to make this shot.

"Last question…"

"I'm ready," Parker answered.

"What would you sacrifice for me?"

Parker stood up, letting the bat hang.

"…What?"

"I know how this works, Buggy, heroes save everyone but you. They'd choose the world every time. That's all they care about, the city."

"..." Parker's eyes widened. "...Did he tell you that?"

Xander looked away, the answer painted all over his scruffed up face,

"Would you have my back out there, or would you sacrifice me for the greater good?"

Parker still remained silent.

"If we were a superhero duo or whatever–"

"A...duo?" Parker cut him off, smiling a bit. Remembering his proposal back at the little pizza joint.

"Yeah– like hell I'm doing this without you– but if we were a duo, what would you choose? The world or me?"

"..." Parker thought long and hard, "...Well, I am a hero, it's my job to save the world...I mean would you sacrifice the world just for me?" Parker laughed, nervously.

Xander lowered his glove, "...Yes."

Parker's face softened into a shock.

"...I would sacrifice anyone, anything for you. Heck, I'm already doing it...guess that's the thing with us 'villains' we'd let the world burn for the people we care about." Xander looked into his beat up leather glove.

Parker sighed, "I...would sacrifice anything to save the people of New York; anything...except you."

The villain looked at his friend, still at home.

"You're the only person I'd save rather than the city, the only person I'd become a 'villain' for," Parker smirked.

"B-But you just said."

"My job is to save people."

"Yeah?"

"And right now I'm saving you," the teen smiled, reading back up, "You're my friend, if I'd sacrifice everything for the city– imagine what I'd sacrifice for you– heck I'd die for you."

"…Really?" Xander asked, astonished by the answer.

Parker held the bat high once more, "**Yes.** Consider the world burned."

Xander breathed, looking at the ball in his hands. He readied up and threw.

Parker swung the bat and with a crash–

A hit.

Parker gasped at the amazing hit as the ball went soaring and flying, and soon it flew off the field into the stadium seats.

Home run.

"YEEEEEEESSSSSSSS! YEEEEEEAAAAAHHH!" Parker screamed and cheered as he threw the bat and ran around the bases. "YOU'RE GOING TO BE A HERO~! YOU'RE GOING TO BE A HERO~! MY BEST FRIEND IS BECOMING A HERO!"

Xander just watched him with a smile as he sprinted around the dirt. The kid flipped and slid on home. Kicking dust into the air.

"LET'S GO! TAKE THAT! I knew I could do it, I–!" He celebrated until he saw a smirk on Xander's face. "–hold on did you…"

Xander rolled his eyes playfully.

Parker started to beam, "You threw me a hit ball on purpose!"

The pitcher scoffed, "Pff– you're crazy."

"You *purposefully* gave me a home run!"

"Maybe," Xander sneered.

Parker ran to him and hugged him, Xander was shocked at first but hugged him back.

"I had to let you have that confidence boost," he assured.

"Mmm hmm~ sure…whatever you say hero."

Xander playfully slapped him away, "Shush! Shut up before someone hears you."

Parker chuckled a bit as he picked up the bat, "Ok, now that that is settled, what else are we doing tonight?"

"Probably whatever you're about to ask me," Xander smirked.

Parker giggled for a bit.

Suddenly the sound of police sirens wailed in the distance, just barely.

Xander looked in a direction, being drawn to the sound, "We should probably go."

"Agreed," Parker added, blood rising as the lights and noise got closer.

Grabbing their bag, Parker and Xander tossed their hoods on and bolted. Running back into the empty halls, avoiding the flashlights and hiding from the footsteps of the police. After a few close calls, they quietly jumped over the fence once more and snuck out. The two ran down the empty lot and ducked behind a barrier, finally catching a breath.

"WOOOO!" Parker cheered, throwing his arms in the air. "That was awesome! I feel great!"

"That adrenaline kicking in?" Xander nudged him playfully.

"YES! Woo! Let's set something on fire!" Parker started to get up.

"Whoa! Whoa! Whoa!" Xander laughed and caught him, "How about we don't?"

"Ok, ok, sorry, just excited!" Parker jumped in place.

"It's ok bud, glad you're having fun."

Parker sighed in relief, "I am! So much fun…but we should get going. It's almost morning."

"Oh– …right."

"What's wrong?" Parker asked, smile fading from his face.

"N-Nothing."

"Are *you* scared?"

"No, I am Xenomorph– I am not scared of anything."

"Dude, you have nothing to fear, Dark Legacy has probably given up and retreated to his dark cave of chaos."

"Tff– it's not him I'm worried about…"

Parker stayed quiet, listening.

"Your boss is going to hate me," Xander warned.

"PHA! Dude you're a superhero, not my date to prom. Besides, he is going to love you! You are amazing, strong, and powerful! You'll do fine."

Xander chuckled a bit, "Ok, fine. Let's go."

"Yes! This is going to be awesome!"

"That adrenaline still working?" Xander smirked.

"YES!" Parker grabbed Xander's arm and off they went, to finally finish their mission.

Chapter 30:

As the orange sun dipped into the city, a new day approached and people were out. The two supers didn't do much, just rested and waited. Avoiding the morning rush.

Parker slipped on his red hoodie and goggles in an alley and he became Firefly once more. He grabbed the bag and started walking out into the street to do surveillance when his reflection caught his eye and he halted. He looked at himself, studying. For the first time liking the kid under the mask.

THUD!

"Ow!" Xeno yelped as he fell over some alley junk, also in his villain gear. Firefly giggled as he realized he liked the kid under that mask too.

"Alright Buggy, let's go!" Xenomorph announced. Jumping up, marching away, and hopping on a garbage bin.

"What are you doing?" Firefly asked, getting ready to follow.

"Taking our transportation to Hero's Tower," He explained as he started to climb the wall of an old brick apartment building.

"But...the bus is that way– also the train, and anything with wheels," Firefly mentioned, as he climbed the bricks.

Xenomorph got to the roof and pulled his friend up, "We aren't taking the bus, we are taking: ...the roof!" He jazzed his hands at the rooftops of hundreds of buildings as the sun shined in the sky.

"Roof?"

"Yeah! Like our job? Superhero transportation. Unless you can just fly?"

"Uh– no! I can't 'just fly'!" Firefly sassed.

Xenomorph paused, "Isn't that why you're called Fire*fly*?!"

"No! Captain Peace chose my name, remember? Can't *you* fly?!"

"Well I could if you could. Or anyone else within my personal bubble could– ...until then; roof!" He announced.

"You can take hero routes for fun?" Firefly asked.

"Yes, silly! It's how I get around all the time! Plus no people, we will be invisible," Xeno whispered as he did a karate pose.

"Well...if we stay out of the public eye, I don't see a problem." Firefly gave in.

"Great!" Xenomorph cheered as he went towards the other edge of the building, leaning back, letting gravity win.

"Xander? What are you doing?!"

"Keep up if you can!" He sneered, and with that, he fell.

"Xander!" Firefly screamed and ran toward the edge, looking over. Scared to find a broken Xenomorph on the floor, but to his surprise a burst of fire flew up like a rocket. Launching Xeno into the sky, back flipping onto the next roof. Landing dramatically as he blew the hair out of his face.

The burst of flames had scared Firefly, yet had impressed him.

"Hey~ I guess you can fly, Buggy!" Xeno cheered from across the way and started to take off.

"Wait– what?! Xander! Xander! Wait for me! Come back!"

Firefly took a running start and jumped across the alleyway gap, rolling onto the next roof. However when he brushed his hair out of his lenses Xeno had already flipped to another roof and was sliding on the tile.

Firefly stuck his hands to his side and blasted some fireballs, and just like Xeno, rocketed off like a firework.

He soared through the clouds a bit, tasting the fresh air, but soon reality had called him back as he fell on the same crooked tiles. Holding onto a gutter for dear life.

Xeno hopped over a couple more cracks and gaps over the streets when he turned around to see his friend. He started laughing as the hero tried to pull himself back up.

"Hey! I've never done this before," He admitted, hoisting himself up.

"Really?" Xeno asked.

"Well– I have planned routes, but other than that, no!"

"What?! Seriously?! How! This is the best part of the job!" Xeno laughed as he helped the hero up.

"Best part?"

"One of many," Xenomorph scoffed, "the wind in your hair, the air racing out of your lungs, no one around? Freedom, the only kind I'll ever get," he smiled as he did an aerial onto another building, crossing his arms dramatically.

"Hey, you'll get your freedom as I promised..." Firefly started as he did his own aerial to join the villain across the way, "Then you'll have way more fun enjoying life."

Xeno smiled, "That's sweet kid, but I only need one thing," He stated as he side flipped onto a fire escape.

"Oh yeah? What's that? Alcohol?" Firefly sassed as he jumped down to join him.

"Well I was going to say you– but alcohol works even better!" He joked, climbing the ladder.

Firefly tried to roll his eyes, but just ended up smiling.

"We are partners in crime now, Buggy! You're stuck with me! Deal with it!" Xeno declared as he balanced over a construction beam and went racing across the building's roof.

"Hey!" Firefly yelled as he ran after Xenomorph.

Soon the fun began; scaling buildings, climbing bricks, walking on skylights, rolling into rooftop gardens (Xenomorph throwing tomatoes at Firefly), and jumping down all sorts of layered balconies and plazas. Even running on the raised subway tracks and little bridges, to zip lining on telephone wires.

The sun shined over the city as the light shimmered off the glass. Firefly and Xenomorph flipped and flew together as if they were invincible. Parkouring over *their* city. Nearly stumbling over piping or falling off windowsills. Firefly even tripped on an air conditioner.

After a couple hours, both supers finally made it to the center of New York, completely exhausted. Hero's Tower sparkling just a few blocks away along with every other glistening building. Xeno sat on the edge trim of whatever building he was on and eventually Firefly joined him, panting.

"Phew!" The hero breathed, "That was awesome!"

"See! I told you, it's so much fun."

"You know what's not fun?" Firefly asked sarcastically. Xenomorph turned to look at him. Firefly whipped the tomato out of his lenses, "Getting pelted with tomatoes!"

Xeno bursted out laughing, "Oh come on! I had to! It's in my nature~, besides you look ridiculous!"

Firefly scoffed as he noticed the tower. Flickering like a ticking time bomb. Xeno's stomach began to swish and sway like a seasick wave.

"...So, today is the day," the teen villain stated, shaking a bit.

"Are you nervous?" Firefly asked.

"I am *the* Xenomorph! I'm never nervous!"

"But after today, you won't be," Firefly reminded.

Xeno froze at the thought, "What are you going to do when this is all over?" He dodged his fate, sitting on the edge.

"What do you mean? I'm going to be a hero with you." Firefly joined him.

"Duh– but like outside of work, and masks, and fluffy hero stuff."

Firefly chuckled, "Um...I don't know, haven't thought about it."

"You never think about yourself," Xeno smirked.

"It's the hero in me."

"Ok well, if you were a villain–" Xenomorph started and Firefly laughed.

Xeno grabbed his friend's arm laughing as well, "No! No! No! Stay with me here– if you were a selfish villain, what would you do?"

Firefly calmed his laughter, "Hmm...well I'd like to write music, play guitar, maybe start a band?"

"Ooouu~ ok ok, and...what about Quinn?" The villain smirked.

Firefly blushed hard, "W-What about Quinn?!"

"Aren't you going to ask her out~?" Xeno sang out as he danced in his seat, nudging the hero.

"W-What?! N-No I couldn't! I'm still a hero!"

"Yeah, but once the systems are taken down, we won't have all these rules! No planned fights! No schedules! We can go out and live a normal life!"

"True–" *Gasp* "I can go to concerts whenever I want!"

"Now you're cooking with fire!" Xeno patted him on the back and Firefly playfully lit up, being ironic. "Ok...well I guess you *are* fire."

Firefly paused for a bit to think about his new life. The uncertainty drove him insane and he took out his little lighter and started flicking it like crazy, in hopes it would calm him down. It sparked and clicked, but no flame.

Suddenly, Xeno slowly took it from him, "Dude, relax—let's not start a fire."

"Y-Yeah."

"Just breathe," Xenomorph helped as he took the lighter and put it in his pocket. He held onto the plastic tube for a bit, for some reason not wanting to let go.

The hero breathed, "Captain Peace will change everything...right?"

Xeno's calm face broke, "He better! Otherwise I'm screwed! Are you telling me you don't know?! You promised–!" He started to flame up as well, getting nervous again,

"No! No! No! No! I know the Captain, you'll be safe with him. He'd be thrilled to have you on the team, and this way heroes are defeated forever! But the schedules and the fights and the routines and lines...will that stay the same you think?"

"You said no one would tell me what to do, no schedules and scripts." Xenomorph reminded, but it was cold and harsh; like a threat.

"I know, I know what I said; but what if I'm wrong? What if nothing really changes?" Firefly asked.

Xeno decided to swallow his own anger as he could see his friend next to him already having a hard time,

"...It would be weird if they did—I mean you only had them in place because your 'dear ol' Governor Jaceson' knew exactly what would happen; once he's gone, we will be set into unknown territory. No one can predict what will happen next, so no need to prepare. You can't schedule crime, well, after Dark Legacy is defeated anyways."

"Yeah, you have a point... although I still don't understand why he'd just give us his plans like that? Doesn't he want to win?"

"Beats me. Monday I came in with that bag of victory diamonds, Boss was not happy—furious even."

"It just makes no sense!" Firefly pondered, holding his head.

"Neither does Dark Legacy, I could never understand what he wanted," Xenomorph added.

"I just feel like I'm missing one final piece of this dang puzzle!" Firefly sighed, covering his face as he breathed.

"Eh, don't worry about it– maybe it's just about control over the city," Xeno added.

Firefly lifted his head, "What do you mean?"

"I mean fear, right? Villains create fear, fear creates vulnerability, vulnerability creates control, control creates power...maybe he's already won?" Xeno solved.

Firefly took a breath, "If that's the case we are going to stop him from his 'winning streak'," he demanded and stood up, "and by the way you didn't create fear. Frustration yes, but never fear."

Xeno smiled, standing up by his side, "Thank you, ...but~ I did– I was awesome."

Firefly giggled, "Well you don't anymore. So, you ready?"

Chapter 31:

Xeno twisted and turned with the backpack as Firefly led the way through the maze that was skyscrapers; he hadn't been to this side of town before. Never seen anything so clean. Glass buildings, green trees, no trash, water fountains and plazas. It was like a palace of quartz.

Xeno hid behind Firefly as best he could; the villain's eyes scattered around, preparing for anything. No heroes were in sight yet but with his black cloak and gray armor he would stick out against all the bright colors.

The sun already started to as a shadow loomed over them. Xenomorph looked up at the large structure. Glass walls and a clean door. He would've mistaken it for an old business building had he known better.

"Yes! We are here! Let's go!" Firefly celebrated and ran towards the tower.

"Wait! Parker!" Xeno whisper yelped after him and followed him inside.

Firefly sprinted up to the door in a hurry and swiped his pass along the wall. He swung open the glass doors and ran in.

"Buggy! Wait up!" Xenomorph yelled as he ran into the door–
"Ow!" and squeezed inside, following Firefly who booked it through
the building.

Xenomorph started to run but slowed down as he looked
around. The windows spewed pink and orange sunlight, highlighting
how empty it was.

"Huh…" Xeno pondered looking through every glass wall he
could, "…Where is everyone?" He asked nothing, and ran to catch up to
his friend.

Firefly bolted down the hall, heart pumping as he slid over the
tile. Running around corners, down halls, and up stairs. Door after door
after door until–

Firefly slammed into the last door and pushed it open to reveal
a large meeting room.

There, standing over the table off to the side, looking through
papers, was Captain Peace. Looking as holy and good as ever in the
golden hour glow.

"Captain!" Firefly shouted, running to him.

Xenomorph followed behind but once he got into the door he
stopped. Seeing the Captain in the flesh was weird, he dressed in
silvery, white armor with dark blue trim. Xeno swallowed nothing as
somehow his favorite color was ruined for him.

Captain Peace looked up, "Firefly?!"

"Captain! Listen I am so, so, so, so, sorry about everything! I
know I messed up, but please listen there is something huge going on

that we never knew–!"

"Whoa, whoa slow down kid, what is going on?! What have you *been doing*?! And why is *he* here?!" Captain Peace asked, pointing to the villain in the room, "You brought a *villain* in here?!" His voice raised.

"No! No, he's not a villain!" Firefly defended.

"…What?"

Xenomorph hid behind Firefly, "…Hi…" he muffled shyly, and quickly avoided eye contact. Looking around the room at the glass cabinets and plans spread across the wall.

"He was forced to be evil! Dark Legacy is Governor Jaceson! He killed all the superheroes! Our parents! He adopted all the villains– and *MADE* them villains. Governor Jaceson is scripting us to fight—like puppets for his sick show!"

"…You– …you figured all that out?" Captain Peace's face dropped.

"Yes! Please sir! I know you're mad at me for exposing the organization."

"Mad doesn't even begin to cover it!" Captain Peace yelled.

"I know, I know– just please believe me– he is not evil!" Firefly said, lifting his goggles like it was nothing.

"You…revealed your identities?"

"…Yes sir," Xeno chipped in, taking off his own blindfold mask. "It…was my idea."

"No, we did it together!" Parker insisted, "Sir we could end the cycle right now, now that we know everything's faked we could save all the villains! No more schedules, no more fights, no more plans! We could all be real heroes! So please believe us–"

The silence was agonizing, but the golden hero finally opened his mouth.

"I do," Captain Peace said.

"Because if you don't– wait what?" Parker did a double-take.

"I believe you. You're a good kid Parker," Captain Peace smiled

Parker smiled back at his leader, feeling proud.

"At first, I was furious about you exposing us, and then resisting arrest– hanging out with a super villain?! But...now it all makes sense! However, you still disobeyed me– so we will talk about that later, but for now, you guys can come with me." Captain Peace started to walk away, Parker following him to the ends of the earth, Xander following his friend loosely—it felt easy, too easy.

But just before they could leave-

"I'm so proud of you Parker, you too, Xander."

Xander froze, world shattering.

"You two definitely surprised me," the angelic figure continued like nothing.

Xander instantly held Parker back–

"Gah– what are you doing?" Parker yelped.

Captain Peace turned around.

"This is it! We've won! You're safe now! A hero, like I promised," Parker tried to assure.

Xander shoved Parker behind him.

Captain Peace still looked at them confused.

"...*How did you know my name...?*" Xander asked.

Parker froze, realizing.

"Y-You guys said you revealed your identities," Captain Peace explained.

"To each other...not you," Xeno added.

"Kid– I think you're overthinking things. Just give me your file and–" The Captain smiled, holding out his hand.

"We never said anything about the file..." Parker interrupted, moving forward.

Captain Peace kept his smiling face but the joy seemed to slip, like he was annoyed.

The super boss scoffed, still trying to be kind and keep his composure, "Ok...fine, don't trust me?"

"...No." Xander spoke.

"*Good.*"

Within seconds Captain Peace pulled out a blaster and pulled the trigger. Firing at the two boys.

The shot seemed to take its sweet time as it inched closer and closer to Parker. Yet, in the last moments, Xander's body moved on its own, pushing Parker out of the way. However, the blast hit him straight in the leg,

"AAAAHHHHOOOWWW!" The villain let out an agonizing scream that seemed to shake the glass and fell to the floor with a thud, holding his stinging limb.

"*This will make things easier...*" Captain Peace declared sinisterly. "And more fun..."

"Xander!" Parker ran to his friend's side, looking up at his hero, "W-WHAT ARE YOU DOING?! HE'S A GOOD GUY! HE'S ON OUR SIDE!"

"...I wasn't aiming for him."

Parker's eyes grew and Xander's heart dropped– and as if things couldn't get any worse–

Xander felt nauseous once again. Like a bunch of powers screaming on top of each other, the same feeling he had back at the party. However, he held it together, trying to collect his stomach.

Captain Peace aimed his gun at Parker once more, but before he could shoot, Xander threw a fireball. Knocking the blaster out of his hands as it shattered the glass table.

"Gah!" The Captain yelped and ran to retrieve it.

Xander shoved the backpack in Parker's hands, filled with all the evidence of this cruel, sick, twisted world.

"RUN!" Xander warned, trying to muster up the volume.

"WHAT?! ARE YOU INSANE! I'M NOT GOING TO LEAVE YOU!" Parker protested, not even daring to give it a second thought.

"HE'S NOT AFTER ME!"

"HE WILL KILL YOU!"

"HE WILL KILL *YOU* IF YOU DON'T GO!" Xander screamed, angry he wasn't already out the door.

"WHERE DO I GO!?" The hero panicked.

"ANYWHERE BUT HERE! I'LL HOLD HIM OFF, YOU GET THIS EVIDENCE FAR AWAY FROM HERE!"

"WHAT?!" Parker screamed as Captain Peace slid and grabbed

his blaster.

"JUST **GO,** NOW! PLEASE, FIRECRACKER!" Xander yelled in his hoarse voice.

Captain Peace fired another blast as Parker ducked. The blast missed his head and smashed a glass wall. He looked back at the wall in shock. Hesitant, he put back on his goggles, grabbed the bag, and ran.

The captain took note; he had to reach that little hero before he left the building.

Xander stood up barely, limping, "You liar...I have no idea what the *hell* is going on, but you are going down." He put back on his mask and readied up.

"How?" Captain Peace did an evil laugh, "You sent your power source away!"

"You– ...you know I'm a mimic?"

His twisted smile turned into a grin that seemed to possess his face, "I KNOW EVERYTHING! You still really think it's just one person pulling the strings?!"

"You– YOU ARE WORKING WITH DARK LEGACY?!" Xeno started to circle.

Captain Peace followed, "Oh- is that what you think? Looks like you don't have it all figured out..." he raised his blaster and shot at Xeno.

Xenomorph rolled out of the way as the blast hit the floor.

Captain shot more blasts and Xeno backflipped, dodging all of them. However, when he landed on the floor he fell on impact. Wincing in pain.

Without a second to waste, Captain Peace soared in and with a heavy punch, sent him flying into one of the cabinets.

The sounds of glass echoed as Xenomorph fell to the floor. Sticky liquid started running down all over his body. He looked down to see red. The nausea kicked in like a cruel reward, and his vision became blurry as he started gasping for air. Something screamed in his brain as he looked down to see broken test tubes, each one labeled with a hero or villain.

Xenomorph gagged as he clicked this wasn't his blood. His dizzy thoughts spiraled as he swallowed the vomit rising in his throat. This was too much power to handle, the raw blood overwhelming him to the point he could see colors that weren't there and sounds he had only heard in his nightmares.

Captain Peace casually walked over as Xenomorph tried to get up, kicking him in his hurt leg, causing him to fall again. Xeno looked up at the cruel angel's face, but he started seeing double as the form blurred in and out of focus.

Firefly ran down the stairs as hard as he could, holding the bag, as he tried to process what in the world just happened. His boss lied to him! Everything was fake! It was all fake– he–

"AAAH!" Firefly screamed as the building started to collapse along with his thoughts, spreading with vines, water, fire, and explosions. On instinct he slid on the floor, holding the bag above his head. Barely making it as a vine came crashing in. He looked back to see Xeno from afar, somehow wielding everything he could to fight.

Xenomorph stumbled about as he sloppily shot off a blast of

fire, a blast of sound, and then a blast of lightning; trying to get a hit.

Captain Peace dodged the askew blast and looked over to see Firefly escaping. They made eye contact as the bug got back up and started running– fear running through his body.

"Damn it!" Captain Peace yelled as he took another shot and blasted Xenomorph right through several glass panes. The villain ragdolled on the floor, as glass sprinkled around him– cutting up his face. "Now, thanks to you…I have a bug to squash."

Xeno looked up in horror, trying to get up.

"Such a 'hero'," He taunted and ran after Firefly.

"HEY!" Xeno tried, forcing himself to get up despite the pain, "G-Get b-back here you maniac!" Xeno huffed, "G-Get up," he told himself, whipping the bulk of blood off, "Get up!"

Firefly continued to run, but soon his heart left his body when blaster shots went off, aiming awfully close to his head. Breaking all sorts of awards and marble.

Firefly kept flipping to dodge, as Captain Peace kept shooting.

"Stay still you–!"

SMASH! THACK!

Xenomorph fell from the roof, landing dramatically, and punched Captain Peace in that twisted grin. The boss took a step back, whipping the blood off his face.

"Oh…ok…wanna play kid?"

"Off the scripts you snake!" Xeno yelled, flaming fist up as his eyes glowed red.

Captain Peace threw the first punch and Xeno dodged. Together they held hand to hand combat, as Xenomorph backed up, throwing spikes of ice, chunks of rock, and shooting lazers from his eyes. Blocking every shot, as Captain Peace kept throwing one hit after another.

Xeno didn't buckle, and he threw a strike, but Captain Peace caught his fist and threw him over a table– breaking it.

"OUGH!" He winced.

"Stay down kid."

"Never!" Xeno bared his teeth, flipped back up, and threw another punch of lightning. He tried to get close to figure out who this liar was, but it wasn't the hopeful and light leader Firefly had thought. It was manipulative and dark. How the apple didn't fall far from the tree.

The mimic phased in and out of sight, teleporting around, and casting shields to block the captain's shots.

While Xenomorph was trying to figure the mystery out and get that blaster away from his trigger happy finger, the captain dodged all his flashy attacks and roundhouse kicked him right out the window–

The world slowed for a bit as he fell through the air, however, his flight didn't last long and he crashed into a balcony (fortunately).

"Mm...ah...ow...," Xenomorph whimpered as he tried to get up, but Captain Peace came crashing down and pinned him to the wall– aiming the blaster at his face.

"You should've stayed out of this," the boss stated, as the blaster fired up.

Xeno stretched his neck thin, ready to meet his fate when–

FWOOSH!

A flaming fireball came rushing in and burnt the captain's face. Only this time the blast didn't come from Xeno.

Captain Peace screamed in pain, but he refused to let go of his catch, only squeezing Xeno's neck tighter on instinct due to the burns.

When the fire flickered out they both looked over to see a furious Firefly, hand full of smoke from his fireball.

"LEAVE HIM ALONE!" He shouted.

"B-Buggy– g-go!" Xeno coughed weakly, kicking and struggling. Trying to raise his hand to summon something.

"With pleasure…" Captain Peace declared as he dropped the villain on the floor with a thump.

Xenomorph gasped for air as Captain Peace slowly approached his target.

Firefly ran in and threw his own hits. Captain Peace dodged one or two but couldn't escape the others as his anger started to escape his mouth.

With one final thwack to the face, Firefly started to back up, and then– he bolted confidently as Captain Peace chased him.

Xeno weakly got up again, "…Being a hero is exhausting," he whispered to himself, out of breath.

Firefly ran through the halls with his boss on his tail. His eyes grew at the threat behind him as he frantically looked around for an answer. He suddenly spotted the sprinkler on the ceiling. Just like before, he aimed and threw a ball of flames, activating the sprinklers.

The fire alarm rang off as Captain Peace shielded himself from the indoor rain. The noise being just another loud, annoying voice in the room to him.

Firefly then kicked down a glass wall, grabbing the shards of glass and melting them together in his own makeshift spear. Without a moment to think, he turned around to throw it only to see the Captain ready for him—face to face.

"I'll be taking that!" Captain Peace jerked the glass weapons out of Firefly's hand and poked him in the stomach with it, ever so gently.

Firefly raised his hands. Gulping at the lumpy blade. He shook in place as the softest little bite pressed on his chest.

"I've been wanting to do this for a looong~ time," Captain Peace quipped.

Firefly's eyes widened behind his lenses, not believing his hero, "...You are sick."

"...Thank you," he smirked, like a true villain.

Suddenly a blur of black and grays came and tackled the fake to the ground, shattering the glass spear.

Firefly watched as the blur became his friend–

"GO! NOW!" Xeno demanded, voice still cracking at the urgency. He used vines to tie the monster to the ground and ice to hold him, beating the crap out of him with super strength.

Although Firefly didn't want to go, he trusted his friend. So he nodded, picked up the bag, and ran through the front door.

"NOOOOOOO!" Captain Peace broke through the ice and roots, bucked Xenomorph off, and rushed to the door. Holding the frames as Firefly ran and ran back into the city. "SHHHHHHH~hoot."

394

Xeno laughed a bit from the floor, "It's over Captain, you've lost...can't fight him in public, can you?" The villain smirked.

"Good thing I have a few friends..." the captain baited. Looking down at his failure.

Xenomorph's smile faded as he realized what that meant. Captain Peace gave an evil smile and dropped his blaster on the floor. Sending it shooting on impact. Xeno ducked as it hit a shelf. The wooden plank fell on him along with the nicely potted plant.

"Gah!" He yelped.

When Xeno looked up, the captain had walked off into the shadows, cape dramatically following him in the wind. He raised a single hand as the building around him started to crack and collapse.

Dust falling from the sky as Xenomorph pushed his sore bones to the limit. Body telling him to stop, but he wouldn't listen. He slowly crawled along, before tucking and rolling out of the way of an incoming beam.

Xenomorph coughed at the dust and looked down at the blaster, and couldn't help ponder about its scary, familiar design.

However, he quickly scrambled up and left. Racing out the doors with a limp to find his firecracker before something else got to him.

Chapter 32:

Firefly ran with all his breath, sprinting down the street like his life depended on it—cause it did. Clouds started to form as the sky turned gray, like a bad omen.

The hero pushed over people and apologized soon after. He slid on the hood of a yellow taxi as he breathed, taking cover behind the object.

The hero took out his phone and dialed a number–

"Hello? 911 what's your emergency?" A nice lady asked on the other side as the hero got up to run again.

"MA'AM CAN I PLEASE SPEAK TO OFFICER JAY!" He yelled.

"Right away sir," After some dialing later, the phone re-rung, "Hello?" a man asked.

"JAY! HELP! THIS IS FIREFLY! I NEED YOU! I KNOW I'M STILL A VIGILANTE BUT MY FRIEND AND I ARE GETTING CHASED BY CAPTAIN PEACE! PLEASE! YOU NEED TO COME

NOW!" Firefly yelled through the phone as he ran.

"C-Captain Peace?" Jay muttered through the phone.

"CAPTAIN PEACE CAN'T BE TRUSTED! HIM AND DARK LEGACY ARE FAKING EVERYTHING! THEY ARE IN KAHOOTS! PLEASE LISTEN TO ME! VILLAINS AND HEROES AREN'T REAL! IT'S A SETUP! PLEASE GET DOWN HERE QUICK WE NEED HELP!"

"Alright! Alright! I'll be right there! Where are you?!" Jay asked.

"I'm at—" Firefly started before he heard sparks and a big flash from above him. Looking up for only seconds he jumped back out of the way of the telephone pole.

The call ended.

Firefly looked at the base of the pole to see a very nice and familiar sports car.

"Wow, no reception? That's Karma for destroying my car..." A voice entered.

The hero looked up to see a cloaked figure in a gas mask with that wretched skull painted over it.

Firefly stuffed the phone in his pocket and froze.

The shadow jumped down in front of him as the lights sparked behind him.

"D-D-Dark Legacy?!" Firefly yelped.

"Hello~ firebrat!" He said and immediately used his powers of telekinesis to lift Firefly up and throw him into the car. Sending the car alarm screaming.

Firefly tried to get off of the car as the villain grabbed his hoodie and yanked him up.

"Well…well…well…if it isn't the kid who started it all."

"I'm not scared of you!" Firefly yelled as he readied a ball of fire.

"*You should be.*"

Firefly swung the fireball as Dark Legacy sent him flying into a brick wall. With no way to turn, the teen scaled up a fire escape and flipped onto a roof, however, he only managed a couple steps before getting interrupted by the villain leader once again. Beating him to freedom.

"Where ya going, Sparky…I thought you weren't scared?" He sassed as he punched Firefly, who toppled over the edge of the roof. The hero misplaced his step and fell.

With a string of luck Firefly grabbed the roof, pulling himself back on the ledge.

While he was busy, Dark Legacy launched a cooling unit at him which shoved him off the roof onto another building. The hero rag-dolled on the cold concrete—

"UAGH!" Firefly groaned, but got up and started to run.

"You really think you can outrun me?! You have nowhere to go!" Dark Legacy yelled and chased after him.

Xenomorph, bloodied and bruised, made it to the streets; still limping on one leg, he looked around for his friend.

Suddenly a shadow flew over him and Xeno looked up; revealing Firefly jumping across rooftops.

Before Xeno even had a moment to breathe in relief, Dark Legacy jumped after him.

Xenomorph's heart fell. He immediately ran over to a building and started climbing it to catch up.

Firefly flipped over everything and even jumped into the unfinished construction from earlier this week—which was a mistake.

The flaming bug wobbled on the loose wooden plank, but sprinted; sliding through all sorts of tight piping and scaffolding.

Dark Legacy entered with ease and started tearing apart the structure with his power and chucking the scrap pieces at Firefly.

The kid dodged the flying debris and junk and kept running.

He ran and ran towards the way out, and just when he looked like he was going to make it—

Dark Legacy threw a giant chunk of cement,

"GAHOW!" He whined as he fell through a couple layers of bare floor work.

Xenomorph jumped into the construction as well, but buckled at the force of impact, "ow…ow ow!" He winced as he held his leg.

Firefly threw a weak fireball and Dark Legacy dodged it. Xeno looked down to see it fly off before he used the telekinesis to direct it to a bundle of wooden planks.

Sending a mass fire erupting in the center.

Dark Legacy and Firefly turn to see the orange glow only to catch Xeno swinging on the hook of the crane, kicking back Dark Legacy into the steel railing.

"AUGH! *Oh that's it!*" The true villain erupted as he pulled down the crane with his power.

The crane started to fall and crash when Xenomorph jumped onto another layer of the building. He tried to ready up any power he had left but the blood had either dripped off or dried up, making it useless. At least Xeno's sickness started to settle and vision became clearer.

"You two have been getting in my way FOR FAR TOO LONG!" Dark Legacy spat as he grabbed a piece of the scaffolding, breaking it off into a sharp piece of steel.

Firefly gulped as he stumbled up.

"I AM DONE! YOU 'HEROES' THINK YOU KNOW WHAT'S BEST?! YOU THINK YOU'RE SO GREAT!?! YOU ONLY THINK ABOUT YOURSELF!" Dark Legacy yelled as he approached, Firefly weakly sprinted across more work, and even slid down a few conveniently placed panels until he was back on solid ground.

Dark Legacy launched the pipe with his power and like a missile, it flew towards its target.

Xeno, once again falling behind, jumped to the ground saw from afar and tried to throw a ball of fire to deflect the blade.

The fire swooshed in and interrupted the shot, but not well enough—

SLICE

"AH!" Firefly held his arm as the pipe whizzed by, barely scraping him, but enough to hurt.

The blast of the fire also didn't help as it landed in a pile of gunpowder— blowing up and launching everything everywhere.

400

Xeno fell onto the ground, giving in once again. He coughed and waved away the smoke as he looked for his friend.

But all he was met with was a surprise attack by Dark Legacy.

Xenomorph yelled as his head was soon slammed into a concrete pillar.

"GAH! Ow! Why! ARE YOU AFTER HIM! I'M THE ONE YOU WANT!" Xeno yelled.

"...*You're not the one I want.*" Dark Legacy said coldly, "Eventually, I do...but now it's a matter of who gets to the press first and *who do you think they're going to believe...?*"

Xenomorph's eyes widened as he remembered that same question back at the gala.

"...The hero..." he whispered, finally figuring it out.

"*You are no hero...*" Dark Legacy finished and threw him again, rolling his puppet onto the dirt ground before swinging his hand to drop hundreds of pounds of debris on him.

Xeno shielded up and screamed as the stone fell, when the rubble finally settled he was stuck.

"But you are right, I am after both of you..." He waved his hand around and the steel pipe flew into his hands, "Goodbye Xenomorph, it truly was not a pleasure..." Dark Legacy taunted as he held the rough dagger high.

Suddenly— a big burst of flames scorched his hands, dropping the pointed weapon on the sand once again. Both villains looked over to see Firefly standing there, on fire, confident, not afraid.

Xeno taught him too well.

"P-Parker, not again, what are you doing?" Xeno struggled.

Firefly's face stayed silent and determined, like he knew something that Xeno didn't.

"Let. Him. GO." Firefly demanded.

"*Excuse me?*" Dark Legacy asked.

"You heard me! It's this that you want…" Firefly threatened, shaking the backpack, "unless you want me to tell the public about your web of lies…"

"WHAT ARE YOU DOING?!" Xeno tried, still struggling.

"Being a real hero and saving everyone, or… 'Getting my karma'," Firefly smiled weakly.

"Well that was a dumb move!" Dark Legacy laughed.

"What's dumb is thinking no one will believe him," Firefly secretly readied a fireball behind him, "BECAUSE I DO!" The hero threw the ball and Dark Legacy screamed as it hit and the little bug bolted.

"Oh. *THAT'S IT!* You are *dead.*" He scolded nothing and ran after the last piece.

"No– NO, NO, NO, NO, NO, NO!" Xeno yelled, trying to escape but he could not move. He hung his head in defeat, breathing, until suddenly he felt an anger he had never known. Like the blood of a matchbox being spilt, yet also being lit. Fire lit his eyes as he had a new goal: *To defeat Dark Legacy at any cost.* With that he started to light a blaze…

Firefly ran weakly, breath in his lungs starting to go out, utterly sore, exhausted, and in pain. He couldn't take the adrenaline anymore and the hero ducked into the crack that was an alleyway.

He ran through the old, secret way, dodging trash bins and garbage as it turned into a dead end.

Punching the wall he quickly turned back around, mortified, when Dark Legacy jumped down as well, blocking his exit.

Firefly froze for a second, before the villain picked him up with his powers and threw him at the wall, pinning him up against the bricks.

Dark Legacy just laughed and laughed, "Wow~ you almost won…"

"Y-You won't get away with this! Xenomorph will stop you! People will find out the truth! …Governor Jaceson."

"…Hm flattering. Lucky for me you've gathered all the evidence in one spot…"

Firefly froze as he held the bag.

Dark Legacy waved his other hand in the air as the sharp pipe came flying into his hand; still covered in some of the hero's blood. Firefly couldn't really think in the moment as the end sparkled in the night light. All he knew was: it was sharp…

"You are not getting this bag! XANDER'S LIFE IS ON THE LINE!" Firefly yelled.

"Now who said I was after the bag…"

Firefly's blood ran cold, "B-But you said the evidence–"

"*You're* the evidence, Firebrat."

"…W-What?"

Dark Legacy dropped him.

"Wha!" Firefly fell to the ground.

"I tried to warn that 'friend' of yours, who is the city going to believe after you spin this drastic tale about how the 'governor is a super villain and it's all faked'?! Do you think they are going to believe a villain?"

Firefly stayed silent, he knew *his* answer…but that wasn't the correct one, was it?

"They *always* believe the heroes. Of course you'll both still die—just need to get you out of the way first… especially after you two RUINED EVERYTHING! ALL MY HARD WORK! YEARS AND YEARS OF GAINING CONTROL! LYING TO THE PUBLIC! PUTTING ON SO MANY FACES!"

"…" Firefly stood frozen, scooting back and trying to pick himself back up, shocked.

"BUT NO MATTER HOW HARD I TRY– NO MATTER HOW MANY HEROES I HAD TO KILL, YOU TWO DESTROYED EVERYTHING! And now you have a price to pay…Sorry Parker…time to disappear…" He spat coldly.

"Y-You know my name too…?" The hero stuttered, finally managing to stand.

"…I *did*…say hi to your father for me."

Dark Legacy quipped and launched the pipe directly at Firefly—

The hero tried to escape but it was too late-

SHLING!

The broken pipe impaled him clean through.

Firefly let out the most blood curdling scream of his life,

awaking the city. He stood frozen for what felt like years, the shock and adrenaline being too much to feel at the moment. Red sticky liquid started pouring from the pipe and his mouth. Any hope of Firefly getting back up was lost as he stumbled back down.

Dark Legacy walked up to him, ready to pull that pipe out and make things so much worse, "Goodbye Firefly…"

When out of nowhere-

THUD! POW!

A figure jumped down and a flaming fist of fire punched Dark Legacy straight in the face, but it wasn't Firefly.

The injured hero looked up to see the impossible;

Xenomorph there, ready to fight, but lit completely ablaze. Mask burnt to a singe so you could see those cold—or rather hot—eyes. As if he were fire itself. The flames danced in reds and yellows and even blue—

Firefly had never seen blue fire before.

Xeno stood still, in his flaming anger, fire in his eyes as he felt the rage fuel him to the tipping point. Like the sun's pain and suffering.

Xenomorph was 'Blowing a fuse'; and it was the strongest one Firefly had ever seen.

"…I told you– *you hurt him*– *I'll rip you limb from limb…it was a **promise, remember?**"* Xenomorph threatened and threw another punch—direct hit.

Dark Legacy barely flinched as Xeno threw another and another landing every swing and kick; like a ballistic mad man. Moving faster than light itself as he kept knocking his ex-boss back. Being unstoppable.

Dark Legacy kept taking hits, trying to throw one of his own, but eventually he stumbled back defeated. His gas mask melted into an abomination as he took a breath.

Finally Xenomorph stopped to see him fall, but he didn't.

"You really think that would work?" Dark Legacy gestured to his cloak, "It's fire resistant, although funny enough my helmet isn't," he informed, so calmly it was a burning taunt.

Xeno stared daggers into him, shielding his injured friend, *"Stay. Away. From him."*

"But 'He started it', right, Xeno? And you two are so annoying…" Dark Legacy scoffed as he slowly took off his burnt mask, revealing the shock twist of fate…

Of Captain Peace.

"W-What…?" Firefly whimpered from behind, still leaking out. Eyes starting to close, feeling light headed.

Xeno's disgusted start to turn into confusion, "But…that can't be! YOU'RE SUPPOSED TO BE GOVERNOR JACESON!" He flared up even more.

Captain Peace took off his super mask and there was their shiny Governor covered in ash and dirt, throwing them a flashy smirk, "SURPRISE!"

Both boys' hearts dropped as he put his hero mask back on, but there was nothing heroic about him.

Xeno's eyes widened as he couldn't believe it—he refused to believe it.

"Y-You're…YOU'RE ALL THREE?! HOW ARE YOU ALL THREE?! THAT DOESN'T MAKE ANY SENSE! DARK— CAPTAIN— WHAT?!" Xeno screamed, his fire getting bigger and bluer by the second.

"You know…I have many names," he approached, slowly and Xeno started backing up. "I go by Captain Peace, or Dark Legacy, or Governor Jaceson…but we are close now, revealing identities and all, so you can call me by my real name…

Ace."

"…What the hell?" Xeno asked, shivering down his spine as his fire started to flicker out. The moon shined its twisted light; how did the day turn into this?

Firefly was still watching everything as he held his wound, trying to keep his head up. Speaking was agony.

"Shocked? I would be too…" Ace smiled, with just a raise of his hand the pipe flew out of Firefly and right back onto his hands.

"NO!" Xeno yelped.

Firefly's blood spilled more, creating a big, red puddle for him to soak in as he tried to cover it up.

Ace leaned on the pole, "Heck, your parents were quite surprised…" he kept taunting.

Xeno flamed up even more, becoming a bright torch, *"you…YOU KILLED OUR PARENTS!"* He went in for a punch when Ace picked him up with telekinesis and threw him against a metal dumpster.

"AAGG!" The flaming super winced.

"Listen! I tried to reason with them! We had powers! We were above everyone—everything! THE WORLD SHOULD HAVE BEEN OURS TO TAKE! Money! Riches! Fame! Power! Control! Life itself! But after a couple 'impulsive decisions'…I was kicked out of the super seven…"

"You were in the super seven? A-As in…Ace Spades…" Xeno solved.

"Damn right I was! And guess who stabbed me in the back! My own mentors, FLAMETHROWER AND MOCKING BIRD! YOUR PARENTS DESERVED EVERYTHING THEY GOT!"

"W-What…" Firefly whispered barely from the corner, "Our parents… w-were…friends?"

"Inseparable…so when the opportunity came I had to make sure that never happened again…you really think it's a coincidence you were assigned against each other?!"

"YOU ARE INSANE!" Xeno flamed up, getting back to his feet, "OUR PARENTS WERE HEROES– THEY DIDN'T 'STAB YOU IN THE BACK', YOU WERE TOO DANGEROUS! And clearly they were *right*."

"I WAS THE *RIGHT* ONE! I will get rid of EVERYONE WHO STANDS IN MY WAY OF WHAT I DESERVE! EVEN A COUPLE OF TEENAGE BRATS!" Ace swung the bleeding pipe around, ready to launch it to Xeno's flaming chest next.

"YOU ARE A MONSTER!" Xeno threw a fireball—but it was small and weak.

Ace dodged like nothing, "How can I be wrong when I've been

successful the past ten years…" he smirked.

Xeno threw another fireball but it was still weak. Ace continued to dodge, "I've been winning this whole time. As 'Captain Peace' I get respect, power, fame! As your beloved 'Dark Legacy' I get the stolen treasure and riches, the power, the fear! And as the Governor I get the people, the votes, the city…and above all else control…I've had this entire world in my hands and you two were just pawns living it."

"…Shut up." Xeno muttered, wielding a huge flame.

"Not my fault you two were dumb enough to fall for it…" Ace gave a big, gut-wrenching smile.

"Shut up!" Xeno warned again.

"And now…finally…after a week of nonsense…I have you in *checkmate*."

"I SAID SHUT UP!" Xeno burst into flames and punched Ace as hard as he could, sending the villain flying back.

Xeno wound his blast up again, but it was the weakest, littlest flame he's ever thrown. It didn't even make it across the alley before fading out.

"W-What…?" *Impossible, Firefly is still here– he is right here.* He kept trying but the fire kept growing smaller and smaller.

Almost as if it were dying…

Xeno's bloodshot was cold as he realized.

"…What's the matter Xander…did we lose something?" Ace taunted.

Before another word, out of nowhere Firefly swung a random pipe at the villain, hitting him back and out onto the empty sidewalk.

"NOW!" The bleeding hero screamed at his shocked partner.

With the last of his rage, Xenomorph blasted him into the streets, burning his face.

The villain got up from the broken street, and was on his way over, walking like nothing happened—like he was happy even.

Suddenly a cop car came racing in and Firefly saw his only opportunity.

He shot one final fireball at the tire, sending the car to spin out and run into Ace. Who flipped on the windshield, breaking the glass and tumbling back onto the pavement.

Xeno was at first in shock, but as the cops got out with the special power diffusers, he only had one thought on his mind—

"Firefly!" He turned to his friend, "Are you ok?"

"Yeah...yeah..." Firefly slurred together, "I...I just...need to lie down..." he said before collapsing.

"FIREFLY!" Xeno shouted and ran to him, sliding on his knees. He looked down at the pool of blood.

Eyes shaking and adrenaline pumping—for the first time—afraid.

"We need to get you to a hospital!" Xeno rushed out, trying to pick him up.

"...A h-hospital? B-But wait, you can't go to a hospital...you'll be arrested, remember?" Firefly reminded softly.

"SO?! ARE YOU CRAZY?! I'M NOT RISKING YOUR LIFE FOR MY FREEDOM! LET'S GO!"

"And I'm not risking your life for mine-...I promised...I-I

wouldn't let anything bad happen to you."

"DUDE! STOP IT! YOU ARE GOING AND THAT IS FINAL!" Xeno tried, ripping off the rest of his mask, as it hung loosely around his neck.

"Xander…"

"NO! SHUT UP! SHUT UP! I AM NOT LOSING YOU TOO!" He started to tear up, trying to hold what was left of Firefly.

"…ow…ow…" the hero whispered as Xander tried to tug him up.

"COME ON! YOU GOT THIS! YOU ARE GOING TO BE OK! WE ARE GOING TO THE HOSPITAL AND–"

"…Xander listen–," Firefly grabbed his cloak with what little strength he had left. "Even…i-if I wanted too…I–…I don't think I'm going to make it," the voice cracked, water welling up in his eyes, trying to smile.

Xander stopped, "…No…d-don't say that! You will! Just stay with me! I'm right here! I'm not going anywhere, and neither are you!" The villain begged as his voice cracked.

Firefly took his goggles off his head.

"W-What are you doing?"

The dying teen grabbed Xander's hand and softly shoved the goggles in them.

"Parker! Stop, this isn't funny!" He bawled.

"You have to protect the city…"

"WHAT?! NO!"

"You have too…because I– I won't be here…"

"NO! NO! NO! WE DO IT TOGETHER, THAT WAS THE DEAL! I AM NOT DOING THIS WITHOUT YOU!"

Parker had a light laugh, "breaking a promise…guess you really did rub off on me, eh parent in crime?"

"No…no…NO, NO, NO!"

"Take care of New York for me," Firefly said, eyes getting lighter.

"STOP IT! DON'T LEAVE ME LIKE THIS!" Xander cried.

"Be the amazing hero you were meant to be…the amazing hero that *I* know you were meant to be…ok?"

Xander opened his mouth to say something, but the police siren went off—catching his attention. He looked to see Ace getting arrested, cuffed and thrown in the car– it was only a second.

Just a split second.

But when Xander looked back at his friend, his hand dropped and his eyes closed.

"…Firefly?" He asked, gently shaking him.

"Parker." He shook again, "Wake up! This isn't how it ends!"

Still nothing as his skin turned cold.

Xander tried to light fire in his hands to prove himself wrong, but nothing lit despite him being right there.

"Firecracker!" He shook again.

"BUGGY!" He screamed, eyes filled with water.

Time seemed to stop. Freezing like ice as the shock was just too much for the new hero to process.

Seconds turned into hours as the coldness of the night slowly crept.

Just like that, Firefly was gone.

With nothing more, Xander caved. His tears started to form slowly. Dropping onto the hero's lifeless body, hugging him tighter than anything. Still holding the goggles, crying his eyes out.

"...I'm so, so sorry..." Xander whispered into his ear, and after another painful silence later, "...I will be your hero."

Chapter 33:

Xander shoved off his villain coat as the rain started. Putting on the blue varsity jacket from the concert. The new hero pulled the hood on, hiding most of his iconic white hair.

Finally, placing his friend's goggles on his face; it felt like a cruel joke. Like it wasn't real.

Xander stuffed whatever was left in the bag, not that he cared anymore. He felt like he had just chugged a bottle of novocaine—numb.

In his new look, he grabbed Parker and carried him out of the alleyway bridal style– although it was the opposite of a wedding.

Police lights blurred his vision in flashing reds and blues as he slowly walked out.

Soon the cops noticed him, cheeks burning red, blank stare. If they could see his eyes, they'd find out that they were lifeless.

The police officers didn't raise their guns, didn't even flinch. It was odd for Xander to see policemen like that. He was so used to running away, dodging tasers, and getting thrown behind bars.

"Kid? You ok?" They asked.

Xander just handed them Parker…or what was Parker.

"…Help him," the teen mumbled.

The officers quickly took the bloodied corpse from his hands—Xander had a hard time letting go—feeling nothing was just as awful. He tried to stay strong, holding back his tears.

The police laid him on the hood of the car and radioed for an ambulance. While one officer (who Xander could've sworn looked familiar) checked his pulse, the other came to talk to him.

"It's going to be ok bud, we will take care of him. Now what happened?"

Xander's mouth quivered, what did happen? In a week his life was turned upside down and if they had time, he'd go into every wonderful detail. But he knew the cops didn't need the full story…just the tragic ending.

"H-He…um…Dark…Legacy got to him," Xander broke, it felt horrible to say that name; how was this the man he'd been worshiping all this time? He really was a pawn, everyone was. The metal spear lying on the side of the road covered in blood was proof that everyone on his team was expendable…

"Alright, don't worry, the ambulance is on its way…who might you be?"

Xander froze.

"I haven't seen you around before, are you a new hero?"

Thanks to his friend, the line in the sand was finally washed away. Xander was officially a hero now—whether he felt like it or not.

While that was one question answered for him, there was still another: Who are you?

Xander searched his brain looking for an answer, a real one. Who was he? The new hero didn't have much time to think, he looked at his partner in crime, trying not to cry…and in honor of him said;

"I…am Phoen-X."

The officer nodded, holding out his hand, "Nice to meet you Phoen-X, glad you are a part of the team."

Phoen-X shook it, "Thank you, but…there actually is no more team."

"What?" The policeman's smile faded.

"Heroes are faked. Villains are faked, nothing was real…Par–…Firefly and I went on a mission…and discovered the truth…Dark Legacy…is Captain Peace."

The policemen stood shellshock.

"And the Governor– we've all been lied to too."

"Whoa– ok, ok– hold on…why don't you start from the beginning," the cop suggested.

So he did, Phoen-X spun the tale just like Dark Legacy mocked, but they *did* believe him, because he was a hero now.

After a while of explaining everything (except the part where he was Xenomorph) the cop looked at his co-worker for an update on the injured super, however the other policeman shook his head slowly, giving a frown.

The policeman who listened to the hero's story deflated, "…I…um…I'm sorry."

Phoen-X started tearing up all over again, hyperventilating as he tried to run to his friend. However, the policeman held him back as the hero struggled in his grip.

"LET ME GO! YOU HAVE TO HELP HIM!" The hero raved like a lunatic as a third policeman helped hold him back.

"Sir, I'm so sorry…but there's nothing we can do," the first cop tried to calm the new hero down as the struggling and grunts from him slowly faded. Knees weakening and surrendering to gravity as Phoen-X was not being held back anymore, but being held up.

"…He can't be," Phoen-X denied.

"Look, we will do everything we can when the ambulance arrives, but there's not much you can do…you did all you could, and you did everything right," the words stung like a scar.

"…Anything would've been worth it for him…" he mumbled, standing back up.

"Have you seen Xenomorph? The two were last seen together," the officer asked.

Phoen-X looked down at the street, eyes widened behind the lenses, "…Xenomorph is dead."

The world was quiet at that answer.

The second police officer handed Phoen-X Firefly's phone and a slew of photobooth photos taken from one crazy roller skating rink.

Phoen-X had to swallow his pain once more—it didn't feel real. His hands shook with the photos and the nice officers noticed.

They looked at each other, "Why don't you head home," the first policeman suggested.

"…Home?" Phoen-X muffled. He hadn't been home in so

417

long—home was the goal, right? So why did it feel so empty?

He didn't wanna go home.

After tonight, did he even have a home? Devan probably threw all his stuff out days ago, even then Dark Legacy– or Ace paid the rent. They'd be kicked out in a week at most.

"I…I don't have a home."

"Oh…" the policeman replied.

Just then a text went off on Parker's phone– it was his mom.

Confused Phoen-X looked at it, he saw her text;

Hi, Lovebug! How's it going? Are you close to defeating Dark Legacy?

Phoen-X scrolled up.

They had been texting the entire time, going over plans, explaining stuff, saying how much they loved and missed each other. All the way back when 'Xenomorph' and Firefly were enemies…

Enemies, wow, things really were different.

Phoen-X didn't want to leave Parker…but he couldn't leave her dangling like that. He found out the hard way…the last thing he wanted was to put anyone else through that.

"I…um…I actually might be ok," He tried.

"Ok, if you say so," the police wrote something down on a yellow pad, "We will be at this hospital in this room if anything changes— we will call you when we can."

With a rip the officer handed Phoen-X the paper. The hero stared at the numbers, as if they meant anything.

"Thank you officers…" Phoen-X mumbled and slowly

approached the car just as the ambulance pulled up.

For the last time Phoen-X held Firefly's cold wrist, rubbing it. Tongue tied as he just waited for his friend's eyes to open, but they never did.

Soon EMTs started running out of the ambulance and surrounded Parker, pushing Phoen-X out of the way.

That was his cue to leave, he took his last breaths of cool air and slowly backed away, heading off into the unknown.

As he walked down the street, Phoen-X couldn't take his eyes off the scene as the nurses carefully loaded the body into the van on a big stretcher.

The teen tried to smile, but found it so difficult, "G-Goodbye, Buggy...say hi to dad for me and...thank you."

The teen continued to walk the wet streets as the rain continued. What a hit to the face. He didn't get a block before stopping under a lamppost, sitting and curling up at the base, and sobbed until the goggle's lenses were practically full. The water drenched him but he didn't care.

All he could think about was what happened. Running the same ten minutes in his head in circles. Finally putting together the puzzle, but at what cost? He started spamming himself with questions and crises. Trying to find hope in the storm, but Firefly was nowhere to be found.

After what felt like forever, he pulled out the phone. Using clues he found an address and followed it. Walking through the empty roads as the street light shined their orange light. It was the same setting, same scene, same painting– but everything just felt wrong. Like the world was broken.

***

Skyscrapers became trees as the lights flickered out. The rain still poured as Phoen-X walked, zoning out. He wasn't all there, and nobody cared. Watching the pavement, as he just kept walking. On that horrid autopilot, still trying to process what had happened.

Eventually the phone led him to a small house in the suburbs. It was nice. White picket fence, stable roofing, a nice eggshell color with black accents. Fluffy bushes dotted the path as the hero slowly opened the gate. The creaking sound felt like a warning, like a new chapter had just begun.

He slowly strolled up the path, taking his precious time as he walked up the stairs. Getting to the door–

What was I thinking?! How in the world am I going to explain what happened?! She's going to kill me.

Phoen-X thought as he was about to knock.

However his fist stayed there, in the air, waiting for something. Something to interrupt him.

However, nothing did.

With his soaking wet hair and shivery breath, he exhaled and knocked on the door.

Waiting for the heartbreak, he stuck his hands in his pockets– but to his surprise he felt something.

The hero pulled out a tiny, red lighter.

Phoen-X stared at it, completely forgetting he took it. Although he couldn't tell if he regretted it or not. He just kept staring at it until footsteps approached.

A lady opened the door, he assumed it was his mom. She looked like him, too much like him. The warm light of a safe house shined behind her.

Her smile disappeared at the stranger in front of her.

"Hello?"

"H-Hi…" Phoen-X started, "I…I um…"

"Am Xenomorph." She finished for him, smirking.

"…How did you–"

She leaned on the door frame, not a care in the world, "Your white hair is kinda a give away, plus you're at Firefly's house– and I've been keeping tabs, you two have been spending a lot of time together recently," she smiled.

"…U-Um, yeah, I hope that's…ok?"

"Of course it is, I want my son to be kind to everyone and see the good in people…and clearly he did…or you wouldn't be here."

"…You…got that right," Phoen-X muttered.

"Anyways, where is he? If you're here, clearly he can't be far behind," She grinned.

Phoen-X had no words, not one. With a sad frown and a silent mind just handed her the lighter.

Her face softened as she looked down. The realization slowly set in as she picked it up ever so carefully.

"…I'm so sorry…" Phoen-X voice cracked.

The lady quickly fell into tears, bawling her eyes out and gasping for air as she wailed in pain. Covering her mouth and chest. Phoen-X just watched her, still guilty about being that awful messenger.

He assumed she would want nothing to do with him now, after all, he failed. He was the reason Parker died. *It should've been me. It is best to just leave her alone—*

Phoen-X started to walk away when she rushed to him and gave him a big hug.

Phoen-X's body stopped in shock. The mom squeezed and cried and after a while he did the same, burying himself into her shoulder. Although he was a lot more silent.

Parker's mom started to slowly quiet down and Phoen-X started to shiver when she noticed.

She pulled back—eyes red and puffy, "Oh honey…you're freezing…do you want to come in?"

"Come in…? You…you want me to stay?"

"Of course I do, please… I need to know what happened," she whispered, eyes breaking.

Phoen-X nodded his head and went inside.

His wet hair dripped onto the hardwood floor as he looked around at the nice house. The yellow glow still felt warm as he looked around. Picture frames lining the wall and doorways that lead into a beautiful kitchen and a cozy living room.

Parker's mom closed the door and froze to watch him.

Phoen-X pondered around brushing the lampshade with his tips and picking up mementos and decor. Trying to figure out the meaning behind each one.

"Your house is nice," The hero finally said, mumbling as he rubbed the edge of a framed photo of her completed family.

"...Thank you..." she drifted, not knowing what to say.

The hero put down the frame and looked at the door but the mother was gone. He frantically looked around, but she soon came back out of the kitchen with two glasses of water. Trying to hand one off to the boy.

Phoen-X hesitantly took it, took a sip, and before he knew it; Parker's mom led him over to their plush couch.

The woman sat next to him and tapped her glass, and in a shaky breath asked, "What happened to him?"

The rest of the night was a blur, but an oddly warm blur. Parker's mom, Nina, listened to the story for a bit, then she made tea and helped her guest dry off. Soon they were back on the couch as Phoen-X kept explaining everything. Every little detail, even telling her how he felt—which he didn't get to do yet.

The lady listened patiently, telling her side, talking about Parker and his dad and how important they were to this world. The crying and chatting went on for hours, but Nina invited him to stay the night.

At first Phoen-X protested, but she insisted; little did he know it wasn't just for that night, he was there the next night and the one after that and so on for years to come.

Chapter 34:

The funeral was just about a week later. Life was quiet and soulless. Xander stood outside as the rain drizzled down, shoes sinking into grass as he stood in his black suit. Nina helped him out. He twirled the single rose he had nervously in his hand, like it meant something.

The service was small, and the turnout was even smaller. Mostly just Nina's side of the family, a couple news reporters, and he saw Quinn, but he thought it was best just to leave her alone. Not a single villain or even hero showed up besides 'Phoen-X' himself. He couldn't tell if he was relieved or absolutely disgusted by the entitlement. Parker laid his life on the line for everyone and barely anyone cared; but no supers meant he didn't have to hide behind some silly mask and dodge suspicion.

Without a mask or goggles (which still dangled around his neck) he could see the gravestone ever so clearly, blue eyes dulling at the stone.

Parker's mom went up to give her speech in the rain as everyone paid attention. Umbrellas up in the air, all except Xander, who refused one.

"Hello everyone," She started, voice already breaking. Xander never felt so much empathy for someone before. "T-Thank you for coming...I know this is probably not the day you wanted to have, but Parker would've appreciated it...he was an amazing son, the brilliant hero Firefly, and a true friend," She looked over at Xander who just stared back at her, focused. "He will be missed, forever and always, but he's finally with his father now and probably having an incredible time up in the heavens, saving the afterlife from whatever demons are running amok up there," she forced a giggle and the audience gave her a soft laugh.

She took a deep breath and started again, tears welling her eyes, "I can't tell you how proud I am of him, for seeing the good and light in everything he did...he would've conquered the world with that type of kindness, so I hope you all vow to do the same..." with another breath she was done, walking back to her spot along the grass, "If anyone wants to go up to speak, now is the time."

Xander looked around, expecting a line but he was mortified when no one offered to go next. It's like they didn't even care. Nina also noticed and began to silently cry to herself. They all looked down and away.

Xander didn't know if it was the anger of revenge, or the disappointment in society, or just the hope of talking to his friend again– but without a word he strode up to the stone, put on his friend's goggles, and faced the crowd.

Nina froze, and all eyes landed on him.

"I would like to speak," he cracked a bit. "I...hadn't known Firefly– or...Parker as long as any of you guys, and definitely not as long as I would've liked to. But I can say with one hundred percent confidence, that he is the best thing to ever happen in my life. I know many of you don't know me, or my past...but it's because of me...he's gone."

The mother put her hands over her mouth in grief as the crowd gasped.

Phoen-X couldn't hold back the pain any longer as the tears began to roll down his cheeks, but they just looked like rain to the average person.

"He sacrificed his life...for me. A debt I could never repay, except to live his final words...become the amazing hero I was born to be and keep the world safe. And that's exactly what I plan to do... From this day on I vow to watch over New York and protect its civilians, the way he would've. Firefly was the fire in my life, and although he's put out...his inspiration and hope will never leave my veins...one day I hope you realize what he stood for...cause it was worth every breath."

With that Phoen-X gently placed his rose down right next to the stone, "You did good buddy," he whispered, still tearing up, "You were super," he softly chuckled, and stood back up, strutting back to his spot in confidence. Nina even rubbed his arm. They looked at each other knowing the truth that no one else knew.

***

After the funeral, everything changed.

Phoen-X told the truth to the world on many live channels and speeches, even resolving peace between the villains and heroes. He tore down both organizations, and with the help of his new mom, started a new chapter of his hero's life. Creating a brand new (non-secretive) organization—one that didn't control everyone with strings and lines and schedules.

He gave every hero and villain the choice to stay or leave. Some heroes retired like they wanted, some villains refused and went to start solo villain careers, but the majority of the supers (both heroes and villains) decided to join Phoen-X in his new era. Creating a whole new wave of true, dedicated, passionate heroes that saved New York every day.

A new Governor was even selected, turns out Michael was more than ready for the role, and was nothing but a blessing to New York—supporting the heroes in full and didn't have two faces or was evil.

Ace was sentenced to life in prison, but Phoen-X decided no ordinary prison would hold such a monster. A new cage would be built, one in which a super could never escape. Creating the Villainary Prison System, making Ace prisoner number: 001. In there he will rot for years thinking about his mistakes and scheming his revenge.

As for Xander himself, life seemed to be turning around. He stayed at Nina's, and by night he was the beloved Phoen-X, the most chaotic but kind hero in all of New York. Some people guessed his past, but he'd always leave no comment or deny it. He trained heroes like

Thunderstorm, Soundwave, Rosethorn, Yellow Jacket, and many others the right way—*and he loved it.*

He loved being a hero.

But by day, he was doing so much more.

Xander went on to become a famous comic book author and artist; ironic. Speaking at conventions, doing interviews, making hundreds of comics and so much more. He was celebrated in his field for his books. His best selling comic series by far was: The Super Tales of Firefly.

In honor of his memory, Xander wrote and drew comics of his friend in all the adventures he didn't get to go on. The book series was nothing but a success and Firefly became one of the most well-known and amazing superheroes in the world. Keeping him alive in some way, and Xander couldn't be prouder.

The teen continued to write his friend's legacy in the sun and fight for it at night dawning his name.

Xenomorph was no more, just like Ace said, but his life had forever changed for the better.

To think, it was all because two boys were caught in the crossfire.

-The End-

www.ingramcontent.com/pod-product-compliance
Lightning Source LLC
Chambersburg PA
CBHW022240020726
47496CB00004B/996